THE
WHISPERING
SWARM

THE
WHISPERING
SWARM

MICHAEL MOORCOCK

GOLLANCZ

LONDON

First published in Great Britain in 2015
by Gollancz
An imprint of the Orion Publishing Group
Carmelite House, 50 Victoria Embankment,
London EC4Y 0DZ
An Hachette UK Company

A CIP catalogue record for this book
is available from the British Library

ISBN (Cased) 978 1 47321 332 6
ISBN (Trade Paperback) 978 1 47321 331 9

1 3 5 7 9 10 8 6 4 2

Printed and bound by CPI Group (UK) Ltd, Croydon, CR0 4YY

The Orion Publishing Group's policy is to use papers that
are natural, renewable and recyclable products and made
from wood grown in sustainable forests. The logging and
manufacturing processes are expected to conform to the
environmental regulations of the country of origin.

www.michaelmoorcock.co.uk
www.orionbooks.co.uk
www.gollancz.co.uk

For

JEAN-LUC FROMENTAL

and a thousand long lunches at the Goncourt

'We do not move in one direction, rather do we wander back and forth, turning now this way and now that. We go back on our own tracks...' *That thought of Montaigne's reminds me about something I thought of in connection with flying saucers, humanoids, and the remains of unbelievably advanced technology found in some ancient ruins. They write about aliens, but I think that in these phenomena we are in fact confronting ourselves; that is our future, our descendants who are actually travelling in time.*

– Andrei Tarkovsky

Through profound metaphysical meditation we reach fulfilment of our deep desires. First comes death; then comes the unending dream.

– Wheldrake,
The Pines of Sparta, 1913

CONTENTS

And Cyrus recalls that from our hopes and fears
We conjure creatures who shed true tears.

– Wheldrake,
The Babylonians

BOOK ONE

For all forlorn was the Bride of Morne,
And sare alone were she,
She sailed that night from Flete's narren sleets,
So to flee the whispering swarm.

– Fourteenth-century English ballad
(coll. Child)

CHAPTER ONE

MY REALITIES

EVERY DAY OF my life, after all I have learned and the many dangers I have survived, I still reflect on the circumstances which drew me to that part of the City of London I know as 'Alsacia', which her inhabitants call 'the Sanctuary'. I learned that magic is as dangerous as we are told it is and that romance can be more destructive than reality. Worse, I came to know and fear the fulfilment of my deepest desires.

I suppose I'm a pretty typical Londoner of my generation. Born at the beginning of the Second World War, in 1940, I was brought up in Brookgate between Grays Inn and Leather Lane. We never moved away, even when the whole city surrounded us in yelling flame. By the time I was born, my family worked chiefly at the lower end of the entertainment business. People had to go on making a living as best they could. And they wanted to be entertained. We were settled Roma intermarried with Jews, Cockneys, Irish. Culturally, we were metropolitan Christians. We had barely heard of Alsacia, which was no more than a bit of local folklore. There was plenty of that in London.

SEEING GHOSTS PROFESSIONALLY

From the age of eleven in 1951, I earned my own living, first in The Gallery, Oxford Street, then, after I left school at fifteen, as a journalist (mostly a stringer for the *Evening Standard*) and writer of fiction. As an early reader, I especially enjoyed P.G. Wodehouse, Edgar Rice Burroughs and George Bernard Shaw, and when I first began writing I habitually used my middle initial because I thought the best authors all had three names. I had been telling stories since I was four or five, mostly as little one-act plays. Adults said they were amazed at my imagination. I had the sense not to tell them that I could see ghosts as well. I knew I could impose images on the air and taught myself not to be frightened by them, that they were a phenomenon which could be explained. Occasionally, I glimpsed trails not much wider than a high wire, stretching off into shivering emerald and silver. I took it for granted that this was some occasional trick of the eye. It went away soon enough. As I grew older and read Jung I became even more convinced that what I saw wasn't real. Not, at any rate, in any other shared reality. Jung had analysed perfectly rational people who believed they had travelled in flying saucers. I was a perfectly rational person and I didn't believe in flying saucers or any of the other stuff Jung wrote about. It soon became second nature to check when I saw something odd and remember that only crazy people had visions.

MY MUM AND SHOW BUSINESS

My mother, who let people think she was a widow, seemed to understand. She loved me unreservedly but didn't spoil me when I was growing up. She was the first to understand what my 'visions' really were and try, with her friend Mr Ackermann's help, to channel that imagination. She ran a tent show in Brookgate Market, where it widens, near the church, putting on melodramas like *Sweeney Todd* or *Rookwood* to audiences of the elderly and lonely. 'And the downright creepy,' she'd laugh. But it kept a few old actors in work. She was a kind-hearted if eccentric woman whose own life, in the telling, was a bit of a melodrama. When I was eight or nine my friends and I grew bored during the school holidays so she let us perform a couple of my pieces on slow afternoons. To the applause of an audience mostly made up of other market traders, *Red Swords of Mars* starred me as the hero, my friend Keith Rivers as the villain and a bunch of little girls we'd recruited in all other parts. It ended with everybody dying, including the hero and heroine. My first successful stab at pulp SF, with the accent on the stab! Mum had encouraged me to channel an overactive imagination into a useful craft. But Mum's shows weren't to last. Public taste changed, so she switched to running mostly short silent film comedies and cartoons until TV got into its stride. Then it was over.

Mum's brother, Uncle Fred, who lived upstairs next to my room, owned The Gallery. This was long before Centre Point was built. The place was bang next door to Tottenham Court Road Tube station, round the corner from Charing Cross Road and opposite the Lyons Corner House where a 'gypsy' orchestra still performed for lunch, tea and supper. They played selections from *Maid of the Mountains*, *The Desert Song* and *The Bandit King*, as well as *In a Monastery Garden* and *In a Persian Market*. Cheap romantic music to go with cheap romantic adventure books and films! My mum used to say I was born out of my time. She loved taking me to the revived silent classics at the National Film Theatre and the Dominion.

MY MUM'S SENSE OF DRAMA

In order to pay for the extra archery and fencing lessons my friend Keith and I took at Brookgate Institute, I worked for Uncle Fred after school and at weekends. I gave change or cashed up the slots. Our family had survived the Blitz but Uncle Fred got a gammy leg at Dunkirk. My dad, a radio operator on Lancaster bombers, was shot down over France in 1943 and hidden by a French family for the duration. He became so comfortable that he stayed on there after the war, with the daughter of the house. My mother said she hadn't minded much – she wasn't cut out for marriage. She had me and the business, which, she said, was actually all she wanted from the bargain. I've never known how much of that was really true but I'm pretty sure I benefited by his absence, and it meant I spent my holidays with Dad in Toulon and Paris when most of my contemporaries were lucky to have a few days at Butlin's every year. I had to tell strangers that I was visiting a family friend. Our immediate family knew the truth about Dad leaving her, but my mum, though sweet-natured, was an habitual fantast. To hear her tell it, she'd travelled all over the world. Actually, she'd hardly been out of Brookgate. She went abroad once, on a day trip to Boulogne, and didn't like it. All foreign food, she would proclaim afterwards, was greasy, fantastic and inedible.

They used to say that Mum would climb a tree to tell a lie rather than stay on the ground to tell the truth. Nobody believed most of her stories. Only Uncle Fred and Mr Ackermann, a local tailor who spent quite a lot of time in our front room, visiting, continued to be sympathetic and supportive of her. Mr Ackermann had lived in Czechoslovakia before the war. A tall, slender man with pale, ascetic features, he dressed like a prewar dandy. His voice was very soft, his face gentle, with long jowls and large brown eyes that gave him the appearance of droll melancholy. He was very well educated. He had been a scientist doing something with radium but he needed fresh qualifications in England, where they were suspicious of him as an 'alien'. He eventually took over his cousin's thriving bespoke tailoring business at the Theobald's Road end of Brookgate Market. He was a kind, rather introspective man, who also gave me books to read. Years later I came across his rather frustrated love letters to my mum. I wasn't shocked. I'd known he loved her and I think, by association, me. He had left all his family behind. Few had survived. He was the only man I ever told about my 'ghosts'. He was sympathetic. 'When they begin to tell their stories, that's when you should be worried.' He smiled.

LONDON SEASONS

Keith and I got bored with the archery but we kept up our fencing, particularly after seeing *The Prisoner of Zenda* at the Rialto, Clerkenwell. I broke my mum's favourite chair trying the trick James Mason played on Stewart Granger and Keith wasn't allowed to see me for a week. Soon after that his mum and dad moved the family out to Epping. They said our neighbourhood was getting too rough. I felt very sorry for Keith, being so far from the centre of things. He wasn't even living in a suburb of London. He was in the *country*!

To this day I still love London. There's nowhere else worth living, even knowing what I know. Holborn Viaduct, that monument to art, science and industry, connecting the West End to The City, spans what used to be the Fleet River, now Farringdon Road, from Brookgate to Smithfield. I liked to stand on the viaduct, looking towards the Thames, inhaling health-preserving fumes from the traffic below. There was Blackfriars Bridge and the rich waters of the river, marbled by rainbow oil, poisonous and invigorating, buzzing like speed. What immune systems that environment gave us! It was an energy shield out of a science fiction story. The city lived through all attacks and so did we. Our bit of it – almost the eye of the storm – was scarcely touched. I grew up knowing I would survive. We all knew it.

BROOKGATE

I think the Blitz only killed twelve people in Brookgate. Thirteen at most. That's luck. And London's still lucky for me. Its familiarity gives me a feeling of security. Repetition is important, too, so when I go through Brooks Passage at lunchtime, Ron the escapologist and his dwarf wife are always there, drumming up trade from the office workers. Gamages decorated their display windows every Christmas. Tinsel and coloured glass and cotton-wool snow. They had a Santa inside. So did Ellisdon's, the big joke emporium on the corner where little drawers of practical jokes stretched from floor to ceiling: *False noses (sm.)*; *nail thru thumb. Blackface soap, bad doggy (lge), black eye, edible goldfish.* Endless entertainment for generations. We went there for dress-up clothes, too. For under a pound they would rig you out as a highwayman, a princess, a pirate, a cowboy or a nurse. Both big stores are gone now.

Few children could have enjoyed growing up quite as much as I did. I lived more or less on the cusp of East and West London, where 'Town' ended and The City began. Everything was in walking distance – cinemas, theatres, restaurants, shops, museums, art galleries, antique places. Pretty much everything you might ever need. And behind the rebuilt main streets there were the endless ruins.

In the '50s London was still characteristically navigated by bomb sites, rather than her midden heaps and church steeples. Almost every little red-brick street had at least one gap in it from some sort of bomb. In the east, people had trodden paths between shoulder-high stretches of rubble. Our hedges were broken brick, stone and burst concrete out of which shot branches of rusted steel rods, vibrating like fresh shoots.

THE DOCKS

The South Bank of the river was even more of a wasteland, with hardly a warehouse standing. It didn't matter. Better roads began to bring goods to the nearest train stations or even to the growing airports. But the Pool of London was still packed with ships, wharf upon endless wharf. You had to take trains between so many docks. For one summer during the school holidays I'd worked for Flexhill Shipping Company delivering bills of lading. But the commercial, trading heart of the city was already beating slower, anticipating the death of the trades which had created it.

Piles of blackened and soil-smeared remains, blazing with purple fireweed, lay between Billingsgate and the Royal Mint, between the Bank and the Monument, St Katharine Docks and Smithfield, everywhere Bow Bells pealed. As if God in his mercy had left us at least a tourist trade. They showed clearly how the city had been designed before Charles Dickens's time. Much of it was seventeenth century, from the Glorious Revolution. If this had happened forty years later they would not have rebuilt it. They would have preserved it as a theme park. Much more profitable. Ye Olde London Towne World. Wrenland. Hawksmooriana. Only the dead worked in London-land.

THE PRESS

There was enough work for everyone. The back pages of the papers were thick with job ads. All the little twittens and lanes around Fleet

Street yelled and clattered with the sound of linotypes and printing machines. They sweated ink and pissed hot air, stank of oil, sweat, exhaust fumes and beer. So many had survived, working through the war, the Blitz and the V-weapons.

There was hardly a basement without a roaring rotary press thumping out multiple editions of national and weekly newspapers, linotypers whirring and rattling away. The entire area ran on electricity and alcohol and was dedicated to the printed page, turning fact into fiction for the magazines and fiction into fact for the newspapers. Interpretation and prejudice; sensation and sobriety; a quarter filled with services for publishers and printers, for block makers, photographic developers, typographers.

Equipped with loudspeaker horns to announce their arrival, newspaper vans ripped through already lively streets or waited with chomping engines for the latest editions to come off the presses before hurtling away to train stations and distributors. Men in crumpled, grey three-piece suits and trilby hats stumbled straight from offices to pubs and chopshops, tea rooms, self-service cafés and automats and back again. Swapping gossip. Putting a bit on a horse. Scouting for a job. Boys ran up and down the streets carrying satchels and bundles or rode their big sit-up-and-beg delivery bikes through the traffic, whistling at the office girls, shouting insults one to the other – noise which became elements of its own symphony as certainly as Messiaen's birds were elements of his. It only stopped on Saturday afternoon and Sunday. By Sunday night it had started up again.

If cynics sitting at bars foretold the death of print, when radio and TV would deliver all the news on three or even four channels, their environment contradicted them. Fleet Street and her surroundings were dedicated to the printed word, to thousands of morning and evening daily newspapers published almost hourly; Sundays; weeklies; fortnightlies; monthlies; quarterlies; magazines; comics; pamphlets; textbooks; paperbacks on newsprint, pulp paper, art paper or vellum, printed by letterpress; offset; photogravure; fuzzy black and white; sepia; vibrant colour. Each publication had its individual scent and texture. I can recall every sound and smell, every glimpse and panorama of a world now utterly vanished.

MEMORY AND IMAGE

For me, linear time continues to be measured by the circulating seasons in St Giles's churchyard, where big chestnut trees drop bright, bronze leaves on gravestones in autumn or stand stark against the grey stone in winter and swell with blossoms in spring and summer. London is the smell of tar from hot streets. Liquorice. Melting vanilla. Sudden quiet falling over Clerkenwell Green on early-closing day. The reflecting rain on pavements, the wet-dog smell of piled snow, veined with mud and topped with dust in St James's, Piccadilly. Blooming spring in Hyde Park, the early daffodils, the scent of summer roses, sight of glinting conkers in autumn. These sights and smells carry me on uncontrollable moods, deep into vivid memory. That smell is a powerful drug, able to drag me back to specific times and places. Too painful. Not fair, that pain. I was a child of the innocent '60s and '70s, we thought we'd abolished misery, when it seemed so little effort was needed to build utopia.

When altruism wasn't silly. Or didn't cost you your life.

LONDON AFTER THE WAR

We had done so much for ourselves since the war. In Britain hunger had been abolished and health care was available to all. Manpower was what we needed. Unemployment was a thing of the past. Poverty was a lifestyle choice and everyone could have a free university education. Best-fed, healthiest, best-educated generation anyone ever knew! We were proud of that. The postwar Labour Party was the builder of our courageous new world. Labour leaders had their eyes on a visionary future. I always had some elder to give me tips, tell me books to read, explain how to make a radio or shoot a gun. The British Museum was ten minutes away. I spent hours there, looking at the ikons of ancient Egypt and Mesopotamia. Strange, beast-headed deities for whom I felt an odd affection. There were film theatres of all kinds. Art galleries from Whitechapel to the Tate. Every day I was introduced to a new book, a painting, a film. At sixteen I was reading Huxley, Camus, Beckett, Firbank. The International Film Theatre showed Kurosawa, Bergman, Resnais, Truffaut and Cocteau as well as the likes of Fritz

Lang, René Clair and Max Ophüls. And then there was Brecht, Weill, *The Threepenny Opera*. Lotte Lenya live on stage at the Royal Court. Ionesco absurdist plays a short walk from home. Camus's *Caligula* at the Phoenix, Charing Cross Road. Merce Cunningham or the Royal Ballet at Sadler's Wells, just down the road from where we lived. There was nowhere better to be in the world than London. Society's last injustices were being taken care of. Slowly, not always graciously, we were giving up the Empire. Abortion- and homosexual-law reform were on their way. In my romantic imagining London was the centre of the cause of the White Lords of Law and I was at the centre of London. It was so good to be a Londoner in those days as we came bouncing up out of the damp, dull decade of the austerity '50s, when we all wore grey and were too cool to smile at the camera. And we had the reality of the Blitz, our defeat of Hitler, only recently behind us. The Gallery had remained open all through the war.

TRY YOUR LUCK

Long and narrow, marinated in the fumes of tobacco and gunpowder, stinking of sweat and damp, the Oxford Street Penny Arcade and Shooting Gallery was an old-fashioned game emporium with a selection of dowdy slot machines and noisy pinballs whose nicotine-stained chrome and gaudy lights promised a bit more than they delivered, and a couple of cranes in glass boxes where you operated a grab to try to pick up a toy, all bundled in there bright as liquorice allsorts. We had a Mystic Mary fortune-telling machine, whose paint was faded by the daily sun, a couple of 'dioramas' where you paid a penny to turn a handle and make a few creaky dolls go through their spasmodic imitations of life against some forgotten or unrecognisable historical drama browned by cigarette smoke on cracked linoleum.

AUNTIE ETHEL AND THE CARDS

For a while Mum's sickly eldest sister, Auntie Ethel, gave tarot readings in a curtained-off corner of The Gallery. She believed in what she did. 'The trick is to put yourself in touch mentally with the person you're reading for,' she told me. 'It's something you do with your mind. Sort of telepathy. Empathy, really. It's only guessing, Mike, but I'd swear you're in touch with something. You tune them in. It's the way they sit or talk. You can either read them or you can't.' I got the hang of it. The readings would sometimes exhaust her. Shortly before she stopped she let me dress up in a bit of a costume with a veil and do a couple of readings on my own. People were impressed and grateful. I got a strange feeling off it. Then Auntie Ethel disappeared. Uncle Fred said she had serious cancer and didn't want anyone to see her. I think she died soon afterwards.

THE GALLERY

The shooting gallery itself was in semi-darkness at the back wall. Rows of cardboard ducks and deer cranked their shaky perpetual progress through a paper forest while men, with skinny cigarettes sending more smoke up to cling against the murky roof or spread, thick as enamel, across hardboard surrounds, leaned the elbows of their greasy demob suits on the well-rubbed oak and killed time banging at the birds with post-1914 BSA .22 rifles. It always surprised me how many of those blokes who were at Dunkirk and Normandy didn't seem comfortable without a rifle in their hands. Shooting back as they hadn't been able to do? A funny, distant look in their eyes. Was it some unresolved terror? Were they trying for what people these days call 'closure'? They played the slots with the same intensity. We had an ancient cast-iron post-office red *What the Butler Saw* machine and that was about it. Uncle Fred reckoned his granddad had been a successful travelling showman, putting on circuses and fairs all over the country. He had a few faded posters to prove it. My favourite was MOORCOCK'S TREASURY OF ANIMALS, actually a rather tame-looking menagerie. 'We go back, our people, to the time of the mummers,' Uncle Fred said. He was deeply and widely educated, my Uncle Fred. All from books, of course. His wasn't the last self-educated generation of his kind (mine was) but his might have been the best. He kept his wisdom and knowledge to himself, only answering when asked. Except within the family, naturally. At work, his longest and most frequent response was 'Right you are, guv'nor.'

He took the *Daily Herald* every day and read the *New Statesman* from cover to cover every week. He gave me my first non-fiction books, like Winwood Reade's *The Martyrdom of Man* or Wells's *Short History of the World*. He was an atheist but his mind wasn't closed. I read Huxley's *The Perennial Philosophy* from his library. All my inspiration comes from those books my Uncle Fred recommended. We'd discuss Shaw's *The Apple Cart* on the morning walk to the arcade but spoke in professional monosyllables all day at work. 'Cuppa?' 'Ta.' Or to a regular customer 'Chilly today, eh?' or whatever the weather happened to be.

MY MUM AND THE WELFARE STATE

My mum kept her wealth of common sense but she got a bit weirder as I grew up. Uncle Fred and Mr Ackermann tried to counsel me, told me not to feel guilty. Her upset was inevitable, they said, as she sensed me making my own life separate to hers. So I stayed away from home a bit longer, just for the peace. Sometimes I went home via the Westminster Reference Library where you sat and read without interruption because nobody was allowed to take books out. We were all serious readers, sitting on wooden chairs at rows of lecterns, turning the pages, united in mutual love of isolation.

I had been born into a world that had learned to value important things. The Tories didn't dare mess with that infrastructure. An air of equality and tranquillity filled my world. Class would still be with us for another generation but it was disappearing and the evidence was everywhere. Cheap travel. Cheap credit. Cheap and gentle little black-and-white comedies. Holidays abroad. As a result of our first great socialist government, we became the freest people in the world, if not the richest. Sometimes you had to make the choice between a nice meal or a trip to the West End cinema. The wealth was spread, the country became stronger and, bit by bit, better off. For a while I saw working-class London grow happier, better educated and more optimistic. Before they took it all away again.

UNCLE FRED'S WISDOM

Oxford Street these days, of course, is far too posh for a shabby little amusement arcade like my Uncle Fred's. His lease came up in 1958. There's a tourist shop there now. They pay a fortune for those leases. Mugs and T-shirts. Postcards and miniature Beefeaters. Union Jacks on everything. Red, white and blue bunting. Bags. Hats. Coppers' helmets. Red double-deckers. 'London,' as my cousin Denny always says, 'is ikon rich. And that makes *us* rich, Michael, my son.' They move thousands of little Beefeaters and queens on horseback a day, they turn over hundreds of thousands of pounds. Their turnover makes you feel sick. And crowded! Push and shove is the name of the game there now. Roll up, roll up! Can you blame me if I get nostalgic for my boyhood, when it was cheap to enjoy yourself and people said 'pardon' and 'sorry'?

'Years ago,' said my Uncle Fred as we walked home towards Brookgate one night when I still worked for him, 'we all liked to make money but we didn't feel anxious if we didn't make millions. We just wanted to nod along like everybody else. We thought in terms of equality and fairness. I'm not kidding, Mike. Of course there's always thieves and troublemakers, people who are predatory and live off the weak. The stock market depends on our getting into debt. All this cheap gelt, it's making us into addicts. It's a drug culture and we're mainlining money.'

He was talking about hire purchase. Pre-credit cards. A different way of getting the poor into debt, but I think he was right. It was nice when ordinary people could take a holiday in Spain, of course, but easy credit is what started the cultural rot. Tourism depends on lots of people everywhere with loads of disposable wealth, which means all kinds of changes go through a place that cultivates it. The real, messy, informative past disappears to be overlaid with bad fiction, with simplified folklore, easy answers. Memory needs to remain complex, debatable. Without those qualities it is mere nostalgic sentimentality. Commodified identity. Souls bought and sold.

'The more lucrative the story,' Uncle Fred said, 'the more it gives way to falsification. Barnum knew all about that.' Barnum and Marx were my Uncle Fred's twin saints, his Freud and Jung. 'My Jekyll and

Hind,' he'd joke. If he'd wanted to, Uncle Fred could have brought in a few props and called the arcade Ye Olde Charles Dickens Pennye Emporium or some such and done very well. But *Das Kapital*'s terrible Puritanism reined him back. When Fred's lease ran out he couldn't afford to renew it without borrowing, so he retired on a modest state pension ('Fair and square,' he always said. 'You gets back what you pays in'). But of course he also had his savings and his stash of sovereigns to sell when the rate was good and hard times came around. Like all sensible socialists, he hedged his bets in the capitalist world.

Uncle Fred gave me books he was enthusiastic about. His generation had grown up on the Fabians' popular paperbacks of politics, philosophy and history and the Thinker's Library. He had a shelf full of such stuff. Herbert Read's *What is Revolutionary Art?* was one of his favourites and Jung's *Modern Man in Search of a Soul*. Various commentaries on the Qur'an, the Bhagavad Gita and the Avesta were among the spiritual studies Uncle Fred had read on myth, human belief and the supernatural in general. He was a secular humanist but he was curious. 'It's always worth knowing what makes people tick, Mike.' He'd read most of *Mein Kampf* by Hitler. 'If you know your enemy and can see your enemy, you can protect yourself against him. Or at least know when to run for it. Everything that monster did was in his book. You only had to read it. That's when I split with Stalin, when he signed that treaty with Hitler.' Uncle Fred, like most of his contemporaries, spoke in a tone of taken-for-granted scepticism you heard everywhere in those days, in almost all the papers, on the radio and in films. You heard it in the language of those who had been 'believers' before the war. That tone reflected the common assumption that religion was a thing of the past and it was now time to build a more rational world. The clergy was represented by dotty old Whitehall-farce vicars and unworldly curates. Only Hollywood made a buck or two from God. Religion and the corrupt romanticism surrounding much of that, and the discredited fascist creeds and their actions, had helped create the horrors of the past twenty years or so. The Church of England, which still turned up on Sunday BBC, and was effectively the conscience of Parliament, was associated with the 'caring' aspects of the paternalistic establishment. Nobody thought much about that. The church created colourful traditions, of course, and probably we were none the worse for having them, but anyone who seriously believed in God as anything but a philosophical abstraction was sadly deluded. Even T.S. Eliot, the Church of England's big catch, wasn't sure Jesus had existed. It was left to romantics like me to ask what a rational world had got for us already if it wasn't Stalinism, Hitlerism and fascism. All of which promised a golden future but without much attention to detail. We would discover romance in a big way in the 1960s.

After Uncle Fred's lease ran out I got a couple of the better .22 rifles and some boxes of cartridges as souvenirs. He wouldn't let me keep Mystic Mary. She was sold off with the rest. He had a share in the Bucket o' Gold down in Leicester Square, which eventually became a rock-and-roll venue and where I opened with the reunited Deep Fix a few years later. Uncle Fred left six figures when he died not long after he retired. He was eighty-one. Left the lot to the Labour Party, for services rendered he said. The gold he divided amongst us the day before he popped off, singing 'The Red Flag' in his reedy old voice. Nobody but me joined in. 'Cowards!' he whispered, and was gone.

CHAPTER TWO

FRIAR ISIDORE

WITH FRED'S DEATH my mum was heartbroken and her nerves began to worsen. Increasingly, she dyed her hair badly and put on her makeup erratically. She rarely got out of the same few cosmetics-stained clothes and gave most of her wardrobe to Oxfam. Mr Ackermann came round to console her, but she was never quite the same after Fred died. She had loved Fred and continued to love Mr A. But she and Fred had memories together going back all her life. Fred had understood her and known how to cheer her up. His love was reciprocated. As well as her talent for fiction, Mum had a huge, almost childish, capacity for unconditional love, and, like Fred, she still celebrated liberty and spoke disparagingly of children whose parents clung to them. When I met a bunch of like-minded teenagers and started hanging out in the Soho coffee bars, she didn't try to stop me. She invited us all back and became quite good friends with some of the people I knew.

By 1955 the times were definitely on the change. Especially for me. And it wasn't just the rock and roll. I was getting more ambitious in general. I wanted to write a novel. And make a record. I learned to play a few chords on my cousin's Gretsch guitar. I became a fan of American folk music. I added Woody Guthrie and Robert Johnson to my pantheon. A bunch of us in Brookgate had formed The Green-horns (who became the nucleus of the first Deep Fix line-up) and we were hanging around Alexis Korner and Cyril Davies, who played blues in the jazz clubs and were regulars at a place near King's Cross. For a while my greatest musical heroes were Gene Vincent and Muddy Waters. I met Gene once and Muddy a few times. I wrote to Woody Guthrie and Pete Seeger and they replied! At fifteen my literary heroes were almost all alive – P.G. Wodehouse, John Steinbeck, Ray Bradbury and E.R. Burroughs. Burroughs wrote the Tarzan and John Carter of Mars books. He was the first writer I tried to emulate. My enthusiasm for 'ERB', as his fans called him, would lead to me getting my first editorial job. But for that, I would never be telling this story. I would not have been introduced to the Sanctuary by the old monk, Friar Isidore.

Between the ages of fourteen and seventeen or so I put out an ERB fanzine, *Burroughsania*. The thing was typed without a ribbon so the keys could cut clear impressions in wax stencils which were then carefully placed over the drum of a mimeograph machine. That was how we reproduced things in those days, before Xerox, before computers. The stencils were delicate things and needed to be used with special skill, particularly if you had pictures or display lettering on them. To make sure they had come out right, you held them up to the light. If the typewriter keys had cut cleanly through the wax, you were ok. Pictures could be delicate as paper lace.

Jacob Egg, Mr Ackermann's dwarfish friend, who ran an estate agent's in Grays Inn Road, offered me free use of their big, modern Gestetner machine. 'Remember who started you off when you get to be Lord Beaverbrook,' he said. He was very indulgent, giving me free paper and stencils. I think he was a little fascinated by me and maybe wanted to be a writer himself. Mr Egg kept copies of all my fanzines – and there were quite a few – and years later would show them, carefully preserved in plastic folders, as from 'before you were famous.'

I called mine 'amateur mags' before I discovered they were known as fanzines. I didn't know there were other fanzines being produced until I put an ad in a print version of Craigslist called *Exchange and Mart*, addressing ERB enthusiasts. SF fans wrote from all over the country and people they knew wrote from America and Europe.

Suddenly, at sixteen, I was part of international science fiction 'fandom'! I was invited to attend an informal meeting of fans which was held on Thursday nights at the Globe pub, Hatton Garden, about five minutes from where I was born. Almost everyone there produced or contributed to SF fanzines! I was astonished. I had never read a word of contemporary science fiction and precious little Verne and Wells and now, at sixteen but tall enough to pass for older, I stood holding my pint of bitter and chatting to the amiably posh John Wyndham, Arthur Clarke, with his benign intelligence and strange Somerset-American accent, C.S. Lewis, all benign Oxbridge behind his good-humoured pipe, and a bunch of others whose work, like theirs, I had hardly heard of. My heroes were at that time Firbank, Aldous Huxley, T.H. White and Mervyn Peake. I had a correspondence with White and would visit Peake later that year, as I would Tolkien, with Lewis's help. Perhaps they liked me because I was enthusiastic but didn't fawn. Before he died, Wyndham said they were all in awe of me, though I was so young, because of my energetic dynamism. I can only guess what he meant.

I was soon on first-name terms with the SF editors, too: Ted Carnell of *New Worlds* and *Science Fantasy,* dapper in his fashionable casuals, with a Ronald Colman moustache; rangy, six-foot-three-inch raconteur Ted Tubb of *Authentic* and bookish little Peter Hamilton of *Nebula* with his heavy Scots accent. Useful contacts? It didn't necessarily pay to know them. Barry Bayley got on well with them all but took years before he sold to Carnell and that was by changing his name. More useful contacts for me in those days were the Fleet Street newspapermen like Peter Phillips or John Burke, who knew when a bit of quick copy was needed. I remained a working journalist for years before I saw myself specifically as a fantasy writer.

At the Globe I became close friends with Barry, Pete Taylor and John Brunner, all recently demobbed from the RAF. Brunner, I think, had been an officer. In those days young men inducted into the national service were, if reasonably intelligent and technically savvy, sent to the RAF to be trained as wireless operators or electrical engineers. The theory was that you came out with a skill. Sadly, the only skill we all shared was the one they'd gone in with, as writers. Barry, the spitting image of Voltaire and not much above five feet high, was a clerk at Australia House and all brain. That twin of the great French comedian Fernandel, Pete Taylor, like me, got work as a supply typist between jobs. We were both superfast, which made us always employable. Only John Brunner was self-employed, somehow running a flat in Hampstead, a Morgan sports car and a Gibson guitar. Maybe he had money. He was rumoured to be from a posh background. His voice was the exaggerated bray of a RAF officer. He wore a Van Dyke beard and moustache, an ascot, a maroon velvet jacket and baggy flannel trousers and smoked expensive cigarettes from a tortoiseshell holder. As the outspoken American writer Harry Harrison put it, John had got himself up in the complete Hampstead left-wing intellectual set. He had a CND button in his lapel. He was a socialist. He had written the Campaign for Nuclear Disarmament's marching song 'Don't You Hear the H-bomb's Thunder?' and was famous for following the Aldermaston March in his Morgan. He wrote science fantasy with tremendous brio. His first, *The Wanton of Argus,* came out in the pulpiest of pulps while he sold sophisticated hard SF to the prestigious *Astounding*. His posh drawl, however, unlike Wyndham's or Allard's, got people's backs up. He had a way of treading on their toes. He never meant to be rude, but he wouldn't learn. I tried to tell him he irritated people. He explained how I was wrong. He would die of a heart attack at an SF convention in Glasgow, an embittered shadow of his former self.

Another friend made through 'fandom' was Ray Napoleon, a kind of modern-day remittance man. Ray's parents had sent him to Europe after he'd refused to marry a girl he had made pregnant. He'd been told to stay there, on a modest stipend, until he matured. The logic was a bit strange. Ray was perfectly happy with the arrangement. He said he had been sent away to save his mother and father embarrassment. From San Francisco, Ray was heavily built with dark, Italianate features. I remember meeting a Bay Area folk-singing couple who brought their baby to a London gig. I asked the man if they knew Ray. His face clouded. 'Ray's not our kind of people,' he said. The woman merely smiled. When I looked into the carrycot, there was a miniature version of Ray looking back at me. At sixteen I went to stay with him in Paris. That was my first big step towards becoming an adult. I met a whole bunch of writers and musicians in the couple of weeks I was there. I even had a brief vision of the four Musketeers walking arm in arm out of the Luxembourg Gardens, coming down

Boulevard Saint-Michel towards me. I wasn't fazed. I'd had similar flashes all my life. I always knew that these visions weren't real. They were just something I could do.

Still relatively sparsely populated, extremely relaxed and unjudgemental, Paris was one huge vision to me. Never scarred by the war, she had a beauty I could hardly believe was real. Foreigners were slowly drifting back to the city. Ray had a Swedish guitarist friend, Monica Helander, who sang old music-hall songs at a little tourist cabaret in Montmartre. On Sundays, she would drive her Citroën 2CV down onto the cobbles of the quay and, under the golden chestnut trees, would wash it with water drawn directly from the Seine. Today, you aren't even allowed to go there on foot! We would take a bottle of wine and play in the bays under the embankment, where you could get a good echo. I took over from Monica for a gig or two, learning to sing interminable verses of 'Clementine' and 'Careless Love', which all the tourists seemed to like and which, happily, I could play. I wasn't great, but you didn't have to be in those more-innocent and less-demanding days. I went reluctantly back to London in an ambitious mood. I would return to Paris at least once a year after that.

My fanzine improved considerably once I was in touch with fandom. Like most British musicians at that time, talented SF people were semi-pro. The fields didn't pay enough, even to the top professionals. From Gateshead-on-Tyne, Jim Cawthorn started to send me stencilled illustrations of extraordinary quality. From Brixton, Arthur Thomson, who already illustrated the professional SF mags, drew me cartoons and headings. Professional writers who had sold stories to *Nebula* and *Authentic* wrote features as I expanded my fanzine's parameters to include writers such as T.H. White and Mervyn Peake. Thanks to my new contributors I had begun to look pretty professional. I tried to get interviews with more fantasts and ran articles on people like Ray Bradbury, Talbot Mundy and M.R. James. When I told them how close to the Globe the weekly *Tarzan Adventures* magazine was, my fellow fans suggested I interview the editor whose offices were below the rooms where Chatterton died, between Leather Lane and Grays Inn Road, in Brook Street, Holborn. It seemed as if I could live my entire life in a bubble less than half a mile across and find everyone I wanted to meet, everything I wanted to do!

Tarzan Adventures was a bit of a crossover between a weekly comic book and a text magazine primarily for boys. I enjoyed it better than most but I didn't like every artist who drew the strip and I thought the features and short stories were pretty pathetic. Still, it seemed a good moment to ask the editor, Bob Greenway, for an interview. He was a bit lordly about it but permission was granted and I went to see him in his old-fashioned editorial study at Westworld Publications. Plump, boozy, aggressive, he knew nothing about Burroughs and of course my piece on him in *Burroughsania* reflected this appalling ignorance.

Mr Greenway didn't bother to send back my next submissions. But then, about the middle of 1956, I received a phone call from his young assistant editor, Alistair Graham. Bob had got a new job on *Gardening Weekly*. A tall, gaunt, cheerful, bearded Scot, Alistair had loved my piece. Everyone there had hated Bob. Now the editor, Alistair liked the idea of carrying some features on ERB characters, then perhaps something more substantial later. He was only a couple of years older than me. Soon I was writing short features on John Carter of Mars, Carson of Venus, Tanar of Pellucidar. Alistair was delighted. The readers loved them. Next I was asked to write a Burroughs-style serial. Could, I wondered, another fanzine contributor perhaps illustrate a story? Agreed. Jim Cawthorn, later to sketch out illustrations for Elric, illustrated *Sojan the Swordsman*. I got a guinea and a half an episode for them! I wrote thousand-word features for the same money. At sixteen I was on my way to becoming a full-time professional. I discovered that Alistair played banjo. We formed a skiffle group with his friends from Notting Hill and rehearsed at the office in the evenings. Then one lunchtime Alistair asked me to come and work at Westworld as an assistant editor. Surprised, I wasn't sure. I enjoyed freelancing. I still worked part-time at The Gallery and did temp typing work when I needed to, but my freelance earnings were improving. He murmured that it might be a good idea to accept. When in a few weeks he left to hitch-hike round the world with the rest of the skiffle group, I could take over from him. I would be editor. But, I thought, I was only sixteen!

Uncle Fred saw sense in accepting the job, a great start to a career. 'You'll be editor of the *Daily Herald* at this rate.' He stretched an arthritic hand towards the teapot. After all, he told my uncertain mum, editing was like show business. 'Still selling illusions,' he said.

So, when a few weeks later Alistair left to travel around the world, busk with his friends and write mysteries, sure enough I was the editor! I must admit I wasn't especially flattered by the wage offer. I was to get six pounds a week. His face scarred by fire from the downed Hurricane he had flown in the war, Donald F. Peters, our sad-eyed boss, was primarily a commercial printer who had sought higher profits in publishing. That dream had faded by the time I turned up. He knew I was prepared to work for a much lower wage than an older journalist! My enthusiasm might prove profitable. As it turned out, he was right!

I was responsible for the whole magazine. I didn't just make the old American Sunday *Tarzan* comic-strip pages fit our quarto format, sometimes with drastic surgery and amateurish redrawing, I also commissioned features, fiction, illustrations and our back-pages comics serial, sometimes bought from Italy, sometimes commissioned. Through my fanzine contacts I had a large pool of talented semi-professionals to draw from. They soon started appearing regularly in *Tarzan*. By 1957 I was producing a semi-juvenile version of the US pulp magazines I loved and which were dying in the US. The circulation began to improve. Donald Peters cheered up a little.

They gave me an assistant, a septuagenarian Fleet Street man, a sub-editor all his life who hated everything I did. He particularly hated fantasy and science fiction, believing it 'unwholesome'. He came in twice a week to Brook Street and took the office at the farthest end of the narrow building piled with bales of Westworld's unsold publications and divided up into mysterious spaces whose original function was only remembered by the accounts people and Donald F. Peters, who had designed them in more optimistic times. Sometimes, if I was alone in the office and had a bit of a hangover, I slept on top of unsold bales of *Marvelman*, *Pecos Bill* and various reprints of other Italian comics stored in the basement. I can smell their musty, yellowing paper to this day! They hadn't been a great success in the UK market.

My ancient assistant's name was Reginald 'Sammy' Samuels. Mostly he did paste-up. His scissors and can of Cow gum seemed a comfort to him. He used shirt suspenders and the green eyeshade Bob Greenway had left behind. He wore a dark suit, shiny at knees and elbows, a frayed shirt, a greasy bow tie and a tobacco-stained waistcoat. He smelled a little sour. He had a long, unhappy face and was bent over with scoliosis. His skin fell in long, discoloured facial curtains which the nicotine from his cigarettes, smoked in long holders, had tanned kipper-gold. I think they paid him less than I got. I found it a little awkward, being the boss of a much older man, and he didn't much like it, either. I would introduce him as our senior editor. He taught me some of the tricks of the trade but probably his most useful tip was how to survive on very little money. At lunch, for instance, he would order two rounds of toast at our nearby greasy spoon round the corner in Grays Inn Road. When the toast arrived he shook salt onto one piece and sugar on the other. 'There you are,' he said, 'the savoury course and the sweet course, and all for threepence!' When broke I frequently used his tip. I already knew how to make a cheap sandwich from a bread roll and a portion of Branston pickle in Lyons teashops!

I seemed to have a knack for the work. I could quickly eyeball a piece of copy and know how much of the page it would fill. Even Sammy couldn't do that as well as I could. He showed me how to draw a title and embellish it to look professional, if a little old-fashioned, and passed along his prowess as a proofreader. I learned the trick of bulking out a short piece and cramming in a long one.

We got our typesetting done by Olympic in Old Bailey. They occupied a basement not far from the courts. I would deliver next week's copy on Wednesday and check it over on Thursday. The typesetters would photograph it and send it to our lithograph printers in St Albans. They would already have the pictures and layouts. The printed copy had to be turned around quickly to coincide with the existing pasted-up pages.

Which was how I met Friar Isidore.

Because I was editor *and* printer's devil, every Thursday I went down to Old Bailey and checked the proofs. I was getting great experience. When copy was late and we were short of time I learned to read type straight from the frame in reverse, making corrections without the type being 'pulled' off on paper, by rolling ink onto the frame, putting a sheet of cheap paper on top of that, then rolling over it to make an impression. If copy was too long I could cut in an instant and if not enough, I could write a short article and have them set it on the spot. They had a couple of typewriters on a high desk so you could type standing up. I was born to the job. I could turn an issue around so quickly, I usually took an hour or two off before going back to the office. On a good day, I didn't have to go back at all.

During these extra hours there was time for a stroll by the river, or a walk to the Tower of London, to watch the Tower Bridge open for shipping, explore the alleys and courts off Fenchurch and Liverpool Streets, or cross the river and dive into mysterious Southwark or Bermondsey. The Blitz had destroyed those Victorian boroughs more thoroughly than the Restoration buildings. Councils were putting up great blank blocks of modern flats where the old alleys had been.

I had known Fleet Street, of course, since childhood. I spent more time there once I had decided to become a writer. I drank and ate the atmosphere. It enriched me. It was the stuff of life. I had developed an unbeatable immune system from it. I had gone there for as long as I could remember but now I was fully part of it! I was a pressman, treated as an equal by most who knew me (though because of my youth some still took me for an office boy), including the other editorial staff members who congregated around the typesetters early on Wednesday afternoons when we put our charges to bed. I carried a pica ruler, which we called an em-stick, for measuring type. I knew the number of words which would fill two or three columns on a quarto page, how to mark up and turn an illustration into a reduced block, how to prepare a picture. We understood the same trade jargon. We were brothers (sisters were not yet even a novelty) of the typewriter. Most of my fellow pressmen only had time for a quick familiar nod as they rushed in and out, but one rather eccentric regular, Friar Isidore, shared my hours and was willing to pass the time of day, to ask me an opinion, to offer a thought of his own on the news as I presented it, addressing me with a kind of mild, respectful good will which was as welcome as it was unfamiliar. His smile, if a little distant, was infinitely benign.

I was fascinated by Friar Isidore. A tall, scrawny, hunched, pink, bright-eyed man, he would push back his hood to reveal a tonsured, stubbled skull. Carefully rolling up his habit's sleeves, he tackled the sheaf of proofs the setter took out of the pigeonhole for him to read. His magazine looked a bit dull to me, mostly closely printed text in double columns with mysterious titles which meant absolutely nothing, using unfamiliar words in Greek, Latin or Hebrew. Some were even in Arabic, he told me, pointing to what looked like shorthand. And Aramaic. The title was equally meaningless: *The White Friar*. I had no idea what a white friar was. Judging by Friar Isidore's appearance, he surely had something to do with religion.

Religion, in a view shared by the majority of my fellow Londoners, was something mostly associated with our superstitious past. All the Jews I knew were non-believers. Occasionally I saw an Hasidic oldster in Hatton Garden but as often as not, he was from Amsterdam. I had never met a Moslem. I knew no-one who went to church. In common with most of my contemporaries I thought people needed to invent a creator to give authority to their ignorance. Our remaining churches were chiefly empty, their congregations almost entirely made up of growing numbers of tourists; impressive architecturally and artistically, but essentially alien mausoleums. Westminster Abbey was reserved for royal pomp, also considered a pleasant exercise in nostalgia. Yet I think we were proud of our 'red' priests and outspoken archbishops. We still heard them on the radio every Sunday. We used an Anglican church, if we used one at all, for weddings, christenings and funerals, yet continued to see St Paul's as the proud ikon of our wartime survival. We'd tell you we were agnostics, mostly to appease any potential Mormon or Seventh-day Adventist on the old door-to-door.

The holidays we kept were essentially pagan with pretty much the same measure of sentimentality reserved for Easter chicks, the baby Jesus and watching the Queen's Speech on Christmas Day. We were vaguely tolerant of others' beliefs, remembered most of the words of well-known hymns and carols, shared the common views about 'low' and 'high' churches (Baptists went to chapels and were tight-fisted and Catholics were more generous but bred like rabbits). The few prominent Anglicans who appeared in the media probably had greater moral authority than equally prominent politicians.

I knew only a little about my ancestors. My mother's father had died of drink in a pauper's hostel. My grandmother had thrown him out years before. He'd been a journeyman newspaper journalist of some kind, a stringer. His family was Jewish anarchist. Hers was strictly Orthodox. The gypsies were on my father's side, just a generation or so back. I was rather proud of my Jewish heritage, through a daughter of Isaac D'Israeli, the great nineteenth-century scholar and writer, father of Benjamin, the novelist and politician. Until I hitch-hiked one summer from Stockholm to Hamburg, I never encountered anything I recognised as anti-Semitism. Brookgate slang was full of Yiddish. We were on the edge of districts traditionally occupied by tailors, clockmakers and diamond merchants. We had a synagogue across the road from us. Admittedly it was attended less and less, but so were the churches. Very few Jews were culturally any different by now from their neighbours. Clerkenwell, and Brookgate in particular, pretty much forced socialism, secularism and self-schooling on us all. We supplied London with a lot of her best taxi drivers, too. I had three uncles who were cabbies and had the traditional left-wing populism and self-education London cabbies were famous for. I have to this day a horror of undertipping, listening as I did to my uncles' opinion of stingy customers. In general, though, the old men cultivated a rather tolerant view of their fellow creatures.

We used as much Yiddish and gypsy slang in our language as Cockney but we swore according to a Christian god. Monks weren't a very common sight on our streets any more than Orthodox Jews or Sikhs. Black faces were still rare in most districts. (My mother and her sisters touched a black man for luck but bridled at prejudice.) West Indians were only just beginning to arrive to replace the manpower destroyed in the war. Three evening papers were crammed with ads for jobs and low-rent flats. We were still essentially the indigenous, white, Protestant people we had been since the Reformation. Monks figured largely in advertisements for tobacco, beer or meat pies, as jolly, life-loving versions of Friar Tuck; manifestations of the Good Old Days, of Merrie England. So this ascetic, kindly, somewhat vulnerable, grey-faced man was a bit of a puzzle, even though I had an instinctive liking for him. I had never seen a monk on the street, as far as I remembered.

I was familiar with Carmelite Street, Whitefriars Street and Blackfriars Bridge, of course, but they had no more religious significance than St Pancras, Charing Cross, King's Cross or the Temple Tube stations. They were names, like the 'gates' – Aldgate, Brookgate, Bishopsgate – non-existent barriers to barely distinctive districts. If I hadn't met Friar Isidore, I might have taken 'Carmelite' for something you spread on bread like Marmite or Nutella. For all I'd known, *The White Friar* was a trade magazine run by a man who liked to go to work in his dressing gown. Yet Friar Isidore had such an air of genial dedication, even, if I dare say it, *godliness*, that, one autumn afternoon, I felt confident enough to ask him what the magazine was about.

He answered with perfect good humour. The white friars were Carmelites, he said. A celibate religious order, they vowed to serve God in poverty, serving outcast and downtrodden people. Like me he was also editor and proofreader of their magazine, which mostly debated theological matters, usually in Latin. He chuckled when he added, 'Well, I am also the chief trugmoldy.' This was clearly a bit of a joke but, when he saw that I was unfamiliar with the word, he explained. 'I go up and down Fleet Street, selling it in the taverns. It is how we've paid up to now for its publication, though we do have a small endowment. You might have seen me at the entrance to the caverns, too – yes, yes, those ill-smelling Underground stations, I should say. I sell it there. Taverns and caverns. Wherever light might help.' He smiled as if for my approval. I was now trying to place his accent. Was it rural? Some kind of American? It sounded old-fashioned.

'So you're a bit like the Salvation Army,' I said. He nodded vaguely. I assumed he was local, though I wasn't entirely sure where monks lived. St Paul's? I asked him how long he had been in the area. He responded with what might have been amusement. The priory was long established, he said. It had been continuously inhabited since the thirteenth century.

I told him this was fascinating. 'I had no idea!' I wasn't kidding. Religious stuff was mostly new to me.

I think he spoke next partly from a sense of duty, as if to a pagan ready for conversion!

'Perhaps, if you have time, we could talk over a cup of tea? I might explain a little...'

History had always fascinated me. At that time I was more familiar with Sir Walter Scott and *Ivanhoe* or *Quentin Durward*, Dumas,

Hugo, Rafael Sabatini's *Captain Blood* or Baroness Orczy's *Scarlet Pimpernel*; Harold Lamb, whose stories I read in second-hand pulps, wrote about Erik the Red and the Crusades: Richard the Lionheart; the noble Saladin. Needless to say, I preferred my history dressed up with a bit of romantic action but it had already occurred to me that I might be able to run a series on London history in *Tarzan*. Would Friar Isidore be the man to do us such a series? Crusaders and Saracens sounded okay, too. There was a new line of toy soldiers I'd seen in Gamages, Holborn. Crusader Knights and Turks. Theology? I didn't know much about that. Perhaps we could angle it on the folklore of either side? I had featured several pieces on old Irish mythology by a friend of mine. Though fascinated by the colour and pageantry of war, I had no interest in war itself. I didn't collect historical lead soldiers, just bright Imperial troops of the kind you could build up into mighty panoramas of Rorke's Drift or even the Charge of the Light Brigade complete with running Highlanders and Russian troops behind the gunners (not that you could ever afford them all). I had a couple of sets of crusaders and 'Arabs' in my toy soldier collection and had already run a series about collecting model soldiers called 'Commanding Your Own Army'. Maybe I could interview this vicar bloke and get material for a series about battles on the Thames?

So that was the ignorant muddle which served me for a decision-making brain when I accepted his invitation. We walked down Old Bailey and round the corner to grey, drizzling Ludgate Hill, as always crowded with busy messenger boys, sergeants-at-arms, girl typists, salesmen and wandering journalists. The Hill's tall, dark, gilded-glass shop fronts displayed stationery, smoking accessories, coffee beans, sandwiches, books, model ships. Down under the railway bridge the street ended with the Old King Lud on one side and The Kwik-U-R, a rapid-service restaurant, employing a lot of staff to get your food to you as fast as possible. You could eat three courses there in fifteen minutes. Then came Farringdon Road and the tall modern concrete offices of Amalgamated Press, following the bed of the old Fleet. Once, Holborn Viaduct high overhead might easily have crossed a river. The traffic flowed around Ludgate Circus and on over Blackfriars Bridge to Southwark and beyond, turning left to continue into Fleet Street and a thousand newspapers, journals, magazines and comics. But Friar Isidore and I stopped at the ABC Teashop across the road.

The ABC Teashop, with its busy clatter and smart, modern, art deco silver, chrome and glass, was fairly empty at this time. Before we entered, Friar Isidore stopped in the street's bustling pedestrian flow and asked embarrassedly if I would mind if we bought our own refreshments. He couldn't really treat me. He was close to tears. 'The white friars are a poor order. Anything we spend comes out of the common purse. I have my brothers to consider.' Then he might have blushed.

When I offered to pay, he smiled his gaunt thanks and shook his head. 'It was my suggestion. But I appreciate the thought.' We went inside. Here was the world where *1984* was conceived. The Aerated Bread Company's teashops all had a smell, largely disappeared from the English culinary landscape, of weak, overboiled tea, grease, brown sauce, sweet pastry, what used to be called spotted dick and thin vanilla custard. As we picked up our metal trays and joined the line, the friar looked around the crowded cafeteria as if experiencing it for the first time.

Reaching into his habit, the monk took out a worn, nondescript leather bag with drawstrings, holding it tightly as we moved down the line, picking up a plate with a toasted bun on it, a thick cup of milky tea, all as if he did not quite understand what he was looking at. He checked the prices carefully before counting the big pennies from his bag to his hand. I was aware of people making jokes about him, a girl sniggering. In comparison he had an air of artless dignity. At seventeen, of course, I felt awkward on his behalf and angry at the other customers. Remembering how he behaved, I now think he knew exactly what was happening.

We carried our trays to the nearest glass-topped table. At his request, I told him a little about myself. He didn't seem surprised that I was editing a magazine at such an early age. But he had not heard of any of the writers I liked until I mentioned a recent favourite book, absurdist Ronald Firbank's *The Eccentricities of Cardinal Pirelli*.

The name seemed familiar to him. 'Oh, really? Are you acquainted?' He meant, I thought, did I actually know Firbank.

'Well, not personally, of course. He died so long ago. Before I was born.'

He seemed startled. 'Surely –?'

'I'm not certain when...' I was puzzled by his puzzlement. I then mentioned Charles Williams but this produced confused babbling from him about theology so I gave up. I thought later he might know a Cardinal Pirelli.

He sipped his tea glancing towards the plate-glass window and the busy traffic of the Hill, at a Number 15 bus, all red-and-gold enamel, splashed with the city's filth, purring and quivering and steaming as it waited at the stop. 'We lose touch with the world so easily in the abbey. You must forgive me if I seem a little stupid.'

'Not at all. Do you like him? Williams?'

'I fear we are a little restricted in our reading. Might I ask when you were born?'

I told him January 1940 and he laughed. 'How foolish of me. I should have realised. I have absolutely no sense of the passage of time out here.'

'Surely you've lived in this area for a while? The whole of Fleet Street around you. You're not exactly far away from the sources of news.' I then became apologetic. I had sounded rude to my own ears. But he was shaking his head.

'Surprising as it may be, Master Michael, we are pretty well shut off from this world.' He glanced down at his cup, wetted his little finger and rubbed at what was probably a smudge of lipstick on the rim. 'Close as it seems!'

I said that I envied him his solitude.

At this, he shook his head again. 'Oh, it's not exactly *solitude* in the world of the Sanctuary.' I think the sound he made was a chuckle. 'Only if you're lucky.'

This was the first time I'd heard him use the term. When he noticed my enquiry, he added, 'You probably know the Sanctuary better as "Alsacia".' And when I shook my head, he gave a small shrug. 'I forget. We're a little off the beaten track...'

'I was born in Brookgate,' I said. 'I thought I'd explored all the local backstreets. Perhaps you could point your abbey out to me sometime. I've probably passed it on a hundred occasions and not noticed it. There are parts of London that are really rural, whole fields, like the ones behind Sporting Club Square. All the allotments. They're disappearing. I've been trying to teach myself to be more observant.'

'Well, it's surely best when you have a guide,' he told me. He seemed to reach an important decision, his expression changing markedly. He frowned to himself. 'Would you care to see it today? This would be an ideal moment. The abbot...'

'I'm free.' I finished my teacake. 'This would be a good time for me, too. They don't expect me back at the office today. I mean, if it's no trouble...' Should I have trusted him so readily? Had he already slipped something in my cup?

'Never any great trouble for me,' he said. 'You always do need a guide, I fear. At least at first. I, of course, had mine.' Now his chuckle was spontaneous, self-deprecating. 'It's practically impossible to find the Sanctuary's gates without help. But you must be prepared for a surprise or two.'

'The other monks won't mind?'

'That's never the question. We welcome to Alsacia all who discover us. We have done so almost since we were founded. Our articles demand we turn none away. Noble or commoner. Saint or sinner. Man or woman. That is the nature of our calling, to provide sanctuary for any who need it. The wealthy give us donations. The poor and the needy benefit, for they can hide here as well as work. Just as we took vows of poverty, to follow the example of the Nazarene, so, too, do we neither judge nor seek to punish. We are bound to forgive and to pray. To take in all who suffer. All who are in danger of persecution.'

I was impressed. This was the first time I had encountered such an idea. I realised how ignorant I was about church institutions. 'Well, I'm not exactly...' Maybe there was a brochure. I got up and followed him from the teashop, out into the grey press of Ludgate Hill. We turned together down New Bridge Street and crossed over to stand at the intersection of Fleet Street and Ludgate Circus. I looked back up the hill to where St Paul's stood washed by the rays of the late-afternoon sun. Suddenly a silence fell over the busy streets. I found myself mesmerised by the sight of the great cathedral, remembering the stories I had grown up with, of the Blitz, the miraculous failure of the Nazi incendiaries to do anything but minor damage, while the surrounding streets all guttered and howled.

As we waited for the traffic lights to change, I asked him, 'Did your abbey suffer much during the Blitz?'

We began to cross Fleet Street. 'Oh, not at all,' he replied. 'We were always singularly blessed, you know. The Plague. The Great Fire. It's believed our covenant protects us.'

'Somehow Brookgate didn't get much damage either,' I said. 'A few people called that a miracle.'

As we walked he told me how the Carmelites had originally lived on the slopes of Mount Carmel, near Haifa, mostly inhabiting caves and shacks, before being expelled by zealous Saracens in the thirteenth century. They had no saintly founder like the Dominicans and Franciscans. Other orders sometimes questioned the Carmelites' religious credentials. Happily, Christian kings wished to show their piety by giving them lands, especially in Britain and France. They had found homes for their order in various parts of Europe, including Amsterdam, Paris, London and Oxford. They were called white friars because of their robes, just as the Dominicans, with their dark habits, who had arrived in London at about the same time, had been called black friars. Both orders had been granted the land under Royal Charter, by devout noblemen.

With passers-by occasionally glancing at us, we continued past the Punch, the Old Bell, the Cheshire Cheese, the Tipperary and all the other many pubs which served the street's journalists; past the offices of the *Daily Telegraph*, *Daily Mail*, *Daily Sketch*, *News Chronicle* and half a dozen other national newspapers. It seemed strange that such a pious man should have his home in what was, after all, a pretty impious place. I didn't notice which side street we turned into. Perhaps Bouverie Street, where that least godly of newspapers, the scandalmongering *News of the World*, had its offices, possibly Whitefriars Street. Another side street and then we were crossing a small Georgian square, one of the minor Inns of Court, where lawyers had their chambers. Then Friar Isidore stopped in another old square, an Inn of Court I wasn't familiar with, and stared at a big, battered oaken gate, one of a pair, bound with huge straps of black iron, on massive hinges. Worn, grimy, weather-stained, it seemed as old as time.

'That must be more ancient than most of the City,' I said.

'You can see it?' He seemed enormously pleased.

I laughed. 'Well, of course I can. It's massive.'

He stepped forward and pushed hard at the gate, ushering me through.

I expected to find myself in the courtyard of an old ecclesiastical building. Instead, as the door closed behind me, I saw that I was in a cobbled street, like several you could then still discover in the area. I was struck by an unusual smell, completely different to anything I'd ever experienced and impossible to identify. The smell was at once earthy and sharp, more like a market at full pitch, a mixture of vegetables, fish, fruit, cooked food, spice, malfunctioning lavatories and all different kinds of smoke. On both sides of the narrow alley leaned tall half-timbered houses, their second, even third storeys pitched at crazy angles out above their ground floors. Such houses, too, could still occasionally be found in my part of London. An entire stretch of them stood minutes from where I lived in High Holborn. Others were at the western end of Fleet Street. Most were all rather too tidily preserved. These buildings, however, had a different air to them, at once decrepit and full of vitality, with crooked wooden blinds, some hanging by a single hinge; paint peeling on doors and woodwork; part of the plaster exposed to reveal lath or brick; creepers, vines crawling up, over and through tiles missing from roofs out of which also jutted crooked stone chimneys gouting sooty clouds into the damp grey air.

The cobbles were grubby and I was just able to avoid stepping into horse droppings directly in front of me. Apart from the gypsies, the Brookgate and Holborn dairies' nags and the occasional policeman's mount, I had never seen a horse in the Fleet Street area. Even more astonishing to me, a couple of fat, red-combed white chickens were pecking at the dung. They were dispersed, clucking and flapping, as a woman in a long, nondescript skirt, wearing a grubby cap on her dirty hair, came running from the house with a shovel and bucket, to scoop the stuff up. I remembered my Uncle Fred doing this when he followed the milkman's cart down Leather Lane during the war, bent on getting the manure for the little rose-and-vegetable garden he tended behind our house in Fox Street.

An early autumn afternoon fog was darkening a day not yet lit by gas. Behind some of the thickly glazed windowpanes yellow light began to flicker and bloom. Their blinds and curtains drawn, a number of windows were patched with oiled paper. Most others had green-tinged 'bottle-glass' panes. Maybe they had been blown out in the Blitz and not yet replaced? Britain was still emerging from that long, grey, hand-me-down period. Some parts of London, too, had either resisted government improvements or been overlooked. The yellow glow grew warmer, steadier, either from candles or oil lamps and not gas, as I'd originally guessed. I began to wonder how on earth I had failed to discover this quaint bit of London as a boy. It was extraordinary. The smell alone, being so much like one of the big London markets, was acrid, sweet, musty, ancient, intense, impossible to identify. Why did I feel uneasy?

From hidden alleys came shouts, the occasional cry of a child, coarse grunts and elaborate curses. I was reminded of the old public slum courts and Peabody estates that still survived around Brookgate, where our narrow lanes wound through to Grays Inn Road. I tended to avoid those blocks of flats in case I was challenged by one of the 'court cliques' which metamorphosed into the 1950s Teddy Boy gangs. Luckily they fought mostly among themselves from echoing court to echoing court. They barely bothered you if you were an obvious neutral.

I couldn't see any gangs in the Sanctuary. A lot of people crowded together here but no more than in, say, Leather Lane market on a Friday. They could belong to some religious sect, judging by their old-fashioned clothes. I saw them strolling, gossiping, chatting on cobbled corners, seated at open windows. We passed a massive coaching inn, with servants' or guests' rooms built out above the central stone-and-red-brick archway. Overlooked by balconies, there was space in the inn's cobbled yard for a full-sized express coach and team, or three modern buses. The odd picture on its sign was explained by the tavern's name: The Swan With Two Necks. What I could see of the stables looked new enough but logically had not been used in half a century at least. Dull brass, black leather, dark green paint, black beams and whitewashed walls, almost fresh. I could even see some tack. Recently dressed up for something. The coronation, probably. Around the time Queen Elizabeth II had been crowned, there had been a lot of 'New Elizabethan' nostalgia for the glorious days of Good Queen Bess. Days that never really were, of course. New myths for a new age. Above was a gallery of leaded glass behind which someone moved swiftly, lighting candles. The entrance's signboard showed the mythical swan encountering three happy greybeards seated in a row on a bench with huge two-pint 'shant' tankards on their knees. It might have been painted by Tom Browne or Phil May, those master-draughtsmen of Edwardian London. I was surprised I had never heard of the place. From it came a smell of strong beer, shag tobacco, frying chops.

I heard a shout from nearby and looked back. From around the corner, ducking beneath the tavern's low overhang, straight from a Dick Turpin story Tom Browne himself might have illustrated, rode a dramatically pretty young woman. Kitted in some sort of eccentric hunting outfit, with shining black thigh-high boots, doeskin breeches, a cutaway velvet midnight-blue coat, frothing lace at throat and wrists, she wore a befeathered tricorn on her long, red-gold curls. Pure Howard Pyle stuff. Even though she probably was dressed to rehearse for a coming pantomime, with herself as the 'principal boy', I fell instantly in love with the woman's huge violet eyes and full, red lips. Almost riding us down, she struck one bold, appraising look back at me before cantering into the innyard yelling, I'd swear, for an ostler. An *ostler*? Was there a film crew in the upper galleries? Her horse was a beautiful chestnut stallion, furnished in oiled leather and silvered steel, his flanks flecked with sweat. Those brass-wrapped holsters on her saddle were big enough for monstrous horse pistols the size of carbines. I laughed, guessing they were making a movie about rural Ireland, and watched her long legs as she swung off her horse. My heart beat rapidly. I recognised her.

She'd appeared often in a recurring dream I'd experienced several years earlier. Probably puberty had something to do with it! Then I'd seen her as my sister. Now the feelings she sparked were not brotherly. I wanted to follow her, find out her name. Of course I couldn't possibly leave Friar Isidore, but the urge to do so was strong. I might never have the luck to dream of her again!

Then the tavern was behind us. We turned left. With the fog still thickening, we reached a large stone building at the end of a cul-de-sac, a narrow Gothic archway and a door whose battered ancient oak and iron were older even than the first. Could that sight or the fog be causing the pressure in my chest? I drew as deep a breath as possible, observing a massive brass crucifix nailed to the door. No, not a crucifix, but more like the looped Egyptian cross. Beneath it, carved on a piece of wood, was a mysterious Greek inscription, *Panta Rhei*. Below this an iron grille was set into the door. Friar Isidore lifted the old black knocker and rapped out what was evidently a prearranged sequence. A dark brown eye gleamed on the other side of the grille, blinked as if in surprise, then disappeared.

A moment later I heard the scrape and squeal of bolts and bars and then, feeling sudden alarm for no obvious reason, I was admitted to the ancient London abbey of that Most Pious Order of Old Flete Carmelite Friars.

Friar Isidore drew a deep breath, as if in relief, and put his arm around my shoulders.

CHAPTER THREE

THE FISH CHALICE

THE DOOR LED not into a building but into stone cloisters running around a small courtyard, much of which had been put to lawn. Surrounding this were twelve squat yew trees whose massive trunks must have grown there for a thousand years. Lit at intervals by lanterns, the cloisters encircled the whole courtyard and were entered on the far side through another door, almost the twin of the one we'd used. The priory building enclosing the courtyard was partly of stone, partly of warm red brick, its black oak beams standing out strongly through the fog, while the stone and mortar, on the other hand, disappeared into it. I loved this effect, especially when concrete was the grey material made to vanish. The smell of the yews and the fog mingled. A familiar stew: London! Town and country were always best when organically entwined.

We took the mossy path leading directly across the lawn to the other door. I heard a robin ticking at us from the ivy as if we threatened her territory. A plump, cheerful, tonsured monk appeared in the doorway, looked up, recognised Friar Isidore and smiled, did not recognise me, and frowned. He introduced himself as Brother Constantine and fussed with a large key attached to the loose belt tied around his waist. Then, before anyone could speak, his brow cleared and he looked at me with an expression of genial welcome. Maybe he thought I was a volunteer? Turning the key again, he beckoned us back into the relative warmth of the priory church. Clearly this did not serve a large group of monks. We stood in some sort of vestibule. Directly ahead of us was a small nave from which emerged a very old monk, beaming benignly at me as if I were a long-lost nephew. 'My dear boy! But you are early, are you not? I was at my prayers and now I have an appointment with our – the treasure...'

'This is our Father Abbot,' declared Friar Isidore at his pause. 'Father Grammaticus is a little absent-minded. Possibly we should...' As he spoke we followed the abbot back into the building. Suddenly the chapel was alive with gorgeous colour! From modern-looking, strangely abstract stained-glass windows poured the most extraordinary vibrant light, flooding across the deep-yellow stones of the small nave. Standing before this on a plinth of its own was a tall, slender-stemmed silver-chased vessel I took to be a chalice. The vessel caught the last of the light as it passed through the rich glass and spread in a shimmering pool, an unstable halo throughout the chapel. Suddenly in that wild, uncertain brilliance the gilded pewter and green-gold-red enamel resembled a moving fish straining upward to the surface. The abbot appeared to hesitate before making a gesture towards the cup. He then turned, apparently baffled, as if listening to a voice we could not hear. By the set of his head he might even be taking instruction. He turned, spreading his hands in apology. 'I had hoped to invite you here for tea, but apparently –'

'We have had tea, thank you, Father Abbot, in those – in that –'

'ABC,' I supplied. 'In Ludgate Hill.'

The abbot stared at me, his mouth forming the words I had just spoken. I felt I had stumped him somehow. I had no idea what to say next.

'Then you must come tomorrow. Around four?' He looked behind us as if someone had brought him good news. 'He saw our gate, did he?'

Reflected light flared in his eyes. Then it was gone.

'Oh, he did.' The friar beamed; but for me, mystified by this exchange, the chapel was suddenly gloomy again and where I had been vaguely aware of a sense of joy I now felt something close to depression. 'I had best be getting home I suppose,' I said.

Friar Isidore answered in surprise. 'The fog. Aren't you unsure? Isn't it dangerous? If the gate has moved you could become lost for ever as others have. You'll be walking back?' His concern betrayed a certain innocence. 'Can you find your way?'

I was charmed by him. I laughed. 'Easily. Thanks.' We shook hands, his dry, delicate, almost transparent skin rustling against mine. I'd felt nothing like it. So old, so soft, so thin I thought I might tear it!

'Meet me here at the bookshop by The Swan With Two Necks, at half past three,' he said.

For another instant the scene was framed in pearly pink light until the surrounding shadows merged and we found ourselves in the cloisters again, walking towards the outer gate. Then we stood in the little cobbled cul-de-sac with tall, leaning houses on both sides. The fog was deeper as we made our way back. From the warm windows of The Swan With Two Necks, that brick and daub half-timbered tavern on the opposite corner, came the stink of strong, bitter beer and the somewhat muted sound of voices lowered perhaps in conspiracy. Next door to the tavern stood the bookshop, still open, with shaded oil lamps flickering outside for customers to read by. A large tortoiseshell cat cleaned herself in the window. An old man with long white hair looked up from the book he was examining. On the other side was a spice merchant's, its shutters already closed against the fog. I looked everywhere, hoping for another glimpse of the red-ringleted young woman who had ridden so furiously into the tavern's courtyard. I pretended that I wanted to look at the books, but Friar Isidore hurried now. He took me hesitantly by the elbow to guide me towards that big gate. Did it, like some Inns of Court, still shut at dusk? A few oddly dressed women stopped their gossiping to glance with greater interest at the two of us. He opened the gate just wide enough for me to squeeze through, cautiously glanced out and waved a worried goodbye. 'Godspeed, Master Michael!'

With its exotic scents and queerly dressed people, this area was more like Soho than the City. I hurried up towards Grays Inn Road. My footsteps gave off that strange muffled echo which defied location. Fog made the world timeless and spaceless. Of course I knew the route well enough, up to Holborn and from there to Brookgate Market, but I was coughing heartily by Chancery Lane. The more I saw of Alsacia, the less my lungs would be able to tolerate the familiar atmosphere of my boyhood, even though I had walked through worse pea-soupers. When the Clean Air Act came into force and it became illegal to burn the coal or coke which gave our fog its distinctive smell, the cities of England lost much of their lethal magic. We would never again see the coalman on his regular rounds, his sacks being counted in, hundredweight by hundredweight, to a million domestic coal holes. His work became a rural or posh-people's trade, along with chimney sweeps and the old reliable street services, like knife grinders and crumpet men you once saw every winter. They were the common cultural-map references we thought would always endure. They vanished before you could turn around, like story papers and gobstoppers. And toy soldiers. While my mum worked I was even looked after by the horse-gypsies who had stabled their livestock in Brooks Mews. They had taught me to ride their ponies through the nearby streets and, like my auntie, tell fortunes with tarot or ordinary playing cards. A few years later, they were gone, absorbed into the rest of the community, lost in the fog of the past.

In 1950 I was in Gamages buying boxes of Messrs Britain & Sons' lead soldiers in all their glorious uniforms of empire and by 1970 I was fingering plastic GIs and wondering what had happened to all that gold braid, scarlet and navy blue enamelled onto tiny hollow-cast military men. Sometime between 1957 and 1963 the world changed completely. I don't think anyone noticed. After the war our world had been generally dull, poor and safe, much like the Depression 1930s. Even when they became Teddy Boys, the racetrack gangsters hung out in two or three pubs we all knew and avoided. By 1965, when money brightened it up, everything became fantastic and more dangerous. The TV seemed to reflect this. Unemployment was part of the cause. We lost the sweets factory, the Old Holborn factory, Cadbury's chocolate biscuit factory, and the B&H dairies all in a couple of years. No wonder the air smelled so sweet. Then warehouses became worth more than the stuff they stored. Houses and factories became 'real estate'. We got more crime, but there was also full-colour advertising, headlines on the front page, umpteen supplements, soft porn on page three, extra TV channels, home-grown horror comics, the Vietnam War and Technicolor Hammer films.

Making my way through that particular fog, enjoying it as I always did, I could pretend I was in a movie, especially one of the Hollywood

Sherlock Holmes stories. Many of my early memories were actually of movies. Anyone was allowed into the cinemas before they made 'universal' and 'adult' certificates. Long before they needed an X certificate. The movies were nearly always in black and white and full of fog. It took me years to realise there were other kinds of films. My mother liked musicals, too, but I associate my childhood visits to the local Rialto with a mood of grim melancholy. There weren't too many happy endings in *The Big Combo* or *They Drive by Night*. Mum loved gangster pictures, preferably featuring misunderstood brutes: James Cagney, George Raft, Robert Ryan, James Mason, Sterling Hayden – the kind of men she would never have allowed into our house in real life.

On that evening I quickly became used to the fog. I pretended I wore a fedora and a trench coat like a character in those American thrillers we loved so much. I experimented with the odd menacing cough. And, enjoying the echo of my own footsteps, I made my way accurately home.

My mother still had her pinafore on, the souvenir Brighton one I'd bought her that summer. Our last holiday together. She had been worried sick, she said, though she seemed perfectly cheerful as she got supper ready. She hadn't lost her wartime habits. Her relief at seeing me safe always overcame her anxiety. She needed to stay busy. Her friend, Mr Ackermann, had given her a job working at his toy stall in the market. She sold mostly Japanese tin toys, cheap and dangerous. I think he only kept the thing running so she had something to do.

Mr Ackermann was of a keen-minded, philosophical disposition. He planned for the long term. Mum was intensely material, mercurial and of the moment. A tolerant woman, too, she fought with herself not to trap me. I've mentioned how she had become a superb liar, one who told and retold her lies until they formed an intricate fantasy so twisted through with strands of intense, bleak reality they often seemed thoroughly true. She became hugely anxious that someone would find out that she invented her stories. From fear of discovery she talked too much. If she stopped talking she knew she would die. She was terrified that someone would successfully challenge her accounts. The stories had almost no intended malice in them. They were fantasies to cheer herself up or give authority to her opinions. When she wanted to be hurtful she wasn't all that good at it.

I felt the strain when she lost touch with her audience! She forgot what she'd told to whom. Much of her energy became devoted to keeping one individual from meeting another in an effort to hide equally rich and intricate lies. Her life took on all the desperate intensity of a Whitehall farce. She would close doors on unexpected visitors, hide others in cupboards and talk loudly over a conversation she didn't want you to hear. Comedy in retrospect, but nerve-racking while it took place. Only Mr Ackermann seemed unaffected. Maybe he believed her. His own early life before escaping to England had been equally fantastic as he was pursued across Europe by Nazis.

I know one or two of Mum's brothers believed she and their other sisters were putting on airs and graces, but they were just the innocent affectations of the petit bourgeois and easily understood and forgiven as mere wish fulfilment. My mother was Sarah Bernhardt compared to the others. Both her sisters were envious, afraid and amazed by what she made of them all. They were simply characters in a mighty novel she carried in her head and, to be fair, her heart. She created a *Comédie Humaine* of her own, longer by far than *Gone with the Wind*. My mother was flattered when men said she looked like Vivien Leigh. They soon discovered she was as confused and vulnerable as Leigh was said to be. And then they tended to fade away, back into the crowded pubs of Brookgate.

Mum went to bed. 'Goodnight, love,' she said. I stayed up reading. There was no late-night telly in those days.

Before I got ready for bed I looked up the Carmelites in my dad's old *Encyclopædia Britannica*. He had bought it on the instalment plan when he had thought to better himself before the war. Mum had made the rest of the payments. It's where she got the details of all the foreign trips she told everyone she was making. It was almost brand-new and the thin pages were a bit damp, tending to stick together. But I found all I wanted to know. The order had grown up as some sort of loose community of hermits on the flanks of Mount Carmel. They might be originally pre-Christian, but Abraham, the prophet Elijah and Mary Magdalene all gave them spiritual guidance. Driven from the flames of Mount Carmel by one of Islam's sudden and passing puritanical waves, they were forced to find patrons amongst Europe's nobles. Slowly they grew reconciled to the loss of the Middle East as

European fiefdoms. They came to London in the first quarter or so of the thirteenth century and had lived there according to their own laws since 1241. Anti-Semitic Henry III, with his reputation for piety, but unable to distinguish a Jew from a Mussulman, had welcomed a great many Christian refugees during his reign. And sure enough there had been an abbey on the site near Fleet Street for centuries and Alsacia (or Alsatia) had been built on the monks' land. According to the *Britannica*, London historians generally agreed that, under the charter of King Henry III, the Carmelites were granted their grounds and priory on land bounded by the old 'Flete' River to the east, the Temple to the west, Fleet Street to the north and on the south by the Thames. Their cemetery abutted the river.

Sometime after 1800 the friars and their abbot had been moved to St Joseph's, Bunhill Fields. They left some dissenting brothers behind, probably due to a schism involving the Jesuits or the Jacobites or the Jacobins or someone. Those monks had apparently been seduced from the paths of righteousness by inhaling an evil miasma coming from beneath the original abbey's foundations. Clearly the various arguments in the church were all about ordinary politics. My own political viewpoint was based on the writings of Prince Peter Kropotkin, the mutualist Uncle Fred admired.

Next morning, I looked through the collection of miscellaneous pre-war boys' weeklies I still picked up whenever I came across them. The other fanzine I did, *Book Collectors News*, was mainly for story-paper collectors. I remembered an issue of *Claude Duval* from the 1900s which mentioned some sort of thieves' quarter near Fleet Street. I only had two issues and I found them easily. *Claude Duval* weekly, Issue 6, Price One Penny, *The Armed Men of Alsacia*, 10 January, 1903, with a fine blue-and-red cover by 'R.H.'. The Masked Cavalier himself! Claude on horseback in all his cavalier finery leaping over a massed pile of barrels while his enemies, corrupt but pinch-lip'd Roundhead redcoats, shoot and slash at him without apparent harm to the laughing highwayman who defiantly doffs his splendidly feathered hat and passes effortlessly over the barricade. A great story, part of a continuing serial, printed in eight-point type, which most adults could only read with a magnifying glass, but from long practice was perfectly legible to me! Claude was in Newgate, awaiting execution, having posed as Lord Wilde, the king's confidant, in order to let the real lord escape. I began to read it during breakfast until my mother stopped me. It was bad manners to read at the table. I started to tell her of the Sanctuary. In *The Armed Men of Alsacia* the quarter seemed to occupy a lot more space than the one I had visited. But she wasn't really listening. She talked about some problems my Auntie Nellie was having with her suppliers and the rotten little Court kids coming over to nick stuff off the stall, thinking she was born yesterday.

Before I left for work, I lied to my mum. I said we had a heavy press day, putting together a special issue. I planned to revisit Alsacia. I had promised to meet the abbot for tea but more importantly I hoped for another glimpse of that beautiful, spirited girl who'd ridden into an innyard calling for an ostler! Now my best guess was that she worked for Bertram Mills' Circus. They stabled a lot of their animals across the river in Battersea.

I was still reading when I headed down New Fetter Lane which led into Fleet Lane which joined Fleet Street. I took *Claude Duval*. Courtly, graceful, handsome and daring, he was a virtuoso on the flageolet. He once played a duet with a lady whose coach he was robbing. He then offered not to take a penny from the coach if she would only grant him a dance. Which she did while her coachman played. Frith had done a famous painting of the scene, much copied by story-paper artists.

I was hardly aware of my real surroundings as I read Claude's adventures, keeping half an eye open so I didn't bump into anyone. Before I knew it I had reached Carmelite Inn Chambers and stood looking up at the great iron-bound door in the far corner. With a sense of anticipation I stepped forward and pushed hard on the left side. It didn't budge. I tried the right. Nothing. Stuffing the magazine into my jacket pocket I tried hammering on the doors but only succeeded in hurting my hands. I looked around for someone to ask if the gates opened at a certain time. But Carmelite Inn Chambers was almost deserted. A delivery boy was leaving on his bike. I called 'excuse me' without any luck. Lights began to burn in offices. I hadn't noticed a morning fog drifting in from the river. If I didn't get back up to Fleet Street there was every chance I'd have to waste time waiting it out in a pub. I started to hurry.

Of course, I was soon lost in that maze of little streets snaking around one another, more or less paralleling the Thames. It took me half an hour to find the Temple and by the time I reached the Strand, heading for Trafalgar Square, the sun blazed in a clear, pale winter sky. I knew what had happened. Somehow I had chosen the wrong square. It wasn't Carmelite Inn Chambers at all!

So I got my hair cut in St Martin's Lane and went back to look for another square like Carmelite Inn Chambers. An old Inn of Court where lawyers worked and often lived. That part of London is still full of them. Some sensible monarch set them up when he was reforming the law. The lawyers, of course, soon departed from the spirit of the institution. Rumour had it that most of the apartments were now occupied by mistresses of barristers or the barristers' mothers.

Remembering that I was due to have tea with the abbot I did everything I could to find the place. Now I felt guilty as well as frustrated. I went back to the Old Bailey, to the typesetter, but they were closed. For hours I tried to find a square that resembled Carmelite Inn Chambers, but I discovered nothing nearby. The more I returned to it, the more I was sure I had been right the first time. I tried pushing on the gates. I asked passers-by what they thought was behind them. Most said they had been sealed up since before the war. Others thought there was a boatyard back there, or some kind of junk business. Some of the chambers appeared to look onto the Sanctuary, but, when I asked to see, I was told those windows had been bricked up since before the war. What sort of delusion could I have suffered? I returned to Fleet Street and had a glass of claret at El Vino while I sat and refused to believe what was happening. When people I knew came in I was cheerful. I didn't say anything about my obsession. There is nothing like an obsession to keep food off the table. I decided to wait until Pete Taylor and Barry Bayley could come with me.

I also decided to keep trying periodically but not to spend my life on it. If I continued to insist on searching for the mysterious gate, I'd really go crazy. However, I was suspicious of comparisons to those stories about vanishing shops or houses, so popular with readers around the end of the nineteenth century. In my world, if a house suddenly vanished it was because Hitler had dropped a bomb on it. Those gates had to be somewhere! Could I be experiencing a trick of the fog?

Although I felt awkward about missing that teatime appointment, I was still mainly intrigued by the young woman I had glimpsed riding into the innyard. She was around my age. Wonderful in her tricorn hat and thigh-high boots, she was quite literally my dream girl. Every time I was in the Fleet Street area I looked out for her.

Three days later Bayley came round to return a *Science Fantasy* he'd borrowed. We went to the Globe, then back to his place. I kept him up all night, going through my little trauma over and over again, showing him the copy of *Claude Duval*. He listened mainly, he admitted, because I was buying. Early next morning I dragged him back to Carmelite Inn Chambers to look for the gate. Barry's hangover had been growing worse. When we reached the gate he pushed it open easily, much to my surprise, and immediately stepped back, holding his nose. 'What a bloody stench!' Then he turned around and began to throw up in the gutter.

It didn't smell that bad to me. 'Come on,' I said. 'Let's go in.'

'Bugger that. It stinks too much. I'll get off home, I think.' He began to stagger back towards the entrance to the court. 'Good luck!'

'Thanks,' I said.

There was nothing else to do. I told Barry I'd see him later. I pushed the gate a little wider and walked in.

CHAPTER FOUR

THE ABBOT'S 'COSMOLABE'

AND THEN I was in the cobbled street where that wonderful swaying signboard announced in cold daylight The Swan With Two Necks. Remembering to close the gate behind me, I only now realised that those who'd caroused last night had doubtless not yet looked day in the eye. A man in shirt and long underwear glared at me as he stumbled past. Cautiously I pushed open a door of the inn. The smell of sour beer had not yet cleared. On the floor was the previous night's swept-up rubbish, scrubbed boards, broken clay pipes, bundles of sweet straw about to be scattered by two little potboys who were of course unaware I had no right to be there. They tipped their caps and called me 'sir'. I took the nearby stairs with pretended authority and walked along a landing giving onto several battered oak doors.

I had no idea what I was looking for or why I was here except, I told myself, that there might be a news story in it. The girl had been very attractive. I was pretty sure she was an actress. If I could find out what her connection with the pub was I might be able to get our regular photographer to take her picture. Together we could make a few guineas. We were always paid in guineas in those days. It separated the trades, who received pounds, from the professions. Working people and the trades were paid in pounds and fractions of pounds, shillings and pence. But, like lawyers and doctors, writers and artists were paid one pound, one shilling. Just as every draper's price always ended in three farthings. The flannel was not ten pounds, but £9.19.11¾d.

This idea of making money, however, was rank self-deception. Pure rationalisation. I had no professional interest in the girl. I had yet to admit my compulsion to get a second look at someone I had previously seen only in my dreams.

Evidently the rest of the place was asleep. Feeling guilty about my intrusion I turned and went back downstairs. I took a side door out into the stableyard and stood gazing directly across at the horses. Horses! Two blacks, a grey and a chestnut. Good riding horses by the look of them. This place was some sort of mews now, I guessed. Maybe municipally owned? People still rode in places like Hyde Park. These horses were probably rented by the hour. If so, they were in beautiful condition, especially the two black stallions. This part of the inn being more or less public, I felt all anyone could do was tell me the place was closed and ask me to leave. The smell of horses was strong as I walked over the washed cobbles. I was still utterly amazed by the sight of them. The gypsies had taught me a bit about horses. I realised that all eight stalls offered a reasonably airy space where riding horses could be tethered. Three stalls were empty. One at the back held an old sorrel mare who did not look ready to ride, but her coat and eyes were bright. She was in great condition for her age.

A tall, pink-skinned, lanky youth of about my age, whose long stringy blond hair was tied back with a simple bit of dark blue ribbon, looked up from where he was raking out a stall. He had a handsome, sardonic, friendly face, with startling black eyes, his thin mouth turned up in a look I took for habitual amusement. He wore a long, old-fashioned coat and breeches, a big cotton shirt, black and white. Almost some sort of uniform, with a big leather apron over it. His voice was straight warm Cockney of the old, refined kind. There were still pockets of that accent all over the City, hangovers from the fashionable upper-class accent of the eighteenth century. 'Joey Cornwall at your service, young sir.' He made a deep, comic bow. 'You look like the devil about to be baptised. Are you lost?'

'I am a bit.' For no good reason I trusted Joey Cornwall. 'I came here a few days ago with Brother Isidore from the abbey. I liked the look of the place. Thought I'd try a drink today.' Unlike my talented ma, my own blushes probably told him I was offering a half-truth. I was always a poor liar. I found it easier to lie on paper. You got paid for that.

He was laughing now. 'Or maybe you're looking for a job? Or for someone you know or maybe a long-lost relative or a doxy you saw last night?'

I joined him in his laughter. 'Honestly, it's true. I went by with Brother Isidore and thought I'd come back to have another look at the place. He didn't seem the type to join me at the bar. It looks like the sort of pub where you can get a decent pint.'

'That you can.' His grin widened. 'In about three hours.'

At that time the pubs were licensed usually from 11 a.m. to 3 p.m. around Fleet Street. They opened again at 6 p.m. and closed at 10 p.m. 'I'll drop by at lunchtime,' I told him.

'You won't regret it.' He offered me a broad wink. 'Come in early for eels and mash and a fresh pie. Steak and kidney, pork, beef and liver, tongue, they're lovely.' Pushing his extraordinarily long pale hair from his eyes, he spoke as if he'd never heard of rationing. This was still austerity Britain. Some things were only available through your ration book. At that time you were still lucky to get a decently filled meat pie of any kind.

That was an outstanding pub! Why, in a fraternity of drinking men, had I never been told of The Swan With Two Necks? Just the name would have sparked the imagination of romantic hacks like us.

Thanking Mr Cornwall I made to leave, turned and found myself almost knocking over the young woman I had seen before. Her eyes were cloudy with sleep. She smelled warm and sweet. She wore a loose smock on top of what were probably her nightclothes and she apologised huskily at the moment I was doing the same. She brightened in an instant however. 'By Gad, boy,' she said – barefoot, she barely reached my shoulder and looked younger than me – 'why up at this hour? Is that the paper?' She snatched my copy of *Claude Duval* from my pocket, glanced at it and, disappointed, gave it back to me. Those violet eyes frowned. 'What are you after? Help? Or are you perhaps an aspiring Runner out for our Claude's reward?'

'I'm on my way to work,' I said, feeling like a fool. 'I'm a journalist.'

She smiled, offering me a mock salute. 'I beg your pardon, then, sir. I'll not keep you.' And she stepped aside for me to pass.

She knew how she had embarrassed me and gave me a friendly wink as I blushed by. For all my early experience with girls, I was still a teenage boy. I could only mumble something, stare at the floor, try not to step on her pretty feet, grope for a non-existent handrail and get away from the source of my embarrassment as soon as possible. 'Will you be here for lunch?' I stammered.

'Oh, if I'm up, no doubt,' she said.

Before I knew it I was running out of Alsacia and was halfway up Fetter Lane, almost at the *Tarzan Adventures* office.

My mind wasn't on my work that day. My hangover didn't get much better. I felt vaguely let down by Barry, who had failed to confirm what I had seen in the Alsacia. Mostly, however, my head was full of the young woman I had seen again. She was everything I had ever dreamed of since I was a boy. Her red hair! Her violet eyes! With final page proofs gone to press, Thursday was always a bit slow. Our boss at *Tarzan*, Donald Peters, usually went home to the country that day. After he left, we, too, tended to take things a bit easy. That was also payday, when I treated myself to a large Dover sole at the Globe, whose lunches I had enjoyed long before I knew about the SF meetings. They used light matzo batter and served thick, crisp chips, fresh green peas or cauliflower, depending on the season. A bit of salad on the side. A pint of best bitter. But this time I put the proofs to press and got down to Carmelite Inn Chambers as fast as I could, back across Fleet Street, through the same Inns of Court and into Alsacia. Over gleaming flint cobbles I entered The Swan With Two Necks, crowded with what I determined was a noisy group of actors, probably from the theatres of Aldgate or the Strand. I understood the costume the young woman had worn. And why she was such a beauty. She was a film star! Being fairly secluded, this pub was taken over by people who might be recognised by the public. They certainly couldn't enter an ordinary pub dressed as they were.

I had hard work pushing myself through men in long leather-and-silk coats, lacy shirts, brightly coloured velvet trousers. The three-cornered hats perched on their wigs made me think of actors in a TV production of *The Beggar's Opera*. The names on the beer casks were unfamiliar, so I asked for a pint of 'best' and was about to pay for it when the grinning girl spotted me and made a sign to the barman. My beer was free. She gestured for me to follow her through a door into a small private bar where she greeted me with her own glass against mine. By their finery the people here were the stars of the production. She remembered me. Her name was Molly, she said. Oh, those eyes and ringlets!

She asked my name and then, jumping onto a chair, called out for silence. 'Now boys, I'd like to introduce you to our guest. This here's Master Michael Moorcock, a scrivener by trade.' Did I hear Irish in her voice? 'Yonder's Captain King and next to him old Captain Turpin and next to him young Captain Turpin. Captain Langley, Captain Jack Sheppard. Colonel Billy Pike. Colonel Carson. Colonel Bowie and Colonel Cody.'

I gasped, barely able to speak. These actors were got up like my boyhood heroes! I was still writing about some of them! I could see them, hear them, certainly smell them and what they were drinking. As I turned to look around, my arm grazed one's unshaven chin. I could practically feel the weight of their greatcoats, noted a grease spot here, a frayed cuff, a tear, a burn mark there. Tom King looked a little redder in the cheeks than I knew from his pictures, Turpin a little too old or a little too young, depending which one was the legendary highway robber. Both looked tired. Overworked, I thought. Jack Sheppard, the same age as me, wore his doom and his youth in equal measure. Jack Rann: 'Sixteen String' Jack. So many Jacks and Dicks! And there was no denying Captain Sheppard to be the only man whose cologne succeeded in disguising any body odour, or that 'Galloping Dick' Langley was shorter than me by at least two inches. What Jim Bowie, Buffalo Bill and Kit Carson had to do in this medley (unless they were in a curtain raiser) I hadn't a notion. But there they stood, glasses raised, enjoying lively conversation with Messrs King and Turpin.

'And,' the violet-eyed beauty murmured over loud greetings, 'I'm known here as Captain Moll Midnight.' She looked at me as if she expected me to recognise who she was but I had only the faintest recollection of her name. Maybe a 1920s heroine in one of my dad's *Boys'*

Friend or *Nelson Lee Library* serials which, with Tarzan, John Carter, Wrykyn, and *The Magnet* and *Gem* had been, by that point in my life, relegated to passing enthusiasms? Currently I was reading Aldous Huxley and Camus, but earlier I would have given a great deal for a good highwayman story by the likes of Stephen Agnew or Morton Pike.

'And this here's Joey Cornwall, our best potboy, or certainly the longest.' Moll slapped the tall stable lad on a back she was scarcely able to reach. He was the same I had met earlier. Just as amiable, intelligent and knowing, with those sharp black crow's eyes that noticed everything. He winked at me as he carried empties back to the bar. He'd had my measure all along.

For some reason only the most famous highwayman, the elder Turpin, showed me any ill will. He scowled a little and turned his back on me. Was he jealous of the attention Moll gave me? He made a coarse joke under his breath. A few smirked unenthusiastically at it. He stank of ladies' perfume, blood and fresh-skinned furs. He also broadcast raw physical power. He had that charisma all the crowd's favourites give off. They are scarcely aware of it and take it all for granted. I was disappointed. Even if he was merely an actor, I felt uncomfortable at his apparent snub.

As Moll made her introductions I knew I had stepped into some wonderful dress rehearsal, a pageant of London's rogues. Too elaborate for TV back then! A film? A *Beggar's Opera*. A *Rogue's Romance*. Even Joey seemed to be 'in character' – playing a part. He gave no sign that he saw anything odd about what was going on. Either these were consummate actors in a perfect set (maybe the Whitefriars Theatre, long since demolished) or they really did believe they were a bunch of infamous highwaymen and frontiersmen, whose main exploits were now mostly reprinted from weeklies and put into pocket-size monthlies. They were actually recast from weekly 1900s text magazines.

I was already fascinated by the way modern mythology took characters from different eras and put them together. *Tarzan* ran strips featuring Buffalo Bill, Davy Crockett, Daniel Boone, Texas Jack and Calamity Jane all together in the same story. Why should I be surprised if a B-movie featured so many heroes from disparate times? I would hardly have been surprised to see Tarzan, Lord Greystoke or

John Carter of Mars sipping cognac in the private snug. But I was also confused. Why didn't I, as a journalist, know about some locally made, reasonably expensive historical film? We got all the film companies' publicity material. I'd heard nothing of a play or a movie featuring so many famous heroes and thieves from fiction and history. The more I listened, the more obvious it was that the general conversation of these men wasn't that of actors. They told stories of horses and transport in general, more like men who worked on the buses. Had they been hired to give authenticity to an elaborate pageant? Re-enactors we'd call them now.

I was beginning to like the slightly more fantastic idea that the whole area was some kind of posh psychiatric hospital, hidden away in the busy, bustling heart of London. It could have been here for centuries, like other, similar institutions. Maybe the white friars ran a madhouse? The 'Sanctuary' certainly sounded like a loony bin. Where I'd visited my mad Uncle Jimmy near Streatham had a name very much like it. You'd think it was a convent or private estate unless you had relatives or loved ones there. That's why it was so hard to find!

Loonies or not, I enjoyed their company. Moll paid me a great deal of attention, which of course was flattering. I remembered the morning warmth of her, through those nightclothes. I was already in love with her smile. She was genuinely interested in my writing. Back in my cups I decided very quickly that she was my soul mate. I'd dreamed of a girl who aroused these same emotions. Clearly she was interested in me. I had seen more than one film where a glamorous star fell for the fresh-faced kid with that special something and a talent for rock and roll. The cinemas currently were stiff with them, trying to catch the 'youth market'. Meanwhile, my beard was well on the way. Other kids tried to look like Elvis or Buddy Holly, but I wasn't modelling myself on a contemporary pop star. The coolest guitarist I knew in Soho was a dandy called Max Stone. He was probably the first mod, with his white button-down shirt, slim black tie, black coat, black narrow trousers. When we met he had this cool, slightly satanic Van Dyke beard and moustache. Sort of cavalier, very self-contained, he played like Django. There really wasn't anyone cooler than Max. A lot of these guys came close, though. I again heard that faintly old-fashioned accent. It reminded me of Edwardian upper-class London and was almost like modern Cockney. I had heard very old ladies in Gamages speaking like that when they ordered school uniforms for their grand-daughters. Years later I met Irene Handl. She had the same natural accent. In fact all the voices, as I listened, seemed to have unfamiliar accents. I think my imagination made Pecos Bill's seem Italian. Buf-falo Bill and Kit Carson sounded what we used to call 'educated' American: soft-voiced and every word and letter articulated. Half their vocabulary was foreign to me but that was true of whichever vocab-ulary was not my own.

While all those good-humoured heroes enjoyed a drunkard's lunch, I didn't drink much myself. My horrible hangover was at last subsid-ing and I wanted to look my best in front of Moll. I was scarcely stag-gering when the big clock over the landlord's station chimed three. I expected the tavern to begin closing. This publican however showed no fear of a copper's helmet. I admired his cheek. I let Moll draw me to her. I was relaxing my guard when Tom King, creeping up from behind, got too amorous. She clearly did not like his touch and wrig-gled away from us both, flouncing upstairs. She paused in the semi-darkness of the first landing and blew me a kiss. Her voice was low, directed at me. 'Meet me here tomorrow evening. Perhaps we'll do something.' She winked.

I nodded, blushed and, feeling the need to escape Tom's boozy glare, made my way out to the street and down to the old bookshop, hardly looking at the titles until slowly it dawned on me what an astonish-ing stock the shop had. There were editions going back to Elizabe-than times, huge books by William Blake with hand-coloured engravings, volumes of *Peregrine Pickle* and *Don Quixote* as sharp as the day they were printed, with uncut pages. There, too, were Vic-torian three-deckers in glittering gold stamping, side by side with brightly dust-wrapped Wodehouse, Edgar Wallace, and mint modern paperbacks. Fascinated, I was tempted to buy a few copies, but I made myself step outside to inspect the cheaper boxes. I remained a little breathless as I swayed above the shop's 'All One Penny' boxes, picking over volumes of sermons and amateur histories with as much concentration as I could muster, clinging a little too firmly to the wooden sides, aware I must be flushed and needing a bucket or two of mouthwash to make myself even modestly presentable. I heard a faint, amused cough behind me. The lugubriously amiable friar offered no sign that he was aware of my condition or indeed that I had failed to keep my last appointment with him. He greeted me with genuine pleasure, thanking me for my punctuality. 'We live by the clock, of course, but I have learned that others are not so quick to note time's blazing.'

'I'm sorry I'm so late,' I said. Was he joking?

'But you are not late!'

'You're very kind. It must be days.'

'Did we not agree to meet at this time?'

'Yes, but –'

'Then if we agreed to meet at this time, this is the time we agreed to meet.'

A bit confused, I smiled. 'If you say so.'

Friar Isidore slipped his arm in mine. Beyond the confines of a few universities, this gesture was rare in a man. If anyone else had made it, I would have felt uncomfortable. He didn't guide me through the streets, but rather assumed we both walked in the same direction. We turned up the cul-de-sac and passed through the yew hedge and across the grassy quadrangle. We came to that same abbey door and entered the Gothic vestibule just as men's voices rose on a single resonant note. Afternoon light filled the place. A rainbow of warm colour. Two monks stepped forward to lay on the altar a living tree branch from which a little green fruit grew. We quietly took the pew at the back. I was fascinated.

Another monk entered carrying that wonderful chalice on a cushion of green and blue. The chalice kept changing its appearance in the light. It resembled a glorious fish standing on its tail. Its almost human mouth seemed to open and close. The yearning eyes were alive with an inner light. The chalice thrust gracefully up towards the sun, moved by the rays into the semblance of a living creature, used almost casually in a ceremony which felt inconceivably ancient. Far, far older than Christianity. I assumed the chalice was only brought out on special occasions. What on earth was it made of? How was the illusion created? The altar was bare except for the branch and cloths. There was no crucifix. The pulpit was occupied by Father Grammaticus, the same little old man with sharp, button-black eyes, whom

I had met before, his frail hands folded in front of him, his head lowered, as if in contemplation.

Their voices falling to a final amen, the monks at prayer all swung about as one to smile at us. A great disparity of ages, races and features. Then they returned their attention to the pulpit, to the Father Abbot who had only to murmur for his voice to be heard clearly. 'Does it ever occur to us to wonder about the real place of religion in today's human affairs?' A conventional enough question I had heard many times on BBC radio, usually at the beginning of a sermon by the radio vicar.

Next followed a set of references so strange to me that I had no idea what was being said. Some words in an unfamiliar language, maybe Greek. Then came a short prayer in what I thought was Hebrew. Some Arabic! I wondered about that service. Few could have had as solid a secular upbringing as I, yet I felt there was something unusual in his words, something moving. Spiritual? Authoritative? Aggressive? I reminded myself that this was a group of people who probably took the ordinary religious stuff for granted. They wouldn't really need the same pep talks as the man or woman in the street. I also felt a bit uncomfortable not knowing the rituals, in spite of their obvious welcome, and was relieved when they finally rose and filed from the pews until all that was left were the green branch on the altar and the Father Abbot beside it, moving it slightly so that it would be in some imagined sunlight the next morning. 'I love these darkening early winter hours, but they are unforgiving to cut boughs or flowers,' he murmured, as if to himself.

When the old man turned he was expectant. He reached towards me in welcome and gestured for us both to follow him. We went out of the side door and into the cloister again. I shivered. It was already growing cold. The sky darkened to grey and a few crows flew over, calling to one another, a foraging family returning home. I could smell wood-smoke mostly, but there was coal in there, too. The dust of a million years. Every ancestor, every invader, almost every relative who had not fought or died abroad was in that air. We opened another old door and found ourselves in a sparely furnished, yet comfortable, sitting room. I saw several holy objects on the walls, including what I knew as an Egyptian cross, an ankh. Yafuz, my Turkish friend at school, had taken one to his eleven-plus exam. It was supposed to bring good luck.

Friar Isidore and I sat down together on a wide, surprisingly comfortable bench. A monk brought tea, milk and sugar and freshly toasted teacakes to the low table. Sitting across from us the abbot himself poured the tea and offered the cakes. They were tasty enough, although the butter or possibly currants had an unfamiliar tinge. I was too polite to take any jam when neither of my hosts did. I had been brought up with austerity manners. Similarly, I had to be pressed to have a second cup of tea, even though it was probably the richest, most delicious brew I had tasted in my life.

Friar Isidore murmured some excuse and left. I remained with the old abbot. Just as if I were drinking tea with a rarely seen relative, Father Grammaticus asked me about my mother and father and my schooling. I answered in a very straightforward way. Unlike a lot of lower middle-class English families mine had no tradition of reticence. The abbot seemed perfectly at ease with my story, nodding as if most of it was already known to him. He was no more or less interested in my religion or lack of it than in my similar failure to engage with mathematics. I told him I had done poorly at school and had left at fifteen. 'And what would you be reading today?' he asked, glancing at my pocket.

A little shamefaced, I showed him the *Science Fantasy* still there since Barry had returned it. He laughed when he saw it. 'Oh, it is not such a fantasy.' He turned it over in his delicate hands. He looked at the bright picture on the front, predominantly scarlet and yellow to represent hellfire, showing a winged Egyptianate cat, a satanic-looking conjuror in white tails and a rather scared-looking young couple. He flipped through. He nodded over it slowly. I could tell that he'd never seen or read anything like it. 'These symbols are not exactly what I recognise.' Then his face cleared. 'Aha! It's a book of fables. I understand.'

'I write such things,' I told him. 'And I tell tales of people like Robin Hood and Claude Duval.' I remember smiling in a self-deprecating way. I was leading up to asking him about all the people I had met at the inn.

'Duval? It's an uncommon name, but we have a rogue calling himself that who comes to mass once a week. More often than most of his fraternity.'

'They're actors, aren't they, sir?' I asked, anxious to get a clearer idea of who those costumed men might be.

'Oh, indeed. Actors, vagabonds, cheapjacks, rum pads and balladeers all of them. I doubt there's one rascal lifts an honest hand, but they're amiable fellows well enough. Plenty of good hearts beat beneath the robber's weeds, as we say.'

So I was disappointed, getting little information for my question, though impressed by the old man's tolerance, if that's what it was. I listened politely while Father Grammaticus told me a little of the abbey's history and the history of Alsacia in general, but I had already read most of it. 'It's astonishing to me that you have managed to remain in this one location for so long,' I said.

'We are blessed in many ways.' He smiled rather sadly. I wondered what price they had to pay for their longevity. 'And we keep our numbers when so many, I read, are losing theirs. It seems a greater darkness than ever hangs over this century.' He smiled again. 'Or did so. God, after all, does not understand time as we. Time is drawn to Him and radiates from Him. Do the living and the dead coexist? Do the real and the imaginary share the same world? Do we bring the myth into the reality by invoking our sense of romance? Does God answer an accumulation of yearning or just a solitary, well-intentioned prayer? The following forty or so years might prove calm, contemplative, even a little progressive in coming to terms with God's purpose for those of us remaining on Earth. Perhaps the atom bomb will frighten us into thinking a little better. And of course, we remain vigilant.'

I had barely followed his train of thought but this last pious remark was one I could easily agree with.

After asking me my age and exact birth date, day and hour, which I could answer because my mother, a believer in astrology, had told me, he rose and showed me around his room. He pointed out relics and holy objects so proudly that I felt obliged to answer with as much interest as I could muster.

'Perhaps? Perhaps that's the secret whose answer we all seek. Peering into the fog.' In front of me a patch of dark grey mist had formed. As I stared into it I heard the abbot's gentle, rhythmic voice.

'Think of nines and threes and twelves. Think of the cards with those numbers. Think of the fool. The child rides from the sun. The wheel turns. Nine swords pierce the hanged man. Nine wands support him. His queen is the Queen of Pentacles. See her?'

Why did I understand what he was saying? My queen was the Queen of the Moon but I gave my fortunes to the Queen of Pentacles and suddenly all I saw was soft, molten mercury. No, I saw silver behaving like mercury. What *did* I see? Silver wall rippling like a curtain. The Phoenix, the Scholar, the Goat and the Lion knew my fortune but it was hidden in the Sphynx. The Ace of Wands and the Nine of Pentacles. The Twin Lovers. Soul mates. The Fool took the road. The mercury parted and something shivered there. I was dreaming. I had lost my bearings.

'Follow the path the Green Knight blazes,' said Father Grammaticus softly. 'If you are ready.'

I wasn't ready. I fell back. The Green Knight? Some Arthurian legend? Something I had done or thought or seen in my mind's eye – perhaps everything I had done, thought or seen – I felt horribly sick. I was frightened. As our conversation continued it seemed that I listened at a distance. I heard my own voice as far away as Father Grammaticus. 'Who is the Green Knight? How do I find the road again? Is there a map?'

'It's there, in your own mind, ordered and prepared since you were born. The dark aether flows there as it flows between the worlds. You need to find it. Most of us have it. An instinct requiring a discipline. An inherited ability. A divine gift. Which, of course, are the same. By means of it you travel easily between our world and its peers. Something which is far harder for us to do, but easy for you once you discover your instinctive discipline.'

'My discipline?' I asked. 'And yours?' I *was* dreaming. Caught in his spell. Fascinated. I wondered briefly again about drugs.

'I suppose I have more than one. By reason of my work, you know. My real love, because it reveals so much of God's plan, is more sophisticated. But here...'

He stood up and touched something under his desk. 'I believe the prince will eventually wish to show you his larger and more sophisticated version.'

Who was the prince? The same as the Green Knight?

I watched the leaves of the desk's top fold back on silent hinges and disappear into the body. A vast, blooming flower. Slowly he turned an invisible crank. I had only once seen anything like it, at the Royal Eise Eisinga Planetarium in Friesland, the Netherlands. An orrery from the mid-eighteenth century. But this was far more complex. From the interior, unfolding on subtle hinges, rose an extraordinary, complicated network of silver wires, slender steel rods, delicate brass cogs and golden spindles, expanding until it seemed to fill the room. Like a mad, joyful clock it vibrated and spun, clicked, chimed and whirred! Then at last it lay before me in silence. How old was it? An orrery, but of such extreme complexity I could not begin to see all it represented, certainly not the sun, moon and planets. Yet there were many spheres of different metals and size. I was fascinated. Delighted. Technically, building the thing was just about within the possibility of, say, seventeenth-century ingenuity. But the skill displayed was astonishing. It was worthy of Leonardo. I was mesmerised by its complexity. I stared unthinking into its rods and cogs, which were spinning and whirling in impossible intricacy.

On the other side of that extraordinary web I saw the beaming face of Father Grammaticus as he reached into the orrery, passing his long-fingered hands to and fro. 'We enjoy certain privileges in the Abbey of the White Friars of Alsacia. Men come here to exchange knowledge as well as to reaffirm their faith in our Creator. The scholars of Arabia. Of Jewry. Of Europe and Africa. Since 1241 we have enjoyed an existence which has been mostly peaceful. According to our charters, everlasting and inviolate, made by those holy monarchs Henry the Third – in whose name we repent the special Sin of the Christians – and James the Second of England – in whose name we repent the Sins of the British, we offer sanctuary to all persecuted sinners in the name of our Creator and His prophets.'

'What –?' I wasn't sure what was happening. I certainly did not feel as bad as I had done when I first turned up, though. My mouth was dry. I had trouble focusing. Again I wondered if Father Grammaticus hadn't put something in my tea! 'The Creator? The Sanctuary? You believe what? – That this is a model of Creation?'

'A simplified one, yes.'

'Nothing bothers you about it?'

'Why should it?'

'You don't feel nauseated? Nothing affects your chest or stomach? You have no pains?' Looking at it was affecting my eyes as well. 'Dizzy? Weak?'

'Not any more. The Black Aether has that effect, I'll admit. The prince's Cosmolabe attempts to represent the Black Aether. The cosmic fog, as it is called. I can represent it but I lack the resource to commission such a superb machine. He had his choice of the world's great instrument makers. Ours relies on more local ingenuity. It is only a crude attempt to represent the cosmos we have explored.'

'Excuse me, Father Abbot, but I still don't know exactly what this is.' I was mesmerised by the rods and webs and spheres. 'Or, indeed, who the prince is you're talking about.' I was beginning to feel a bit scared, thinking in terms of black-magic cults and human sacrifices. Had I been lured here for a purpose? Would the *News of the World* be running pictures of my strangely twisted body in next Sunday's edition?

'On the other side of the Black or Second Aether is what is sometimes termed the Third Aether. We call ours the First or White Aether purely in order to make some rough plan of the heavens. There are seven other known planes or branes, depending upon your choice of model. Our orrery shows a simplified model of Heaven and Earth, which, of course, seems far more complex than the one you know from your lessons. In Prince Rupert's model the Black Aether is represented. It begins to explain certain mysteries. As I said, we call ours the White Aether, but there are thought to be five other colours. Some report a blue aether and others a yellow. If we reach seven with anomalies still recurring, we shall assume further branes.'

I was still transfixed by this particular wonder, his Cosmolabe. Not only had I never imagined anything like it, I had never seen or read about anything like it! And yet it looked so ancient! The abbot's voice had become just then simply music soothing me as my brain tried to grasp the idea of a universe utterly alien to anything I had been taught. I was sure this would interest Barry Bayley, who was fascinated by weird theories and inventions. A little part of me was already working out how to use the idea in a story. Father Grammaticus was still apologising because the prince's orrery, once complete, would be so much more sophisticated than the abbey's. 'But ours serves to demonstrate the fundamental universe. Also the movement of Radiant Time. So!' He passed his hand carefully between the various moving parts to show me golden wires spreading outwards from the base. He opened his fingers. The golden rays fanned out from them. His hand was the trunk, his fingers the branches. The orrery represented both models. The natural and the geometric. Or so I guessed. By now I was almost entirely without conscious thought, as if I were entranced by some perfect piece of music.

Father Grammaticus's soothing voice continued to stroke the webs and strings, making them vibrate. He had the air of playing a complex instrument. 'Not only does this model show the movement of God's Creation,' he explained, 'it also allows us to measure the passage of all the worlds, visible and invisible, including what we sometimes call the half worlds, or ghost worlds, through time. Indeed the whole aether is, as the prince proves by his mathematical logic, a dimension of time. Time and space follow the same laws and enjoy a similar condition.'

Later it would take a lot of discussion with Barry Bayley and others to reconstruct what Father Grammaticus told me. To this day, in spite of all the experience and knowledge I've gained, I still have trouble understanding those astonishing mathematics. It takes a special kind of mind to imagine two models at once and navigate through them, as Father Grammaticus did. But I was losing the thread, through no fault of his explanation. The whirling and twining of the so-called Cosmolabe was making me feel pretty weird.

I hoped I could reach a bathroom before I lost it.

'It's impressive.' I tried to stand up. Then I tried to remember why I wanted to stand up. The Cosmolabe still had my attention.

I was desperate to hold on to familiar beliefs. They had been reached logically enough and with quite a bit of effort. But my hard-won reason was melting before everything I was now learning. Was my physical state merely an echo of my mental turmoil? I think if I hadn't read a bit of science fiction I would have gone completely nuts trying to understand it all.

The slender gold, brass, steel and silver wires shivered delicately.

The rods swung so gracefully, the cogs connected to the wheels, the regulators to the springs. Spheres circled other spheres. What had this to do with me? What had Friar Isidore seen in me which made him bring me here? And why was the old abbot so keen to show me this weird invention?

'Are you – is this –?' I could get no closer than that to framing a question. The abbot took pity on me and smiled: a teacher happy to help a curious pupil. 'Who is it for?' I think I meant to ask him *what*, but he seemed to understand.

He made an expansive gesture. 'It is for everyone who needs it. Are we not all part of the same brotherhood?' Did he mean himself and the monks, or the monks and the Alsacian congregation, or the entire human race? 'Aren't we all presently drifting in troubled waters? Once the scale of the Creator's plan is known and our power is recognised we shall understand its function thoroughly. Do you know what it is?'

The orrery continued to mesmerise me. I was reminded of a description I'd read in the H.G. Wells novel. My eyes were transfixed. 'It's some sort of time machine, isn't it?'

He smiled again. 'Oh, if life were so simple! It's merely a model. As I said, it lacks the refinements of the prince's great orrery. But you can imagine the light sphincter and how it works to draw and expel the ectoplasm creating a perfectly balanced cosmos. We cannot begin to demonstrate here the suggestion, as yet unpresented in any coherent way, concerning the infinity of such objects of balance and the meaning of Scripture in their respect.'

'Scripture?' I was growing dizzy again. I leaned back in my chair. Now even the whizzing spheres and weaving rods were hard to distinguish.

'Believe me,' he said, 'you must not fear that we are practising the black arts. We take our plans from Scripture. We know too much to want to meddle in those. We are trying to save all we value. No soul was ever sold here. No reasonable bargain was ever struck between man and devil. The only bargains we make are honourable...' His voice now seemed indistinct. 'And they are usually with our Creator or His agents in the best accomplishment of His will.'

I missed much of the meaning of what he said. I tried to rise. I still found it difficult to get up from my chair. I sat down again. He had changed the subject. 'No doubt she loves you as much as she ever did.'

'Who loves me?'

The old man frowned and glanced around him, puzzled. 'Ah. I am so sorry. Your mother?'

But he didn't mean my mother.

'The prince knows a better method but this gives a certain verisimilitude to our model.' He reached in and sprinkled something into the elaborate mechanism. 'This will help you understand why we were so glad you came to us all those years ago.'

I was absolutely baffled. 'What do you mean, Father? I came here a few hours ago, at your invitation. Out of curiosity. And before that...'

He was hardly listening. His expression was wonderfully benign. 'Your curiosity helps you see the roads. Soon you'll learn to walk them. The time is upon us. Those hunters have increased the frequency and intensity of their attacks. We have to get our Treasure to a safer place. The Green Knight cannot. His prophet needs him. So you shall help us.' His voice seemed to come from some distance off. I wanted to ask more but the beautiful machine drew my attention. Darkness flowed through the Cosmolabe forming shapes I almost recognised. I feared I was being hypnotised.

Time passed quickly and, in spite of feeling increasingly ill, I remained sitting transfixed in front of that astonishing arrangement of gold, brass, ebony, silver, platinum and ivory. I watched clusters of crystals, some like diamonds, others like rubies, emeralds, sapphires. I peered deeper into the thing. I saw shapes, faces. I had no power to move and I didn't care. I thought I heard another, drawling voice. Perhaps I was imagining the entire experience. Was this astonishing concoction of alchemy and baffling cosmic theory actually created to reach deep into my inner self? Must I believe I owned a soul before I could see it at all?

I tried to break the connection by imagining the tarot deck until all I saw in my mind's eye were the cards. The swords and the cups, the wands and the pentacles became webs and rods and planets and suns whirling before my eyes.

I still heard Father Grammaticus's faraway voice speaking to me.

Radiant Time, he said. *The Black or Second Aether. A greater darkness lies within the familiar darkness of the void.* 'Here the black sun sits, drawing us all into its insatiable orbit. But on the other side of that sun are the anti-worlds thrown out by a blazing light bursting fresh. And so it turns, throughout Creation! The Great Galliard!' There were so many kinds of light: crystalline, fiery, gaseous, sharp. He passed his hands through the orrery again. I felt powerless to look at his face. I saw the Queen of Pentacles dancing with the high priestess and the emperor dancing around the sun. I saw the King, Queen and Knight of Swords form a circle. And in the middle of all was the fool. The fool, poor Pierrot, who had let his Columbine dance off with her Harlequin.

The black energy pulsed and coiled between the stars. The silver threads arced and twisted making impossible connections. Heavy drops of blood fell like summer rain. Huge shadows spread to obscure a mass of suns. I was in agony. My sickness had become an intense burning sensation. I did all I could to shrink it and rid myself of it. *Mass is present but invisible, explained by the presence of identical worlds unseen by us. They nest, one inside the other. Frequently, the only clue we have is the Dark Flow! Step this way, then that,* between *the worlds. Step and step. So and so. You dance the Great Galliard!*

He was teaching me something through hypnotism? Was I learning what he wished me to learn? Should I have listened better? Perhaps if I had been in a different situation I would have done. My new interest in Moll Midnight kept me involved. I felt all this had something to do with her. The science involved was over my head! Was it time I turned to Harlequin in pursuit of my love? I was crying hard now. I gave no further attention to Father Grammaticus. Silver roads? An illusion? Still crying I stood up. I tried to shake my head to rid it of all the images. I closed my eyes. Began to sway. It felt like dying.

I came to know what death was. I couldn't tell anyone. I knew what it felt like when they said they were in God's hands. Even now I had almost no control over my thoughts or my limbs. I watched the black tendrils snake amongst the brightness, appearing to absorb it. I saw what looked grey and yellow like flames flaring and dying. I felt I was actually outside the universe. From Limbo I regarded it. The universe was a rippling pool of many dimensions. My hands especially burned but were numb at the same time. Everything had the familiarity of a recently remembered dream. All kinds of strange, uncomfortable thoughts came to me. They blossomed into images. Faces leered. Faces cried out, begging me for aid. Molly? She was there in a thousand aspects. Faces showed pity, love, pain. I couldn't help them. I had no volition. My whole being, every part, every inch of me, wanted to rest, to sleep. Slowly I became unable to move or think. I lost any sense of identity, any memory, any emotion. Yet still Father Grammaticus continued to talk in that calm, cultivated voice. I wanted to escape. I could neither move nor think. I felt myself grow entirely numb. I wept until there were no more tears.

CHAPTER FIVE

PROTECTING THE PROTECTOR

A ND THEN I was standing again in the chapel as an exhausted old man said goodbye before handing me back into the keeping of Friar Isidore.

Another pat on the shoulder from the abbot and I was led from the abbey grounds. Friar Isidore was childishly excited by what he called our successful séance. When he kissed me as we parted at the gate, I was in no way surprised. The act was entirely spontaneous and without any kind of sexual overtones. I cheerfully agreed to see him the following Wednesday at the typesetter's and I shook his hand. Afraid of hurting his feelings, I didn't mention that I had agreed to meet Moll Midnight the next day. I could think of nothing to ask him about the beautiful young woman whom I'm sure he would not have known. Besides, I felt at liberty to come and go for reasons which had nothing to do with him or his church. I would have found the pub eventually, I was sure. That said, I did feel as if I betrayed the monks and didn't want to lie to them by omission.

Turning to make my way home I was surprised again by the fog's rapid descent. Suddenly I could recognise nothing. The street lights would not come on again for an hour or so. As carefully as I walked I could not avoid crashing suddenly into a hard, masculine shoulder and gasped, feeling for a bruise. At the same time I apologised as the English always do. I expected an automatic reply in kind but the an-

swering voice was surly, affronted, haughty. I smelled danger. The
Brookgate Courts were full of it. I had always been able to sniff potential violence on the wind. This ability to anticipate threat is the
urban form of a countryman's sixth sense.

Here we go again. I tried to guess what happened next.

'What's this? A king's weasel slips from its lair, hoping to do the
Protector and his people some evil.' This rolling Welsh brogue had a
sinister music to it. Out of the fog loomed a massive red head, all bris-
tling orange eyebrows and whiskers. The black halo of a befeathered
hat brim shrouded his glaring blue eyes above a vast, wicked grin.
'Did ye think ye could avoid our defences?'

'Steady on,' I said, playing the shocked citizen. 'You've got the wrong
person. I don't know you from Adam and, as for "defences", London
hasn't had any wall for centuries, certainly not in these parts. So I'd
be glad –'

'*Glad* is he? Hear that, Corporal Love? He's *glad*. And he's just an
innocent young fellow strolling home through the fog without a lamp
to light his way. Correcting his betters on the subject of walls. Happen he can see in the dark? The way a *witch* can, is it?' The Welshman's voice was fractured limestone. 'A *witch*, Corporal Love, do
you see. *Tsk, tsk, tsk.*'

'Them witches, colonel, sir, are as wicked and devious as they come.' A
dangerous toady, this, by his ingratiating tone. 'Consorting with Romans,
I don't doubt, sir. Gypsies are all slaves of the pope, sir. Falsely seeking
God's protection. Very bad, sir, them *gypsies*.' The unseen speaker, dialect
less pronounced than its compatriot's, imitated its master's *tsk*-ing.

All this menacing melodrama had the desired effect. I was frightened. I paused. I had been talked to like that before by Teddy Boys in
the Brookgate tenements. I knew the colonel's tone, the self-righteous
taunting voice of a bully who thinks he's found an easy mark.
'Corporal Love', lurking like a sly ape in the folds of his cloak, was a
classic bully's creature. I had been taught by my mother always to resist them or, if necessary, report them. She knew crime dressed as the
law. In Berlin in the thirties my mum would have been arrested. She
recognised that tone in policeman and gangster alike and never let herself be cowed. She was, in that respect, a typical London working-class
mother. I had yet to prove her wrong.

I laughed as confidently as I could. 'Witches? You poor superstitious buggers.' I walked on. But now they threatened to lay hands on me. Wide brims partly hid their faces. Corporal Love's was all but fleshless with planes of bone from which grey eyes gleamed. I saw long rapiers at their belts as they pressed towards me. I had a police whistle but no time to reach it. I got a good look, through the strands of fog, at the colonel's tall, crouching companion, the cadaverous corporal, and guessed their ranks to be self-given, for neither wore uniform, just stage clothes like the rest. The colonel was all lace and brocade and feathered flounces. He even had a big black feather in his hat. The corporal wore a Quaker's plain black and white.

'Don't be silly, lads. You're really out of your depth here. Go on, get back to your panto or your puffed-wheat advert.' Although scared, I spoke with the quiet authority I had learned from all the serious local gangsters. But this didn't do much more than give them a moment's pause.

'It is not *we* who are silly, knave!' The red-headed Welshman sneered dramatically, as only Welshmen can, his eyes bright with aggressive malice. 'You need a lesson, look you. Something to teach you to respect Parliament's laws and its keepers. It would do you good to cool your heels in the Bridewell!'

I realised I might not be able to talk my way out of this. Those blades looked real. I was in serious trouble. I'd determined all this even as I laughed spontaneously at his self-impressed tone and his weird accent. But this encounter in the fog was not the same. Bent coppers? I wasn't much of a mark. They meant business and I didn't want to find out what that business was. Fog was guaranteed to cloak an evil deed. The red-headed Welshman had more than a few evil deeds written on his lean, satanic muzzle. He now thrust his head forward with a 'Colonel Clitch', by way of introducing himself. Off came the greasy, plain black hat. A horrid smile. A sarcastic bow. 'Upon Parliament's service.' He was about to pounce.

I heard a low sound like someone clearing their throat. Another figure stepped out of the fog, a short man also wearing a wide-brimmed hat, a sash around his waist in which were stuck two large pistols. He, too, had a sword in his hand. 'I do not believe, gentlemen, that this young lad is of any threat to man nor God. But if you wish to contest that opinion I'll be happy to oblige you.' The pair immediately lowered their weapons and began explaining themselves. While that was happening, the short newcomer, possibly their employer or a feared enemy, called to me to get on home. I was happy to oblige. I cried out my thanks and took to my heels as if I were a kid running from those particularly nasty Clerkenwell Court Teds who had tried to set up a kind of juvenile protection racket in the market area until the men of our families had a word with the chief Teds and that was that.

I had remembered Mr Ackermann's advice that it was always best to run from danger if there was a good chance of getting away. 'One big punch and then run like buggery, my boy.' Wondering why they showed such fear of the third man, I ran like an Olympic athlete, looking for the nearest crowded place, preferably a pub or a restaurant, but discovered myself somehow at the same gate. Opening it for the second time, I expected to be back in the Sanctuary where I could at least find allies. Instead I was again standing at the far end of that Inn of Court through which I'd come. Maybe Clitch and Love had been unable to follow me any further. Local statutes? A genuine fear of God's wrath if they drew blood outside their established precinct? And was the third man still around?

Clearly, visiting the Alsacia was more perilous than I had first realised. I was very happy that the Alsacians seemed confined, for whatever reason, to their own particular manor. Custom or superstition or both? I knew in my bones I was afraid of that pair for good reason. I recognised them as men of terrible, gleeful sadism, like some serious East End gangsters I'd been around all my life. Unlike the Teds, the Kray brothers had real ambition to do murder. I had no intention of getting beaten up or killed by their like on that foggy night. They recognised my saviour and feared him, but who was he? Tomorrow I would make sure I reached Alsacia when it was still light. I would tell my mum I was going to a late-night movie with a friend in Earls Court and would probably stay over. That way I could leave at daylight on Saturday morning.

I got home breathless. Now I was completely uncertain about the nature of what I'd witnessed. The costume party at the pub? The old monk and his Cosmolabe? The cloak-and-dagger stuff in the square?

Part of me was a sceptic – even a cynic – but part of me was also romantic and gullible. I felt distinctly dizzy. Was I in some waking dream? Maybe someone wasn't telling me all they should. Had I gone mad? Could the supernatural really exist? If the last were true, I was in a serious moral dilemma. I was still young enough to try telepathic experiments with my friends; gullible enough to wonder if, just possibly, the tarot could tell the future. But I believed there were scientific, not magical, explanations. I was determined to know the truth, fully prepared for some perfectly ordinary explanation.

Of course it never once occurred to me that I might simply forget the whole thing, as one does a dream, and not keep the next day's appointment with Moll Midnight, whose reality or lack of it had me so thoroughly mesmerised. She was not even, I told my teenage self, my type. I should have recognised the symptoms. This wasn't the first time. I had fallen in love again.

CHAPTER SIX

MOLL

THAT FOLLOWING NIGHT, I swapped my jumper for my knitted black tie and a stiff stud-at-the-back white collar, with cufflinks showing at my wrist, and a black duffel coat. Pretty damned dapper! Definitely stylish. I skipped my Woody Guthrie railroad hat. To my own eyes I looked as much like Max Stone as possible. Even more presentable. I was, however, still awkwardly self-conscious as I went to meet Moll Midnight on that darkening Friday afternoon. I planned to go to Greek Street, Soho. Romano Santi was one of London's best restaurants. They would take several pounds out of my earnings, but it would be worth it. I believed in treating a girl the way my mother always expected to be treated.

Even then, as now, I thought in terms of what a piece of work would buy. A short story brought me a minimum of a guinea a thousand words, often two, sometimes three. That was the rent. The slick magazines were at that time beyond my aspirations but later I would earmark so much for new furniture, so much for utilities and so on. Once I had earned what I needed, I would take it easy for a while. Anticipating a stiffish bill at Romano's, I knew I could always do more freelance work to improve my fortunes. A posh meal for two was the equivalent of six pages of text in *Tarzan Adventures*. I had more than enough cash to cover tonight.

Running down a virtually deserted New Fetter Lane, I got to the inn gate in a hurry. It was growing dark by five and I wanted to be early so that I should not be caught by Messrs Clitch and Love at night. I would ask Moll how much I should fear them. Maybe I should find a new way out of Alsacia?

The square was lighting up as the lawyers' offices completed their week's work. Solicitors' clerks scampered from one door to another carrying briefcases of every size. Messengers ran to and fro with large manila envelopes under their arms. Wigs on heads or in hands, QCs walked briskly from the Law Courts or the Old Bailey to their chambers. The lamplighter rode around the square on his solid black bike, igniting the gas in the globes of the big-bracketed wall lamps and the diamond-shaped pole lamps. The Inns of Court worked a little later on Fridays but rarely opened, these days, at the weekend. Even then the City was beginning to stop working on Saturday mornings. The neighbourhood would be almost deserted by Friday evening.

I rarely noticed it back then, but I always had a very faint humming in my ears. Too faint to be a nuisance, it was almost below my consciousness. I don't think I even realised that it had stopped. In some momentary conflict, I pushed open the big gate into Alsacia.

There was no sign of last night's aggressive duo. I was relieved and instantly relaxed. A few more steps and I was outside The Swan With Two Necks. Two more and I was in the snug camaraderie of the private bar, looking for Moll. I knew I was earlier than we had arranged but my need to avoid that pair of self-elected 'Parliamentary' policemen had its boot on the neck of my thoughts. Who the hell were they? But now I was through the gate and in the pub I worried about Moll standing me up. Several of her companions of the previous evening were there, including a tall, rather gloomy man with a silver streak through his black hair, dressed up as Pecos Bill, the legendary hero of Texas.

Bill seemed a little grey and haggard, rather like my Uncle Larry when he was treated for cancer. Here he wore a simple suit of dark tweed. In his comic book he sported an exaggerated cowboy outfit, with wide chaps and a heavy, tooled-leather vest, as well as a white shirt, a red bandanna and a gun belt with a single holster for his .45, and he carried his lariat. Bill kept his own counsel at the bar and I was far too shy to introduce myself. I sat on a bench against a wall in the shadows and watched as Bill was joined by Colonel Carson, in a well-cut, if Victorian, three-piece suit. Kit's hair was shorter and less fair than in the comics, as had been Bill Cody's. He was trying to cheer up Pecos Bill, recruiting the older Turpin to help. He kept holding his hand to the light and pointing. I realised then how old he was. I could almost see through his skin. His friends shook their heads and smiled supportively. But the Texan hero refused consolation and eventually the others shrugged and parted from him.

By the time Moll arrived I was talking casually to Galloping Dick Langley, one of the younger actors who had joined me on the bench and remained in character the whole time. He talked of the great steel toby and robbing double-decker coaches. I had begun to enjoy the game.

I was surprised by Moll's costume. Perhaps she'd had no time to change. She wore the clothes I saw her in when she rode past me that first day – a tricorn on her red-gold ringlets, a linen stock at her throat, over which frothed a luxury of white lace, matching what she wore on her wrists. A ruby velvet military-style coat covered a calf-length brocaded waistcoat whose buttons were as bright as her violet eyes. She wore doeskin breeches and, unsurprisingly, good riding boots, their cuffs turned at the knee, their spurs blunted. On her arm she carried a cloak and in that same hand a sword and gloves. She grinned when she saw me and signalled for me to stand.

Still amused, stamping in her boots like a soldier, Moll guided me out of the bar and up a short flight of stairs to a landing and what appeared to be a closet. She opened the door. I saw it held bottles. A quick glance around and she opened the door supporting the shelves to reveal another door. Sliding a catch on this, she swung it open, showing me into a small room full of costumes: shirts, waistcoats, overcoats, boots, stocks and hats. She made me strip and get into clothes she found for me there, including a pair of riding boots into which I tucked my ordinary trousers. I now wore a long waistcoat and overcoat much like hers, a hat and a wig which she fitted firmly on my head. I also carried a cloak, sword and gloves. So much for my mid-twentieth-century dandyism, I felt a bit of an idiot.

'They'll do you, Master Michael!' She hurried me out of the room, closing the two doors carefully behind her. 'Do ye ride?'

Wasn't this taking authenticity too far? As it happened I had grown up bareback-riding the totter's ponies in our mews and knew a little about keeping my seat and guiding my mount. But I would never call myself a horseman!

'I'm no expert,' I said.

She laughed. 'We'll make you one soon enough.' She saw my sardonic glance at her feet. 'Barefoot Maggy's riding as Moll Midnight tonight, sir.' She smiled. 'Maybe you should choose a nom de guerre for yourself? "Cock o' the Highway", perhaps?' She laughed at my look of disgust.

My initial surprise and hesitancy subsiding, I now thoroughly enjoyed the masquerade. Within minutes we were trotting from the stableyard on our way through streets I hardly recognised though they pretty much followed familiar routes. Fog became mist as we galloped out of the city. I felt trapped astride a cement mixer, rattling and bouncing on Jessie, my amiable, forgiving mare, while I desperately tried to find my seat.

In heavy tooled-leather holsters already attached to my saddle I found two monstrous flintlock pistols, almost the size of rifles. It was as well I didn't really know how to use them. They looked fearsomely lethal, even if they were stage props. Not that they seemed fakes. The flints were real enough. I could see that powder already primed the pans. I could smell it, too. The metal parts were good quality. The steel barrel was bound to the dark oak stock by glowing brass bands and the steel ramrod was fixed firmly in place in its own slot beneath the barrel. I knew weapons like these from local museums, films like *The Highwayman*, Noyes's poem, and in Olivier's hands on stage in *The Beggar's Opera*, so I knew how they worked, more or less. You hauled back the hammer as far as it would go, pointed, and pulled the trigger hoping the spark would catch the primer to ignite the gunpowder and discharge your massive lead ball in the general direction of the target. These brutes looked as if the recoil would knock me backwards off Jessie. The good-natured chestnut was a clattering, jolly hunter in her prime. She enjoyed a long-striding gallop if given her head. Concentrating on keeping my seat and posting as I'd once been taught, I gave her that head as little as possible! For a while, as we went by taverns and a few shops, we slowed to a trot, according to the law. Riding close beside me Moll took these moments to fill me in on what was still a rather murky plan. I have to say I barely understood her. Sometimes I thought I felt reality tearing like rotten stage canvas behind me. I remained determined to enter as fully as possible into the spirit of the scenes. Charade it might be but I had little to lose and I was fascinated to see how the game unfolded.

In darkness we rode on for hours. At one point the moon was bright enough for me to see a church-steeple clock, its hands set at midnight. This was by no means the romantic evening I'd planned in the warmth of Romano's. My bones began to ache. I was unclear how we had passed through London and I had only the vaguest idea where we were. Hertfordshire, perhaps? Essex? In my whole life I had not travelled so far north, certainly not on horseback!

Before long, and much sooner than I expected, we had reached wilder country than I'd ever thought to find so near the city. The landscape felt unreal, lacking a single living soul, save for the owls and nightjars calling from the thickets. The only light in this open country came from the slowly sinking moon and the stars. From horizon to horizon the sky was a sprawl of sparkling points, wide and deep, as if the galaxy were a jug of mercury splashed against black slate. I loved the smell of gorse, heather and still water as we made our way along unpaved roads and out onto a wide expanse of yielding grass full of flying insects and the chirr of crickets. The cold air tasted sweeter than any air before. Where was this primitive, prehistoric wetland? Moll knew the low-lying marsh well, guiding us along narrow paths of relatively firm ground. Were these the legendary Hackney Marshes I'd heard about in old Cockney songs? What an adventure! I felt as if I had galloped beyond the edge of the known globe and was in another wilder, simpler, easier world where such things as the atom bomb and the Cold War were unknown and all you needed to emerge victorious from a passage of arms was a sense of honour and a bit of courageous resolve! What a simple, invigorating world! Every sensation was new to me! No surprise, really, for I was a true Londoner. All I had ever experienced of the countryside was Hyde Park and what

I could see through a train window on my way to Southend. The experience really was making me drunk.

Moll reined in beside me, handing me a wad of dark silk pulled from her pocket; the hood went over my head and settled on my shoulders. I adjusted it until I found eye and mouth holes then sat hat and wig back on my head. 'What now?' I asked.

'Now,' said Moll, with a wild grin, 'we rob the Hackney mail. Check your barkers, Master Michael! Be sure the powder's level in the pan.' When I showed hesitation, she reached over and showed me how to cock and prepare my pistols, flipping up the covers of the priming pans. Then we were off again, with a light rain flickering through the sky. We followed what I thought at first was the bed of a narrow-gauge railway until I realised it more closely resembled a tram line. In 1952 the last trams had rolled through the London suburbs but I still remembered them with nostalgia. You knew exactly where a tram line went. The trams were built to outlast the pyramids. But they had been sacrificed anyway.

Moll brought our horses to a halt in the shadow of a grove of oak trees. The moon came out intermittently and showed nothing but gorse and clumps of trees: Hackney Heath as it had not existed for centuries. I began to realise I had a serious problem. Might I really be experiencing some sort of waking dream or delusion? Madness, in other words...

I had read Twain's *Connecticut Yankee in King Arthur's Court* and L. Sprague de Camp and Fletcher Pratt's Harold Shea stories, but purely as satirical fiction. I didn't believe in so-called 'parallel worlds'. Twain's at least had been familiar. This half-known England was far more complicated and troubling. I had ridden on trams as a kid. I had read dozens of books and comics featuring Turpin, Duval and the other legendary highwaymen. I had been as fascinated by them as I had been with the James brothers and Buffalo Bill, Texas Jack, Pecos Bill and Kit Carson. And Buck Jones, of course, who, according to legend, died heroically in the 1940s, saving people from a terrible fire.

In this waking delusion I felt I had entered an existence obeying entirely different notions of time and identity, exactly like a vivid nightmare. If there were rules, no-one told me what they were. Kafka, indeed! The eighteenth and twentieth centuries somehow overlapped. Absurd! Surreal! I had speculated, very crudely, on such things in the odd science fiction story, but never expected to experience them. I was alarmed. This went quite literally beyond my wildest dreams.

At Moll's prompting I looked across the marshy flatland. In the distance was a fuzz of yellow light I took for a farmhouse until it came creeping towards us. I heard a faint clanging like a distant, off-key bell. The air around me buzzed and the ground underfoot shook so I suspected an earthquake. Moll handed me her spyglass. Putting it to my eye I was amazed to distinguish a big Feltham double-decker tram of a kind I thought vanished from the urban landscape. London Transport livery, all flashing brass, bright sparks and crimson enamel with a bold black-and-white destination board indicating exactly what her route was: Hackney Downs to the Theobald's Road depot, less than half a mile from my own Brookgate home! There was her number picked out in gold above her single, brilliant headlight in the centre of her bow, below the driver's cab.

'A long-hauler going via London Fields carrying the registered mail with a full complement of recently paid company officials. And Universal still pays in cash!' Moll sounded excited as she heaved back the hammer of her right-hand pistol and sighted along its barrel. 'We'll leave the mail for them as waits for it, but the rest are our particular prey. Ready?'

I could barely lift my flintlock to the saddle and hold it so that I could rest it over my left arm, sideways on. I laughed.

Then, lamp and lights glaring, the rattling monster pounded towards us, blazing and roaring like a military brass band. Moll took a bead at an unseen point in the sky. Her pistol flashed and boomed. I heard a hiss and something whistled past my face, just grazing my silk-covered cheek, followed by a crash as the tram's overhead power line hit the roof of the vehicle, sending the conductor rod on the roof swinging crazily, back and forth, swishing like a gigantic windscreen wiper, scarcely visible against the sky. Her emergency brakes automatically squealed on. I saw the driver in his cab trying to fight the tram's momentum and hold his position. The monstrous vehicle shrieked and swayed like a stricken dinosaur, shaking and gasping, until at last she settled back on her tracks and shuddered to a stop.

Out of the cooling night I glimpsed only Moll's breath rising like ectoplasm into the darkness and then her voice came calm and authoritative, absolutely chilling as she called with sardonic good manners in Kensington English: 'Throw down your lever, if you please, Mr Driver!' Within seconds there came a thump nearby and I saw something bright in the grass. Moll made no attempt to pick it up. From his cab the uniformed driver stared furiously unseeing into the blackness.

Moll's voice was still a drawling, lazy half shout. 'Now one of my men will come among you for donations while another will keep an eye on the platform. We want you gents to put your hands deep in your pockets and this bein' the last Friday in the month you'll find those fat wage packets. Packets, gents, you tell your workers you can't afford to share, times being so hard. The company must be more generous than you credit 'em. They're divvying a bonus or two, I hear.' Then, with military impatience, 'Stump up, gentlemen, for our barkers have sensitive triggers, liable to go off at the slightest disappointment. My lads here are hungry for some target practice.' At Moll's signal her 'men' swung from my horse, as we had rehearsed on the way. Carrying my saddlebags over my shoulder I leapt onto the tram's platform, my pistol in my belt. Full of the thrill of adventure I took the outer stairs to the top deck first, bowing to the cursing executives and waving my heavy barker, which I stuffed back in my belt as I collected the big white fivers, twenty pounds or more a head, from the well-fed, grumbling Universal Transport Company executives. As Moll had predicted, not once did I have to do anything more than show them my pistol.

Dream or not, I was enjoying the game. I tipped my hat and bowed to them as if I'd been a tobyman all my life, then stepped down the steel stairs to the lower deck and demanded the same from the red-faced bureaucrats in dark suits and loud ties blustering their threats as they parted with more than half their pay, counted out from their monthly packets. You could smell their outrage. From the size of our 'take' it was clear these men were doing well behind their desks. My Uncle Willie, who had been a Japanese POW, had worked for the tram company until 1952. He told me how the weekly wages of drivers or conductors were half or less what these office workers received. Where I could, I took the empty packets, too. It was Moll's idea. Here was proof how much more these elevated clerks received compared to the drivers who faced the responsibilities and dangers of the 'steel toby'.

A loud shot. Part of our agreed signal. I lifted my hat to the growling executives and headed for my horse.

Then, as musket balls yelped past our heads, splintering wood and thumping into the turf, with our saddlebags stuffed with rustling fivers, fresh oncers and ten-bob notes, our cloaks flying behind us, we were off at full gallop the way we had come. The rushing adrenaline ensured I kept my seat. A louder bang. Something hissed by my left shoulder and hit a willow with a great thunk, showing how serious our game was! Another shot and Moll, a black shadow, swerved, still at full gallop, to lead me along a series of narrow paths through the marsh. 'They've unshipped the top-deck cannon!' Her big stallion took a hedge easily with my mare following. I, however, threatened to remain behind, almost flying clear of saddle and stirrups. I lost my seat more than once and pulled too heavily on the reins, but patient Jessie looked after me. By jumping more gates and streams we reached open fields and avoided the larger, better-lit towns. I saw a wooden signpost for Shoreditch, Stepney and Stoke Newington. The first time we slowed to a walk Moll reached over to pat my arm. 'Good work, Master Michael! This cash will go to the Road Transport Workers Union to help their members pay for a planned strike. Meanwhile the bosses will have learned a lesson from us. They've just received a taste of what we can do if we decide to act. There'll be a thousand pound in our bags tonight. We'll take a levy of five per cent and the rest goes to the union. Workers – and bandits – of the world unite against the bosses. This is how it should be, eh?' Her eyes were alive with excitement.

How it should be, maybe, I thought, but rarely how it was except in fiction.

Her rhetoric was remarkably similar to my Uncle Willie's. He had worked as a turntable man at the Camden Roundhouse when it was still a tram terminal. He had taken part in the General Strike of 1929. For a while he was a member of the Communist Party, having huge arguments with Uncle Alf the pacifist anarchist. Alf believed in mutuality and claimed Trotsky had betrayed the Russian Revolution by reneging on his promises to Makhno.

In spite of the realities I was still at a loss to know how this could not be some sort of dream. The only bandits I had heard voicing such sentiments as Moll's were in fiction and film – Pancho Villa in particular – but my Uncle Alf had told me about Nestor Makhno and his Ukrainian irregulars whom Trotsky, for political motives of his own, called bandits. They had systematically redistributed wealth from the bourgeoisie to the peasants and punished pogromists. I had read how Jesse James and others had preserved their popularity by distributing money at random to poorer people, often signing themselves 'Jack Sheppard', the popular London thief and escapist, fully conscious of the legends they created. Just as calculating, Pretty Boy Floyd left hundred-dollar bills under his plate to pay working people for meals they offered him, confirming their romantic expectations. As far as I knew, Moll was the only highway thief who spouted Marxist rhetoric while stealing on behalf of a trade union. Making everything all the more dreamlike!

I was almost eighteen years old. Dream or not, the rush in my blood convinced me I experienced a sort of 'super-reality'. As real as my desire to make an impression on that beautiful young woman. No girlfriend had fascinated me like Moll, nor had I ever cared about impressing one. Moll's words stirred my soul. I was determined to prove myself as bold and brave as she was. All I wanted at that moment was to ride side by side with the dashing Captain Midnight and the legendary tobymen of The Swan With Two Necks! Anxious to seem a better rider than I actually was, I sat the horse by sheer willpower. Occasionally I looked over my shoulder to see if we were pursued. Those shots appeared to be all they were prepared to send after us. In spite of the real danger and discomfort, I never wished to wake from this dream. I smelled the sharp, wild air of the heath changing from open country to village to town to the great City herself, with the tang of soot and strong air, carrying the immunising bacteria allowing sturdy Cockneys to live indefinitely, some said for ever! It's no illusion. Many Londoners, uprooted to the countryside, die miserably from autoimmune diseases. They went off to St Dunstan's-in-the-Wold to breathe healthy country currents and were dead as doornails within days of arriving. In later years I almost died in rural Texas.

At last I saw a tinge of deep blue on the eastern horizon and recognised the outlines of St Bart's, St Paul's, the Monument and the other tall City landmarks.

It was almost dawn. I was in no way tired. I wondered at the speed with which the night had passed. We were coming home with a fortune in stolen cash! Laughing together we shared a swaggering moment as we slowed our horses and dipped our heads under the various gates and arches which brought us, without hazard, to the courtyard of The Swan With Two Necks.

Still in high spirits, we dismounted. I ran after Moll as she carried the bags up the outer stair and along the landing to more stairs, another floor at the very top of the tavern and finally the double doors of a large apartment. Opposite these were several shorter doors closer together, probably what the French call *chambres de bonne*, servant's quarters. Moll unlocked the double door and, glancing around to be sure we were unseen, led me into a comfortable apartment, with books and a writing desk, through to a small drawing room. Off to the right, presumably, was a bedchamber. The apartment probably occupied most of the space on this side of the building. Were they her rooms or did she share them? Perhaps all her colleagues used the place? She made no effort to enlighten me as, laughing, we emptied the saddlebags onto a table. At Moll's instigation, we sorted the notes into their various denominations, counting as we did so and bundling the money into amounts of £5, £10 and £20. We had cleared a thousand and eighty pounds, a huge sum for 1957, before decimalisation caught us short. Our haul would let a lot of men go on strike without their families having to suffer. 'At this rate we shall defeat the bosses!' With considerable satisfaction Moll planted a sudden kiss on my cheek. I thought my face caught fire. Then, careless of what she had done, she carried on.

'They're more afraid of us than ever before. That's why they've set thief-takers on our tails with a vast reward.'

I told her I'd already encountered two of them, Clitch and Love. She nodded, unsurprised. 'They ride under the Protector's colours and claim to work for the law. In reality they're hired by the transport bosses to catch us. They know where and why we congregate. The UTW is our most powerful union. They help us, even though we rob the trams their members drive. Their bosses would give much to see the back of us.'

'Dead or alive?' I asked, a little hesitantly.

'Alive in some shape or another. But it's our business not to be captured at any cost. Not until I've signalled the union's couriers. Quick. We must rid ourselves of these costumes and get back into our ordinary clothes.' Tying the sacks with twine, she placed a small bundle of notes on the mantel. 'That's our share. We pay ten per cent to the landlord. He'll square the ostler. Then we buy all the drinks tonight in the private bar.' I began to wonder how profitable, if at all, this trade was. Clearly not the best paying in London. But I saw already how the attraction was not in the money but the game. I could easily become addicted to it. The chances were, of course, that this would never happen again. I could still wake up. And, when I did, I could turn that night's adventure into a whole series of shorts and publish it in *Tarzan*. Or even one of the better-paying markets, like Amalgamated Press or Odhams, who did *Eagle*. I had a twinge of conscience. I was learning how to turn every significant moment of my life into money. Not yet eighteen and I would soon be a true Fleet Street hack!

Leaving my jacket, shoes and scarf on the sofa for me, Moll pranced into the bedroom and quickly came out again in her women's petticoats and pinafore. A little embarrassed I climbed quickly into my regular clothes, leaving the highwayman togs neatly folded on the sofa, the riding boots on the floor beside it.

'You're learning all the tricks of the nighthawk chevalier. Eh?' Another kiss brushed my cheek and burned it. Handing me a wad of notes she led me quickly from the room.

I felt almost sick as I put my share into my trouser pocket. There were at least two fivers and who knew how many pounds and ten-shilling notes. It had to amount to over £25! I had never earned so much in so short a time. This was contemporary 1950s money: big, crisp, white fivers, printed in black and gold, watermarked in silver; new pound and ten-shilling notes. In Fleet Street I could spend it anywhere without arousing comment. Elsewhere they might grow suspicious of someone of my youth with so much money. Yet no matter what sort of delusion I suffered I would not be exonerated should the money be traced. It was stolen. I hated stealing, even from pigs like those. I had no need of it. I told her I would buy my rounds and give her what I had left to add to the union funds. She offered me that

sweet, sorrowing look women reserve for harmless idiots or their hus-
bands. 'Don't expect to begin a tradition,' she said. 'The tobyman's
life is an expensive one.'

I left money on the bar for my rounds and handed the rest to
Moll. Now that dawn was rising on another noisy day, I bowed and
thanked her for the exciting night. 'We must do this again.' I was still
fired up by the adventure. Grinning she moved towards me and kissed
me on both cheeks. Fire! 'Adieu for now, Michael, me lad.'

I had to return home. With her warmth and her perfume still
lingering about me, I walked briskly up to the gate and hauled it
open, relieved to see the sun already shining on the ivy-grown walls of
the unoccupied weekend offices. As I pushed the gate further open I
was suddenly face to face with a tall, handsome man of about my
own height, wearing long curly hair, a moustache and goatee, his
eyes half-hidden by the wide brim of a soft hat. He was all wrapped
up in black and brown, a sort of vast, sleeveless overcoat, under which
he carried something hidden in one hand. Taken aback he paused and
looked me over. Then he begged my pardon. I begged his.

'I seek the Abbey of the Flete Street Friars,' he declared. I realised
he spoke a rather odd French, no different in character to the English
of Alsacia. What surprised me was that I could understand him. My
French was notoriously bad.

'You turn left past the inn and keep going until you see it. Impossible to miss.' To my surprise, I replied in the same language.

'I am at your service, sir,' he said. 'Do you by any chance already
follow the oak leaf?' He was charming. I found myself liking him at
once. But I had no idea at all what he meant and he quickly realised
that.

Off came that wide-brimmed hat again. 'Forgive me, sir. I understood you had already put yourself in his cause.'

'Your grace. Please, sir! To the Sanctuary or we are all lost. The
Sanctuary, sir, and quickly!' Friar Isidore's voice. I was embarrassed.
The stranger saw my response and seemed a little taken aback.

Friar Isidore rounded the corner in haste, clearly concerned for the
man who addressed me.

'My dear sir, I apologise. I lost my way. I thought I knew London
well enough, but not this city. And all the time you were here.' The

tall man laughed and clapped me on the shoulder. 'Forgive me, sir, if my hurried manner startled you.' In a swirl of loose clothing he took off for the nearest side street.

Friar Isidore made an apologetic gesture and then went in pursuit of the tall aristocrat. I thought he said, '… we can afford no further fracturing.' I suspected the other man was a patient in the monks' care. Brother Isidore turned once. 'Good morning!' he called apologetically as he followed his charge around the corner.

'Good morning,' I replied. Still feeling flustered, I closed the gate and set off across the empty square. I hurried over the grass, through an archway and up the little maze of alleys which led to Carmelite Street and the familiar sight of Fleet Street, deserted apart from one or two empty taxis and a night bus returning to its depot, all but silent in the dawn light. My mum wouldn't like me coming home so late (or rather early) but I would concoct a story about a quarrel with my mate. I was sure she would not believe the truth. I was inclined to doubt most of it myself!

As it happened I got to my bed before Mum woke up. I began to wonder if the adventure were still going on when, reaching to close the curtains, I saw a large raven perched outside on the windowsill. The bird was glorious, cocking his head to look enquiringly up at me. I smiled, preparing to talk to him. Then he opened his beak, seemed to wink at me, spread his shining wings and flew away to the southeast. I watched him go. I had always been fascinated by corvids of every kind. The raven, I guessed, was heading back towards the Tower of London. Perhaps his flight feathers had grown faster than anticipated. I understood they clipped their ravens' wings in the belief that when the ravens deserted the Tower, then England would fall.

I feigned sleep when Mum looked in on me. It being Saturday, I was able to rest until noon, rise and make myself breakfast, since she'd be working the market stall until six p.m. at least. I still wondered if I had experienced some sort of hallucination. But my body ached from the ride. My bruises were visible, proving I had not had a conventional dream. I even had a very faint but persistent murmuring in my head which I thought was some sort of hangover. This left me with only a couple of unlikely explanations. The most fantastic was that I had actually been in some parallel London! Surely the raven wasn't from there?

Maybe, I thought, feeling a little sick and smiling at my own predicament, I had overdone the fantasy reading, yet somehow this had a different quality. Where in history or legend, for instance, had anyone, dressed and mounted like mid-eighteenth-century highway robbers, set off to hold up the great metal trams of the early twentieth? On behalf of a trade union? This wasn't just impossible. It was truly absurd! And those 'thief-takers'! They weren't even from the same period as the others. Clitch and Love, as well as the man who had interfered to help me, dressed like men from the mid-1600s, the end of the English Civil War. They claimed to work for the Puritan Parliament of Oliver Cromwell. What place did they have in the fantasy?

I thought of Smollett, Peacock, Firbank, Jarry, Vian and the other absurdists I loved so much. They somehow confirmed my own strange familiarity with this experience. All through my childhood, when I grew overtired, I had seen things others said were not there. 'Christmas lights in August,' my mum called it. She was used to me doing it. I *had* to be hallucinating. And who was the handsome man I had bumped into when leaving? He had also dressed in seventeenth-century style. Some foreign nobleman? Had we really spoken French? I was tempted to laugh, but the mystery scared me a bit, too. My sanity might depend on solving it. I would return as soon as I could and find someone prepared to tell me what was happening. I was sure Moll took pleasure in keeping me mystified. She might have known how mysteries make women all the more interesting. Was I in love with her? Not a good idea. Even then I recognised the danger of creating your heart's desire out of a particular waistline, a smile, a haircut and some makeup. I didn't know her at all. I was perfectly clear in my young mind about what was going on in that respect, but of course I still remained fascinated.

After dropping in on my mum's stall to tell her I was fine, I strolled back down to Fleet Street, Carmelite Street and, eventually, into Carmelite Inn Chambers. I almost burst into tears when I realised what was happening again. The gates had gone. As if the buildings of the square had somehow drawn together and made them vanish! For the life of me I could not find the way back into the Alsacia. I felt strangely helpless, as if a terrible trick had been played on me. If I kept staring at the building standing where the gates should be, I would eventually be arrested and taken off to the loony bin. I became confused and enlightened at the same time. There was only one explanation: I had experienced some sort of hallucination. I had better keep it to myself in future. I wouldn't even tell Barry or Pete.

But my senses still believed it had all been real. Wouldn't Barry confirm it? He had been so hungover, he might not remember. I knew exactly what a shrink would tell me. Because of my very active creative gift I was, when tired, very good at imposing my imagination on the world around me. Probably, they would say, I had found that gate precisely because I had wanted to find it. By 'closing' the gate, my mind was warning me that I shouldn't try to go through it again. I really had suffered an incredible hallucination! But Friar Isidore was real, surely? If I met him again next week at the typesetter's wouldn't he tell me the truth? Had I conjured those two Puritan rascals out of whole cloth? To scare *myself*? As a child I had been able to see ghosts. Even then I had been aware that I was imposing the images on the world, because my imagination was stronger than most. I was baffled, yet oddly reconciled. I had a nagging association at the back of my mind which recalled that last encounter at the gates. What *was* 'the oak leaf'? Something to do with the Jacobites?

When I got back home the daily papers had been delivered. They were late as usual. One of the magazines was *The New Scientist*, which had started coming out a year or two earlier. I flipped through it, intending to take it to my room and put it on top of the stack to read later. And then, looking at a brief article on the future of psychiatric drugs, it struck me. LSD! It was just becoming generally known. The talk of those Soho friends who reflected the zeitgeist would be all about *The Doors of Perception*, Aldous Huxley's description of his experiences with mescaline and his rather mystical reflections. Later he said that LSD was superior. The only thing stopping us trying the stuff was the price and difficulties of getting it from John Bell & Croyden in Wigmore Street, the retailer who stocked it. It was not illegal and not that hard to get a prescription. A few people had taken it and described its effects. I recognised the symptoms. Although I had not experienced intensified colour and so on, I had lived out those last hours and days functioning perfectly well but, in my time off, I had experienced a detailed waking dream in which I had done all those strange things. It was 1958. LSD-25 had been around since 1938 but only in recent years had Sandoz put it on the market as Delysid. I had read about it somewhere else, perhaps in one of those American magazines I found in second-hand shops. Everyone agreed that LSD was a drug which could quite literally change your view of reality.

I felt a sickening sense of loss when I realised that truth. I had been the target of a trick or possibly even a well-meant experiment. I was the victim of an hallucinatory drug which someone (perhaps that so-called monk?) had slipped into my tea. On Monday I would probably learn from friends that I had been babbling at them, believing I was in an eighteenth-century highwayman's hostelry or riding to hold up a long-distance tram!

Moll Midnight had no doubt been simply a creature of my secret desires. No wonder I was fascinated! She was my waking dream. Everything I wanted in a sexual partner. I was suddenly deeply depressed. Moll was an illusion. I would never ride beside her again while she challenged me to dare what she dared, taste what she tasted – the thrill of the pounce, the relish at making the powerful suddenly powerless, the chance to right wrongs and reverse injustice! Even now, as I went up the stairs to my room, I saw her standing regarding me with quizzical humour. I knew what that was, or thought I did. I must still have been experiencing flashes of memory, of moments in her company. What on earth did I think I was doing? I was yearning for a woman I had invented.

For a day or two I pined and then other things began to distract me. I told myself I could keep Moll in my company for as long or as little as I liked. If she was a product of an overactive imagination I'd channel it all into something practical. I would do it by writing about her in a new series of stories. If only I could lose the murmuring in my ears, so faint that I was only aware of it when I remembered it. I had begun to wonder if I shouldn't perhaps leave my steady job and go over to Paris for a bit. Ray Napoleon was still there and I was sure he would help me find an apartment. I could write just as easily from there. Cheering up a little I decided to get my artist friend Jim

Cawthorn, who had just moved from Gateshead-on-Tyne to London, to draw her with an unsheathed sword swinging in a soldier's harness from her pretty shoulders. Maybe a four-part serial in the back pages of *Tarzan*. 'Sweet Polly Oliver...' I sang. '*When sweet Polly Oliver lay musing in bed / A sudden strange fancy came into her head...*'

On my slow way to my own bed I wrote the first tale in my head. It would be conventional enough to begin with. By day she was sweet Polly Oliver, whose father once owned the Cross Keys until shot by hirelings working on crooked thief-taker Jake Jekyll's orders. As Meg Midnight she was determined to bring the killers to justice. No-one along the Ratcliffe Highway or beyond laughed at Meg Midnight nor took her lightly. Her threats and her wits were spoken of from Land's End to John o' Groats. She brought justice and hope to the poor. Although no more than seven and ten, she was fêted by the best of them. Forever seventeen, forever riding with the wind in her hair and her enemies far behind, a merry laugh on her lips, she would enter the consciousness of a million boys and girls as soon as I found her a publisher. I would link her adventures to actual history and set her story around 1745 so I could deal with an interesting time in British history, as Scotland and England merged and tensions flared between French and English and their native allies on what would become the Canadian border. Jacobite plots and complications in India. I was too impatient to wait for Jim. I'd do a text story first.

I looked forward to getting back to my sturdy Imperial 50/60, a wartime utility typewriter I still own, winding a sheet of quarto and carbons onto its platen and starting the first story: *Queen of the Road!* But by the time I woke up a few hours later I was depressed. It had dawned on me that my imagination had provided only a passing consolation. I had to accept the fact: whether she was real or imaginary, the invention of my ideals and desires, I would never ride with Moll Midnight again!

CHAPTER SEVEN

LOOKING IN TO LIFE

MY MUM SAID I wasn't getting out enough. I was pale and 'nervy', she thought, conditions I now know she associated with masturbation. What, she asked, had happened to all those 'nice girls' I'd been seeing? 'Quite a few used to come chasing round here.' (It had been two and they were just mates from school, Vera Small and Marie Booker. Both their dads had shops in the market.)

I didn't feel ill at all. And I wasn't wanking myself to death. I was depressed and trying to come to terms with the idea that I might be crazy. I read a bunch of books on hallucinations and how they affected people. I wondered about the faint persistent murmur I had heard since riding out with Moll. I missed my Uncle Fred. I wanted to talk to Mr Ackermann but he was in Austria visiting his remaining relative, a cousin. Mum would be too worried if I told her what I thought had been happening to me. Should I find a psychiatrist? But, over the next few weeks, my natural good humour returned. I joked that I was too shallow to have a serious mental problem. But I did plan to leave *Tarzan* and live in Paris for a while. As I anticipated my trip, memory of Moll slowly faded and Barry Bayley helped convince me the gate had been partly an illusion and what I'd seen behind it a waking dream. He had a lot of theories. Barry always had a lot of theories. But he got me refocused on the skiffle group, which was slowly turning into a blues band and would soon be an R&B band. I wrote a bad song, 'Galloping Mary', and put the Alsacia behind me. We performed the song at the Princess Louise, just down the road in High Holborn. That was where I met Alexandra Taylor, a posh girl whose Pakistani stepfather was a dentist in Belgravia and only let her out at weekends. Sandy was beautifully blonde and not very bright. Eventually she got to be a model and was actually on the cover of *Vogue*. Before that, however, she told me a funny story about how her stepdad had caught a man flirting with her mother and had arranged it so that the man woke up one morning without a tooth in his head.

Soon after ending the affair with Sandy, I began writing the Meg Midnight adventures in earnest. They grounded my fascination for the girl in the Alsacia until I could scarcely tell my character from the Molly I had dreamed about. By now, in spite of aching all over the following day, I had convinced myself that it had been nothing more than a dream. Meg Midnight would now become one of those dreams that keeps on earning the cheques. Her adventures were the best story-paper work I had done so far. In those days there was a shrinking market for text fiction as opposed to comics but a few papers took a typeset story or two because it offered them some sort of respectability with schools. Amalgamated Press's *Comet* and *Sun* seemed to like the older style and at the same time were the comics the department was proudest of. When I had finished the first two Meg Midnight adventures I showed them to the editor Dave Gregory. 'Authentic history,' he said. 'Teachers and parents love that.' Everyone was looking for that edge: to be a comic, like *Eagle*, which parents tolerated. AP had at one time used a female highway thief-turned-thief-taker in their Jack o' Justice series, so Len Matthews, one of Dave's bosses, who had written them, was also reassured.

If Clark Gable had lived and gone to seed, that was Bill Baker, the hard-drinking Irish-Canadian, who edited *Sexton Blake Library* and who had introduced me to Dave and the others. Outside, he wore a snap-brim fedora and a trench-coat-style mackintosh. Sometimes at work he chewed a cigar, wore a green eyeshade and held his shirt-sleeves back with special bands. He called you 'sport' if he liked you and 'chum' when you were in his bad graces. He had known little of Sexton Blake when he started and got his mate Jack Trevor Story to collaborate on one. An odd mixture. Jack's pastoral comedy like *The*

Trouble with Harry mixed with Bill's mean streets and casinos. In the end Jack became a better friend of mine than Bill was. Bill loved the old story papers he had read as a boy – *Magnet, Gem, Popular, Union Jack* and *Thriller* – and was very enthusiastic about Meg. She would be perfect, he decided, to feature in one of the remodelled comics they were bringing out. *Lion* and *Tiger* would take over from *Comet* and *Sun*. She was exactly right for them. These comics carried about six to ten series strips a week. Bill planned to run a text serial and two shorts based on recurring characters or themes. They were trying to make the paper broaden its appeal to girls. Meg would be a great character for the ongoing series of shorts. I turned them in and they sold very well from the start. Circulation jumped whenever Meg appeared. I got to write a text story in *Sun* every week, then a two-page serial strip in *Comet*.

Of course, what I really wanted to write for AP was a Sexton Blake novel, only because Blake was the last continuous character they had from before the First World War. I had collected *Union Jack*, 'Sexton Blake's Own Paper', during my story-paper phase. The *Sexton Blake Library* had lasted the longest. *SBL* published two issues a month and paid 150 guineas for a story, usually paid the week after acceptance. Thirty-five to forty-five thousand words – about half a hardback novel. A small fortune. You relinquished all rights by signing the back of the cheque. AP could retitle your stories, rename your characters and alter the plot to suit an editor's whim over and over for ever. But for about half the time it took to write a full-length novel, the pay was so much better than a trade publisher's first advance of between £75 and £100. When that was the only concern there was little incentive to worry about who owned what rights. Jack Story would take a Sexton Blake tale he'd done, change the name, make Sexton a solicitor, sell the novel to Secker & Warburg and get great reviews. I learned from him that most reviewers didn't judge you by your writing but what format your story appeared in. Most Blake novels only ever saw one edition. Many AP writers, myself included once or twice, kept themselves going by recycling and resetting stories and giving characters new names. Once I sold the same story to three magazines as a western, SF and historical tale. In comparison, literature, as my fellow hacks were fond of saying, did not pay.

Meg Midnight soon made me one of the best-paid scriptwriters at Fleetway and Odhams. I specialised in the posher scripts and non-fiction. I became the go-to bloke for 'historicals'. With a little name change, to satisfy an ever-tolerant Fleetway Publications (these were the days when corporate execs thought a feast was as good as a feeding frenzy), I also sold Midnight Moll adventures to World Books as paperbacks – *Midnight Moll, Moll and Turpin, Moll o' the Road*. She was a more grown-up version of my magazine character. The same plots, a little modest sex for the ladies. As a highwaywoman she had amorous adventures in what became a more specific eighteenth century, using real people for walk-on parts. I called myself Kathleen Barclay and they sold exceptionally well to a mainly female audience. Yet I felt increasingly as if I were betraying a real person.

Moll became more and more the woman of my dreams, less and less of a reality. I gave the stories a mild love interest with a boyfriend, Gentleman Jeb Collins. Moll became the feistiest highway robber in the business. She made more than one foray into the world of fantasy. She had ancestors and descendants. I did a couple of haunted horse tram and ghost stagecoach stories but real trams, of course, were out as far as Midnight Moll went – a part of my dream which would be impossible for the readers to accept. In fact Moll/Meg soon didn't do much conventional coach robbing, either. Mostly she got involved with the machinery of the nineteenth-century Gothic and its secret caverns, glowing horsemen, hooded figures, phantom ships, mysterious castles and sinister dwarves. Pirate episodes. An American Indian story. The Spanish Inquisition. The Jacobite Rebellion. Hardy perennials. I had hit gold. Or at least silver. Editors as well as the public loved Meg.

For a while her popularity was pretty big. They gave her a modern descendant who could summon Robin Hood whenever she blew Robin's horn. Molly Midnight became a kind of Batgirl who fought crime. She featured for a while in *Tiger*. I wrote almost every other character in *Tiger* except her! Soon she was awarded Fleetway's highest accolade: her own *Thriller Picture Library* – sixty-four pages for a shilling.

For a while I returned to editing *Tarzan* but I was losing interest. Our skiffle-and-blues band was getting a little bit of attention. A bloke with a Polish name was keen on us to try a bunch of the outer-London pubs. We were flattered. We began to have musical ambitions.

The next time I went down to Metropolitan Typesetters in Old Bailey there was no sign of Friar Isidore. Had I imagined him too? Another week and he still didn't turn up. Quite a few people remembered him. 'I think his paper folded', said one of the apprentices. He had read something about it in the last issue of *The White Friar* he composed. I got Sammy Samuels to do the proofs after that.

I was bothered by the very faint humming in my ears. I wondered if it was caused by being too close to the stage when a jazz band was on. It was hardly noticeable most of the time and was only irritating when I was overtired. I worried it would affect my playing but our local GP, Dr Dillon, told me it was nothing to worry about. I believed him. I had been seeing him since he delivered me. The Greenhorns had become Killing Floor, giving up our smart grey Stetsons, matching box jackets and string ties. We had our biggest gig coming up at a jazz club in West Hampstead and I didn't want to blow it. That gig got us a demo at EMI. I suppose it was probably just as well it was so dire and I wasn't lured away from writing for a while.

Before I was nineteen I had left *Tarzan*, promising to continue writing for them while looking after the Tarzan strip. Once again I went to Paris to stay with Ray Napoleon. Ray still kept his San Francisco contacts and hung out with the Beats. He took me round to a tiny hotel at the back of George Whitman's Le Mistral bookshop, and introduced me to Gregory Corso and Allen Ginsberg. I thought they were nice, polite, clean-cut young Americans. They were kind to me. At that time I had never heard of them. Although I knew a lot about the music, I was almost entirely ignorant of modern American literature. That faint humming in my ears remained but I was having so much fun and I didn't care.

Ray and I busked outside Le Mistral. George Whitman was happy. Any money we made outside the shop was spent inside. Le Mistral eventually became Shakespeare and Co. That was where I bought the first modern SF novel I read, a serial in *Galaxy* of Alfred Bester's *The Stars My Destination*. I loved it. If that was SF, I was a convert. I found more old copies of *Galaxy* and read Pohl and Kornbluth's

The Space Merchants. Eventually, tired of sleeping uncomfortably in Ray's living room, I went home. I had work to do.

Moll remained my most popular character, running in *Comet*, *Tiger* and *Thriller Picture Library*, for a while at the same time. I rewrote some as science fantasy for *Tarzan* simply by beginning 'On Mars'... and making Moll a tough space rat in the manner of Leigh Brackett's Eric John Stark. I didn't do many. Sammy had been awaiting his chance. The moment I left he took *Tarzan* swinging and whooping back to the early twentieth century. I dropped in one day and found my stories and Jim's illustrations actually in the wastepaper basket. 'Healthy boys don't want that stuff,' he said of everything I loved. There weren't enough healthy boys, apparently. The paper lasted another ten or so weeks.

CHAPTER EIGHT

LITERARY LIFE

I MOVED TO Earls Court. A big furnished flat by the Tube. Of course I was as profligate as any young man capable of earning large amounts of money. I became a teenage drunkard. I became attractive to women. I put it down to playing in a group and making money from writing. Whatever it was, I got on well with women. At eighteen I had a reputation. It was mysterious to me but every time I turned up at the Globe I was with a new girlfriend. I enjoyed their company but felt no powerful attraction to the girls. Until I fell in love with Maria Papadoupolis.

I met Maria at a party of *Outsider* author Colin Wilson. People had brought Colin and me together because they saw us as *enfants terribles* but we didn't have a lot in common. I got on better with Colin's friend Bill Hopkins, another self-styled 'angry young man', who wrote a couple of rather lush novels. They lived together in a big flat off Portobello Road. When I was there, most of their anger seemed to do with who had used up the last of the milk. Maria was a friend of Charlotte, Charlie Shapiro's sister, whom I'd taken to dinner a couple of times. Charlotte, Colin and Bill had got into tarot reading and Ouija boards for some reason. Probably because of the gypsies and Auntie Ethel, I'd shown a surprising aptitude for the usual silly party tricks like who was being faithful or unfaithful, where something could be found and so on, but I wouldn't do 'talking to the dead' stuff.

Maria had pale skin, dark curly hair cut to the nape of her neck, dark eyes, spectacular lashes. She was short but she had the figure of a Greek goddess, over which she wore a scarlet velvet frock. Her high heels matched that frock. Her earrings probably weren't real pearls and diamonds but somehow they looked real on her. She wore just the right amount of Shalimar. She leaned against my shoulder while I dealt the cards and huskily asked me to read her tarot. We were soon in bed, courtesy of Bill, who luckily had his own plans for the evening, as did Colin. She clearly wasn't the virgin her dad insisted she remain.

Maria had slept with some pretty useful communists. She knew a lot more about pleasure, how to find it and sustain it, than I did. I was soon more than willing, as Charlotte joined us, to risk the wrath of the most feared communist gangster in North London. But, as the weekend wore on in Charlotte's little Bloomsbury boarding-house room, I understood that wasn't really the problem. Mr P. believed his daughter was visiting family in Cyprus, which gave her a lot of freedom in those days before everyone had a phone. The problem was me. I had fallen in love with a woman who wasn't in the mood for love and I was, as far as she was concerned, something of a wimp. I thought I came out of it pretty well. I learned how to give her multiple orgasms. I did several kinds of threesome. Drugs were harder to find in those days, but I found them. I refused to let her try heroin or morphine and hadn't tried them yet myself. Slowly but surely I became protective of her. She was seventeen, bursting out of her convent school full of frustration and ready for everything. And of course, within weeks I drove her away. Now, I can sympathise with her state of mind, but then I was shattered. She simply disappeared. Charlotte didn't know where she had gone. Her father, of course, told me she was in Cyprus. I think it was at that moment I started to cry.

My old posh girlfriend Alexandra had been sent off to finishing school almost as soon as we broke up. After Maria, I started seeing Alex's sister Memphis. Her parents were heavily into Egypt for some reason. Memphis Gupta had to be the coolest name in town, especially in 1958. We had a lot of fun. For a while Alex's friend Indigo joined us.

I wined and dined everyone and drove a few real friends away. I wanted to share my good fortune, that was all. It took me years to understand why they would feel insulted. Some came to dislike me for flashing my money about. Some could handle it. Some wound up despising me. I berated others for their lack of imagination and sensitivity while often completely lacking it myself. I had come to all this money a little too soon. Certainly it didn't occur to me to save it. I could always earn what I needed by writing another Moll story.

I made even more money by doing the odd bit of guitar work. At that time there were a lot fewer people in London who could play blues. I got around twenty quid an hour. Union rates. Some people liked my weird half-banjo sound. Open G, picking, the bass string as a kind of drone. All sorts of weird tricks. I also got gigs with the little Dixieland bands springing up everywhere. Sometimes I played a couple of blues songs while they took a break. The customers thought of me as some kind of one-man skiffle group. Gradually, though, I got anonymous work on British rock-and-roll records. I was very grateful for the anonymity.

At last I began to sell short science fiction to the English magazines. There were three left: *New Worlds*, *Science Fantasy* and *Science Fiction Adventures*, all edited by Ted Carnell. I met Jack Allard in Carnell's offices, when we were both delivering stories. I was not overly familiar with his work but one novella had struck me as outstanding and I was able to tell him. He took my praise graciously. We began to meet intermittently, sometimes with Barry Bayley, first at a nearby pub and then closer to Jack's editing job in Knightsbridge. We shared a frustration with the contemporary novel only matched by our disappointment with science fiction. It all looked old-fashioned to us. Nostalgic. Profoundly sentimental. We loathed nostalgia and bemoaned its dominance of American and British literature. William Burroughs was our favourite SF writer. I had been introduced to him briefly in Paris and had a desultory correspondence: a few postcards. I had introduced Allard to Burroughs's work after I returned from Paris with a bunch of his Olympia Press stuff. He was the only Beat I really liked.

The fiction we visualised would be printed on slick paper in a format large enough to reproduce good art, in a magazine with an up-to-date title designed to appeal to a modern, educated audience. Not generic SF, but borrowing from it. I showed Allard some mock-ups I'd done for a new kind of publication. I couldn't think of a decent title. We were looking for a fresh vocabulary and narrative forms to explain our special experience as the postwar generation which had known the war as children and were embracing modern scientific ideas, computers, psychosexuality, new social interpretations and so on. Allard was older than me and his ideas of how the magazine should look were in my view a little outdated. He thought my visual notions were driven by fashion rather than the zeitgeist. I thought his a bit 1940s. We argued but rarely fell out because we agreed in general. We joked that if we ever got what we wanted we would be like Trotsky and Lenin, quarrelling over who knew best, who should have the most power. The amiable, superbright Barry, who chuckled approvingly at our ideas but saw no chance of them reaching any kind of fruition, said that as long we wanted to take his stories, rejected by Carnell, we had his support.

I admired Camus. I'd been introduced to his work in Paris with stuff by Jarry and Ionesco. I thought Philip K. Dick was a bit like that but I was disappointed by the rationalisations he provided to please his publishers. Allard liked Bradbury, noir films and the Nouvelle Vague in French cinema. I joked with him that if he hadn't been tone deaf he would have liked bebop. But existentialism and absurdism were in the air we breathed. He loved surrealism. I loved pop art. We would have long, fierce, friendly arguments about all this. He had read very little, preferring to get his culture via the screen or from the radio, but this didn't stop him having strong opinions about literature. I had grown up between two great public libraries in a neighbourhood and surrounded by second-hand bookshops. I had been an early reader. He had read mostly American comics and science fiction magazines. We didn't even have the same tastes in those!

After the liberation of Guernsey, where he had grown up under German occupation, Allard had gone to posh schools and Cambridge. I had barely been educated formally after I was fourteen. But we got on well and were soon warm friends. Allard was married with two little children so we rarely met in the evenings. We talked a bit about the unusual stories we had written and how there was nowhere to sell them now that *Lilliput* was a shadow of its former self. We looked eagerly for particular markets. We kept on submitting to *Argosy* and the posher monthlies, like *Encounter*, which occasionally bought imaginative fiction. Whenever we were rejected we comforted ourselves that we were proving how out of touch those editors were. He spoke of Kafka's rejections. I said they only accepted what they could recognise. Even when Allard sold to *Argosy* he claimed it was one of the most ordinary stories he'd ever written, thus underpinning his argument.

I didn't much share Allard's enthusiasm for the New Wave French film-makers and he didn't share mine for Vian, Cendrars, Henry Green and the American avant-garde. I eventually realised that the only fiction he liked was his own. Meanwhile, he wrote brilliant, lyrical, existentialist stories which were a bit like Ray Bradbury, a bit like Graham Greene and were as original as anything the genre had ever seen. By contrast, I found a profitable facility for reviving the pulp sword-and-sorcery story for which I still had a fondness and which Carnell began to commission from me.

A great Mervyn Peake fan, I publicised his work whenever I could. I had known Peake for a couple of years and his health was failing but we all held hope for his recovery. I didn't really think of his work as fantasy. To me he was closer to absurdists like Peacock and Firbank or Maurice Richardson, whom Allard also loved. Peake had a better sense of narrative than any of them but his grotesque characters dominated his work. There was nothing supernatural about it. Some people called it Gothic, I think because it was set in a brooding castle, while others compared him to Kafka or even Lovecraft. Peake was a vorticist with a sense of humour. But manifestos weren't his thing. I'd discovered that as I came to know him. *Gormenghast* was an intensely personal response to the world, eschewing movements yet having much in common with the surrealists or even the pataphysicians. I'd never properly read *Lord of the Rings*. Seemed a somewhat reactionary response to the Modern, having much in common with Germanic folklore and much American SF, and probably the secret of its success. There was something about Tolkien's comfy, conspiratorial tone which reminded me of the *Daily Mail*, BBC *Children's Hour* or Winnie-the-Pooh, and actually repelled me.

I found my heroic fantasy masters in the pulps, old and new. They were almost all American. Robert E. Howard was their king and Fritz Leiber the best literary stylist. I loved Jack Vance's *Dying Earth* and Frank Owen's strange pseudo-orientalism. I struggled a bit with James Branch Cabell but enjoyed Lord Dunsany. Lovecraft and horror fiction in general had no attractions. Lovecraft's contemporary, Seabury Quinn, who was his greatest rival in *Weird Tales*, was much more to my taste. Allard had no interest in any pulp but *Black Mask*. *Galaxy* was his favourite contemporary SF magazine, as it was mine. No spaceships. Lots of dystopias. I don't think either of us read the other when we weren't doing something unusual, but we pretended we had. For me literature had to be thoroughly stunning (like Eliot) or pleasantly numbing (like Sexton Blake stories). My enthusiasm for SF faded when so little of it engaged with the day's issues. I wasn't interested in middlebrow concerns or middle-class tastes. That was what kept us friends, our lust for the excellent and the extraordinary. And Barry read everything we did, as I read his. He and I even wrote a few stories together. The most ambitious of them anticipated miniature computers and M-theory and examined largely metaphysical worlds and ideas. We had intense intellectual conversations and then earned our livings as best we could by writing Gothics for the comics. Allard continued to edit his trade magazine but flirted with the idea of selling an SF novel to the US and getting a thousand dollars. As long as he worked rapidly it would earn enough to let him chuck in his job. Barry and I wrote mostly educational stuff for *Look and Learn*, *Did You Know?* and *Bible Story* and every so often I did another Meg Midnight story for Fleetway.

Dave Gregory at AP soon wanted more 'historicals' as these costume melodramas were called, so I came up with *The Phantom Cavalier*: a cloaked and hooded vigilante before the Restoration. Remembering Claude Duval I made my hero an exile from France and a loyal servant of the Stuart Cause, so that many of his adventures could be lifted whole from Stevenson, with a few tweaks, reversing the political polarities, setting them in Cromwellian England and making them over-the-top romances in the spirit of the old 'bloods'.

The bloods had titles like *The Blue Dwarf* and *Colonel Jack, The Gentleman Highwayman*, *The Brotherhood of the Heath* or *Black Bess* – dozens of them. The Gothic was one of the most popular genres of the nineteenth century and I revived the writing of it single-handed, to be lauded as something of an innovator in the world of comics and fantasy fiction. That stuff was directly in the Gothic tradition.

Doing a great deal of lucrative hackwork, I was still in a slightly uncertain position. Freelancing, while well paid, was unpredictable. At that point – 1959 – Bill Baker asked me to come and work on his editorial team. I liked the idea. Keeping a steady ten-to-five editing job and, with luck, selling the odd feature would give me time to take a crack at a proper novel. I had moved from Earls Court to Notting Hill and couldn't write a novel until the rent was paid, and the freelance work could always dry up without warning. The editorial job on *Sexton Blake Library* solved my dilemma. Really, I was just delighted at the chance to work on the last of the AP story papers!

So of course I took the job. In loyalty to my younger self, if nothing else. It was my last dream come true! And the work scarcely proved to be arduous! Bill explained that, because there wasn't really a full-time job on Blake and because of my experience with type and text layouts, I would also be doing some other editorial work, mostly on the annuals. These were hardcover versions of the weekly comics. I could write a good many text stories and some comics when not doing editorial work, and be paid top rates for them. The annuals paid more. Pretty easy work after the one-man band I'd been on a weekly magazine. The surrounding offices were crammed with young editors, all with enormous literary ambition. They loved lecturing me. They knew all kinds of stuff: foreign films, untranslated literary masters, obscure English writers and painters. With my patchy cultural background, I brought out the worst as well as the best in them, but they were great enthusiasts and really well educated. Because I started so young as an editor, I was at least three or four years younger then the rest. They were my professors. New Fleetway House was my university.

Soon after I got the editing job, Dave asked me for two more Meg Midnight stories a week – one in text for *Tiger* and the other a strip in *Lion*, the new versions of *Sun* and *Comet* – to see which form was going to be the most popular. Even though they'd already reprinted one of my long stories as a serial, with a bulked-up Turpin in place of Moll. I agreed. They also turned her into first Turpin's girl pal then

Jack o' Justice's girl pal, who loved investigating the paranormal. The department head, Len Matthews, had earlier created his own girl highway robber who had not been as successful as Meg, but he seemed perfectly happy with my version. She settled into the rôle she made her own. My *The Haunted Blade* sold twice as many as any other issue of *Thriller Picture Library*. This was a big break for me. Fleetway generally paid much better and quicker than the other publishers. I was glad they'd taken my rejigged character back into the fold.

Memphis went on a cruise with her grandmother. I briefly went back to seeing Sandy. Mr Gupta saw me as young, ambitious and destined to be a good breadwinner. He started talking about marriage. I was already the son he'd never had. So that was the end of my association with that family. Their upper-class assumptions and opinions had become increasingly hard to take anyway.

By now, of course, I completely blamed LSD for what had happened in 'Alsacia'. Life was getting very full for me and Alsacia had dropped below my horizon. I talked about it sometimes, but only to illustrate the power of LSD to create hallucinations.

By 1959 I had written, with Jim Cawthorn, the Sexton Blake story I always wanted to do and was selling regularly to the British SF magazines. I was also still in Killing Floor, a skiffle group-cum-blues band. But now I was more into Carter than Cash. I played banjo and sang some Guthrie songs, which I quickly discovered wasn't sexy, even though I wasn't bad at it. I went through a bluegrass phase. I bought a Gretsch guitar on hire-purchase payments but kept the G tuning, dropping a string so I could carry on fingering the same as the banjo. I wasn't bad. Slide guitar is pretty easy with that tuning and gave Woody some beaty phrasing. I could stop a show with 'Pretty Boy Floyd' or 'This Land is Your Land'. People said I put real emotion into my singing.

For a year or more we earned a bit of money on the side doing small gigs, pubs and dances, briefly becoming a C&W band before we morphed into the Big Six, a moddy R&B band doing Chicago blues and Chuck Berry hits. Your influences and your tastes change rapidly when you're young. A familiar route.

In those pre-Swinging days everyone seemed to wear grey. That was when I first understood fashion as not just a passing Ted thing. We wore Italian suits, pale grey bum-freezer jackets, overcoats to the knee, Italian shoes, short pudding-bowl haircuts. Slender, knitted ties, sharp white collar and cuffs. Earlier, my buff pullover, corduroy bags, chukka boots and a duffel coat identified me as a beatnik. My only touch of originality was the black ex-army ski cap on my head. I wore it because it was like Woody Guthrie's railroad-man's hat. There's a picture of me at *Tarzan* wearing it! Later Bob Dylan would put on much the same outfit. I wrote to Woody. Woody wrote back. But Bob made the physical pilgrimage.

Later we changed to black. Cool blokes wore black. Black car coat, tight charcoal trousers, cuban-heeled pointed shoes, old-fashioned detachable white collars and shirts with links, showing a fair bit of bright, white cuff below the sleeve. Early mod, my children call it. For a while it was The Who, Faces, The Action and us. Can you guess who didn't get a record deal?

Through the late '50s we performed in Soho venues like Bunjies, Sam Widges, the Skiffle Cellar, the Gyre & Gimble at Charing Cross. The Nucleus in St Martin's Lane, across from the As You Like It where John Baldry and Reg Dwight hung out. Both of them could belt out blues in those days. I was with John when we met Willie Dixon. John was at least a couple of inches taller than me. Known as Long John, he could belt out blues better than any of us. Now we were on the Rik Gunnell circuit, playing the Flamingo, the Railway Hotel and Eel Pie Island. And Moll rode on, to almost impossible popularity in the years when WW II's *Battler Britton* was taking over everything except soccer. I've often wondered how things would have gone with the band if I'd been able to put my whole talent behind it.

Amongst my writer colleagues there weren't many I bonded with, apart from my closest friends Allard, Barry, Pete, and Max Stone. Allard, as noted, was of an older generation and tone deaf as well. Max the dandy was now a cartoonist and an outstanding Django-style guitarist. Pete played what he called classical washboard. Barry had become self-conscious and dropped out, taking his harmonica with him. With Max on guitar we had a nifty little trio with me on bass, sometimes doing banjo where appropriate.

Max and Barry had been in the RAF together and were a year or two older than me. I had just escaped the call-up by a month or so. Originally we had met at the Globe because we had an interest in science fiction. The pub was only a street or two from my mum's house. I was still looking to science fiction as a means of confronting what were particularly contemporary problems.

Confined as a child when the Germans invaded Guernsey, Jack had innocently given his father up to the authorities when an avuncular German officer asked whose dads had radios. He had what some thought a skewed view of the world. Admirers of his short stories (he had yet to write a novel) said he was something close to a genius. I was, needless to say, an admirer. I had known nothing as terrifying as a German camp, but had come through the Blitz and the V-bombs.

We were not concerned like the middle classes with shivering at the future and seeing doom in every scientific development. We embraced all innovation. We weren't even standard bohemians, wanting to ban the bomb. Allard had seen the bomb as a sign of release from the appalling cruelty of the Germans and Japanese. Bayley wondered about its philosophical meaning and symbolism, while I, who had experienced so many V-rockets and known friends who disappeared suddenly as a result of those explosions, did not feel especially bothered about a lethal instrument which took you out instantaneously. So while progressives marched with the CND, we were inclined not to. The beneficiaries of most wars were the survivors. That's how we saw ourselves. Fortunate.

When we did march it was to please our friends. The experience sharpened our sense of what lay in store for us should our democracies break down, both politically and socially. John Brunner, with his goatee, yellow stock and corduroy sports jacket, was very disappointed in us. I knew his inner RAF officer was tempted to order us to volunteer. Instead he forced a smile and said our hearts were in the right places. That wasn't true, either. Turning his back on his earlier romanticism, Allard was developing his bleak, existential parables of contemporary life. Influenced by the English absurdists and French existentialists, I was thinking about a character looking for a contemporary urban identity, who could relish and examine what most people considered the nightmares of the present and near future, who took

being a fictional character for granted. Bayley considered the most grotesque notions and imagined their logical outcome. Of the three of
us, he was the most interested in using science fiction to examine and
formulate ideas in theoretical physics. We proved we could suspend
disbelief with the best of them. Now the trick was how to *retain* disbelief. We were strong on theories of alienation in those days. I loved
Brecht. Allard found his inspiration in Freud. His work was becoming that mixture of austere romanticism which out-Greened Greene
and was totally idiosyncratic. Max took to writing lyrics. And, eventually, jingles.

We still dreamed of creating a glossy magazine, about the dimensions of *Playboy*, which would run features and fiction, all examining the world around us. We needed to create literary forms to carry
the maximum number of narratives. We needed art paper so that we
could reproduce modern paintings, photographs and good illustrations. We would use photomontage for some of those features. It was
not for us to bemoan the 'death of literature'; it was for us to create
new ways of telling stories and attracting audiences by embracing
their anxieties, examining their nightmares and offering them unfamiliar forms and unconventional elements which at the same time embraced all the methods we saw around us and were still rarely
considered respectable literary forms. We were hugely idealistic and
had no practical understanding of how to fund such a venture. But
talk was good enough for those days. And I had my new girlfriend.

CHAPTER NINE

ROMANCE

BY 1960 I was twenty. I had enjoyed some brilliant affairs with spirited women and I'd come to know several of the writers I most admired. Some I read after I'd met them. Some became friends. They were my teachers. Lastly I enjoyed a fine education in the arms of Christina Vandeleur, an older woman who taught me a lot more than how to have fun in bed. She taught me about wines, food and travel. When I went to Sweden for a while she met me in Malmö and we had a tremendous month together. I think she said she was reindeer hunting in the Arctic Circle. Those were the days, before mobile phones and computers. Later I did go up to Norrlands, as it happened, and climbed there. A remote part of the world in those days. You could feel wonderfully isolated, hundreds of miles from the nearest civilisation or doctor.

Christina Vandeleur was a cousin of the Queen. A friend of Princess Margaret. I met her first at a gig. I think she was slumming with her husband, a rather remote Tory MP who had, she said, an American boyfriend. He had to be in New York a lot. On business, she told me with a jolly wink. Most of the time, in fact. She preferred London. He went home that night. She stayed, she said, for a one-night stand. I wasn't disappointed. Some generations seem to produce a lot of handsome people. Mine was definitely one of them. I think I owe a great deal of my finish to Christina Vandeleur. Perhaps every young sexual savage, naïve, shy and brutal, delicate and clumsy at the same time, should get his training in the art of love from the likes of her. I passed her education on to some younger women. Those girls have much to thank their mothers for.

Born Christina Bright in 1933 to the Rev. and Mrs Bright of Havercombe Morley, Somerset, cousins to Lord and Lady Bright of the same address, Christina's was a face well known to the scandal sheets and gossip columns to which she also contributed as a skilful journalist. She had negotiated her way out of Godolphin & Latymer School for supersmart girls when she joined forces with the teenaged Lord Acreman to be the youngest pair of consenting English adults married in the month of September, the day after her sixteenth birthday. She was soon persuaded to dissolve the marriage on grounds of nonconsummation. Apparently Acreman wasn't the most interesting of lovers. A year later she had married John Calvert, a dashing RAF officer. Almost at once both bride and groom were involved in some infamous and highly publicised affairs. She was nineteen when she married the named co-respondent in her divorce from Calvert. Jimmy Vandeleur was a bit of a walking cliché. Newspaper readers probably remember him as the daring young Formula One driver tragically killed during a practice run. Christina mourned him publicly and far more discreetly than before. She had later married Lord Mackenzie of Mourne and Jute, the newspaper owner, and wrote a column for the *Daily Graphic* which most people agreed was all that kept the paper afloat. It was a marriage of equals. While he was off buggering boys in Bangkok she indulged her not-dissimilar pleasures in Brighton.

We met again at a posh dinner party given by Monotype for all the editors on their lists. That was how I knew her name. They put little tags in our places. By chance I was seated across from her. Vandeleur was the name she kept for her journalism. We have all forgotten how, before personal computers, the makers of typefaces pursued us trying to persuade us to use their products. I still have a measuring stick I was given at a similar party. Christina was flattering, fascinated when I was introduced as the youngest editor in Fleet Street, which I might or might not have been. I, of course, had no idea how much I appealed to her. I thought she was being kind to a young, rather gauche fiction editor. News people generally despised us. We'd had a perfectly good night after the gig but now she showed genuine interest in my story and background. I thought she perceived me as some kind of Ettrick Shepherd. But in fact, as she crowed later, I was everything she wanted for her birthday tied up with blue ribbon and delivered to her door.

Her Mitsouko worked on me a bit like Viagra. I vaguely remember her giving the taxi an address in Chelsea which in those days was part of a run-down bohemia. She had an apartment at the top end of King's Road in a block of flats called Mackintosh Mansions. Yeats had lived there at some point. Designed to supply everything to residents they could possibly want, 'the Mack' had its own restaurant, hairdresser, newsagent and grocer's shop. Twentieth century, here we come! The idea was that residents were just beginning to feel the lack of available labour as well as inherited money. The flats still had servants' quarters, one room for a valet or lady's maid. Turned into spare bedrooms or even sublet by some. Many residents were forced to run their own errands after the Great Depression of the 1880s. So the young moderns were lured with services and exclusive shops all under one roof. If they liked to pose as painters they could also rent one of the studios where Augustus John and others worked. Sporting Club Square, where I went to live years later, was a similar idea on a much larger scale.

After the first passionate days, I saw Christina at the Mack about twice a week and went on dates with her more often. Affectionately, humorously, quietly, most of the time, she taught me an extraordinary range of sexual techniques so subtle that I never once felt a moment's resistance or nervousness. I even discovered a range of fantasies I might never have imagined for myself and enjoyed what others, I suppose, might think of as perversions. 'It depends on your attitude,' Christina would say. It was from her I learned the great mantra: Lips. Tongue. Eyes. Teeth. Swallow. Everything depended on the mood of those involved. If the mood wasn't right not much else would be. I suspect attitudes changed after 1980 or so. We'd learned which drug induced what response. Before then, before AIDS, a sort of glorious Golden Age ruled much of the world, promising peace and prosperity for everyone. The sexual adept was much higher on the social scale.

Then somehow it all darkened. Later I would feel oafish and unsophis-
ticated because I needed no special stimulus to fill my cock with
blood. Until then I enjoyed the whole range of sexual pleasure and
was willing to enjoy other people's fantasies, although I never needed
fantasy to be stimulated. Many, I learned, did. By the cocaine-snorting
1980s it was almost impossible to find a sexual partner who wasn't
into something weird. At that time my lifestyle was entirely different.
I had anticipated the end of the Golden Age. I'd wanted it to last
for ever, but it was pretty clear by the time Reagan and Thatcher so-
lidified their power that we had missed our chance. I remember the
moment in 1983 when a sadness swept over me and all I wanted to
do was stay in bed and dream.

CHAPTER TEN

THE STOLEN ALBINO

I HAVE TO admit that my attraction to Christina Vandeleur was distinctly Pavlovian! My friends came to recognise her 'type'. A little older. Very pretty, with shortish brown hair, small breasts. Other aspects which remain more elusive. Why? Her certain way of dressing? Of responding? I didn't feel any special lust for violent fantasy but she knew how to tease out the brute in me. And she wasn't alone. Women were quite open in those days. Eventually, I stopped being surprised. I played the games, acted the fantasies, but I was often sad, feeling a distinct loss. All the women I came close to loving were like Christina, with a couple of exceptions. I began to see her as the norm. Maybe she was.

After a year or so, as if she had done all she could for my sentimental and fleshly education, Christina tired of me. I had grown used to her, thought myself in love with her. I became jealous, morbidly self-involved. When you catch yourself watching a TV situated at the end of a single bed, weeping to Garbo's self-sacrificing dismissal of Robert Taylor in *Camille*, you know you're in trouble. Christina was kind according to her own lights. 'I never strive to hang on to the joys of youth,' she said, a bit mysteriously. I think I was that youth.

As a going-away present Christina introduced me to DiDi Dee, as she was known. The Honourable Deirdre Dee was the daughter of a blended-whisky robber baron. I liked her quite a bit but she was as controlling in her way as I was in mine at that age. And relentlessly intellectual. She painted. She had started a review and wanted me to contribute. I held back. I'd had enough of bluestockings. For a while I seemed to attract women who felt I could teach them something more intellectual or romantic or even technical that was the secret of their need. Really, I could only teach them what Christina had taught me. Christina was a huge influence on the sexual fashions of several generations. She deserved a statue or at least a plaque.

After DiDi I'd had a series of girlfriends. I refused, against all natural instincts, to commit. My weakness was that I committed far too readily. And then caused problems. I wasn't the bastard who buggered off, I was the bastard who hung around. My romantic, overblown, melodramatic self-image was beginning to be grounded in Meg Midnight's adventures with various Byronic villains. Somewhat to my surprise I found I preferred my lovemaking on an equal basis. I think that was what my grandma had drummed into me. I don't do moody or wounded or stern. I can't play head games. Sadly it left a lot of unhappy women who eroticised inequality so triumphantly and inescapably they identified it as their deepest self and defended that self against all attempts to expose it. They offer you so much power. All that patriarchy! So tempting to take advantage of it. It doesn't last all that long, not for me at any rate. Cheap thrills aren't my style any more. Eventually even the old temptations get satisfied once too often.

Naturally, I made a melodrama of all this.

I was in the office one evening when Harry Harrison, an ebullient American SF writer living in Europe, dropped in. He and an editor friend, Andy Vincent, were about to cross the road to the White Swan and have a drink. Why didn't I come? He was seeing Ted Carnell and John Wyndham there later. So I went. It was one of those watershed moments.

Talking to John and Ted, we mourned the passing of the old fantasy adventures done by the likes of Robert E. Howard and C.L. Moore in *Weird Tales*. The best remembered of these were the Conan stories. As it happened, I'd done half a Conan story at the request of Hans Stefan Santesson, the editor of *Fantastic Universe*. I'd tried it out but wasn't all that enthusiastic. John said I ought to come up with a character of my own for *Science Fantasy*. 'That way they remember the character when they've forgotten who you are.'

Thinking that over, I remembered Elric. Elric had been the central character I'd discussed with Jim Cawthorn when talking over doing a comic. I hadn't read most of the 'classics'. At that time *Lord of the Rings* hadn't been published in America and become a cult. It was considered just one of several offbeat books. I had read the Conan stories and Poul Anderson's first published fantasy *The Broken Sword*. I would want my own story to be as different as possible from all existing stories of the type. So, influenced in spite of myself by Poul Anderson and Blake writer Anthony Skene, who created Blake's opponent Zenith the Albino, I came up with a sorcerer-king too weak to fight without drugs or his sinister sword Stormbringer. Elric was born.

I never planned to write more than one story. I had no strong desire to write more. Then the readers' letters started coming. Carnell was amazed at the number. Most were enthusiastic. So he asked for another. I had started the first story well into Elric's narrative. I had to do my best with that. Off he went looking for his identity or at least *an* identity, enslaved by the demon lurking in his blade. And then Carnell wanted a third and a fourth and a fifth. And in between the Elric stories Carnell wanted novellas. As many as I wanted to write. From being an obscure writer who occasionally published in *New Worlds* or *Science Fiction Adventures*, I now had the lead story, illustrated on the cover. I was, Carnell said, his best discovery since Allard. Of course the stories initially made less money than my journalism. Yet they were a better investment of my time. Books might pay less, but they kept reprinting. If you made sure of your royalties, you could also leave something worthwhile for your spouse and children.

Elric was proving popular, not entirely from luck. All that reading of Freud and Jung, an absorption in metaphysics and the existentialists, paid off for a young lad earning a living from weird fiction. Knowing the Victorian Gothics helped, too. There's a lot to be said for going back to basics and for the existence of a good public-library system.

When I met the next girl of my dreams, I didn't think I had a chance. I discovered your knees really can knock together if you hold them close enough. It was horrible. As a rule I scarcely noticed a girl's advances yet I never lacked for female company. I thought incuriously, for I was supremely self-confident, that my attraction was something to do with my editorial power.

I honestly didn't think in terms of looks, but I was by no means the only one to decide that Helena Denham was the prettiest young woman in a world of good-looking women. Existentialist chic had at last brought a plethora of female beauty to the creative world, even if that world was one of mostly commercial fiction. Juliette Gréco set the standard and many women were well above it.

I caught sight of Helena at a party given by a friend of DiDi's, Ildiko Hayes. I had gone there on my own, having just broken up with a young woman who had dumped me and returned to her husband, a sergeant in the Household Cavalry who made me nervous, so I was a bit relieved. I had also resigned from Fleetway.

Helena had recently split with her boyfriend and, determined to have nothing further to do with men, had made herself as unattractive as possible. She had given herself a pudding-bowl haircut and wore frumpy tweeds but I still knew she was beautiful. She was posh, slightly awkward in a cute sort of way, a million times better educated than me, with a double first from Cambridge, a job at the Ministry of Information and the reputation, Ildiko told me, as a bit of a *belle dame sans merci*. That probably came from her preference for long, Left Bank cigarette holders, pageboy haircuts and big black jumpers.

There are only a few photographs of us and they show us trying to dress conventionally. She's in a fashionable 1961 Courrège suit, Sassoon hairdo. I have short hair and a neat Van Dyke. I'm in a white button-down shirt with a thin black tie, black car coat, tight grey trousers and cuban-heeled winkle-pickers. I didn't think I was dressing in any particular style. They were the clothes my peers wore. Later we'd all wear feathers and velvet. In reality most of the time Helena wore existentialist chic: black stockings, big jumpers. A Beat. People said we were the image of cool, the spirit of the age. Natural partners.

I wanted her. I was determined to have her. Against all habit I crossed a room full of half-dancing, half-talking people, went straight up to her and had Ildiko introduce us. She seemed startled when I stayed but then relaxed. We made a few jokes. Later, when she was about to leave with the group giving her a lift home I simply said, 'You're not going. You're staying.' And she stayed.

That was the beginning of my courtship. And it *was* a courtship. She slept with me but she wouldn't commit to me. I had never fought for a woman before. I was famous for it. But now I fought for Helena. For a short while she went out with both me and an Aussie friend of mine called Gordon Gaines. I think I'd introduced them. I'm not naturally possessive but I would have done almost anything to win her. I actually considered killing Gordon while I simpered and displayed my pretty feathers and fine accomplishments to the object of my desire. I wrote her songs and poems and begging letters full of sticky self-endorsement. Despite this she eventually agreed to marry me and that was that.

CHAPTER ELEVEN

ENGAGEMENT

I REMEMBER THE smell of the November air the evening Helena accepted me. We were on a Number 25, muffled upstairs, smoking
at the back, a little drunk from good food and wine in Soho. I took
her to meet my old friends. Masked against the fog I felt sudden
pleasure as I pushed open the pub door for her to enter and the warm
air carried her perfume briefly to me until we were inside and I was
introducing her.

Bitter beer and Gauloises were the predominant smells at the New
Hanged Man, the last of Brookgate's Victorian People's Palaces, only
a short step from the Globe. This was the pub used by a bunch of
young Brookgaters and others involved in the arts, mostly film. There
was jazz and folk upstairs. St Martins and the Slade were not far
away. In a few years some of the regulars would form bands and become Akhanon and Sadness and so turn into producers, A&R men,
media personalities. The New Hanged Man still hosts bands and became one of the best punk venues in the early, wilder times. It's been
turned into a much bigger place. Glen Matlock performs there.

I was proud of my friends and enjoyed introducing them to Helena.
They all congratulated me on my catch. She said she felt like a giant
cod.

I'd told Helena about the Alsacia. I tried to take her to Carmelite
Inn Chambers where I'd seen the gates, where that pair of thieftakers

had tried to arrest me. She didn't believe in the supernatural, she said. She believed only in the rational. She was only recently out of Cambridge. She was a sceptic. She argued that if Alsacia did exist then it had to be supernatural in origin and we both agreed there was no such thing as the supernatural. Therefore it actually *couldn't* exist. 'You'll believe in God next!' Her point was a good one. For us a belief in God and the supernatural went arm in arm with reactionary politics and was anti-progressive at best. My own fascination with metaphysics was, I insisted, purely sociological. My own imagination was so wild I had to control it with the tightest, most rationalist of reins. Yet I responded negatively to Helena's certainty. She argued that if you accepted the existence of, say, zombies, then ipso facto you accepted the existence of God. I took her points. Some of them would go into *Behold the Man*.

Helena and I would have those arguments all the way through our marriage and well beyond. I think they bound me to her more strongly.

CHAPTER TWELVE

SCENES FROM URBAN LIFE

OF COURSE I still dreamed of the Alsacia and everything I'd experienced there. I dreamed of my frustrations at being unable to find the gateway. In some dreams Father Grammaticus and Brother Isidore tried to help me. In others they resisted me. Molly often rode beside me, her red hair blazing in the wind, a devil-may-care grin on her lips. But I no longer felt that same fascinated yearning for her. I associated her with other dreams I had had when emerging into puberty. I told Helena all about them, of course, and she congratulated me on my imagination. She was fascinated by that, if not by the Alsacia. Helena's scepticism was well honed. Her mother had argued rationally for years with her grim Methodist parents and Helena had learned to be a rationalist at her mother's knee. They relished Mormons, Seventh-day Adventists and others calling at their house. They could scatter them. They knew Greek and could quote whole chunks of the Greek New Testament. Chapter and verse.

Mrs Denham wasn't so sure about freelance writers. Those days were perhaps the last when a young man had to prove himself worthy to his girlfriend's parents. Helena thought if I had a regular job then it would make things a lot easier. I could give it up later. Alistair Graham again came to my rescue. He was back from his travels and was working in the Liberal Party publications department. This was the time of the first so-called 'Liberal revival' when it seemed the reforming party of Lloyd George was making a comeback. Slightly euphoric, they were hiring speechwriters and people to work on their policy documents. So I got a job which mostly involved trying to make sense of work done by young men fresh from university whose parents had connections. The party leader was an amiable man who clearly thought there was something corrupting about power and did everything he could to keep from getting it. Jo Grimond was mild-mannered, good-humoured and not the brightest star in the political firmament. Almost as soon as I got there I saw how much money they were wasting, and when one of their favourite young chaps made a complete hash of the type and design for a whole set of policy pamphlets, Alistair and I had to sort out the mess. The pamphlets were delivered late so were not much use in the elections.

My main job, as a writer, was to go to the Tory and Labour central offices, pick up their policy statements and rewrite the best of what we liked. Voilà! Liberal policy! Our opponents were fond of saying that we had no policy. That wasn't strictly true. We had a policy. It just happened to be theirs. The experience did help me write some political SF, however, and since the Liberals weren't paying much I could pick up reasonable money by selling to Carnell and continuing to write for *Look and Learn* and the other AP publications. But I had a regular job. Helena's ma would approve. Helena could safely announce our marriage.

Before we both knew it we had parents and other relatives involved. We managed to tell my mother and Helena's that we weren't living near them, got both mothers' blessings, kept them apart as much as possible (Mrs Denham was a strict rationalist and my mother was anything but) and, on 29 October, 1962, we married at Caxton Hall, in those days the most fashionable registry office in England, across the road from the Houses of Parliament. Just up the road from the Liberal Party. Next door to Methodist headquarters. That was a sop to Helena's ILP Methodist grandparents and a compromise with her fiercely atheistic mother and her mother's communist boyfriend.

Our wedding reception was held at Mrs Denham's house in Dulwich. Because she couldn't afford to do much for the reception we made it a bring-a-bottle affair. There were three hundred guests, hippest of the hip and most bourgeois of bougies all cheerfully mingling.

At first everyone got along very well, the way they're supposed to in Richard Curtis movies. Through the course of the evening, however, the reception became more of a Richard Lester affair.

Because Helena's mother was a widow and not very well-off I paid for everything including the first tailor-made suit I'd ever possessed. Neither of us look that spiffy in the photos. We were doing and dressing as convention demanded. This was just before the swinging-London revolution when dandyism became the norm in some circles. I also paid for the photographer but unfortunately he got into a fistfight with my brother-in-law and used his camera as the weapon of last resort. Therefore we had very few photographs of the wedding. Which was just as well. Everyone was pretty drunk. My cousins taught Helena's posher Cambridge chums to do the knees-up and my Uncle Alf, who had been on the bill at the London Palladium, showed the local MP how to play spoons. My forty-seven-year-old mum met my dad for the first time since the war and Ted Tubb, the lanky charming science fiction writer who edited *Authentic* before it folded and who never missed a party or a chance to chat up a woman ('pick the ugly one – they're always grateful...'), offered to lead my still-good-looking and much-flattered mother to the bottom of the garden to look for the fairies. My dad even revealed a glimmer of jealousy. He left early, since he was on a cheap ticket from Paris.

We heard later that my best man, David Harvey, had driven my cousin, David Roberts, home in Cousin Dave's car and then left him sleeping in the alley outside his own house while the others went joyriding. He could have caught pneumonia and died, my posh Aunt Dorothea later complained to my unconcerned mother.

Helena and I were the last to go home. We helped stack dishes and then Dave Harvey drove us back to our tiny, newly rented top-floor flat in Lancaster Gate, directly across from the bell in the church's tower. We both decided later that we would rather have plighted our troth in some other way and maybe found a nicer flat first. It was a depressing dump. All our furniture was handed down to us. Very little light came through the high windows. And, when you flushed the toilet, black ooze bubbled up into the bath. Even I couldn't pretend it was an attractive love nest.

In the bed I'd been born in I held her in my arms as she cried. 'I wish I'd never got married,' she said.

I knew how she felt. But in those days social pressure was strong. We did not have a constituency as powerful as our parents'. That balance of power would change soon and rapidly but we were just on the brink of it all. My romantic twenty-two-year-old self became a bit depressed until I was reassured by her evident decision to stay. Passive-aggressive? I was used to simple aggression. My family never bottled up anything. Although a bit manipulative, my mother was volatile and she said whatever was on her mind. Rows came quickly, took furious form and then were over, thoroughly forgotten. When Helena first witnessed my mother and me arguing she thought surely WW III had broken out and that neither side could possibly ever speak again. She was astonished when a few days later everything was sunny and my mother and I had completely forgotten the point of the row and indeed the row itself. I wasn't used to middle-class repression. Helena's family brooded on a supposed wrong for months. They generally aired their terrible accusations over Christmas dinner when everyone was drunk.

Before our first Christmas the Liberals had begun to complain about the hours I kept. I had edited Jo Grimond's book and begged them to tell him not to publish. Even I could see how naïve his logic was. My conscientious point wasn't welcome. As for the job: I had to admit that the work wasn't very arduous but the pay reflected that. To earn what I needed I continued writing for AP and others, which meant I had to see editors. When my immediate boss, Harry Cowie, asked why I was so frequently out for hours at lunchtime I explained to him reasonably that I couldn't live on what the Liberals paid me. I had to get other work. A week before we celebrated the big holiday, and just three months after our wedding, I was fired. I was shocked. If I had needed the money, I said, that sacking was callous. My respect for the amateurs who worked there went down a little more. But the job had served its purpose even if Helena was disappointed at the end of my brief career in politics.

CHAPTER THIRTEEN

MARRIAGE

Our tiny Lancaster Gate flat was at the top of exactly one hundred stairs in what had been a *chambre de bonne*. I'll always remember that wedding night, and the next morning, a Sunday, when the church bells started chiming. The entire tiny apartment shook and I thought the windows and then my bones would shatter. My ears rang and the persistent murmuring which had been with me since I left the Alsacia was drowned out for a while. 'That's what I call a welcome,' I said. We laughed ourselves silly. We were unprepared.

On Christmas morning, we woke up to find the whole square covered in thick snow. The sun burned in a cold, clear sky. I got up and went out to Hyde Park. I paused at the gate. The entire park lay beneath a deep fall of pristine snow. The only prints were those of a large bird. A few minutes later I heard the call of a crow as he flew across the sky between the black branches of chestnut trees. That was the winter of '62/'63 when the Thames froze at her fringes and the cold was bitter. The snow didn't melt but turned to ice. A month later the weight of it had me muffled in all the warm clothes I could find, staggering about on the collapsing roof high above the late Georgian square, trying to shovel snow from the gutters running between the high buildings on a level with the church spire, into the unpopulated backyard, before the stuff melted into our bedroom. More black filth bubbled up into the bath. The old concierge stole the bucket and shovel I had bought. We kept our spirits up as best we could. Helena still had her job at the Foreign Office and it was easy enough for me to make up my earnings to what they had been when I worked at the Liberal Party. We were not there very much, but we started looking for a new apartment.

That January, while the snow still covered Hyde Park, Helena discovered she was pregnant. She had already had one abortion and didn't want another. She tried a few old wives' remedies to stop the pregnancy, but nothing worked. We were now, not four months into our marriage, anticipating our first child. Helena kept going into work, but she was very depressed. I reassured her. I could earn enough for two – or three. The first thing to do was to find a larger flat. That was when Joyce Carter, Ildiko's friend, took pity on us and offered us temporary use of her place in Kensington Park Gardens, off Queensway. And so we got out of our snow-burdened flat in Lancaster Gate. Another month or two and Joyce must have liked us as tenants. She was marrying her boyfriend and going to live with him in Malta. She couldn't sublet her Queensway flat but she could sublet her other flat in Colville Terrace, Notting Hill, the core of slum landlord Peter Rachman's empire of exploitation. I actually liked Rachman. When work was slow I had done a bit of painting and decorating for him a couple of years earlier. He had paid decently and on the nail. I had lived briefly in the area and liked it, for all its association with race riots, crime and prostitution. We had a larger flat up fewer stairs, close to the shops of Portobello Road. It seemed like paradise in comparison. I was sure this would cheer Helena up.

No matter what our situation, I soon learned that, without apparent reason, Helena could resist cheering up better than Queen Victoria at a Prince Albert retrospective. Periodically she fell into the blackest moods, refusing to eat or talk. I think these days we'd call it clinical depression. I did have the sense to wonder what caused her descents and try to ease them by changing my own behaviour. My ego often got into the equation back then. I always thought it was my fault, my failure. I would go out for long walks, to leave her alone. I wasn't used to people not speaking their minds. Helena would never discuss anything, so I never knew whether she blamed me or whether her moods had any link to my actions at all. I needed some pointers. I remember a time when she'd spent all day trying to buy a hat to wear to a Royal Society of Literature function. It cost a fortune but she looked stunning. She spent about half an hour at the party and then wanted to leave. As we walked home she took off the hat and threw it over a hedge. I didn't know why she did it. All I knew, conventional as it sounds, was that I wanted to support her, help her get through whatever it was. The more she withdrew, however, the more tired I became. After a while I despaired.

Typically, I was prone to guilt. I even shared survivor's guilt as further news of Nazi atrocities was detailed through the '60s. Certainly some of the blame for Helena's moods was probably mine. Her mother said my wife had been prone to those moods since her father had died suddenly of a heart attack at a concert. His favourite child, and just fourteen, she had hardly spoken for two years after she heard the news. The first month we were married, Helena told me she knew I was going to leave her. Being *sans* fathers, hers permanently, we shared our anger at the common experience. I swore I would not leave her.

But generally she couldn't see me as an ally. Men always divorced their wives, she predicted, to take up with someone younger. I was no better than the rest. My mum being who she was, I wasn't used to indirect, despairing or masochistic women. My mother had stood up to everyone, especially in my defence. I'm sure I caused Helena pain. I'm sure I delivered many of those small insults and diminishing remarks, the kind men still unconsciously delivered to women in the early '60s. But whatever else, she always enjoyed my lovemaking. Maybe that's what kept us together. She had been attracted to me by my generosity, she said. Good-natured and generous by inclination, like so many writers, I was probably monstrously insensitive, utterly self-involved, but genuinely out to give her a good time. I seemed able to sympathise with her but not understand her. I retreated under stress. I sought the few dark spaces of the apartment for my demonstrations of misery, just as she did. At any time you might find one or both of us in some cupboard or under some table or other. Slumped in any available furniture and bemoaning the futility of life. Those bleak '60s playwrights were very influential.

Two such personalities as ours were doomed, I suppose. Maybe Helena never had a chance to tell me anything because I was too caught up in my own ambition, imposing my own vision on reality. Yet I know I learned from her. I was already conscious of two different kinds of author in me. One was practical, able to make money commercially. The other was predominantly analytical, experimental and not at all commercial! My imagination was forever imposing vision on reality. I constantly saw things which weren't actually there. If I was over-tired, an entire scene might present itself to me. I could take pleasure in it, even though I knew only I could see it. I wasn't psychotic, but a cycle of intense work followed by terrible exhaustion could somehow enslave me. With others depending on me, anxiety was also now part of my creative habit. I must have been horrible to live with. Yet I craved equality. I was used to it. Maybe Helena wasn't. As a better and faster typist I edited and typed her stories for her. But there had to be some-thing more.

I always delighted in my friends, for whom I frequently felt an unconditional loyalty. I began seriously to cultivate an interest in oth-ers, beyond being generally sympathetic. I wanted, in a dumb sort of way, to alleviate their discomfort or pain but still had only the vagu-est sense of why they were hurting. If I had been a dog I would have brought them my best bone.

I was not thin-skinned. Because I had been raised with consider-able self-confidence I could take quite a lot of banter, criticism or in-sults. Helena was really the only one who could hurt me because I had so much emotion invested in her. God knows what it was I did to her! Looking back, I wonder about my own casual verbal cruel-ties. I rarely lied and must have been horribly frank. I joked about the most profound experience. Having been brought up among strong women I only felt comfortable with women who generally gave good account of themselves. As an autodidact I was in awe of Helena's for-mal education, her ability to learn and understand things for their own sake. I taught myself to watch and listen more acutely, studying what lay beneath any surface not because I was driven by shame or regret but because I was curious and needed to improve my range. To that end for a while I read only modern writers. T.H. White had told me to read everything I could learn from. Sometimes I'm astonished at how lucky I was to have known such writers as a child. Commercial writers and literary writers, including my aunt's genial neighbour, the thriller writer Edwy Searles Brooks. He began his career combining fantastic subjects, with the traditional Wodehousian school story set in a Sargasso Sea populated by the descendants of pirates. In my school holidays I stayed with Auntie Connie and used to go to tea with Mr and Mrs Brooks. They lived in a leafy south-western London suburb, which always seemed magical to me. Those suburbs were endless. Brooks had written dozens of Sexton Blake stories which he now turned into his Norman Conquest thriller series published by the prestigious Collins Crime Club. He gave me a lot of practical advice. Mervyn Peake, though, was probably my greatest mentor. The Peakes lived not far from Brooks, in Wallington. Around 1960 the family moved to Kensington. Peake encouraged me to be dissatisfied with the mediocre and to hoe one's own row. In some ways it helped me create several subgenres, but it made me a slave to the conventions I'd put in place.

My worst faults I only saw in retrospect. I was arrogant and blunt but apparently my sense of humour and self-deprecation made up for it. I remained supremely self-confident and somehow had the ability to take others with me. Maybe our mutual curiosity had something to do with it, too. And there was something about our chemistry. We were, after all, in love.

I remember racing to get something sorted before the baby was born. While I hammered out scripts and features and novellas and novels for money I also studied form and narrative method. Hoping to train my eye to see overlooked details of every kind, I probably did develop a greater sympathy and humility. I doubt if any of this showed in my work, most of which was melodrama: SF, fantasy, allegorical stuff, maudlin autobiography. But I was determined, by the time I was thirty, to have faced the devils driving me and take a broader interest in the world in general. I admired writers like George Meredith, Angus Wilson, Elizabeth Bowen and Elizabeth Taylor, all of whom could do what I couldn't. I wanted to write moral novels of character dealing with important social issues. I needed to understand others better. In particular I wanted to make my love for Helena into something positive and useful to her. I did my honest best to learn how to support Helena emotionally during her terrible brooding silences but I suppose I was at root too selfish myself to be of any fundamental help.

And then I betrayed her. The worst thing I could have done to coun-teract anything positive I had tried to do. Pregnancy, of course, didn't help. I began to feel serious anxieties about my ability to provide properly for a mother and child.

Most of what I learned about Helena's early life came from her mother. Mrs Denham had married a director of Vickers-Armstrong, the arms and aeroplane company. They made the VC10. The best jet-liner ever. Helena always said her dad was an arms manufacturer. She had been his firstborn and his favourite. She had adored him. She was fourteen when he died listening to Bach at the Wigmore Hall. Mrs D. said her husband had Jewish blood on his mother's side. 'And they're prone to heart problems, aren't they? As well as brooding.' Helena's ma was at once fascinated by and suspicious of anyone who might be Jewish. Or anyone who wasn't Anglo-Saxon, for that matter. At six foot two, with blond hair and blue eyes, with my professional back-ground, I fit her bill perfectly. No matter what I told her about my heritage, she was profoundly convinced of my racial purity. Before I came along, Helena's succession of small, neurotic men ('Jews, Scots, even Australians!') before me hadn't suited Mrs Denham. I had never lied to her. She insisted my family history was speculative. We had an authentic family story of how my grandmother's Jewish parents had mourned her as though dead, not because she married a goy but be-cause she married a secular Jew. Mrs Denham insisted the story was myth and that my grandmother had made it all up! I was genuinely puzzled by these mental convolutions. In London, in the middle of the twentieth century, only loonies cared about your racial origins. Shortly before I was fired, Mrs Denham stood for Dulwich as Liberal MP and missed by a narrow margin.

To make life as stable for Helena and the baby as I could, I did my best to earn more money, upping my output of Meg Midnight stories and a new character, time-travelling Jack o' London. I also did 'The Man from T.I.G.E.R.' for, you guessed it, *Tiger*. I took on 'Danny and His Time Machine' weekly for *Lion* and started a weekly feature, 'African Safari'. I wrote scripts for the monthlies, *Buck Jones, Kit Car-son, Dick Daring of the Mounties, Dogfight Dixon, RFC*. I wrote features for *Look and Learn*. I did Zip Nolan and Speed Solo stories for the regular weeklies, Karl the Viking and Olac the Gladiator and historical features for the annuals – anything I could write to start saving a bit of money so we might at least make Colville Terrace a little more congenial. I wrote fantasy novellas and science fiction short stories for Carnell. And the rest of the time wasn't too bad. We were a couple. Helena kept her job for as long as she could. She also planned to freelance. We started to see a lot more of the Allard family and others. He and I would sit and talk literature together while Helena and Shirley talked of more serious matters and wondered if they were ever going to be able to afford a holiday.

In those days I loved Notting Hill and Notting Dale for their increasing diversity. Everybody rubbed along. Only occasionally would a few white lads from the predominantly Irish population go wild when they perceived their girls were being lured into the life. The girls weren't being lured but they did prefer the sweet ways of the West Indians. A few bottles thrown with the insults, a few oy oys and a bit of a tussle was usually the worst it got and then there were the manly exchanges of compliments. Shouts in the street at night. Checking it out from darkened windows.

We did all we could to get ready for the baby so that when she came she was very welcome. September 1963. In those days mothers counted off the months just to make sure a child had been conceived in wedlock. I still relied on AP and other periodicals for most of my income but I was writing more for Carnell all the time. I began doing more science fiction novellas for *Science Fiction Adventures* and *New Worlds*. I even began a feature in *Science Fantasy* calling on writers to raise their horizons. My own ambitions were growing all the time.

CHAPTER FOURTEEN

CHILDREN

1964 BROUGHT ANOTHER two novels, a demo and Kitty. Kitty took so long coming that the hospital sent me home. Sally was being looked after by my mum. To keep awake until the hospital rang I played poker with Barry, Max and a couple of other blokes. At dawn I walked to the hospital next to Wormwood Scrubs and there was Helena and another scowling miniature Capone. I had lost all my cash at cards. I had to ask Helena to find her purse and let me have my bus fare home. Of course, she never forgot that.

Now I was definitely Father, but not my father. Helena was Mother, not my mother. I was determined not to become my father, whom I didn't much like. I loved my mother, Helena, my daughters. I wanted to be with my family for ever. I took on that job. I wanted to be all they wanted of me, Father. I loved them; delighted in them. I bought a massive, industrial-strength, battleship-grey pushchair so the children could sit one behind the other, as if they were in the cockpit of a DH-4 biplane. I dreamed of fixing a Lewis gun on the front as I rushed them through the streets at great speed, through the crowds of Saturday tourists in Portobello Road, up to Holland Park and Hyde Park where we'd settle. As they became toddlers, they could run about on grass while I read or wrote and gave their mother a rest. I got ideas for stories in the parks and on top of Derry & Toms department store. Their huge roof garden was unknown by most Londoners. Many a character description came from the people I saw there, many a background scene was from something I'd observed. I loved being with my girls and they were always an inspiration. Twice, what I swore was the same crow I had last seen in the snow turned up, perching on top of the fake wishing well and on the wall of the Tudor Garden. He turned his head and seemed to wink at me. I suppose I should have thought it sinister, even when he hopped along the wall staring at the girls, but to me he was only comical. He seemed a happy soul for a carrion bird. I had always felt an affinity for crows. They are among the smartest creatures on the planet.

Mysteriously, and for a short while after both children were born, I again heard the Whispering Swarm. That faintest of distant murmurings in my ears would briefly grow into a torrent of unfamiliar voices. I made out no words, but after a while I thought I heard something, because of certain repeated notes. I would lie in that old double bed worrying what was best for the baby, where we should move and so on, and before I knew it the Swarm would begin to whisper in my left ear. I thought at first that it was Helena, but she always slept on my right. I hardly heard it at first. Perhaps she was snoring? I washed my ears carefully in case I had picked up a virus. But the whispering voices – and I was now convinced they were voices – were just as insidious. I tried hard to detect words but heard nothing coherent. And then, in the darkness, they went away, leaving a questioning silence. At night I was in no doubt that they represented some kind of intelligence. By daylight, however, they became an irritant, a minor hallucination: I thought it might be acid-reverb, when LSD taken months earlier suddenly kicks in again. Or maybe a subconsciously originated distraction from my responsibilities, suggested Arthur Paine, the local shrink, when, at the pub one night, I told him about the Swarm. He hardly listened, though. He wanted to talk about his son. Dr Paine had asked him what he wanted to be when he grew up. 'A suicide!' the boy declared.

I took my responsibilities seriously enough, though it meant a lot of hackwork. I never regretted having our children so relatively young, but Helena and I weren't prepared for babies, especially two in less than a year. We knew so little about what to do. Mothers offered conflicting advice. Other wisdom sounded like superstition to us. Thank God for Doc Spock.

Abortions were still illegal. But at that moment in our lives a third young child would have been ruinous, both financially and emotionally for everyone. Just in time, female contraception became widely available. Of course we accepted our responsibility as parents, buying the special foods, the books and the clothes, negotiating the convictions of well-meaning relatives, doing the best that could be done by conscientious, uninformed young people. I wasn't exactly a New Man, but possibly I did more than most men of my generation to take on my share of the domestic work.

The children were never a burden, though it wasn't easy in our two rooms, a bath in the kitchen and a toilet downstairs on the landing, but we managed reasonably well. We had been raised during austerity and were used to making do. There was virtue in it. We had a TV. Although Len Matthews and I had fallen out at the end of my time with AP, I still freelanced for all his editors. They just asked me to contribute under Helena's maiden name because Len had put it about that I was some kind of commie agitator, maybe because I knew too much about his ruthless careerism. My freelance earnings were reasonably good and we had only minor money worries. I had given up music for the time being. Our girls were huge, healthy and generally happy even though their cot was a little close to a record player constantly broadcasting The Beatles and Beethoven, which preserved our sanity. That flat couldn't have been more than three hundred square feet. For a bit I rented a daytime room from my brother-in-law, where I could work. It was miles away in Southwark. I started looking for a bigger flat we could reasonably afford, but for eighteen months we lived in very cramped, somewhat noisy conditions as the babies became toddlers with their own increasingly complex personalities.

Colville Terrace then was a mixture of brothels, bohemians, old people and young parents. A couple of years earlier we had the so-called race riots, running fights between Teddy Boys and West Indians. Now the neo-Nazis were trying to exploit the situation from their headquarters in Princedale Road. We had a steel band rehearsing next door. Outside, at three a.m. every weeknight, a big whore called Marie got drunk and wielded a giant kitchen knife and needed three policemen to wrestle her down and take the weapon away from her before she killed her pimp and her client. The cops never charged her. They were too scared. Nobody accused Marie to her face. She was the sunniest of neighbours when sober. But she always carried that knife.

During the day people were generally friendly to young couples with children who shopped in what then was a cheap Portobello Road market. In a pushchair solid enough to go up against a Sherman tank, Sally and Kitty sat chuckling and waving as their massive, wheeled battering ram charged through knots of tourists adding our junk-and-antique market to their itineraries. Secure in their machine, the girls were a big hit with the local shopkeepers, especially Mrs Pash who, with her companion Mr Skinner, ran Elgin Music in Elgin Crescent. We spent a lot of time in Mrs Pash's. She loved the kids. Mr Skinner had opened the shop in 1905 when he closed his father's old place in Kilburn. 'It was all banjos and ukes until the 1930s,' he told me, looking at a fretless banjo I'd picked up in the market. 'This is off a minstrel show, isn't it?' He admired the sunburst surround, the gold-and-scarlet resonator. 'We saw a lot of these once.' He loved the Epiphone guitar I found. 'They used to tune these classical,' he said. 'Bit of a mistake. Because of classical orchestras, that's all. Always best in G, though.' The Epiphone had a huge resonator on the back and was used for dance-band work before electric amplifiers. He talked of old customers, of Jack Jackson, Caroll Gibbons and his Savoy Orpheans. He wasn't aware that half the most famous popular musicians in the world were now hanging out in his shop. One afternoon I walked in to find Jeff Beck, Jimi Hendrix and Martin Stone all there together.

After Mrs Pash's husband died in the 1940s Mr Skinner moved into the basement and ground-floor flat at 87 Ladbroke Grove, W11. Mr Skinner had taught her grandsons to play every fretted instrument there was. One of them, David, became a guitar prodigy and appeared on the cover of *BMG*. Mrs Pash was as enthusiastic about Sally and Kitty as she was about her own grandchildren, one of whom was a foreign correspondent. Cheerful, enthusiastic David worked in the shop part-time. I admired his classical training, he envied me my idiosyncrasies.

For that series of articles on fantasy fiction for *Science Fantasy* I immersed myself in nineteenth-century Gothic fiction. Bayley and I were still making most of our money from journalism while Allard kept his day job as editor of *Science and Industry*. We needed every penny we earned.

When *Science Fiction Adventures* folded suddenly it was the writing on the wall. We weren't surprised when Carnell told us his magazines, which had put a bit of jam on our bread and butter, were under threat of extinction. We started looking for more work. We sent a few stories to *Argosy* and American magazines and had them accepted, but those markets, though they paid a little better, were even more conservative than *New Worlds*. We had no market for our ambitious fiction.

Next, to my surprise, Ted Carnell phoned me to say *New Worlds* and *Science Fantasy* had been bought. He would not continue as editor but he had named me as his successor because of my editorial experience. It turned out, however, that Kyril Bonfiglioli, the accomplished fencer and art dealer, had been suggested as Carnell's replacement by Brian Aldiss. Like them, the new publisher lived in Oxford. They all used the same pubs. I was almost relieved, certainly reconciled, that I would not be editing the mags. I had lost any enthusiasm for commercial SF and most fantasy and was hardly reading it any more. I had a different sort of novel to write.

In the end a compromise was proposed: Impact Books offered me first choice of the magazines. Against expectations I picked *New Worlds*. It was the best vehicle for what I had talked about doing. The title was at least a little ambiguous. And so began what others would call the 'SF New Wave'. While Bon followed a policy similar to America's *Magazine of Fantasy and Science Fiction* concentrating on improvements in characterisation and more sophisticated writing, I was determined, with Burroughs, some British poets like George MacBeth and the British pop artists, to take what we needed from SF but drop some genre clichés and rationalisations, moving on to create our own kind of fiction. Using methods developed from both modernism and SF, the work remained rooted in popular traditions but also encouraged innovation. I wanted the general reader. I wanted women like Helena to buy it. I wanted art paper, large quarto, colour. They let

me have a bimonthly paperback magazine printed on already disin-
tegrating cardboard – the nearest thing an English magazine of its type
ever came to actual pulp.

Some saw this as a refreshing change from a degenerated modernism. SF was threatened with losing precisely what made it work for
Allard and myself. Richard Hamilton feared the same. He thought
SF should keep its popular vitality, by which he meant spaceships and
robots. People knew little of my taste for Ronald Firbank, Jarry or
Vian, abstract absurdism, or of Allard's fierce intention to engage in
bloody experiment where he invoked to his own requirements the
ikons of Anglo-American culture. They didn't see us coming. Certain
readers and critics became disenchanted. Early allies deserted us. Some
distanced themselves, citing my youthful naïveté. Others recognised
and celebrated what we were doing.

The weight of responsibility settled on me for a while and then fell
off. Our mothers were pleased. We were procreating as fast as we
could. I spent most of my time working. Now I would have to start
producing novels in earnest. When, as an editor, I couldn't get something I liked as a serial, I wrote a two-parter for *New Worlds* and then
sold it to Ace Books in the US. They paid between $750 and $1,000
and ran short novels back to back. Some of the old SF hacks accused
me of writing all *New Worlds* myself because they'd never heard of
anyone they saw on the contents page, but I was finding good new
writers, bringing good old writers into a more sympathetic environment, only writing what I hoped were exemplary stories and not paying myself for them. The money was passed on to pay contributors
a little better. Any pseudonym I used had already previously been in a
Carnell mag. Criticism was done as Jack Corbal. A fitting name for a
critic, I thought. In those columns I talked up Bill Burroughs, Borges
and others, new and old, demonstrating that the realist rationale wasn't
important to visionary stories. We needed to find new ways of telling
such tales and we needed to stop the modern novel comforting itself
and the contemporary novelist and only addressing part of a certain
class. We wanted to get rid of the retrospective narrative as the only
significant factor in separating one genre from another. We could
parody it and did, but we were tired of a device which made it
difficult to confront the actualities of the modern world. I stepped a

little cautiously in our early numbers. I knew from revamping *Tarzan* and Sexton Blake that in time most people accepted change and that change attracted new readers. You lost perhaps twenty-five per cent but you gained fifty per cent or more. You built from there.

The new publisher also wanted a line of SF novels. I offered a couple of my own but mostly I bought what was available from friends, Carnell's clients, or people I enjoyed as a boy. I bought what I knew from experience of the SF fanzines would sell and what would probably sell. Roger Zelazny, E.C. Tubb, L. Sprague de Camp, Kenneth Bulmer, Judith Merril, Dan Morgan, Daphne Castell, Jack Vance, Connie Stern and others all came aboard. I wanted to buy some P.K. Dick and went to see his agent who offered us a deal: £150 a book or four for £500. He had rubber bands around each batch. I would have bought them instantly, of course. Many were Ace Doubles just like mine but their quality was so much superior to mine. He deserved more than our miserable advances, so I wrote to Phil and told him his agent was selling him short. I and others spoke to Tom Maschler at Jonathan Cape, thought to be one of the two or three top publishers of literary fiction. I got John Brunner to write the first ever article which saw Phil as a serious writer. We talked him up as a unique visionary in *New Worlds* and soon Cape was publishing barmy, brilliant, treacherous old Phil. Maschler was soon taking cues from us. He would ask me who were the next new writers to look out for. I had already recommended Allard. Maschler suggested I send him something but I knew I wasn't ready. I was happy to keep the obscurity of paperbacks and learn my craft a bit better.

A year or two before that brief Golden Age of the revivified novel, around 1965 when we were just beginning to emerge as an identifiable group based on the magazine, I was still doing Fleet Street hackwork in partnership with Barry. He tended to write the science articles and I did historical, geographical and 'social' features. I still have our rubber stamp: Moorcock and Bayley, 8 Colville Terrace, London W11. The history of London was my speciality. Alsacia was never that far away. I was sometimes tempted to look for the gates again but resisted. I stopped thinking about Moll, the abbot, The Swan With Two Necks or any other complex acid trip I'd enjoyed!

Although I sometimes referred to 'Alsacia' to demonstrate the power of an acid hallucination, I was increasingly focused on the magazine, my family, my work. Gradually we built up readers. Helena was at once relieved and unhappy about my taking over the magazine. We weren't making much money from it but it offered me the chance to ask her for a real story. She had already sold one story to Carnell. She was a natural. I knew she could do well.

Helena's brilliant novella *The Haul of Frankie Steinway* appeared in our second issue. She wrote reviews. Her periods of depression grew fewer. And, perhaps best of all, Mrs Pash persuaded her landlord to let us take over her big two-storey flat in Ladbroke Grove for six guineas a week. The flat had been occupied by Mrs Pash for thirty-odd years. Into the bargain, Mrs Pash left us her mighty player piano, an impressive Banning and Goethe Model 97 which had rolls from Gilbert and Sullivan to Schoenberg. It had been brought in the back way over wartime bomb damage and through some big French windows. The damage had since been repaired. Consequently there was no way the pianola could leave what became the kids' room. So the Moorcocks became stewards to that clangy, old, hardly tuneable, beautiful instrument for another thirty years or so.

The flat was part of a substantial house originally built for a wealthy Edwardian doctor in the days before the financial crashes of the 1890s. It occupied two large floors, ground and basement, on the corner of Elgin Crescent near the 52 bus stop. It became ours, first to rent and eventually to buy, for more than a third of a century. With its own little walled garden letting out onto a short alley into the huge communal square, it proved a marvellous home in which to bring up children. The square was nearly four acres, wooded and with rough lawn. Children could play there all day and never use the streets while always in sight of at least twenty responsible adults. It was a wonderland for the working-class and bohemian families who then lived around the square. We could not have wanted anything better. There were good schools within walking distance and a huge range of independent shops, including grocers, electricians, hardware, stationers, booksellers, bakers, greengrocers, butchers, toy shops, tailors, and, of course, the second-hand emporia for which Portobello Road was famous in the years before the gentrification, of which we were ironically the pioneers.

By the time we moved to Ladbroke Grove, my marriage was pretty happy. I had started to learn not to take Helena's moods too personally. I understood a little better where I was failing her. I was determined not to abandon my family as my father had abandoned his.

We were busy but we were young and energetic. Things seemed to improve yearly. I profoundly relished the company of my children, taking them to parties, to gigs, wherever we could. We particularly loved nearby Holland Park and the Derry & Toms roof garden, still providing many scenes for my early novels. Given my situation as the main breadwinner I gave Helena as much time to work on her own stories as I could. I took kids to the Disney cinema in St Martin's Lane, enjoying the museums all the more when it came on to rain. Our life was pretty idyllic. I looked forward to the days when Helena and I could go on holiday on our own. Of course, I had to tell her about the one time that I'd gone down to Carmelite Inn against my promise, looking for that non-existent place! So, when I came back from a trip to Manchester, I found she had painted my Windsor chair, and anything else she could reasonably lay hands on, a bright royal blue. Scarcely grounds for divorce either way. By the time we'd had our rows and counter-accusations, make-up sex and all the rest of it, and I had repainted that beautiful armchair a sober black, we returned to some sort of even keel, able to settle down and take a holiday with the girls to see my dad in Toulon, which turned out to be a minor logistics disaster. We had the odd weekend on our own, here and there. My mum was their favourite grandma, thanks to her talent to amuse. She still had an old projector and some silent movies she could show. I think that was how Sally and Kitty became Douglas Fairbanks's greatest fans. They learned to read from the silent-picture cards. (When she was thirteen Sally ran after Douglas Fairbanks Jr's limo and asked the beaming old chap for his autograph. She probably added ten years to his life. I still have the book, signed upside down at the back.) *New Worlds* was improving with almost every issue. A new generation of young Americans was attracted to the magazine and began arriving on our doorstep, quite literally. An older American SF critic, Judy Merril, had been talking us up for a year or two and had even, to my dismay, published my home address. 'When in London, all roads lead to Ladbroke Grove,' according to Judy. She was the first reverse pioneer, moving into a flat Barry Bayley found in the house of which he was concierge. Jim Cawthorn also lived there and soon Rex Fisch, the elegant, funny, flouncing Texan, and his equally funny straight friend Jack Slade, small and shaggy in his dark hair and beard, also moved in, until I joked I could take out at least half of our best writers with one well-placed bomb.

I tried to avoid hearing that whispering, faint as it was most of the time. Only twice had it grown loud enough to be a major distraction. I continued to associate it with the Alsacia, whether the place was a mirage or not. I did all I could to ignore it. When Helena had a slump or was writing a new story, I looked after the kids. I cooked a bit, the usual blokes' limited menu including a lot of omelettes, jacket spuds and baked beans, got the kids ready and took them to nursery school, trying to give Helena space. I usually went for a short walk before I returned to work in Ladbroke Grove and sometimes I saw a big dark green sports car with a long, old-fashioned bonnet and running boards. The car would follow me when I dropped them off at the school gates, so I had no suspicion of the driver being a paedophile. Not that we thought much in such terms in those seemingly more innocent days. The driver wore sunglasses and some sort of uniform which matched the car's livery. I was not in any way disconcerted but I was a bit curious. I had inherited my dad's prewar cigarette card collection. From a series called 'Fifty Famous Motor Cars (1938)', I saw I was being shadowed by a green 1937 Lagonda. Like the US Duesenberg, she was almost a fantasy sports convertible saloon. I tried to find out if there was a club of Lagonda drivers. I copied down the number, also prewar. But I couldn't trace it. Nonetheless, I took precautions and told my girls to go nowhere near that big green car or its driver. I didn't pay it much attention after that. I was focused on a shift in the dynamics of my career.

My first Elric book, *The Stealer of Souls*, had come out in 1963. I felt I could properly claim to be an author. The second book, in 1965, was *Stormbringer*, in which I killed my hero off. I really did think the public had had enough of him. In the meantime I had found the character, 'voice' and method I needed for what was really my first novel, the first time I had left genre behind, like the booster rockets of the *Discovery*, and done something influenced by Firbank and Raymond

Chandler yet really my own! In ten days of January 1965 I had written *The Final Programme*, featuring a young man with the physical appearance of someone I had seen up at Notting Hill. Behind him had been the name I looked for that could not be easily identified with one European nation, Cornelius of London, a local greengrocer. No publisher was interested. One publisher told me to learn to write before I sent in another novel. Judy thought it was evil. I published a few cut-up parts in *New Worlds* when I was short of material. And forgot about it. The magazine had started as a bimonthly, alternating with *Science Fantasy*, but had quickly become a monthly, requiring more work, more talent. I wrote another serial, *The Shores of Death*, until I could get a good novel from a decent writer. I was growing quickly bored with science fiction, which had never been my first love. But the circulation was rising and Impact was pleased. The number of novels of mine published in 1965 is alarming, looking back. In a very short period I wrote three sword-and-planet novels, three comedy thrillers and a couple of short science fiction novels, as well as editing the series and the magazine. I didn't think my output all that large. The generation which trained me was familiar with hard work.

The Americans had arrived in the nick of time. Rex Fisch and Jack Slade, travelling in Europe on the equivalent of a world tour, brought their best work with them. Rejected by most of the American magazines, they hoped to sell a story or two to me to help finance their trip, which had foundered when they both got hepatitis from bad acid in Spain. Fisch turned up first, six foot two of blue-eyed, fair-haired mincing theatrical Texan angst and wild humour, wanting to sell me his fiction and also to recommend his friends, among them Polly Zuker, who was already living in London, Jerry Mundis, still in New York, Johnny van der Kroot, somewhere at sea, and Jack Slade, dark, sardonic and utterly original. Zuker and van der Kroot had not yet written much fiction but Slade had a bunch of unsold stories, every one of which was a winner! I could not have been better pleased. And we all soon became good friends. Fisch and Slade were two of the funniest men I had ever met and our sense of humour was very similar. We bonded. Soon we were sharing almost everything and they were joining Judy at Barry Bayley's rooming house, 34 Princedale Road, where a few years later Rex would set a story series with the location changed to Manhattan. It seemed that we were about to hit a new high in *New Worlds*.

Then, near the end of 1966, we got news that our distributor was going bankrupt, taking us with him. Another crisis! Just at the point when we had a full inventory of first-class fiction. I couldn't bear to see it disappear. I began looking for a new publisher. A campaign organised by Brian Aldiss, with the Arts Council at its centre, got us a grant. We had two allies on the AC literary committee we hadn't known about, Angus Wilson and Giles Gordon, and they persuaded the others. We began planning the magazine I had always wanted to edit. With one of the old Impact directors as a partner I planned a large, slick magazine which would display the good new writers at their best. However, we couldn't be sure of going ahead until we had costed everything. I would pay the authors for the first few issues and my partner would receive the grant and put it towards printing costs.

By December 1966 we were all a bit worn out by events and were determined to end the year with a merry Christmas. Helena and I thought it would be a good idea to have my mum, her mum and our American friends for Christmas day.

CHAPTER FIFTEEN

CHRISTMAS DAY 1966

R EX FISCH AND Jack Slade were still living in Portland Road, while Polly Zee, as she preferred, was living in Camden at the flat of an ex-boyfriend. To everyone's astonishment the dramatically gay Fisch had recently announced his engagement to Polly who, to tell the truth, did not seem as enthusiastic about it as Rex.

We hadn't been able to do a Thanksgiving Day meal for them that year. The previous year Rex had gone to Turkey for Christmas, having decided that in a Moslem country he would not get infected by the holiday. He wound up eating a lonely traditional dinner at the Hilton Istanbul in a restaurant occupied mostly by single businessmen. Typically, he made great fun of his situation. His pale blue eyes twinkling, he pushed his thinning fair hair back from his huge pink forehead and swore that this year he'd come in a red suit with a white beard if he could enjoy a traditional Christmas. We had a long sturdy table, bought at Habitat, but, with all the food and the decorations, it was only just big enough to accommodate the adults. Anticipating this, I had bought a little round table and chairs to put over in the far corner of the kitchen so that the children could enjoy their meal without need of adult interference (although I warned them I might change that if they got too boisterous).

This turned out to be a much more dramatic day than we had anticipated. It began well enough. Mrs Denham arrived wearing what looked like a military jacket and boots, her white hair newly red-washed. My mum came next, her hair dyed raven black, her usual rather wildly applied makeup brightening her face, a large bag in her hands packed with extra puddings, pies and other Christmas fare in case we should be snowed in and run out in the course of the following months. The three Americans all turned up together. They had been enjoying an early drink. Mrs Denham sensed a bit of an atmosphere amongst the Americans, or as she put it to Helena, 'Something is up with our Yankee cousins.' Astonishingly, she had recovered from her own Christmas Eve hangover. She had spent the previous evening with her Irish politician boyfriend and whatever he recommended as a cure was working. She was in fine enough form to judge Jack Slade drinking his way through several bottles of Riesling and getting so soused he could hardly move his legs when the meal was announced. I don't think he heard her refer to him as 'that dark little dwarf' as he absently plaited coloured streamers into his thick black hair and beard. Polly – lush, gorgeous, plump, sexy – had become engaged to Rex after she had given her Lebanese boyfriend, whom I only knew as Oz, his marching orders from his own flat. We all wondered at this development. At that time we didn't know Polly particularly well and were surprised she hadn't noticed Rex's exaggerated flounces and gasps. Not that he had recognised anything in himself apparently. He finished up another bottle, still before lunch was served, with the clatter of expressive pans assuring me that the usual kitchen tensions were being vented. Then we overheard Polly having some sort of hissing row with him just before lunch was ready. The point of their dispute was never mentioned. Since the previous Easter, Rex's appetite had brought him heroic status in the eyes of Mrs Denham who admired him, with his blue eyes and blond hair, for being what she called 'a good old-fashioned trencherman'. Poor boozed-up Jack Slade didn't get a thought. In swarthy, brown-eyed people, she saw indications of degenerate greed, probably Jewish. Drinking steadily, Rex still managed to get the best part of a whole turkey down, together with big helpings of various side dishes. Jack seemed introverted and hardly managed two or three bites of turkey in spite of Polly's determination to make him eat more. While extending his rather elaborate Texan courtesy to everyone else, Rex occasionally took a moment to glare bitterly in his friends' direction.

'I think Rex and Polly have something important to tell us,' announced Helena with forced cheer. And then a child caught her attention for the moment and she had to leave the table. I hoped nobody had heard her. Rex and Polly already knew they were getting married and thought everyone else did, too. I didn't make any effort to follow through. My mum, who had kept out of everything pretty successfully, stared at her plate, eating automatically with steady stolidity. Every so often she looked up at me and winked. She knew she was in a madhouse. As soon as she could, she joined the children for a seasonal game or two.

'Important?' enquired Rex in anticipatory relish. As usual he hoped for a scandal.

Polly, raising her impressive eyebrows, frowned at Rex and was spotted by Helena's mother.

'I thought you were going to announce your engagement,' said Helena, a little lamely.

'I thought we had,' said Polly. My mother started to clap.

Shortly after the pudding was served Jack felt sick and rushed off to throw up rather audibly while Polly and Rex had another argument climbing the stairs to the living room. We enjoyed the big Christmas pudding as best we could. Meanwhile another diversion came when Kitty accused Sally of pinching her silver threepenny bit out of the pudding. I reminded her that the rare coins were redeemable for use next year. An IOU would work just as well for wishing on.

There was a break in the action when Mrs Denham, in the absence of her daughter, glared at the ceiling and asked why on earth the children couldn't eat at the same table as the adults. Hoping to divert a row between her and Helena, I told her I had bought them their table and chairs as a step towards adulthood. 'Aren't they having a great time?' They weren't breaking anything and apart from the odd bit of arbitration, they didn't need supervision. Their maternal grandmother thought they did. A lot of mysterious giggling then recaptured her attention. My mother had gone off to hide. The children began to count. Grandma rose to her full height, set her face like a knight lowering his visor and reached for her metaphorical sword. Still desperate to distract her, I pointed out that the kids were clearly having a much better meal than anyone else and they didn't even need alcohol to do it.

'Is that a dig at me, Mike?' asked Mrs D., firmly readjusting her paper crown. I knew that tone as well as I had known the tone of the Clerkenwell Kings, our local Teds. She was looking for trouble, just as her clan traditionally looked for trouble at this season. Their end-of-year settling of scores. Helena and I hated her family when they were like this. The sounds were still murmuring away in the back of my head. I didn't reply to my mother-in-law, though I couldn't help thinking her crown increased her resemblance to the Queen of Hearts in *Alice* (or was it the Queen of Spades in Tchaikovsky). I was relieved that she had no actual right to a crown or she might have sent a few of us to the chopping block that day. I almost felt sorry for the poor woman, being denied her regular family rituals. My mother leapt out of a cupboard. The children shrieked.

The whispered conversation from upstairs had taken on an added sharpness and reminded me of two cats spitting.

The entertainment might have been further refined if the majority of the guests had any idea what the row was about. Somehow curiosity encouraged my own mother to stick her black-dyed fuzzy mass of hair back through the door and ask, sotto voce, what the hell was going on, then regret her question. We didn't know anyway. We wouldn't discover the truth for a while because the front door slammed. Below, in the kitchen, we fell silent. I got up and went to the bathroom next door. I came back out and crossed the hall to the girls' big room full of toys and Christmas stuff. Beyond that were the dark French windows into the dark, glittering garden. I lifted the lid of the piano and played a few bars of an R&B riff. The whispering had grown louder, almost like running water. I needed to pull myself together.

'I'd guess Jack won't be coming back for his pudding.' My mum stood in the doorway grinning. I shook my head and smiled back at her. We went into dinner again. Polly and Rex had grown drunker and more strained until suddenly Polly leapt from her chair and disappeared upstairs. Another slam told us she, too, had left, probably off to find Jack. The children, giggling and pulling crackers back at their little table, noticed nothing.

'This is getting to be like a French farce,' said Mrs Denham, and we all pretended not to hear her.

The Princedale Road house was only about ten minutes' walk away around the corner. We looked to Rex for an explanation but he was too busy pretending nothing had happened and wouldn't reply. He had found the mince pies and drawn them towards him. Almost defiantly, he took a large helping of Christmas pudding and brandy butter which he began to eat with steely determination before jumping up and heading for the toilet. A short while later the front door slammed for a third time.

'It sounds like a lovers' tiff to me,' said my mum. 'But who on earth are the lovers?'

For a few minutes there was silence broken only by the occasional snort or bray from the children's corner.

A ring at the door. I answered it. Helena joined me. She had a look on her face I recognised. She was beginning to enjoy the melodrama. Polly hurried back in, apologising but not illuminating. Then, ignoring us, Rex walked through the open door and the subsequent whispering row gave us a better clue. Rex had been betrayed. It seemed by Polly. His best friend Jack was probably the other betrayer. But still nothing was explained. We watched the drama: silent spectators. Eventually the girls joined our mothers and us just as Jack came back in and began to cry. He sat on the upstairs sofa and sobbed some sort of confession, told us all how sorry he was. He had a mug of coffee and another glass of wine. Helena patted him on the back and made comforting sounds. Suddenly Rex came in, saw Jack and left, slamming the door. He returned in a few minutes, indicating an afterthought on his way to Princedale Road. He and Jack then had some drunken words. Jack put out a pale, quivering hand which Rex refused to take.

Jack got up and unsteadily made for the front door, still weeping and asking for forgiveness. We heard it open and close behind him. I wondered if I shouldn't go after him. Helena shook her head. He would probably be all right on Boxing Day. She found a bottle of claret and poured herself a glass, leaning back on the sofa.

About five minutes later Polly came in, a look of concern on her large, gorgeous face. She was afraid Jack really did intend to kill himself, as he'd indicated through his snuffles. Should she go to him? Enthusiastically, we sent her after her lover. She, too, departed through the front door. Another pause and Rex decided that he had better go to make sure Jack was okay. A little later Rex returned, apparently to use the toilet. Soon he could be heard vomiting downstairs. I was grateful we had not yet gone on to the old Hine cognac which I'd been looking forward to for several months and didn't want to waste. I was wondering if I could possibly sneak it off the sideboard and secrete it away somewhere until New Year's Eve.

Now Mrs Denham became as vociferous as she normally did about this time. Except instead of attacking her daughter, son or grandchildren, she wanted to know 'exactly what' had got into Rex and company. 'Aren't they Catholics?' she asked, introducing another prejudice so far unaired. Emerging from the bathroom, Rex declared, with elaborate courtesy rather spoiled by his intense, arsenical pallor and the vomit on his tie, that he was extremely sorry and would explain. Then a phone call from Princedale Road caused him to put off the moment. He announced with a gasp worthy of Garrick that Jack had attempted to kill himself.

So this time I accompanied Rex round to Princedale Road where Jack was sprawled in their bathroom having just thrown up his bottle of sleeping pills. Polly was crying. I remember noticing how large her tears were as they fell off her nose into a wad of damp Kleenex. It was, she told me, all her fault. I hadn't heard so many mea culpas since Helena had dropped and smashed a bottle of spaghetti sauce at Sainsbury's. I simply couldn't share what I saw as my friends' overreaction. Rex told me as icily as he could that Jack had betrayed their friendship. He was always a 'backdoor man'. He'd been having an affair with Polly. Polly acknowledged this. She said the affair had happened only because Rex 'like an idiot' had decided to keep himself pure until their wedding night.

Rex was embarrassed by this. Having warned me to guard my own marriage, he became inarticulate and left, presumably to return to Ladbroke Grove. A phone call from Helena confirmed that Rex had, indeed, come back. He had wandered into the girls' room and had fallen asleep in Sally's bed. Sally was complaining bitterly about not being able to get into her bed. Of course, she had no intention of going to sleep at all if she could get away with it. Time I went home.

Polly cried on my shoulder and asked me if Rex hated her. He probably did just then. She didn't dare, she said, leave Jack in that condition. By now he was also sleeping. So I plodded home to Ladbroke Grove.

When I got back Mrs Denham had her coat on. She stood in the hall on our mustard-coloured carpet and darkly demanded a taxi while managing somehow to judge her daughter as the cause of all the chaos. She couldn't, she said, stand it a moment longer. I reported what I'd discovered about Jack's affair with Polly and went downstairs to get a cup of tea. While I filled the kettle Rex began to shout incoherently from Sally's bed before falling backwards into our little girl's pillows and snoring with impressive volume. Sally meanwhile had given up negotiation for a while and was sitting in the corner with my mum watching the seasonal fun on our dilapidated black-and-white TV. I phoned the only taxi rank I knew, the cabman's shelter at Notting Hill. Surprisingly a cab was ready. Two minutes. Suddenly he had materialised outside our front steps.

Naturally Mrs Denham was frozen by a human desire to learn what happened next. She hovered between the taxi and the living room until her daughter, taking her firmly to the outside door, got her down the steps to the street. Here the taxi murmured and grumbled to itself, waiting for the expensive fare to Norbury, in South London on the other side of the river. Considering the cost, Mrs Denham wondered, perhaps we should cancel it. I went out, shoved a bunch of fivers into the contemplative driver's hand to keep him long enough so we could get Mrs D., her various presents, massive handbag and some sewing patterns she'd brought for unknown purposes down into the seats of the cab and on her way to Pollards Hill.

The following year Rex at last discovered he was gay on a poetry tour organised by the Poetry Society which put him together with the notorious bisexual junky Lin Carwood ('man, woman or dog, I just throw 'em on a bed'). Only Rex was surprised. He stopped trying to marry some puzzled woman and his relationship with Polly and Jack improved. Jack took up with Ellen Voight, the gin heiress, and lived with her as a kind of pet in her big Chelsea house. Polly married Gordon Perry, who did the Fix's light-show. They eventually moved back to the States and put on mixed-media festivals underwritten by Polly's millionaire dad. She almost stopped painting entirely. Her father once asked me what was the best thing he could do for her as a painter. 'Do you really want to know?' I asked him. He did. 'Then cut her off without a penny,' I said. This idea appealed to him but he couldn't bring himself to put it into practice. Polly only eventually developed her talent.

The year 1967 came with more plans for the new-style *New Worlds*. Allard drove over with his kids on New Year's Day. Helena thought we should go up to the pub together. He had become rather sad and a little erratic since his wife Shirley's death, even though I had introduced him to a new woman he liked, Cathy White. Cathy had briefly been my girlfriend and didn't much like coming over on these family things. Helena said she'd look after his kids while Jack and I went up to Hennekey's for a drink. His spirits seemed to rise when he talked about the magazine and he fired off a whole lot of ideas, most of which didn't really suit what we wanted to do, yet at the same time I saw him as the soul of the magazine. His were the stories I ran as exemplary. Cathy said he was jealous of me, but I couldn't see it. I never could.

Jack's career was moving him into a different direction and he was seeing more of a mutual friend, Malcolm Bix, a regular of John Brunner's 'at homes'. He ran a little magazine, *ajax*, and shared some of our contributors, such as George MacBeth and D.M. Thomas. We had always been wary of little magazines, but they asked Jack to be prose editor and, disappointed that I didn't let him decide the contents of the magazine, he accepted. He liked their willingness to give him his head.

Jack hated the first cover we did by Escher. He thought it should be Dalí. I pointed out that Dalí or Dalí-esque artwork had been appearing on covers for years and Escher was less familiar to readers. We were after all a newsstand magazine with a general readership. The Escher I had selected for the cover appealed to a wide audience. I told Jack he had only his own career to think about. I had a lot of careers to worry about. Jack did do a good story for the first issue, however, along with Fisch, Slade, Zelazny, MacBeth, Aldiss, Masson, Zee and Ratz. Dr Christopher Evans, our own tame mad scientist, wrote a feature on computers, sleep and dreams. It was a great issue, featuring some of our best writers, and the general press gave us a generous reception. We doubled our circulation. When it came out I, of course, was already working on the fourth issue. For a few great months everything seemed to be going our way. A good many established literary writers were submitting work and I found myself in a rather uncomfortable position of power.

Although I had written *The Final Programme*, I was still not sure I had found exactly the tone I needed for the work I wanted to do, which would deal with identity and the modern city. I had written some well-received SF novels but nothing really stretched me. I began another series of Meg Midnight stories, setting aside some of the money to pay *New Worlds* contributors until we received income on the first issues. Most of the AP earnings were needed for our growing expenses as a family. I still found myself writing features because Helena became pregnant again. Three children so close together would break the bank and exhaust her. You could get an abortion at that time if a psychiatrist said your mental health would suffer if you didn't. Doctors who performed abortions usually told you which psychiatrist to go to. We discovered that, once you had a baby, you found the abortion option much harder to accept. I had the 'new baby' visualised, even named. Nothing morbid about it. It simply happened. It was hard for both of us. Harder for her of course.

After a very depressing time of it, Helena at least came away from Harley Street with a new coil, an effective birth-control method which did not depend on my clumsiness or our erratic memories. I was depressed and puzzled because for some reason I suddenly developed a strong desire to visit the Alsacia. After delivering a feature to Ted Holmes at *Look and Learn*, I found myself wandering around Carmelite Inn Chambers, looking for the gates. But I had no luck. I was relieved, later, when I sat on top of the 15 bus going home. I felt obscurely guilty and said nothing to Helena, though she sensed my secret. The business of running a new magazine soon drove thoughts of the Alsacia away.

We had fallen in love with our Ladbroke Grove flat. The noise from the traffic at the front was impersonal and at the back, with the big gardens, it was often tranquil. Helena was much happier and, because of the gardens, the children didn't require our complete attention. But I needed to earn more and help keep an ambitious magazine going until we started getting income. I became busier than I liked. My anxiety had begun to manifest itself in bouts of bad temper. I never attacked anyone physically of course, but I could become, briefly, a roaring monster with my friends or Helena. I wouldn't have blamed Helena if she'd left me. Of course I experienced the usual guilt but I

wasn't happy with myself and wanted to change without quite knowing how. Helena would occasionally take the kids out to give me the
space I was demanding but it didn't help much. I still felt abandoned.
I saw a shrink up at St Charles Hospital but all he did was prescribe
valium, tell me to drink Guinness and warned me that if I smoked
marijuana I should be careful because dealers cut it with cocaine. I
left his surgery wondering if everyone in his profession was as ill-
informed. To work I had to pull myself together but I was growing
increasingly melancholy. Helena had plenty of ideas about what was
wrong with me, but her theories seemed no better than mine.

Helena and the kids had gone out one warm, summer afternoon. I
think it must have been early-closing day, obeying that benign law
which insisted on a shop assistant's half holiday midweek, before
Thatcher smashed protectionism and gave us freedom to choose between a rock and a hard place. The sound of traffic dropped almost
to nothing on those lazy afternoons. The whole city grew drowsy. I had
taken a break from the typewriter to stretch my legs, going downstairs
through the kids' room, inching my way between the pianola and a
toy castle, round the vast rocking horse we had bought from Ham-
leys during a flush period, and walking out into our little patch of
ratty green garden with its orange brick walls, its briar roses sturdily
climbing their makeshift trellises. On the warm, dusty air came distant sounds of adults and children playing in the gardens on the
other side of the wall. The air, carrying the scent of roses and car exhaust, was a perfect mixture of town and country. I felt pleasantly
alone. Relaxed, I lit a spliff.

I was enjoying the moment when a large bird hopped on top of
the old brick wall, put its beautiful black head on one side, fixed me
with a sardonic jet-black eye and croaked, 'Hello.'

Though this was not the first talking bird I had encountered, I was
still surprised. 'I've never met a talking crow before,' I said.

'No and you're not likely to,' said the bird with astonishing elocu-
tion. 'I'm a raven. I was sent from the Alsacia because no other messages got through to you. Apparently everyone's been calling you. They
even sent the green Lagonda but the people said you had moved or
that you were not who you distinctly are. You might have several enemies hereabouts. This is nice, isn't it? Like being in the country.'

Once again I suspected LSD, increasingly popular in the area. And I had just lit a joint. I frowned.

'Now the neighbours will hear me talking to myself and will be sure I'm barmy,' I said.

'They'll think *they're* barmy when they hear me talking to you,' said the raven. 'Shall I caw?'

'If you like.'

'Sure.' He lifted his head, opened his beak, drew breath and let out an incredibly loud cry which echoed around the square. His next words were a whisper in comparison. 'Okay. So shall I hang around like an omen, perched on your backside as you pray for release? Or will you waddle back indoors and see who can get to that open upstairs window first? I'm here to say Moll Midnight asked after you and sent her best. She says to drop in any time. More importantly, Friar Isidore would like to see you urgently at a place of your own choosing.'

Surely this was too much of a delay to be another late acid reaction. If anything, this was a good old-fashioned psychotic episode. I'd read about those, too. Could I be experiencing serious psychosis? I didn't believe it. There had been no warning sign. Pulling myself together I remembered when this had happened before. I had met a talking jackdaw when I was a kid climbing on piles of weed-grown rubble. He had hopped on my shoulder and we'd exchanged a few words before he no doubt flew off home. It had nonetheless been a magical experience. 'Why would Friar Isidore send a talking bird? A raven at that. Aren't you a harbinger of something?'

'Doom? I think that's because the word "doom" is tellingly croaked. You've seen me around. I've been keeping an eye on you. But I'm not a spy. I'm not a soddin' harbinger, either. I'm just a regular messenger. I work part-time at the Tower. Well, not your Tower. The old Elizabethan Tower. I had an idea for a story, incidentally...' And the raven began to do the thing an author most fears: he outlined the plot of his novel to me. I had to stand there, smoking a Sullivan and listening to what seemed a pretty banal story about a bunch of birds who enjoyed tricking people into thinking they were schizophrenic. 'Believe me, I had this idea long before Hitchcock!'

'Short on irony,' I said when he had finished. 'Try it in the States.'

'Oh what a witty man the boy's become. I remember you blushing away in the stables. Seems like yesterday. You didn't even notice me. Anyway, they'd like to see you for old times' sake at the Carmelite Inn entrance. That's all I was told. And I'll be looking out for your next book. If it's anything like mine, I'll sue.' With this empty threat he hopped ostentatiously to the flower bed and waddled across the lawn to admire himself in the reflecting window glass.

'You're probably an illusion,' I said, 'so why should I listen to you?'

He paused in his grooming. 'Why shouldn't you? You're short of tin, aren't you?'

'I'll be fine when I finish the story I'm working on upstairs. I'm not exactly looking for fairy gold. Any particular hour of the day?'

'If you've just started the story, make it this time next week. If you're still writing them in three days, that will let you recover.'

'It's the only economic way to justify doing this one,' I said, 'since Fleetway gets the royalties. But with a few names changed and giving horses a few extra legs I'll probably sell them as sword-and-sorcery novels in the States.'

'So you're still doing those awful historical fantasy things?'

I was sensitive about my hackwork. I turned my back on the raven. I went inside and upstairs to my typewriter where I was, of course, working on the first of another series of Meg stories: *Black Sword of the Dales*. The window was open. He must have peeked.

I looked for bird shit on the carpet.

CHAPTER SIXTEEN

SUCCUMBING

IT CAME ON me the way an affair can happen, suddenly, when everything at home is fine, knocking along okay, and then, there you are in some sleazy Bloomsbury bedsitter, doing what comes naturally and with such unwelcome complications...

A day later the book was done and I went to Fleet Street to give it to Bill Baker. Helena, remembering what happened the last time I delivered a script in person, told me not to wake the children when I stumbled home. I thought it wise to skip lunch with Bill. His lunches were likely to last into the small hours of the next day and never leave licensed premises. So I tried to hand in the manuscript at the ground-floor reception desk. But the uniformed old jobsworth on duty insisted I deliver it myself. On entering the lift I recognised Les Brown, a former colleague from my editorial days, who suggested we go to get a few pints for old times' sake. I made an excuse, reached my floor, threw the envelope on Bill Baker's desk then legged it to the annex and the back lift generally used by directors.

In Farringdon Road I found myself without thinking heading for the Old Bailey and was soon in the familiar grey backstreets which took me to the great Courts themselves and Olympic, our *Tarzan* typesetters. I walked down the steep steps into the clacking office and the crowded proofing room, full of the same men in waistcoats and felt hats who had always seemed to be there, and asked someone I half recognised if he'd seen Friar Isidore. 'Does he still come in?'

'Yeah,' said the sallow old hack not looking up from his galleys. 'Usually on a Wednesday.'

'Know much about him?'

An expression of disgust. 'Well, he's a bloody monk, ain't he? Not that much to know about a monk, is there? Why?' He became alert. 'Done anything he shouldn't?'

I grew automatically wary. 'You've not heard anything? About LSD?'

'Why, is he a millionaire?' That was gullible old Fleet Street for you. Nobody more behind the times. Nobody wanting to believe a sensational lie more than the journalist it's being told to. Sniffing the same old trails. Some of them honestly believed they printed the truth.

'I mean drugs,' I said. Did he make a habit of slipping Mickey Finns, say, into young editors' cups of Darjeeling? In the semi-darkness the few men standing about waiting to receive their 'pulls' pricked up their evil little ears.

I looked around, rather regretting what I'd said, and then it dawned on me why I'd rushed to get the manuscript in today: so I could be paid by the Thursday after next. It was paysheet day at Fleetway. Leave it any later and you didn't get paid for two weeks. We used to think that was slow. Wednesday? Proofing day for *Tarzan* and…

I turned.

'I had just left! Some instinct brought me back.' Friar Isidore stood in the doorway. He shrugged. 'Or perhaps I forgot these galleys!' In white cassock, taller than anyone except me, his eyes mild and twinkling and his long fingers tightly twined before him, the friar regarded me from above rimless glasses. He seemed genuinely happy. He was radiant. 'Oh! How delightful! Wait a few minutes and I'll be there. I wasn't expecting you until next week.' He ran up to the desk to receive his forgotten envelope. He waved it. 'Doubly blessed, eh?'

So I stepped outside with him and we went down to Ludgate Hill to that same clattering, chattering, giggling ABC Teashop where I was careful to watch that he put nothing in my cup. It was not so much for himself, he said, as for Father Abbot who asked almost every day about me. Had he made me nervous, showing me too much, too soon? He had tried to give me what was needed to persuade the prince to throw in with us. 'At present he is adrift, dragged along one brane and then another by time's awful gravity…'

'So he sent a talking raven rather than a billet-doux,' I said.

Brother Isidore seemed to be humouring me rather than I him. Perhaps the LSD had permanently affected both of us? I let it drop. I don't think he had any idea what I was talking about. I smiled to myself. Suddenly this wasn't a very sinister rabbit hole at all.

'What's wrong with the abbot?' I surprised myself. I felt genuine concern.

'He had set great store by you. Will you come to see him?'

I was wary. 'Not for tea. Or coffee. Or lemonade.'

He frowned, puzzled. 'No refreshment of any kind shall be offered if that suits you,' he said.

I loved his gentle innocence. If it was assumed then I was completely fooled. And if he had anything but the best of intentions, at least in his scheme of things, he did not betray by the slightest expression or tic that he was lying.

'And how is Father Grammaticus?' Was the abbot manipulating this sweet-natured man?

'Well. As ever, well! He has a great spirit and enjoys robust health.'

I thought I had last seen a rather frail, delicate old man. Apparently he had been ill when I saw him first.

Friar Isidore led me back through that rich, strong-smelling rat's nest of lanes, alleys, courts and twittens, more intricate than a North African souk, to Carmelite Inn Chambers, until we again pushed open the thick iron-bound doors of the Alsacia. No illusion there! So parts of my delusion *were* true! Before we ever reached Alsacia's massive doors I had walked under old stoneworks which might once have been gatehouses, like parts of abandoned baileys around which buildings of all uses and eras had grown.

And there was The Swan With Two Necks, quiet at this time of day, an enormous, rambling, ramshackle building linked to other ramshackle buildings, leaning hard against each other to form the inner yard. And in front of that another cobbled square. I looked for the tavern's inhabitants. I thought for a second I saw the potman, Joey

Cornwall, rolling a big barrel through the doors. A few others stood at rest, chatting, leaning on brooms, setting down pails. An ordinary lazy Wednesday afternoon in a quiet, domestic bit of London. Their costumes were rather drab, their long hair dirty. They did not look especially old-fashioned. I saw no beautiful girl in highwayman costume. No sign of anything at all romantic. Only the sweet scent of horse manure told me the stables were still in use. I laughed to myself, shaking my head as we rounded a corner and passed under an archway opening out into a forecourt planted with shrubs. We entered the old abbey, now smelling of rich summer flowers, mould and dust, dust which curled and fluttered in the afternoon light; and there in those mellow cloisters I again came face to face with the patrician Father Grammaticus.

I shook the abbot's hand. His huge purple veins ran like maps of mountain ranges across the thin, white parchment skin of his wrist. His age and vulnerability were almost repulsive. How could Friar Isidore believe he was in better health? Smiling, the abbot took my young hand in both his frail ones. 'I am gladdened you came at last, my boy. There is a growing urgency. You are so badly needed here. He will only trust one who resembles the silhouette whom he insists on calling Mercury. Fate alone has given you that rôle, even though you are now bearded. You are Mercury. I can see the resemblance to his poor brother.' He led me from the cloisters back through the low doorway into the little chapel itself.

His grip was far too strong.

I felt suddenly sick with anxiety. I worried how to retreat. I told him about my happy marriage and how much I loved my children, how I devoted so much of my spare time to them, how I loved to get up, cook them breakfast, take them to school on my bike – one on the handlebars, one on the saddle, while I pedalled between them – and how proud I was of them. I told him that this was not something I was prepared to jeopardise. I checked my watch. 'They're expecting me home for tea.'

He nodded. 'We thought you would visit us a week from today. The raven is one of our most reliable couriers.'

'My fault,' I said. 'I came in early. Needed the money.'

He released me, then reached out to touch my lips and I was

suddenly, awkwardly silent. I said I was sorry. I got up to leave. Too much time had passed. The gorgeous light fell in shafts through the stained glass, fell on the altar where in the cool, rippling air suddenly a writhing living fish stood on its fluttering tail, as if straining to break out of its natural habitat, its body running with brilliant greens and blues and a dozen different shades of gold and red.

'Ah –!' He sensed something I did not and reached for the goblet.

And then it was gone, popping out of existence and the light with it. 'Radiant Time… Brother Armand's greatest discovery. Revealed to the prince. And now the dreadful Spaniard. The Inquisition. Radiant Time. And Cromwell. I wonder. Is he as savage, as cruel as they say? Their hatred of us is palpable. Yet we hold many of the same principles. Tom Paine was here. We sheltered him for weeks. Or will… Radiant Time. He said we practised what they only preached. Every branch in harmony. It can be achieved, I know.' He seemed to be finishing a sentence, not beginning one. 'That is why it is so important you be here when the prince is also present.'

He bent to his left, to an ecclesiastical cupboard on the nearby table. The cupboard was of thick, simply hewn oak with long strap hinges of blackened iron. He put in a dull brass key and opened it. I blinked. The indigo light shivered from the box, changing to ghastly yellow then blue-green fluttering like living storm-shredded rags. How had he conjured it from one place to another? The fish stood upright again, flicking its tail, straining for the surface, changing colour as if to escape recognition when it tried to flee. I looked towards Father Grammaticus and Friar Isidore but the light was too white and bright for my eyes. I couldn't see their expressions. 'Which prince do you mean?' I asked. I was growing uncomfortable.

I heard a great swelling noise that was discordant yet sublimely beautiful while distantly the abbot spoke of God's vast universe, worlds without end, and the significance of humanity, *'perhaps the only sentient creatures of our kind in the whole of material Creation! Can you believe that? We are creatures blessed with souls and advanced intellect! God's image. With material bodies. Alone to give God the praise He deserves for His wisdom and His Grace. Did God create the universe or did the universe make God? That was the only question in the end. In the name of the Creator and the created, created and Cre-*

ator. Evolved man or God? Shall we ever know or cease to care which began the cycle? We live in a world of duality and paradox.'

These didn't sound very likely words for a Christian clergyman. So this, in spite of all the Christian trappings, actually was a cult.

I got up slowly. 'I must go. I'm sorry.'

'You will come back. We do not lie. We cannot swear, but we do not lie. The divine – the divine –' He bowed and led me to the door. He was babbling, a madman. 'Those simple-minded Puritans want our Treasure. They will do anything they can to steal it. They think they can use it. They fear us. They fear the power of the old religions. Yet we pray for them, also. We cannot fight if we are not free. We would not harm them. Free will is at the heart of our –' Echoes, as if in a great, empty house. 'We believe. Light is substance. Light is gravity and time. Next week. Same sun's ray – same moonbeam – same hour… the moment will be made. Each moment ordered in a state of linearity. It can be done.' That, when I wrote it down later, was the best I recalled.

'Of course.' I pretended to agree. I was holding down my panic. Maybe this *was* an asylum as I'd first thought, and the loonies really had taken over the bin? Or maybe we were experiencing some sort of social experiment? I chose to take what he said as a question. With Friar Isidore beside me and the blue-green flames still fluttering before my eyes, I said goodbye to the abbot, left the abbey and Alsacia, waved farewell to Friar Isidore and caught a 15 bus all the way home. I felt guilty.

I was back much earlier than Helena had expected. She was pleased, full of curiosity. 'You've got a telegram from New York,' she said. 'Your agent. I'll make some tea.'

CHAPTER SEVENTEEN

THE TEMPTATIONS

THE TELEGRAM WAS from my agent, Bob Cornfield, in America. I was invited to attend a big SF convention in New York and Doubleday, who were enthusiastic about the 'historical fantasies' I was publishing with them, had offered to pay my fare while 'an anonymous donor' would pay my expenses. I had a good idea who my benefactor was. Doubleday were now her publisher and she had recommended Allard, Fisch, Bayley and me, among others. Judy Merril saw me as an ally in her one-woman crusade to improve the quality and critical reception of science fiction. After the Labor Day convention another conference would be held and Rex had been invited, too. Most Americans had not seen *New Worlds* and very few had any idea of what we were really about. Helena thought I should go. I was reluctant to make the journey without her. She deserved the break more than me. She laughed. My being away would be a break for her, not to worry. Get her a nice dress at Saks Fifth Avenue, something for the kids at FAO Schwarz.

Aboard a cheap flight via Dublin, I arrived in New York with a babbling, crazed Rex Fisch in August 1967. Rex was going home on some personal matter but would meet up at the writers' conference in Milford, Pennsylvania, a relatively short ride from New York. The Vietnam War was the big issue of the day and the Aer Lingus jet was packed with priests and nuns divided on the rights and wrongs of the conflict. While the Catholic-born Rex sat purse-lipped beside me a bunch of Irish priests argued furiously up and down the aisle of the 727. We arrived a lot more tired than when we had left and New York was almost overwhelming, but Doubleday had booked me into the Park Plaza, looking over Central Park, and I began to feel a touch of euphoria. There were twin beds. I offered Rex the other and was glad that he only stayed in New York a couple of days. The big convention was coming up. In those days the smells of coffee and strong tobacco made up the distinctive scent of the city. Brilliant neon reminded me of the wonder of my childhood after the war when streets had come alive again. And Central Park was beautiful. Early russet among the green. I was entranced!

Labor Day is when Americans rather reluctantly celebrate the dignity of manual work, though a red flag hasn't been seen flying in Union Square since 1945. Yankees still had a puritanical reluctance to give ordinary people the day off. Joe McCarthy continued to be a vivid memory and the anti-communist hysteria was only just starting to die down while in the South things were just better than intolerable. Primed by TV and movies I had come prepared for violence and found only good will. I fell in love with New York, of course. And I met people with whom I'd previously only corresponded. Rex disappeared off to Minnesota.

Four days later and thoroughly corrupted, I visited my publisher on his beautiful farm in the rolling foothills of the Poconos and I fell in love again. At last I understood the American dream! There was only good to say of it! I had never been nor never ever would've, or whatever it was they wanted you to say in re communism, the Red Menace, and had no problem with that, but I didn't necessarily swallow the right-wing view of the engine of Western prosperity and how it had arrived at its current levels of success. I knew how much American wealth had been built on the backs of dead natives, illegal immigrants, slaves and destitute refugees from starving Europe. But the people I met now lived only in a happier present. The future was an optimistic dream. Infectious stuff. I cheered up instantly. The depressed habits we identified as virtuous in England were considered doom-laden nightmares in the US. New Yorkers seemed as intolerant of historical analysis as they were forgiving of psychoanalysis and self-regard.

Back in New York, Rex had copies of *New Worlds* containing his serial and although he wasn't in the best mental shape for it he planned to offer it to Random House. He hoped they would be impressed. He did not want a publisher even remotely associated with genre fiction.

Leaving it with an editor he knew there, he set off for Milford, Pennsylvania, with me and a bunch of women SF writers including Judy, Anne McCaffrey and Joanna Russ. The Science Fiction Writers of America was only about a year old and we had all been invited to attend a conference at the rambling Victorian house of Damon Knight, an intelligent and ambitious writer and editor determined to raise the genre's writing standards. As well as more established writers, Knight had also invited Samuel R. Delany, Harlan Ellison, Gene Wolfe, James Sallis, Norman Spinrad and a few others just making names for themselves who had sold to Knight's anthology *Orbit* and to *New Worlds*.

There was much interest in my magazine. Knight had worked for years to improve the literary standards of science fiction and was something of an ally, although I had no particular interest in the genre beyond what was useful to me. We enjoyed some heady arguments and I found another contributor. Highly argumentative, with no special background in SF, Spinrad had already published some fairly run-of-the mill titles but he brought part of his unpublished novel *Bug Jack Barron* with him to the Milford conference. I fell in love with the book and asked him to send me a copy in London. The language and subject matter, although not derivative, were the closest I'd found to Bill Burroughs. One of a number of friendships begun in Milford which would last a lifetime.

In the USA for the first time, I was witnessing the modern economic liberal state in all its glory. Most of the checks and balances with which I was familiar were gone. Big-buck euphoria. Big numbers. Big heads. Pierrot and the Politics of Plunder. The Panto of Faux Prosperity. Rapacity at Full Ahead. The Ego, astride its favourite mount, was coming into its own! Yet the place was strangely old-fashioned. The strongest feeling I got from New York at first was nostalgia. A 1930s vision of the future.

Within a week I was exuding confidence and self-worth. I shudder to think what an old friend, meeting me on the streets of downtown Manhattan, would have made of me. Mistaking bright American good manners for admiration of my genius I became thoroughly convinced of my literary superpowers. Here I was, bringing the future to America. The Innovator! What would have got me jeered off the planet as a prig and wanker and stuck-up all-round bounder in Ladbroke Grove made me merely a man with a sense of his own worth on Broadway. This unbashful Brit, modest in tone but arrogant in content, sat across the dinner table from editor Larry Ashfield, charismatic bullshitter of his golden cage, feeding him anecdotes Larry could make his own, and talked up a planned book which would use the tropes and methods of popular fiction with the structural ambition of modernism and would bring the great British novel and the great American novel back together.

I write, I told him, for money. The better the money, the better the book.

'So what would you give me for a million bucks?' asked Larry, flying high on my spiel.

'*War and Peace*,' I said.

'You got it,' he said. I was thinking of Jerry Cornelius, whom I was just reviving in short stories. I made some notes and typed them up on my agent's machine.

Two days later I sat with Bob in Larry's office and signed the contract in the middle of a press conference, going instantly from work-for-hire hack to literary novelist. Jerry Cornelius was a character Mick Jagger felt was too freaky to play in the movie; a smart alec, eccentric, working-class, dandy rock-and-roll scientist, an urban rôle-player who understood he was several *commedia* characters, as familiar with the languages of science as with arts and politics. A man of the New Renaissance, he was entangled in absurd stories conceived against the background of Vietnam and an ex-Imperial Britain re-imagining herself as part of Europe. His career would last through a dozen books and various spin-offs, comics, a movie and more. He was as much a technique as a character. The nearest nineteenth-century character I could think of for comparison was Vautrin/Jacques Collin, Balzac's wonderful villain.

Balzac was one of my heroes because he did reams of hackwork before doing reams of ambitious, innovative fiction. Why shouldn't I identify with him? My uncles wanted me to emulate Disraeli, the legendary ancestor. Meg Midnight was the nearest I got to *Sybil*. I planned nothing in conscious imitation. Those linked stories came naturally to me. Theme echoes theme. Image sparks phrase. Phrase strikes theme. Image carries narrative. Anthony Powell's comic *Dance to the Music of Time* wasn't Proust but it was the nearest he could get to tell his story. He lacked a method for our postwar age. We do our best with the techniques and ideas that come to us. But only so much can be done with the retrospective tone before it becomes sentimental and nostalgic.

Bullshit? Maybe. But Ashfield bought it.

The best form for carrying the weight of contemporary concerns was a modified SF. But I was trying to suspend belief, not disbelief. I borrowed as much from noir, Ubu and Firbank as I did from Bester. I rejected *Horizon* as well as *Galaxy*. Drunk on my self-awarded authority, my urgent persuasion, Ashfield applauded the dawning of a new art. I had to move fast and get the contract before other voices persuaded him to think along different lines. Of course the money wouldn't all come at once but it was enough to pay the rent and allow me to work at a more ambitious level.

Naturally, some, including me, would always wonder if I wasn't just another '60s con artist who had found a sucker to back a Fun Palace project. Yet I believed my spiel. I wanted to appeal to that modern audience who helped *Sgt. Pepper* stay so long at number one when there had never been anything like it ever before and that, in the more modest form of modern fiction, was my offering to the common pot of innovation and egalitarianism. Jerry Cornelius was modern man who had given up looking for a soul but needed to discover a rôle. At least one. A modernist rejecting the failed ideas of the twentieth century, accepting the impossibility of drastically improving the human condition, Jerry sought instead to remain constantly adaptable, constantly able to change the script, even the nature of his own character.

The culture had started to cook, I told Ashfield. Many more ingredients would go in my particular pot and many sips would be taken from my dipped ladle before it simmered into its fullest flavour but it would take decades before the goal was fully achieved. Now I was preparing the recipe I would create from the coming interaction of world cultures... and here I began to falter, having extended, as it were, my brief. But Larry had drunk enough Chateau Prude to see the dawning of the Age of Aquarius. That beard and burnoose still worked miracles. He could see I was an authentic prophet. A guru! Advised by Marc Haefele, a bright young man who worked as his assistant, Larry was caught by the euphoria of highly paid innovation. I was his first hit of acid. He had his own trip. He was the publisher of the English New Wave and to prove it I got my *War and Peace* advance. Larry would buy Allard's *The Savagery Show* in the same spirit. And, in the spirit of another age, his bosses would have it pulped.

I got so many gifts for Helena and the girls I had to pack some big parcels and post them straight to the house. I was quite the conquering hero. I was pleased with myself on another count. Given the considerable opportunity, I had not given in to any sexual temptation. I came home on a cold Tuesday morning and the first parcel arrived about an hour after I came in. Helena snorted as she held up a dress to look at it in the light. 'Lovely,' she said. 'Too good for me.' She was in one of those moods where she didn't believe she deserved anything. Or that there really was such a thing as altruism. Or love. 'What did you get up to in the States?'

The girls were pleased with their toys and cowboy outfits. I also got them BB guns like Colt .45s, jeans and shirts and cowboy wellies. And that night Helena made love as if there were no tomorrow. I consoled myself that she didn't like to say what she felt. There were plenty of other perfectly good ways of welcoming me home. And while there were a few ways I cared less for, there were few others I preferred more. I felt virtuous and deserving. I had brought back a pretty substantial elk. I had learned to stop looking for my father everywhere and not to sleep with and expect to marry every woman who wanted to. We stayed up in the bedroom until it was time to go together to collect the girls from school. Life was getting alarmingly sweeter by the minute...

Then the war against *New Worlds* heated up in earnest. The British Bill of Rights, written in 1689, was too early for free speech to be covered. And we weren't protected. W.H. Smith & Son booksellers, that old Quaker family, decided that Langdon Jones's protagonist, entering into a perfectly respectful conversation with Christ on the cross in a story dedicated to Olivier Messiaen (that most devout of composers, whom Jones revered), was an obscene, blasphemous or libellous act, maybe all three. They weren't too sure but there had to be a law against it. There was also *Bug Jack Barron*, Norman Spinrad's novel using the language of the LA streets and the Hollywood studios. That might be even worse, since it contained much F&C and all the other disgusting words ever created by human ingenuity. They wanted it axed. Or no sales. Our circulation had grown wonderfully before the Quakers determined we should not foul their racks. I was sorry. I had always liked Quakers, found their religious beliefs and practices admirable and, for my pleasure and health, regularly ate their oats.

Sadly the battle for *New Worlds* became the context for everything else we did, just like the Vietnam War. For months, growing increasingly exhausted, I struggled to keep the mag going. We were ultimately saved by a press outcry which shamed Smith's and newsagents Menzies into reluctantly taking us back, but by then we were all exhausted. The battle lines were still drawn. There I was in my long hair and lace and feathers and there they were in their drab suits; hard, grim haircuts and letterbox mouths. It was the English Civil War all over again. Roundheads primly putting down Cavaliers. And, as usual, the Roundheads were winning. Temporarily. Also as usual.

We needed a holiday.

But when I suggested it, Helena refused to come with me to the Alsacia. Even though she refused to believe it existed, she also seemed afraid of the place, associating it with madness. She said she would leave me if I started all that again. I understood her concern though she seemed to be overreacting. I was soon so embroiled in trying to save the magazine that I didn't have time even to think about the Alsacia. Or a holiday.

CHAPTER EIGHTEEN

RALLYING THE TROOPS

THE FOLLOWING YEAR, 1968, would prove an extraordinary one. The novel versions of *Behold the Man* and *The Final Programme* came out to great reviews, *New Worlds* received enormous amounts of publicity from a mainly sympathetic press; my work published in hardcovers had always been reviewed as literary fiction, while my fantasy paperbacks were almost never reviewed by the mainstream press. That suited me. I refused to use pseudonyms for my books but the paperbacks, most of which I wrote in three days, were distinguished at that time by the format. Critics were not confused. They knew that hardbacks were 'serious' and that paperbacks were not. I took ten days to write *The Final Programme* and about the same to write *Behold the Man* while it only took three days to write a fantasy 'historical'.

As a result of the press interest a new publishing partner presented himself for *New Worlds*, a man who had produced *Drum* in South Africa during the years in which it fought against being banned, so he seemed naturally sympathetic. I was slowing down on the fantasies. I only planned to complete a few more. The magazine no longer needed the influx of cash. I had three more Jerry Cornelius novels to write. I had signed with Ashfield.

By now the Ladbroke Grove area was turning into the future. This was where all the rock bands began to hang out. Every other kind of experiment went on around us. Because my books somehow caught the mood of the times I had turned into some sort of guru. Our ups and downs with *New Worlds* took on the character of a fight against authority. We mingled with poets, painters, film-makers and musicians and our activities were enough to get us in the gossip columns.

Around us there was less and less street noise as the hippies took over and became what they called the boss culture, and we all began living in wonderland, dressing up in our feathers and lace, our lovely clothes with our beautiful hair and hats and monstrous bean-crusher two-tone Saturday nighter shoes ready to strut into the Age of Aquarius. Light blues and dark blues and deep greens and luminous scarlets, silver and gold, long hair and dreadlocks and profound postwar desires gave us that peacock poise, swinging our guitars like lords with their swords, Death with his scythe. As far as the culture went, *we* said who lived or died. *We* had the moral high ground. *We* were the wonderlads. *We* had the secret. At parties merchant bankers asked our advice on the latest trends, as if we knew. Astonishingly beautiful and intelligent models were interested in what we thought about Vietnam. Had I been single I could have gone home with a different stunner every night, or it might have been the same one. They could be hard to tell apart. No temptations. Not really. I was perfectly at ease with domestic life at last. God, I felt happy. Content. Peter-fucking-Pureheart. No thanks, I'm married.

And so happy again with Helena and the kids. And my confident self. Don't fix the effect, fix the cause. But fame is power and power is a drug. You fascinate everyone, including yourself. You start getting as interested in you as they are. Life is so easy. Power is thrust at you from all sides. They want you to lie to them. Screw them. They wanted you to tell them stories. Sing them songs. In return you could do whatever you wanted. Women in particular just loved to give you power. *Take it. I don't want it. I don't have the strength or the taste for it.* They came up to you and offered their liberty to you. *I'm yours.* But what if you didn't want it? Then you got some weird reactions. *You don't love me. We need to discuss our relationship.* I don't know why, but at the very period when I was most happily married, women were intriguing me more and more. I was fascinated by their attitudes. I was infatuated by their femininity, by their motives and ambitions.

I wrote *The Adventures of Una Persson and Catherine Cornelius in the Twentieth Century* from them and to them. I wanted to know and understand them, each fucking individual, every bloody friend. There was no such thing as 'women'. People want to know how I turned from MCP to pro-feminist. Well, that was how. But it took a long time.

I was learning my guitar better. Keep it simple. Keep it soulful and keep it cool. I loved slide at home. At home it was: *I can't break with you baby because the stars rule my loving heart, I'll give anything to keep you, babe, nothing will ever tear us apart.* On stage it was: *We are the veterans of the psychic wars. We are the cruel, the cold, the unkind. We are the lost, we are the last, unfeeling, blind.* We had followed a familiar arc from rhythm and blues to psychedelic and experimental, from mods to hippies, riding the zeitgeist, possibly even tugging the wheel a little.

Psychedelia by night, Willie Dixon by day. Footprints in the sands of time. I took the kids to gigs whenever possible. Sometimes they would sleep behind the stacks. The pounding speakers were better than a lullaby. The rhythms were primal. A giant loving heart. That's why so many rock-and-roll kids are secure and well-balanced. Even the survivors who snorted their first line before they were nine. Just like my generation with the Nazi bombs, nothing could ever keep my kids awake. I remember going back to where they were sleeping in their carrycots seeing their seraphic faces glowing with contentment as their little chests rose and fell, their little noses snored in unison to the music on the stage out front. It was even better when you stopped having to change shit-filled nappies. When they were clean they smelled so good, so warm and sweet. I still get turned on by the smell of Johnson's baby oil and talc. Especially when one of our records comes on the radio at the same time. *City guerrilla, I'm a shitty psycho killer,* sings poor old dead Captain Crackers, that genius of the stage and studio. Talented bloke. Magic on stage.

What with sex, drugs, rock and roll and writing novels I didn't have a lot of extra time to think about the Alsacia or its messengers. I'd made it clear how I felt to the abbot. There wasn't much to make me nostalgic for the Alsacia. The murmuring was constant and getting louder but not especially loud. I was having a very good life in the real world. The kind of life most people dreamed of. I had already enjoyed the full catalogue of male fantasies. And a lot of interesting female ones. But sometimes, even when I was on stage, in the middle of a performance, getting great riffs out of my Rickenbacker, the murmur would grow suddenly louder, at first like a faint hum in the amplifiers, a badly stacked cabinet, some feedback; then the intensity rather than the sound level increased, an insistent whisper threatening to throw me off completely as I played. This felt like an attack and I decided the best way to deal with it was to ignore it. The worse it grew in my head, the more frenzied was my playing. Audiences loved it!

I still had no idea of the sound's nature. Its insistent quality appeared increasingly aggressive. I began to wonder if there was more than one force sending messages to me from the Sanctuary.

Although *New Worlds* now had to use a different distributor it looked as if the customers could find us. I broke with Stonehart Publications, who were neither passing on the Arts Council money nor supporting me in my struggle with authority, and became the sole publisher and owner of the title. The magazine had begun to do well again and I was considering handing it over in good order to someone else. My books were getting generous reviews. I appeared on radio and TV, became a subject for Sunday supplement interviews. Sales went up accordingly until we were seized in a raid on England's Glory, Manchester's alternative bookshop.

And then we were back in a new nightmare, another campaign. We were never alone, but the fight went on for ever and everyone was getting so weary and I wanted to keep with my kids. I wasn't going to wreck it, hurt the woman I loved. We'd been tested and found true and trustworthy. But at some point where the coke and the speed met the mary jane and the wine my poor, puny little ego decided that promises were negotiable, for ordinary people. There was no brain in the equation. Not a gram. I decided I must go to Alsacia and, as I put it, face my demons. But I didn't do anything about it until I saw the Lagonda again.

I went into Fleet Street to meet old friends who still worked there. I needed to see them. They were barely interested in my career or my fame, and they kept me grounded. Until, sure enough, one day I turned a corner into Whitefriars Street off Greystoke Place into Carmelite Inn Chambers and saw that the gates were open. I had a glimpse of the Alsacia. I was almost hyperventilating as I paused to look. Backing into the stableyard of The Swan With Two Necks was the same green Lagonda that had followed me in Notting Dale. The car, the raven said, had been sent from Alsacia to pick me up. I wanted a better look. I moved towards it as its long bonnet slid backwards out of sight.

Then the gates closed in my face and I burst into tears. I went home. I didn't say anything but Helena was concerned. She was sure I was cracking up. She wanted me to see a doctor. I raved at her. I didn't want a doctor. And of course I watched my wife begin to doubt her own judgement. So what did I do next? You guessed it; I made another trip to the Alsacia, or at least to the gates, and began hanging around, trying to get in. I would drink myself silly in one of my old favourite places and then stagger down there. Eventually the police were called. They took me home in a police car. Helena was even more worried about me. Again I told her I didn't need help. I was fine.

Helena wasn't fine. In spite of my obsession I saw that she was growing miserable. Her face was drawn. She doubted herself worse than ever. I couldn't let her think she was going crazy when I was the cause. I spilled the beans to her. I'm so sorry, I said. I told her what was happening to me. It was the whispering voices, I said. I can't get them out of my head. I expected a tearful reconciliation. Instead, she set me up with another shrink. I was delusional.

I saw that guy once, too. Largactil again. He was useless. Resentfully, I decided I must face the Alsacia. I *had* to find out what it was all about. I told this to Helena. I told her that the noises in my head went away in the Alsacia. So someone or something was sending the Swarm from there. Why was that? I had to try to get back there and learn what was going on. I begged her to come with me.

'Mike,' she said seriously, 'I love you. I like being married to you. But if you insist on pursuing this delusion I don't think I can stay married.'

'I can't make a promise, Helena. I wish I could. The noises are driving me nuts. I've got to get rid of them!'

'See a doctor. That's all I'm asking.'

'I've seen a doctor. He didn't know anything. He couldn't help me.'

'Then do what you like, but remember what I'm saying.'

'I'll be altogether better as a husband and a father if I can get all this behind me,' I said. Helena refused to look at me.

'Please yourself,' she said grimly.

CHAPTER NINETEEN

THE LARKS

The next time I went to Fleet Street to drop off copy I had a quick drink with Bill Baker and then made for Carmelite Inn Chambers. Whether or not I was justified, I felt betrayed and desperate, determined to know whether I was experiencing an hallucination or not. I wanted Helena with me. I wanted to show her the truth. By the time I got into the maze of streets between Fleet Street and the Thames I was on a mission. That was when I saw the big green Lagonda driving down Carmelite Street, admired by more than one passer-by. The raven had mentioned it. So I knew it wasn't an illusion.

When I reached Carmelite Inn Chambers the gates were not only there, they were partially open and the Lagonda was vanishing through the gap. Without any hesitation I ran forward and opened the doors further. Then I paused. From the other side I heard the shouts of angry men and, amazingly, the sound of steel on steel, as if some kind of brawl with knives or swords were taking place. Perhaps I had been right, years ago, and these actually were the premises of a small movie studio. My drugged brain had just made a lot of a few props from old Hammer pictures.

My impression was confirmed as I squeezed through the gates and saw, directly in front of me, three men in clothes I associated with the mid-seventeenth century. One faced two others. All held naked steel. They were fighting. One had his back to me. He wore the befeathered hat and lace of a military fop. A blue silk tabard! He stood with his sword point resting on the cobbled ground casually baiting the other two who had paused in their assault.

I had seen that nasty pair before! The short untidy man was dressed like his antagonist, a Cavalier, but wore the costume badly. His tall companion wore drab black and plain white, a stained high-crowned black hat on his cropped head. This was the couple who had come after me on that distant foggy Friday night and been challenged by the mysterious soldier. The plump untidy red-headed scarlet-faced Welshman was self-commissioned Colonel Clitch. At whose side was his faux pious, cadaverous compatriot, Corporal Love. Cromwell's thief-takers! A dangerous pair! I stood there gaping in confusion.

When their opponent turned his head a fraction I recognised him with delight. He was a self-professed thief, Moll's friend, who bore the name of one of the characters I wrote about. The laughing Cavalier highwayman! The gallant musician! Captain Claude Duval!

Duval was a brilliant swordsman. He was happy to rest and goad the Parliamentarians until, full of fury, red-faced and breathing heavily, Love and Clitch rushed him. With an air of reluctant good manners, he re-engaged them with a silver blur of steel. 'Good day to you, Master Moorcock!' he called over his shoulder, laughing with pleasure as his sharp sword cut the plain homespun worn by the Puritan, who swore in a very ungodly way and retreated. Duval's adversaries were good swordsmen but he was more than their equal. This clearly was more than a rehearsal for a drama. Duval moved suddenly. One of the pair had scored a hit on his left arm. The spot was darkening. This was either real blood or very good imitation stuff.

Now there was a thin scratch on Corporal Love's cheek which looked suspiciously like a sword cut. Those foils were not blunted. I began to wish I'd chosen a better moment to drop in.

About to murmur an excuse and step back around the gates, I heard a cry from the other side of the cobbled square. On the street-side balcony of The Swan With Two Necks tavern, above the big main gates, stood a figure in a blood-red cloak whom I recognised as the mysterious man the friar had called 'Your grace'. Around this prince's waist was a broad sash of the almost tasteful Stuart plaid. Into this was jammed a couple of big pistols. His hat held more feathers than the posteriors of a whole clutch of ostriches, dyed a dozen vivid colours. As he settled this on his head he saw me and called out, brandishing two rapiers in one hand while, in a great swirl of scarlet edged with foaming lace, he jumped the parapet shouting, 'Ho, sir! Hold your place. I'll bring ye a blade to defend your faith!' And before I knew it he had landed, laughing, on the ground and run towards the fight, throwing a sword to me straight over the head of the startled Puritan. I caught it automatically. A well-balanced épée rather than a rapier. I had never used one in a real fight.

Also, apart from a few friendly passages with Kevin at the old Brookgate sports club, I had hardly picked up a sword in years. This weapon definitely had the heft and balance of an épée though, not the sabre I favoured. The real blood on the Puritan's cheek proved this bout wasn't all that friendly. My first impulse was to throw the sword down and escape but before I knew it the grinning, unsavoury Love had turned his attention to me and I was defending myself with the distinct impression I was fighting for my life! Then the prince was in front of me, protecting me from Love's advances.

My heart was pounding and my legs were shaking. Why bother to throw me a sword?, I thought. As the prince turned his man so that his back was to me I signalled puzzlement. 'What is the sword for?'

'For them!' called the prince in response.

'For them?' Love and Clitch were no longer threatening me.

'No, blockhead, for *them*!'

I turned to look behind me.

To my baffled surprise through the open gates rushed men in steel war hats; woollen shirts; long, leather waistcoats; breastplates and greaves. Their short hair and russet homespun identified them as Cromwellian soldiers of the New Model Army. These Roundheads or 'redcoats' already had their swords drawn or halberds at the ready and ran confidently towards us. The halberd was a horrible weapon, half spear, half axe, much favoured against cavalry. Now I found myself standing back to back with Duval, hearing Duval speak in that same rich, old French. 'My prince! You should guard thine own safety. I can deal with these arsemouths.'

The prince laughed. 'I know it, Monsieur Duval, but ye'd not begrudge this lad and myself a little sport, would ye?'

That was one of those moments when I wish I had been offered the chance to speak on my own behalf.

Sensing my discomfort – you might almost call it fear – Corporal Love managed somehow to sneer and grin at the same time. He pressed his advantage for a moment until suddenly the prince was engaging Colonel Clitch and Duval's sword blade lay across Love's shoulder as, paling, the puritanic Welshman turned.

Thwack! The tall, black Quaker hat went spinning, knocked from Love's head by the laughing highwayman. In haste the thief-taker put his back to me while Duval pressed him further and further across the cobbles. Meanwhile I had another opponent in one of the Round-heads who worked a big pistol from his sash as he engaged me. Now I faced the prospect of being shot as well as stabbed! All I could do was to press him as hard as possible, relying on my advantage of height and reach, for I was pretty much a foot taller than any soldier and could give the tallest a good six inches. Here, I was virtually a giant! For all these advantages, I couldn't see how we were going to escape from the situation. I was reconciled to capture or death. In my present mood of self-pity I didn't much care which.

It was then I heard a further commotion. I inched around, driven back by my opponents. With a wary eye on a pistol, I saw four more brightly dressed Cavaliers running from the inn. Drawing their swords they cried in the same warm brogue as the prince, '*Aux armes, mousquetaires! Tous pour un! Un pour tous!*' Sure enough. No schoolboy of my generation would fail to recognise the war cry of the Three Musketeers (actually four with D'Artagnan) as, all for one and one for all, they threw themselves joyfully into the battle, instantly turning the tide with their astonishing display of unified, disciplined swordsmanship. These really were men who made an art of their calling and I could only pause and watch for a moment as the huge Porthos, perhaps even taller than me; the handsome Athos; the cool, smiling Aramis; half saint, half killer and hot-headed, stocky D'Artagnan took on an enemy outnumbering us three to one. Somehow they also managed to protect me as the fight went back and forth across the cobbles.

Meanwhile, escaping the conflict like the cowards they were Clitch and Love directed their soldiers from afar now, refusing to be drawn back in by the jeers of the Cavaliers.

Bang! More than one pistol exploded! Balls of lead flew across the little square outside The Swan With Two Necks. *Bang! Bang!* The Roundheads, losing swords, relied increasingly on their massive pistols. Ignoring the whizzing lead, the Cavaliers pressed the Roundheads before they could reload. They had begun disarming some of the soldiers when Colonel Clitch called the order to withdraw and they fell back to the still-open gate, helping their wounded. And vanished. No great damage had been done, but where had they gone? Not into the London I knew, for certain. From the way local citizens appeared so suddenly I wondered if this was an unremarkable event these days in the Alsacia. And why was everyone wearing clothes of a hundred years earlier than the last time I'd visited? I looked down at the sword in my hand, then looked up again. One Parliament man still stood at the gate, glaring at me.

For all we had not insisted on our advantage, that retreating Roundhead stared into my eyes, making me shiver as if in a fever. He was the embodiment of vicious evil. 'Ye've made an enemy of Jake Nixer, my lad. Only fools and rogues side with the Stuarts. Parliament and the people rule England now, in God's name. We'll meet again, ye papist pup, and when we do Jake Nixer will lead. We'll have no need of mercenary cowards like Love and Clitch. I'll meet ye again and I'll be sure to spare ye no advantage.'

The prince was immediately at my side, his hand on my arm. He was almost as tall as I. 'Well done, young man. Ye fought well for a towny 'prentice.'

'Which I'm not,' I insisted.

Which of course brought more teasing from the Cavaliers, who seemed to have adopted me as a kind of mascot.

'Let's celebrate our victory,' suggested Duval, leading me towards The Swan With Two Necks, 'and then you can explain to us, M'sieur St Maur, how one such as yourself, a –'

'My name's not Maur. It's Moorcock. I'm not an apprentice. In fact I'm a paid-up member of the NUJ and have been for years. I'm a writer.'

'– a snivelling scrivener, yet able to give such soldierly account of himself. Cocky Maur it is, then!'

'I had lessons at the local institute,' I said, not really hearing this.

'I have to thank you, m'sieur. I think you saved my life at least five times just then.'

Duval seemed of a naturally cheerful disposition. 'As you'd have saved mine in the same circumstance.' He clapped me on the back.

We approached the inn. One of the street doors opened and from it stepped my companion of the steel toby. My heroine. Laughing and glorious. Moll Midnight with a huge white dog beside her. 'Boye! Here, lad!' called the prince. The dog ran up to greet its chuckling master. Moll's red hair was still in ringlets which bounced as she ran to throw her arms around me and give me an enthusiastic hug.

'Why, it's Master Michael, all grown up!' She still seemed much younger than I. She was as beautiful as ever with her pale skin, those violet eyes and crimson lips. Even though she mocked me it was pretty clear she rather fancied me now I was bearded, well dressed and aggressively assured in most things except the duel to the death.

I realised that the whispering in my ears had stopped.

CHAPTER TWENTY

RETREAT

'LET'S LIFT A bumper or two to welcome young Master Maur's Cocke, who might be my own nephew.' Still teasing, the tall prince locked his arm in mine while Moll took the other. I had never felt so free from care, so fully among friends as I felt that moment at The Swan With Two Necks. Prince Rupert of the Rhine recalled his beloved brother Maurice of whom I reminded him 'in all but size'. Duval spoke nostalgically of his days at King Charles's Court and the French musketeers drank to the death of all cardinals. They swore the present pope was bad enough to turn an honest papist Protestant.

I assumed Prince Rupert, being a Stuart and the nephew of the king, to be a Roman Catholic, too, but when I said something to that effect he showed real anger.

'I am a Protestant, young Maur's, through and through. I have defended my religion against all threats – and I assure you, sir, they were real. Neither defeat in battle nor Jesuits and Inquisition have converted me to their cause. When I was imprisoned, sir, King Ferdinand sent priests to me almost daily. For two years. I am in every sense a confirmed Protestant. To the marrow. My sword was always in service against the pope, though that's not why I fight in England. Here, my uncle, King Charles, goes to stand upon that scaffold not because he chose the pope over his sworn religion but because he refused to bow to the dictates of holier-than-thou fanatic Puritans who believe a papist lies under every bed and every lapdog is a familiar.' He put his arm about my waist. 'They'll find they've been duped and their cursed rebellion no more than the instrument of the few to enrich themselves. The majority fight not for liberty but for gold.' His flounced lace rustling, he called for more ale and patted the bench. That large, unruly white dog came to stand with its forepaws on his leg, panting for an anticipated treat. 'Ain't that so, Boye.' The dog was a huge poodle, one of the original hunting dogs from which the smaller breed came. He seemed a good-natured animal. I heard he travelled everywhere with his master. I would learn that a Puritan propagandist's favourite trick was to accuse an enemy of witchcraft. A faithful dog was a 'familiar', their equivalent of suspected WMDs in your palace.

Later, and more thoroughly in his cups, Prince Rupert confided that he fought in this case not for faith but for blood and friendship. 'An adventure you would find most satisfying, Master Maur'sson. Had you any inclination to join our cause.'

I smiled and shook my head. 'My vocation is to watch and note,' I said. 'Participation is forbidden me, your grace.' I recognised someone as good at talking people into ideas as I was.

The prince's expression was almost melancholy as I lifted my tankard in what I hoped was a graceful salute.

'Your help would greatly facilitate us,' he said quietly.

'I have responsibilities,' I said, feeling a hypocrite. I took a long drink.

To break the moment, Prince Rupert drew us all in with a gesture so that he could tell us a story. His oddly accented English was pleasant to the ear. His long hair was naturally curly and kept falling into his eyes. His beard and moustache were as well groomed as my own. I was astonished that his exaggerated linen stayed as clean as it did. He used a shake of his lace cuff to emphasise a point. A direct and charming man, fond of bad language and casual insult, he commanded considerable loyalty. He was a great general. If he had been a better courtier he might have beaten Cromwell and saved his uncle's crown. Now he seemed tired and I wasn't surprised when he made his excuses and stumbled off to bed.

Cavaliers were skilled at the art of celebration. It had been a long time since I'd heard so much good-natured laughter in one place. These men were hard drinkers and eloquent speakers. They had magnificent stories. I particularly enjoyed Porthos's account of a spy and a case of poisoned wine. It was wonderful to be accepted into that legendary company and for the moment at least I stopped trying to explain what was happening. I was thoroughly distracted and really had no incentive just then to ask questions of myself or this place.

Moll flirted with me all night. I felt no guilt when I responded, just elation. Harmless pleasure. I wished Helena had not been such a sceptic and had come with me. I knew how much she would enjoy herself. I was sure she would be no happier in the middle-class world her mother wanted for her. I had not, of course, turned my back on Ladbroke Grove. I loved my children more than anything. Was I learning, like Henry Kissinger, that power was the greatest aphrodisiac? So many temptations! Sweet threats to my dream of domesticity.

As the evening progressed I relaxed as if into a warm bath. I was scarcely refusing responsibility to my family in the material sense. In the Alsacia I had as much emotional responsibility as in a dream. Two shants of porter helped me towards happy compromise. Moll's attitude towards me was different. She said I was masterful. Time had gone forward *and* backward in the Alsacia. I had left Moll when I was a boy. I was returning to her a man of the world. And now she seemed several years younger than I. I was glad. So when Moll suggested we retire to some privacy, I hungrily agreed. If Helena wanted to divorce me, I'd give her grounds. Later I would know regret and guilt, but not now. Now I was free of the Whispering Swarm.

Somehow I said goodnight to my new friends. I followed Moll up that same old wooden stair to the apartment on the third floor of the tavern. Once we were inside I began to kiss her but she pulled away, unbuttoning her frock, laughing in that deep, throaty way I still love. I was aware of her perfume, her soft, curling red-brown hair, her violet eyes and that delightful smile at once challenging and yielding.

She took my hand. 'Let's go to bed,' she said.

BOOK TWO

Fear the fulfilment of thy deep desires.

– The Book of Ariach

CHAPTER TWENTY-ONE

COMRADES ALL

I WENT UP to Fleet Street to phone Helena and tell her that I was fine. I would arrange to have a few things picked up. I had signed myself into a retreat, I said. A monastery. I thought it was for the best. After a pause she agreed and asked how she could get in touch. I told her the monks wouldn't allow us phone calls and for a while I couldn't have visitors. I would come to see her at my first chance. Meanwhile if she needed me urgently she could contact me through Barry Bayley, who knew how to reach me. I spoke to the girls and told them I loved them. I was doing research for a book. While I was out I dropped in on my mum and gave her much the same story. I phoned Barry, told him where I was and how he could contact me. I asked him to get some stuff for me from Ladbroke Grove. He was the only one who knew where the gates were. He met me just inside. He wouldn't come any further. He didn't like what was happening.

'Mike, this is all a bit weird. Are you sure you know what you're up to?'

I told him Helena didn't care what I did. She'd had enough of me. I was accepting the inevitable. He was still concerned. He asked me to come back to Ladbroke Grove with him and when I refused he shook his head. 'I think this is a mistake.'

'At this stage all I have is a choice of mistakes.'

Barry's inclination was to do nothing until circumstances changed, but that wasn't how I handled things. As Helena said, I made decisions even when there was no possible decision to make.

Molly found us a fine suite of rooms in the south wing of The Swan With Two Necks. They were across the stableyard from the first set I had seen. The apartment was furnished snugly. It had an air of calm. I at once began to relax. I realised that I had forgotten what it was to stop worrying. To know peace. I had been anxious for years, trying to reach deadlines, making sure the family was fed and sheltered, keeping the magazine going, not listening to the Swarm and making sure I generally took care of everyone. I got authors jobs or publishers. I was persuasive, even when I wasn't trying. I had a gift, that was all. My mother said it was for blarney. My Uncle Willie had had it. After he retired from the trams he sold high-end cars to toffs. Mr Ackermann said Willie could have talked Hitler into becoming a Zionist.

The pace of the Sanctuary was peaceful most of the time. All my life I had rarely found the quiet my temperament craved. Life with Moll was like a holiday. She was as sentimental as I was. She saw the world romantically. If anything, Helena was a cultivated doubting Thomas, a rationalist from a home of rationalists rebelling against a Methodist background. Although hard-working, Helena made a bohemian virtue of chaos. Molly's rooms were neat and tranquil. At night you could hear almost nothing. In contrast, our home in Ladbroke Grove was like a lunatic asylum. Yet I often missed the noise, the upheavals, the quarrels, the intellectual arguments around the big rectory table. Realistically I knew why this thing with Moll felt like a holiday. Because it *was* a holiday. It wasn't really supposed to last. I knew life was only simple when focused by the beginnings of a love affair or the prospect of sudden death. I felt horribly guilty. I really was desperate because I did love Helena. And the children. But I went ahead anyway.

What made me want Molly so badly? I have tried to analyse her appeal to me. She wasn't really my type except she struck a chord in me. An echo, a powerful resonance. She was my dream girl. Even in the throes of love and lust, I wondered sometimes if maybe she wasn't more than one person's dream girl. Maybe that was the secret of her success.

Very shortly after I moved to the Alsacia to be with Molly, my anger subsided. I began to feel homesick as well as guilty about what I was doing. Like most of my friends I was essentially a family man. I missed my children. I had never fantasised about having affairs. I had sown plenty of wild oats. There was almost nothing sexual I hadn't tried more than once. I knew myself fairly well. I knew what I needed. Simple. To love and be loved. Ambiguity was my enemy. I grew nostalgic. South Kensington, with its museums and posh shops, is nearly always sunny in my memories of those early years with Helena. I told Molly that I felt as if I were the character in the folk tale who visits the fairy village for a night and can never find his way back. Or perhaps I'd get home to find that like Rip Van Winkle I had slept for an age. I was almost afraid to leave. I was hoping for reassurance, rather than an answer. Molly seemed sympathetic. But she didn't share my anxieties.

'There's no secret to it,' Molly insisted. 'Nothing but fast-growing grass and a certain trick of light and fog.'

Yes, that was what she said and I did not bother to ask her to repeat it. I thought I had caught her meaning, the way you do with an unfamiliar slang. I wonder if I heard only what I wanted to hear, as Helena claimed.

Molly knew the Alsacia pretty well. We spent some of our time wandering around the little streets and alleys. She wanted to show me favourite places. She had been born here but her mother was originally Iranian. Moll wouldn't talk much about her. After a while the smell became familiar. Its thoroughfares were mostly narrow lanes and cul-de-sacs resembling the maze of a Moroccan *mellah*, where Jews were confined to a tiny area of a city. The cobbled alleys were slightly canted to the middle, forming crude gutters carrying off waste to a central sewer and from there into the fast-running Fleet. All the streets and gutters had to be washed down by hand using big yellow cakes of soap and boiling kettles. The few children to be found in the Sanctuary loved to play in the foaming water. It was the only time they were bathed. Yet they all showed signs of good health in spite of the unsanitary conditions. I could only speculate about the toughness of the immune systems in the ones who survived.

Many of the Sanctuary's streets weren't cobbled at all but were made of hard-compacted wood, grit, mud and old stone put down in Roman times and hardened over the centuries. While it often misted or fogged, the Alsacia never knew real rain while I was there. The streets would have turned to deep mud. People were not short of water. They drew it from the Thames by bucket or hand pump. There was no modern embankment then. Strangely, they could never see to the far bank. The fog was always thickest on the dockside. While watermen occasionally rowed back and forth, they spent most of their time together ashore in an unwelcoming quayside pub called The Lost Apprentice. It was painted in the same murky shades as the fog itself and was only identifiable by the brownish angles of its walls and the obscured sign bearing a few faded letters – ST APP. All kinds of dark superstitions surrounded The Lost Apprentice. Nobody else in the Alsacia ever went there without an excellent reason.

Few others lived along the riverline. In the winter the water froze. It was always dank; bitter cold at night and not much nicer by day. In the streets running back from the river and to the west of the abbey, little shops sat next to houses next to potteries and breweries and slaughterhouses and bakers and warehouses and all the other trades and crafts of an old-fashioned community. From one alley you might suddenly see an eruption of complaining goats or glimpse through an archway a courtyard where a pair of big Jersey cows were milked. People drew the line at pigs. Chickens were more populous than the midden heaps they favoured and eggs were frequently covered in dung. There's sometimes a fine line between what you are about to eat and what you have recently eaten. I have never tasted better eggs.

The Alsacia had very few customs or practices I associated with good hygiene. But the livestock showed how the Sanctuary was able to remain self-sufficient. I think they bought flour or grain and had it delivered by river. You were fine if you had the sense to boil all drinking water over your mule-manure fire. Many Londoners I knew identified the Alsacia's predominant smells with good health, the cure for everything from TB to the monthlies. I had grown up playing in sewage outlets feeding the hidden Fleet, covered for a century or more. I could easily see how the district had become a zone of safety, able to withstand attacks from the outside world. As far as the authorities were concerned it wasn't worth the effort to try to catch the average crook who was anyway contained by the Alsacia and rarely likely to leave. Most who fled to the Alsacia's protection were only occasionally worse than debtors or petty thieves and the prisons were already overcrowded. So, until now, that was why the place was tolerated. Alsacia judged murder as foul as those on the outside and their justice was swifter than any to be found at the Old Bailey. For these reasons no city watch could ever recruit men to die in the Sanctuary of the White Friars, where the inhabitants were known to defend their territory with well-kept weapons – to the death. 'We cause them no discomfort, they'll cause us no pain' was a popular motto.

As to a scientific basis for the Sanctuary's existence, I was sure one would be forthcoming. I rejected any kind of supernatural explanation. Helena was fond of saying that, if the supernatural should ever manifest itself in a form impossible to refute, then logically it would suggest the existence of God, whatever we meant by the word. But why was Alsacia under attack by Cromwell's Puritans and hireling mobsmen like Clitch and Love? When had the Sanctuary needed to hide itself this way in time and space? And what was the exact nature of its enemy?

Whatever the answers, the Alsacia had hidden itself cleverly in recent centuries. How was that? Some trick of light and atmosphere? I had already seen one example of the abbot's sophisticated scientific instruments. No matter how the trick was done, it was achieved at the very heart of the scandal factory where so many of the British 'red-tops', the tabloids, had their headquarters. Fleet Street would have loved the story. I could imagine the *News of the World* headlines: SECRET LONDON DEFIES THE LAW. **Where Was Scotland Yard?** An irony. A bit like hiding from the escaped lion in his own cage. How they did it remained a mystery. Some fluke, I thought. A bubble in time. But of course there were other factors I refused to let myself consider.

The Alsacia was the closest I had seen in Europe to a complete mediaeval town, yet it had incongruous aspects of modernity. A couple of bicycles were near useless on the cobbles but were always parked near the main gate. The only music was performed on slightly weird instruments. Electricity was unknown. Records were played on wind-up gramophones. Nothing requiring batteries or gas worked. Electric music couldn't exist. I missed that almost as much as I missed my home. No TV. No radio. Even the records were pre-electric 78s. I used an old

Imperial 50/60 manual typewriter and bought my supplies in a tumble-down shop which sold paper, notebooks and accessories for typewriters going back to the 1880s. Some people dressed in nineteenth- and early-twentieth-century clothes, some in a mixture of several periods, though the seventeenth century was increasingly favoured. Some signboards had modern lettering or painting. One shop sold almost nothing but Cadbury chocolates, Rowntree's sweets, Jacob's and McVitie's biscuits and Wall's ice cream. All from the outside world and all retailing for silver rather than copper. Another offered books of all periods, including some vividly coloured contemporary SF, detective stories and, perhaps most incongruously, a lurid French Foreign Legion series of paperbacks, side by side with the 1910s Aldine *Dick Turpin Library* and mint-condition 1930s *Schoolboys' Own Library*. I found a Robin Hood *TPL* with one of my stories. All were too expensive for what they were, from 5/3*d* to a guinea. A few hundred yards outside Alsacia, where they still existed, they were 6*d* and 1/-. When I remarked on this the bookseller said the prices were fair. The titles were imports. There were dangers involved, arcane laws could be invoked. What 'dangers'; what laws? Surely he exaggerated! Those were the days when in the England beyond Alsacia inessential imports were banned and it was hard to obtain anything from America or even Canada. I still get a buzz when I see those big Sunday pages from the *Toronto Star* sent to us by relatives and friends. They were free supplements. The 'funnies', with *Flash Gordon, Terry and the Pirates, Prince Valiant* and Burne Hogarth's *Tarzan*. Wonderful stuff. But when a newsagent had the nerve to charge for them, I would get furious.

In Alsacia I was especially irritated by the high prices charged for paperbacks and pulps, many of them produced so close by, actually printed on machines in Fetter Lane and Farringdon Street, home to the famous Amalgamated Press, where Meg Midnight's adventures were still being told. 'Imported from where?' I asked once, waving a recent copy of *Thriller Picture Library* featuring my character Dogfight Dixon, RFC. The newsagent was charging five shillings for a one-shilling comic book. Pulling me away, Molly told me they were expensive not because they were saying they were American, as in the world beyond our walls, but because here few people ever managed to bring in stuff from outside at all, often risking a great deal. I found that a bit hard to swallow but I didn't argue. I stopped manhandling Dogfight and put him back on the rack. That was actually the first time I noticed that the newsagent also had magazines from the 1920s and '30s side by side with more recent comics. Time and space were truly skewed here. *The Passing Show* and *Detective Weekly* were as spanking new as my own *Thriller Library*! Many mint prewar story papers were cheaper than the prices dealers charged in the world outside.

Finally one day I swallowed my fear and asked Molly some questions. I hated to ask them. The answers might explode this dream and I might lose her for ever. But I went for it anyway. How could Alsacia exist with so little apparent intercourse between it and my familiar world? Why was there such an erratic connection in time with that world? Was Alsacia set up this way for a reason? 'Why can I come and go and others seem to be prisoners? Or are we *all* prisoners of our own half-imaginary habitat? There aren't many rational theories about Alsacia, Molly. None that ever impressed me as more than supernatural gobbledegook. Honestly, the place goes against all logic! There has to be some kind of scientific explanation for it, unless we're dreaming it somehow. Or it's dreaming *us*.'

As usual she took her time answering. 'You will hear convincing arguments at some point, Mike, but from learned, wise men. Not from me or marketplace thespians or all the rogues of the rookery, but from people who understand the nature of the Alsacia. Most ordinary Alsacians won't go outside the gates because they're afraid they'll not get back. And ultimately death waits for them "outside", whereas here they can practically live for ever. Death itself, they say, protects this Sanctuary. But of course these are superstitions. They cannot grasp the subtleties, so content themselves with romantic, superstitious, imaginative nonsense, plucked from a fairy tale. We all do it.' Her violet eyes held a candour I trusted. She made light of our situation, but understood more than she cared to admit.

'What are they really afraid of, Moll?' I spoke almost without thinking.

'As I said, it's mortality.' Sometimes she sounded like a bored teacher to a child. She treated me the same in bed when she thought I was naïve and too prudish to play some violent game which I'd previously tried and disliked. Sometimes I felt so much older! My experience of most ongoing threesomes, for instance, was that ultimately they created emotional confusion for someone. Too many conflicting agendas. Some games also involved a loss of privacy, of self. She didn't believe that I hadn't particularly liked them. In the right circumstances I could play as cruelly as the next man but I was virtually incapable of objectifying a sexual partner. I had friends with open marriages and could see they managed their lives well enough. When I tried it, I became confused, emotionally and psychologically.

Amused by what she thought of as my prudery Moll loved me enough to accept how I felt. I in turn loved her for what I thought of as her courage and curiosity. The power of the imagination could create a positive monogamy. But I knew it couldn't really last.

CHAPTER TWENTY-TWO

MY GAMES

I TOLD MOLLY I hated games. But really both of us played a game. We didn't know the rules and we didn't know what there was to win or lose. To a greater degree than I realised at first, our rôles were changing. They weren't especially healthy. Against everything I had ever felt like doing I now encouraged other fantasies. Ah, the taste of them. Power and submission. It dawned on me that she had no boundaries. I, like many, had determined my own. Autodidacts like me worked out some rules for ourselves, a moral position. She had no rules except what she borrowed from me, what she interpreted as my desires. She now possessed a not unattractive ambiguous quality. Was she auditioning rôles? Had she turned herself into a quasi-child whom I could fuck whenever I felt like? What was happening? I didn't like women who liked that crap! All it did was feed a hunger, something which must be exorcised or satisfied and accommodated. It felt vaguely nasty. We hovered on the edge of a terrible temptation which I knew in my bones would become an addiction to poison my life and very probably hers, too. She wanted the experience again. The sweet, fantastic, all-consuming sensations she had shared with her first important lover, whom she called her 'cavalier'. I was jealous of him. I saw him as a rival. I was competing with him, following not my own desires but his. Her mentor? I asked. Did he live in the Alsacia? Sometimes, she said. I was pretty sure at that point it was Turpin, which was why he was off hunting double-deckers on the Cambridge Express run. I had hardly seen him or any of his compatriots since I arrived. The 'cowboys' had all disappeared. They had met in Oxford. I couldn't imagine Buck Jones in The High. Or could her old lover be Duval? D'Artagnan? One of the other musketeers? All were great horsemen, of course, and as such could be called 'cavaliers'.

I refused to admit to myself that Molly so thoroughly engaged my emotions. I think she believed it was possible to compartmentalise her life because she had seen men do it. But not all men do it, and it's usually harder still for women. It drives them crazy. They're not trained to kill feeling. Moll wanted to enhance it. I could never really see it like that. Slow, romantic foreplay was what I liked, no matter what we followed it with. I favoured a romantic calling, and harnessing my nature was what I was about. Between my craft, my magazine and my rock band, I could have my pick of what most young men would consider unobtainable. I was constantly offered what old perverts craved and could only find by paying whores. We hadn't become avant-garde only in terms of the arts. We changed the norm for lovemaking. We were in the vanguard of the sexual revolution, in those brief decades from sexual liberation to the New Puritans, to HIV and AIDS. I would come to understand how she was addicted to fantasy and the indirect uses of power and how that addiction would become the main problem in our relationship, threatening break-up. But that day was still far away. I believed I was helping her feel more secure and that if she was secure she would not need fantasy to bring pleasure. Yet, when I could and because I loved her, I did my best to play the games she wanted. The days rolled by, passion still unspent.

Perhaps because I was so relieved not to suffer the Swarm, I did not recognise the signs of a weird kind of depression. A depression which still haunts me. I did not want to admit that I was missing the children and Helena. No matter where I am, that strange, overheated period of my life sometimes returns to mystify me.

There was Moll, as beautiful as always, as attached to me as ever. My angel. My muse. My damnation. She occasionally sensed my sudden moments of terror. There were periods when I got a flash forward to the future, times when I dreamed a scene accurately and in detail, something she would actually be doing, perhaps, and hadn't told me about. I had done that since childhood. Women thought me psychic. I didn't know what it meant. My mother could consistently pick winners. Auntie Ethel had taught me to read the tarot with an accuracy which scared me. I hated that accuracy. But Father Grammaticus also spoke admiringly of 'psychic' talents I remained sceptical about. More than once he talked about Radiant Time. What was that? Part of the rational answer I yearned for?

'Why are they afraid of the outside world?' I repeated the question to her more than once. Her answers were never entirely satisfying. She was often amused.

'They fear they will die of plague or be attacked. Or eaten by cannibals,' she told me one day. 'They have so many stories of the World Beyond, as some call it. Your London will swallow them up or turn them mad or the law will have them and cart them off to jail or transport them as indentured servants, even slaves. The Sanctuary has been under attack almost constantly since the war between Parliament and the king. They have seen Cromwell's Roundheads make a little headway. Though they've made the place their headquarters, don't expect the Cavaliers to be here at all times. They trust neither king nor Protector. They fear the monks have been compromised in their compact with God. You've witnessed one attack by Nixer and his militia and seen how easily we beat them back. But Cromwell's power increases. I think we are now truly under threat. Should that great threat come, we have a fighting chance. A good one. The Alsacians will defend this place to the last man or woman.'

'And child?' I asked. She had already evaded my questions about why we saw so few small children here.

'It's a tradition with them to defend the Sanctuary, as it is to go armed. This place is, after all, a rogues' rookery.' She laughed. 'And you must defend what's your own. But really they fear those who hate them and would see them trampled into nothing, remembered by no-one.' I noticed that she again evaded a question but I lacked the will to challenge her.

'Well, I'm not sure the local council would go that far.' I joked, but Molly, who usually made light of things, was almost grave. She was no longer self-mocking. Her seriousness took me aback.

'We are freeborn English people and will stay so,' she insisted. 'There are those who would do us grave harm from within and from without. Corporal Love and Colonel Clitch and Jake Nixer, too. The first two are little better than mercenaries, though dangerous enough. We truly fear the likes of Nixer, who sincerely wish us scoured from the face of the Earth. You've met the Intelligencer General? Cromwell's former London Intelligencer Jacob Nixer? Once he was little more than a spy – now he is, after Cromwell himself, the most powerful man in the city. The two offices are the same. The Lord Protector acts under pressure from his own Puritans. Jake Nixer has full power to arrest and interrogate whomever he pleases. This man is charged to detect all crime, all wantonness, all witchery, all evil and devilry and pagan worship, all servants of Lucifer and his horrid angels including any others, mortal or supernatural, who threaten the Realm.' Her smile was humourless. 'He is perhaps our greatest single enemy, Jake Nixer, with Old Thunder and his growing band of cruel cronies. Privately, and do not ask how I know, Nixer fears he dreams and cannot wake up. I suspect he believes the Sanctuary to be sentient. Satan personified or the Colchian Dragon protecting our Treasure. He is possessed. Our Treasure and our deaths will release him, he says, from his dream. Odd fellow, eh?'

'And have you no hint of what he fears?'

'Hope you never discover.' She loved teasing me in that way. I could be quickly irritated by her constant flirting evasions.

Every day I remembered, with increasing bad conscience, that I still had a wife and children to support. At least at first Moll didn't seem to mind me spending the time I needed to bang out a book or two or write the odd feature. She seemed content just to be around, doing a bit of drawing, serving in the bar, going shopping, getting us an evening meal. Playing house. Much of the rest of the time we smoked hashish or sniffed coke and made love, still determinedly in the throes of first passionate romance.

One evening, when she came up late after serving in the bar, she was amused to find I had painted some Britain's toy soldiers I'd bought in a backstreet shop. They were an elaborately uniformed Indian Cavalry regiment from the mid-1920s in bright reds, yellows and greens. How they had ever got into the shop I couldn't think. I was fascinated by British colonial uniforms but had absolutely no interest in warfare. I used to say I was more interested in what caused wars. Painting those wonderful uniforms, using little pots of enamel and tiny brushes, helped me think and work out stories.

Moll smiled. 'Another man would be growing bored by now. Don't you feel confined by Alsacia's crowded streets?'

'Well,' I said, 'perhaps I'm too patient. I feel stimulated. You're my muse.' I had belted out three new Meg Midnight books in a new series. Twelve days' work. I was worn out.

Prostitution, she said. She didn't like me writing commercial fiction, particularly when it was about a fictionalised version of herself! To celebrate finishing the books, I was smoking a monstrous spliff she had rolled.

I needed the money and she knew it. 'If you don't want me to go on writing hack books, you might want to get back to the steel toby,' I suggested, remembering our raid on the tram. 'After all, I'm supporting two and a half households.' But I had enjoyed doing the books, I won't lie. There had been no demands in writing them. Smooth as silk, I said.

In so many ways this was an idyll, taking me away from all my emotional responsibilities. I hadn't worked so easily and at such a speed even at my fastest, not since I left my mother's. My only fear was that I would never be able to leave there. I wanted to know *how* Alsacia existed. And my curiosity threatened to separate me from my children. That was my main concern. I was, I realised reluctantly, increasingly homesick. But I would be missing them more if I were in America. Or even out of London. I was faintly surprised then that I called Ladbroke Grove home. I still did and still do.

I made an effort to recall how terrible my marriage could sometimes be, remembering my awful fits of temper taken out on innocent inanimate things in a shower of broken glass, pottery, woodwork and angrily twisted metal. Arguments in which I fought like a gorilla, constantly growling, displaying my strength as I backed away, never engaging in straightforward war. I hated violence. I hated threatening those weaker than myself, even if it was inadvertent. The anxieties were entirely to do with work. During those tantrums I became a horrible, monstrous child. Moll knew how to calm me down and I loved her for that. By treating me like a child she helped me check myself and behave like an adult. At other times she simply sucked my cock.

'I think the Restoration architects imagined the whole thing on classical lines so that as you approached from below you would walk up vistas of columns, trees and statuary. But commerce won, of course. Like so many British dreams of order, that one dream was eventually realised in Washington. Which in turn became the most glorious temple to Mammon the world had ever seen. Yet I have such a massive emotional investment in all it was supposed to mean. Hitler finished much of the work the Great Fire began!'

'I know.' Moll hugged my arm. 'You're hallucinating, aren't you? How big was that last hit? Won't you help them? They are all brave men of great resourcefulness. They need your special senses.'

I thought she must have taken a much bigger hit than I had! Why on earth would she suddenly ask me to join in a plot I'd almost be ashamed to offer in one of my Meg Midnight books? I found myself laughing. 'I'm not sure what's involved but I'm pretty certain my life insurance wouldn't pay up on it,' I said. I was an obsessive buyer of life insurance even then. I couldn't bear to think of Helena and the kids left like the family of so many writers I had known. Then Moll continued to chat on as normal. Ladies love normal. When they don't love weird. Chat, chat, calm, calm. Almost sent you to sleep. 'Alsacia offers so much but needs so much from us. And you can get lost – beyond our walls. Lost for ever…'

'Yet I used to lose the way *here*,' I reminded her. 'I feared I would never again be able to find my way back to the Sanctuary. And now I'm afraid I won't be able to get back to the kids.'

We had gone out onto the balcony for air. Either she understood or she made a very good pretence of it. I was alone and almost all that I loved had gone from London. Lost to me, invisible. London, my London, seemed as hard to enter as Heaven itself. Radiant Time. Did each different ray carry me further and further away? I had chosen the securities of a simplified past. I thought of Father Grammaticus and what he had told me. Time fans out from the massive and mysterious black star. She was here, with me. Here. No terrible future had opened up and gulped us down. We were safe. We could always get back. This was only one of many timelines. I could not lose my children. Who could pursue us into this version of the past? We had good and powerful friends who were inducting us into their secrets, perhaps preparing us to become adepts. 'So why do I have these terrors?'

'Dope,' she said. I missed her meaning. She did not elaborate. 'Yes, you're absolutely right, dear.' She stood up on tiptoe to kiss me. 'Hard to find and harder to leave, we say. But as to a proper scientific explanation of the phenomenon, which I know has good logic to support its existence, for that, darling, you'll have to ask someone else.' She had never called me darling before. A violet wink. 'I don't have the brains for it. The brothers and a few Cavaliers are the educated ones here. There's Friar Isidore crossing the quadrangle. Look!'

I told her I would see her later and on impulse off I went like a terrier after a ball. Down the outside steps from the gallery to the street and over the cobbles in pursuit.

I eventually caught up with Friar Isidore a few yards away from the abbey walls. Although reluctant to make a formal call on him I had been hoping to bump into him casually. He was delighted to see me. His thin, delicate skin rustled loudly and I was worried for him until I realised he'd hidden some papers in his sleeve. He showed me a glimpse of what looked like a freshly illuminated manuscript: gold, scarlet, blue and glowing green. He smelled faintly of mint and roses. And linseed oil.

As I panted for breath he waited patiently. Then I explained how I now had friends in the Sanctuary and was no longer merely a visitor, having made a home here. But as a new and enthusiastic resident I was curious about it all and wanted to know the secret of Alsacia's strange and stable position. How, for instance, could it be approached from the river? Invisibility existed only in stories and I'd grown out of *The Wizard of Oz*. I still discounted any supernatural explanation. There had to be a physical one. Were we – or most of us – quite literally its creations? Our ancestors could well have known far more than we did, and been closer to the truth. A pantheon! Think of that. Odin and Freya and Loki, Thor and the rest, each with their favourites, like the gods and goddesses of Mount Olympus. I was born into the first atomic age. Like Oppenheimer, say, I was a rationalist fascinated by metaphysics. What kind of bargain had the occupants of the Alsacia struck with some pantheon of superior beings? Was that bargain theoretically possible? I considered all the baroque language and images, the ritual and the colour of a fashion long passed. The very symbol of what rationalists hated? Overcomplicated? Or too simple?

'Why are so few able to find the Sanctuary? And what about the children? Why do adults live so long?' All these questions and speculations tumbled out of me.

He almost retreated in the face of my urgency. 'Master Michael, I am a simple monk. I am guided by our Creator. I know little of these questions. I live by my faith, not my intellect.' He smiled, his eyes as mild as always. 'We await the Conjunction of the Days. Then, I understand, all our questions will be answered.'

'The Days?' I asked. But he had scurried off. He did not want to be confronted. It sounded like an apocalyptic visionary notion. In the 1950s and '60s we had relatively few big cults or pseudo-religious groups. We tended to reject them, being deeply suspicious of them, from the Flat Earth Society to the Rosicrucians. Even in America, land of so many fake philosophers, Ayn Rand was still small beer, seen as the loony she was, and associated by most with the reactionary neofascist John Birch Society. Scientology and the rest had yet to offer the illusion of effect to large numbers of unhappy men and women. They were still down in East Grinstead, not yet, for the sake of the taxman, calling themselves a 'religion' but a 'science'. We were only at the very beginning of the new Age of Superstition. The Scientologists and flying-saucer nuts were mostly only known to the science fiction community, who were generally pretty sceptical, too. Religion was something we identified with Victorians and their forebears. Darwin, Freud, Einstein, even Marx had introduced us to scientific rationalism and we had felt a cleansing wind blowing across the world. But had reaction already set in? The reforming '60s were to become an environment of superstition, nostalgia and sentiment. Progress would prove lucrative! Consumerism was the enemy of education.

I'm still not quite sure how or when the '60s became an age of uncertainty, when crooks and charlatans suspended our disbelief, exploited a public made gullible by a series of astonishing ventures into space, when amazing advances in democracy and the popular arts combined with shocking barbarism in southern Asia. Even a sceptic like my Uncle Fred, before he died, began to talk about there being a lot of truth in stuff I still considered gobbledegook. I made my income by appealing to people's sense of wonder. I was a professional liar. I knew how it was done. And how easily it could be manufactured. I respected people's imaginations as much as their bodies. I wouldn't ever want to steal someone's faith or their crutches.

Sometimes Alsacia reminded me of my days in mass-produced fiction, when dozens of us created new characters and their backgrounds. We committed to a common illusion. We worked like they did in the old film studios. At the moment the Alsacia picture lacked a quality of authenticity, maybe? It only began to assume complexity. I felt a chill. It couldn't be a trap? The Days? The phrase was faintly familiar.

Apart from the monks, I didn't know anyone in the Alsacia who might have a reasonable scientific idea of how the place preserved itself. I would like to hear any kind of explanation, however farfetched. Duval advised me to ask Prince Rupert when he returned from France and the Low Countries. They said he vainly attempted to raise an army to free his king. If my reading of history was right, that wasn't going to happen. Assuming our history was the same!

I continued to work. They had begun to call me a fiction factory. I had kids to feed. Maybe because I was now living there but still had an outside connection, I could, unlike most of the inhabitants of the Alsacia, come and go as I wished. I soon arranged with Helena to visit the kids regularly. I took them to the pictures, to the zoo and the various parks and museums. Their mother seemed reasonably content, getting on with a new novel, living quietly, she said.

When I wasn't enjoying Moll's company I was writing another tale that was one part Jung, one part Freud and one part pulp. Nobody spotted it. I wasn't cynical about writing the stories, just about selling them. The outline had been approved. Sometimes I would go to the Westminster Reference Library, the London Library or the British Museum Reading Room and look for what I could find about Alsacia. Certainly no existing mainstream theory even began to touch on the phenomenon of somewhere remotely resembling the Alsacia, let alone explain it. I read folk tales which described similar places like

Les Hivers in Paris or Amsteldorp in Amsterdam. Then, of course, there were the rural 'fairy circles' and the like, where people disappeared and woke up days or years after they had disappeared. God knew how many of those there were! Only SF, or marginalised scientists like Haldane, would ever propose the existence of *pockets* of reality within a larger reality! Anomalies defining the generality.

Barry and I had discussed all this once, but marriage has a habit of discouraging abstract intellectualising. Older writers like Brian Aldiss and Jack Allard told me to lay off the wacky baccy. My contemporaries were interested and sympathetic, but were a bit sceptical when somehow I could never find the gates in their company, even though Barry had once slipped through ahead of me. Barry continued to believe me, but the trouble was very few people believed Barry. Everyone thought me an oddball genius pursuing all sorts of wild ideas. Where were the gates? Where the gates *should* be we'd see a neat pair of narrow eighteenth-century houses in Carmelite Inn Chambers. Lawyers' digs and offices. I'd even managed to get through to the back of one of the houses and seen a neat bit of lawn. I very easily doubted my own mind at those times.

If I had a healthy rationalism, common to my generation, I still loved a lot of the old, romantic stories. And so did my friends. It's what we shared with a previous generation. *The Big Sleep. Casablanca.* I needed someone like Barry to talk this over with. He had the most open mind, the most questing intelligence I ever knew, and could have helped me work out the puzzle, but unfortunately, soon after I began staying in the Alsacia, Barry and Dolores left for Telford to look after his sick dad. Even if he'd been sympathetic, Jack Allard was busy with his own concerns. He was planning some kind of pop-image exhibition and that was all he wanted to talk about. Max, my mentor and rôle model, was now permanently touring with a Hot Club of France tribute group, supporting George Melly. Temperamentally, he needed regular work. Rex Fisch and Jake Slade were back in the USA for the moment, raising dough; Lang Jones was newly married. Pete Taylor was fighting to save his marriage and other friends were drinking themselves to death in Spain, touring in mega rock bands, doing something brainy in academia, doing something romantic in Paris or pursuing errant lovers to Lima. Mervyn was in the Priory. I could never burden his wife, Maeve, with my problems. I had let all my other friends slowly slope off as I became less and less the man they recognised.

I only went out of Alsacia to see my mum, meet the girls, or perform an occasional gig with the Deep Fix. 'This book's taking you longer than normal,' said Helena. 'Have you sorted yourself out yet?' She knew more was going on than I'd told her. 'Maybe something in your retreat is slowing you down?' Of course, I was still fascinated by Molly and the Alsacia or I might have done something more to save my marriage and change my lifestyle. At that point I had come to care for my dream more than I worried about reality. I was reluctant to leave the Sanctuary for several reasons, the chief one being what the place sent after me when I left: the Whispering Swarm, rising, falling, crying and laughing, murmuring its inaudible secrets. Driving me nuts.

As a writer I wanted routine, consistency, and quiet more than I wanted sex. Ambiguity was the enemy of my ambitions. I *liked* monogamy. I *liked* investing in one person whom I got to know better and better and love more and more. But I chose the worst ways of demonstrating this. Maybe I was what Johnny van der Kroot, now *New Worlds*' lead critic, called me: a serial monogamist. When I visited Helena and put this to her, she retreated into silence, at least until the next bit of coke turned up.

Helena had probably been talking about me with people like Jill, who still worked part-time as my assistant, coming to the flat to deal with any correspondence and messages for a couple of days a week. If I hadn't been so involved with Molly I might have wondered which of my friends was already sleeping with Helena. But my instinct didn't tell me anything. Charlie Ratz, our designer, had decided I was schizophrenic, but the facts didn't support his theory. By then I really didn't care. I compromised in a way I'd decided worked for us all. I wanted everyone to be as happy as I was. I was still on holiday. Of course, I didn't put it quite like that to Helena. I had a bit of sense left. What I did notice was how much healthier and relaxed Helena had become, how well her novel was going, and how well the girls were getting on at school. I almost took credit for the lot. I had two wives. My ego had never been in better shape.

Full of Molly and work as most days were, I still continued to wonder about Alsacia's secrets. I knew there must be rational causes for the phenomenon. I was a materialist, perhaps because I was such an expert fantast. I knew there had to be a scientific principle for Alsacia, no matter how hard to grasp. But nobody wanted to talk about it. I thought they were afraid analysis would destroy them. They weren't the first to believe that, of course. I had the same superstition to a degree. If anything, it's easier to understand nowadays. They didn't want to be deconstructed. Their experience and instincts told them that deconstruction could be the preliminary to commodification. In that respect they were prescient. Nonetheless I was determined to know *how* the district was hidden from other Londoners.

I was pretty sure Father Grammaticus could have helped but he did not volunteer. Of course I did wonder if that machine in his office might be the 'engine' driving Alsacia, but the thing seemed only an elaborate model. Might it *represent* an engine? Perhaps Prince Rupert's machine was capable of more? But Prince Rupert was still away. And when I asked Friar Isidore, the subject made him sink increasingly into a kind of sadness. I could never get him to discuss what was happening, even though he often seemed astute about the outside world. Indeed, everyone in the Alsacia knew about the outside and still fancied they risked profound danger if they stepped through the gates. And it wasn't necessarily *my* familiar world they feared. Some thought they would find wild and menacing terrain where only fools or specialists would go without being killed or being damned to madness for ever. 'Risking Their Reason Each Night On The Road', as a popular rogue's ballad had it.

Why was my world so menacing and mysterious to Alsacians? A child told me the World Beyond was Cromwell's or Queen Anne's but ruled without justice or mercy. Save for large monuments and palaces, most of London had looked like Alsacia before the Great Fire. Tudor mostly. Perhaps, in my past, Alsacia was destroyed in the fire? I still didn't believe in the supernatural. I remained a firm empiricist. So I gave up and decided to wait for answers. For the moment at least I would take things as they came and make what friends or allies I could.

The less I questioned, the more I grew to enjoy the unselfconscious, accepting fellowship of those great, life-loving Cavaliers. Kind-hearted, even intellectual and artistic sometimes, believing themselves tolerated by a generous God and His Son, they were men of action. They were on one side of the French Enlightenment and I was on the other! Their politics were so remote from the twentieth century's we had little to disagree on except possibly the rights of slaves and Huguenots. In general these people were the soul of humanity who could, while keeping none of their own, grade slaves as well as they graded horses. They treated both, when they encountered them, as they believed God wished them treated. They could guess a man's religion at a casual glance, yet they hadn't an inkling as to the workings of the human mind. They caricatured Jews, Arabs, 'Moors', Englishmen and Germans at every turn, believing them all they were alleged to be, except of course the ones they knew personally, who were wonderful exceptions proving the rule. I felt privileged to be witnessing the birth of modern self-serving racialism.

Both Aramis and Athos were God-fearing intellectuals, and their grasp of ideas was as quick as any twentieth-century philosopher's. While D'Artagnan was comfortable only with his closest friends, Porthos had made me his special mascot, though I was a little taller than he was. He would include me in affectionate jokes against the others, helping me build my confidence until I no longer felt callow and self-conscious in their company. Compared to the giant musketeer, I was slender. I admired but simply couldn't handle the huge consumption he expected of me. 'Every man is required, as a matter of loyalty, to build his strength, the better to serve his king.' I think he had an idea he could feed me up, make me a better roisterer! Enough wine and ale and I would be the son he never knowingly had. I thought of him as a grand mixture of Falstaff and Don Quixote. Maybe Rabelais, too. His pretensions to the nobility seemed to me more an invention of a nineteenth-century satirist than a seventeenth-century historian, but perhaps such stereotypes change rarely in France. The Musketeers were the king's secret emissaries, they said. They had been summoned here by Prince Rupert to help defend the Alsacia from any attack, to serve King Charles's interests, and to guard the abbey Treasure with their lives.

One night grave Aramis told me the prince was due to arrive back the next day. I was delighted to welcome the king's nephew home.

Moll had no interest, she said, in hearing his manly talk, and found excuses to do other things, much as I implored her to join me downstairs to welcome Rupert when he returned. But she was insistent.

'I don't dislike him, Mike. I only dislike the way you all fawn on him. It's a man's pleasure, I know. But I don't choose to add to his admirers or hear his tall tales. Your Prince Rupert, I think you'll agree, is a man's man if nothing else.'

So I went to the party downstairs on my own.

I joined Duval, the Musketeers and Pierre Ronet, a fellow highwayman visiting from France, in the big private bar to be greeted with a friendly cheer by the prince, who held a bumper in one hand and a scroll in the other. Boye, his big white poodle, was at his feet. The prince was dressed in ordinary soldier's clothes, with the dust of the road still on his boots. A great tartan sash over his shoulder supported a heavy, basket-hilted rapier. A brace of big horse pistols lay on the bar. He demanded I drink a shant of scrumpy with them, it now being the season. Against my better judgement I accepted a massive mug. To roars of drunken approval, we drank King Charlie's health and we drank to the queen and their sons, Rupert's cousins. We drank to their spaniels and, without disrespect, their spaniels' fleas. We drank to drink and after an hour or two of this I stopped wondering if Moll would join us. In fact I rather hoped she wouldn't. Some instinct told me she would not be sympathetic to our condition.

By the third hour I was still sober enough to remember the question I had waited so long to ask the prince. 'I am glad you found us once more, sir. How, your highness, can it be that this place, this Sanctuary of ours, cannot be seen from any direction, nor even from above?' I think I smiled drunkenly at him, proud of my ability to form and complete a sentence. 'Why do people age slowly – or sometimes rapidly – sometimes, apparently, not at all – and why are so few children found here?' I almost fell forward at that moment but held my balance, steadying myself on the bar. Suddenly, I wished with all my heart that I was sober and capable. He was looking at me with some amusement, brushing pork pie crumbs off his leather waistcoat.

I began to feel sick.

A little later, when everyone's attention was engaged elsewhere, Prince Rupert murmured to a quieter and more sober me: 'There are answers to your questions. They are a little too widely scattered, in shreds, waiting for a certain breeze to blow them together again. I will summon you when the time has come. I promise you, St Maur's whelp.'

Soon after that, he disappeared. Half an hour later, Moll came down into the bar, curtseying to her Cavaliers and rather than scolding me for my drunkenness, she joined me in another jug of Rhenish. And so we passed the evening, with me able to take greater pleasure from the company and the wine now that I anticipated an answer to my most pressing questions.

Prince Rupert was glad to take me under his wing in the following days. He told me tales of warfare and plunder in the Americas and the Indies, on land and sea. His dog Boye always with him, both in the telling and the tale. This time I saw him, I thought the dog grew greyer about the muzzle. I said nothing then. Any observation I made on age or death was generally ignored or laughed down by my new friends. I remember asking myself why, except in the stories I wrote, French musketeers were in England. These four were, after all, usually in France, either retired to their estates or being drawn reluctantly back into a Parisian life at once vigorous and rewarding. I reminded myself that I would soon have answers.

CHAPTER TWENTY-THREE

MY GHOSTS

APART FROM THE specific fashions of the day, I could imagine these beribboned dandies, with their puffed chests and exaggerated gestures of chivalry, belonging to any period. For all their attention to fashion, they were brave, intelligent men, who wore their learning lightly, preferring to talk only of old times, good friends and of the sinister villains they had defeated. All my life I had heard veteran soldiers speak and behave the same. The subject and consequences of war were only good for a comic yarn.

I must say I remained in awe of their vitality. They roared through life, impulsively pledging their swords to all good causes, never thinking of their own safety. If there was an innocent to be rescued or woman's honour to be redeemed, they would spring to volunteer. They were loved by the whole Alsacia and were only larger than life in their tireless adventuring. They had great generous hearts. The best men of their time, they were cheerfully physical in showing affection, pity or insult compared to modern friends. They smacked one another about the head, kicked and hugged and kissed and swore that there had never been such friends since Roland and Oliver, David and Jonathan, Arthur and Lancelot! And they came mainly in pairs. As did we. With Molly, they all swore loyalty to Rupert (Count Palatine of the Rhine, Herzog von Bayern, First Duke of Cumberland, First Earl of Holder-ness, close heir to the throne of England and Scotland), though an infamous Protestant.

'Why is everyone gathered here?' I asked Molly one night while my friends argued and whispered downstairs. She was drunker than usual and saw nothing wrong with telling me.

'Why, to create justice, of course. Always! To save King Charlie from the scaffold. There's a plan. It will involve that squalid London thief-taker, Jeremiah Jessup, being substituted for his grace. Jessup deserves to die. It will not be the first time he's 'personated his grace! He's a murdering coward who burned down the house of my mother's dear friend Lord Mettlesfield with the poor man's aunts and uncles and aged parents all in their beds when it happened.' She glared up into my face. Did she know she was playing a part?

This Moll favoured a nondescript blouse and skirt when not dressing up as the highwayman. She looked great in anything. But I noticed how, gradually, she had changed her clothes. Now, with the blouse cut low, she looked like a kind of low-budget all-purpose Nell Gwynne. When I first met her she belonged to the eighteenth century and the tram we held up to the nineteenth. When I put this to her she looked blankly at me and carried on, just as the others did if I asked simple questions about their business in London and so on.

I think most of my ideas were far too abstract for them. They had an air of waiting for something or someone to happen. I had thought at first the event was Prince Rupert's arrival. Dressed these days in civvies, a long wig, lots of lace, a silk waistcoat almost to his knees and a coat just a shade or two darker than the vest, he often carried a beribboned dandy cane in his left hand. He kept me close to him, doubtless from mutual liking, and we saw much more of him, back from facing a thousand dangers. Although she was inclined to be bored by his wonderfully entertaining monologues, Moll obviously admired him, pretending to listen intelligently and never interrupting. Like me, he was a man of the world and I knew it was stupid to be jealous, but I could have sworn I saw her blushing once or twice. When I asked her if she found him attractive, she said quite the opposite.

The highwaymen from the later century – Turpin, Sheppard and the rest – were rarely at the tavern these days. I asked after them and Moll was a little vague.

'Their work takes them far and wide across the country. They continue to support working men from Land's End to John o' Groats.'

'Riding to York and that, I suppose. Are they all tram chasers?'

She shrugged.

'Come on, Moll. Is there still a moonlit heath where bold tobymen hold up brass-and-steel electric double-decker trams?' I was growing impatient again, challenging her. I wanted to know how and why this town within the city existed. Did I threaten her? 'Do Turpin and company still make war on Universal Transport?'

'Some of them,' she told me evasively. 'Things change...' And, though at first she considered answering, she suddenly, regretfully, refused to tell me any more.

'Turpin has no love for me, Molly, and I little for him, but you must admit it's surprising. When I first started coming here, the Swan was full of Turpin's kind. His son, Tom King, Jack Sheppard, Jack Rann, and a whole gang of famous tobymen. Now we see them once in a blue moon.'

In spite of this goading, she refused to respond. 'I'm not sure I remember,' was all she would say.

Maybe she was genuinely amnesic. Molly was typically extremely frank in her answers. When she was entrusted with a secret, she would simply tell me that she couldn't speak of it. I never quite got to the truth of what was going on amongst all these heroes of popular folklore. I wouldn't have been very surprised if Sherlock Holmes and Doctor Who dropped in for a beer. Ironically I, who had earned such a large part of my income in what I called 'the popular folk hero business' was now drinking side by side with their actual manifestations. It was almost as if I'd brought them to life myself; conjured them from thin air. Maybe I was addicted to these inventions now like a smoker to nicotine? There were behavioural addictions just as powerful as others. These ideas brought a frisson of fascination which made my senses suddenly more alive than ever.

I had such a lot of questions. Many I was reluctant to ask. Could I really make a world? Were all these people just shadows of my childhood imagination? What we called 'ghosts'? It was too simple an explanation. And too terrifying. I had a lot of myself invested in remaining rational! But I knew in my bones I had not made up Alsacia. Many others had written about it, such as Scott in *Sir Nigel*. The ancient Sanctuary of the White Friars really had been here since the thirteenth century. Very powerful vows that had been exchanged in order to receive holy protection.

Not too wild an idea if you accepted the existence of God. But I'd be crazy if I applied it to real life. To believe in a supernatural deity with limitless power and a set of rules for mankind to follow seemed to me like a special kind of sin, a rejection of the power of Man. I was tolerant enough about what others believed. If they thought God was a winged goat, that was up to them. I respected whatever logic or tradition had brought them to that point. But I despised it in myself. Early on I'd learned to curb the kind of imagination others envied or loathed. The fact remained that the abbey and the town had been here, under charter from a pious king, for nearly a thousand years. They believed that God fulfilled His compact. I thought I knew why they evaded my questions. They could not afford to think about it, either. As realities went, this was a pretty strange one. Sadly my own identity depended on my belief in reason, my inability to accept the supernatural, including God.

The matter of these men and women being creatures of folk tale and myth remained. Some of those very fleshly phantoms were becoming good friends! They weren't ghosts in any sense I understood. Body heat fairly burst from them as they sang songs and told stories, funny and sad. They had pasts, relatives, ambitions for the future. They believed profoundly in a Creator. These people were far more lifelike than any characters I had created or read about. Surely I could not, in some extraordinary psychotic state, have invented all this – the Alsacia, my friends, our enemies?

Meanwhile, Helena chose to issue a bit of an ultimatum, one I didn't find at all unpalatable. She wanted me to come and look after the children so she could go out once or twice a week. I wanted to see as much of the children as possible and agreed immediately. She told me she did not want me making excuses to stay in the retreat until I was certain I was 'well'. Or at least had finished my novel.

In the end I could only take Helena at her word and stop arguing.

We had a few unexpectedly pleasant conversations and I remembered how we had fallen in love in the first place. I felt a little guilty when I returned from a call like that but Moll didn't seem to notice. She appeared determined not to make waves. All that I wanted was someone who loved as loyally as I said I did. Molly and I seemed like that.

I didn't use my brain much during those first weeks of spending more days with the girls. I wondered if I could come up with a way of spending time with Molly Midnight and her violet eyes and keeping near to Helena. I didn't want to stop seeing my children, whom I loved more than anyone. At that point I don't think Moll liked them coming so close. She was living with me, however, and that gave her an advantage. She began to see things in better perspective. My way.

Moll grew nervous. She worried, of course, what would happen if Helena demanded I leave 'the retreat' and come back to Ladbroke Grove. I wasn't much help. I was in a daze of sexual exploration and infatuation. I was deeply selfish. Greedy. Guilty. Missing my children. Molly had become everything I had ever desired in a partner. I suspected that her intentions might be short term, but intentions frequently changed. She reflected everything I had ever desired. She was companionable, like a younger sister, passionate as any woman can be, and smarter than I was in many manly conversations concerning the art of warfare and the nature of horses. I loved her humour. Her big smile. If she had changed from the ringleted tomboy I had first met to the cheerful, sexy companion I now knew, then doubtless so had I changed. She said I was completely different. No longer a boy.

Sometimes, Molly said, I seemed decades older than when we'd first met. I thought I knew what she meant. When I had first seen her she had been the initiator, the leader. Now I frequently led. I thought of us as equals. With equality, so my old Grandma Taylor used to say, comes trust. She'd been a Labour councillor in Clerkenwell. She was talking about societies, but she was a wise old bird and she could just as easily have meant couples. But were we equals?

'With equality comes trust.' I can see my granny laying out the tea things as she talked. She died when I was eleven. 'And a trusting society is one which takes it for granted that all their fellow citizens work for the common good. Keir Hardie told me that himself. Which is why those who allow themselves to be corrupted in a democracy are worse

than those who merely do what the ruling autocracy tells them to do.'
Granny wasn't with us long enough. Cancer.

Molly told me little of her background. She had been born in the
Alsacia but her mother was not from there. For a while she had lived
abroad in the Middle East before returning with her mother for a bit.
When she was twelve she was sent to Godolphin & Latymer in Ham-
mersmith and later went to Oxford, studying classics. 'I got into Somer-
ville.' She laughed. 'Somehow I received a decent degree. But the night
I was celebrating, still in Oxford, I met this wonderful-looking man.
I called him my long-haired cavalier. He was a bit eccentric, but ec-
centricity tended to be cultivated at that time at Oxford. I thought he
had to be doing a Master's or was maybe a young don. Perhaps an
artist. He could be very mysterious about himself. He wore cordu-
roys and a neckerchief. Sometimes he even had a kind of cloak. Otherwise his clothes were fairly ordinary, yet I called him 'my cavalier'
because of his hair and beard. It came to a point like yours. You remind
me of him now. I thought of him like that from the start. My cavalier! Romantic, I know. But you saw what I was like when I was first
here. He's who brought me back to the Alsacia. And left me here.
When he grew bored, I suppose. I had nowhere else to go. That's how
I fell in with Turpin and the others and took to the steel toby.'

'Your parents...'

'Not sure about my dad. I believe he died when I was young. Mum's
abroad quite a lot of the time with her job. I'm pretty sure she didn't
approve of the relationship. And I had my pride.'

As Moll grew a little older, she said, she stopped being a tomboy
and relied increasingly on what used to be called women's wiles, almost as if she were exploring that side of her nature or finding out
how it was best done. 'You met the men I fell in with. Rogues and
adventurers. Some girls went after musicians. There weren't many in
the Alsacia, so I fell for highwaymen. I was romantic. They offered
all kinds of attractive dangers.' I had known other women like Moll,
who plunged into experience determined to know the lure, as it were,
of the lash. In the '70s they began to call it 'empowerment'. In Ladbroke Grove, the rock-and-roll world, many girls scarcely survived
the adventure. There are a lot of addictions. Few of them wind up
making you feel better about yourself.

Then, without any warning I had seen, Helena decided I'd been in exile long enough and announced she wanted me to leave my retreat and come home to Ladbroke Grove. We had to think of the children. She expected to have a serious talk about things. And there I was, unable to tell fact from fiction, living pretty literally in a fantasy world.

I had to think seriously about what we were doing. I had enjoyed my break from responsibility, but I couldn't ignore it much longer. I must start making serious choices.

CHAPTER TWENTY-FOUR

SOMETHING LIKE REMORSE

'I THINK YOU really are altruistic,' Moll told me one night as we lay exhausted in our big soft bed.

I, of course, felt even guiltier than before. I was already planning to return to my 'real' world. But I was flattered. Thinking about it later I'm not sure she meant to be flattering. She might have meant I was naïve or gullible. Did she mean I really loved them both? For a while, the convenience of two wives, regular contact with the girls and plenty of time to write tended to overshadow other considerations. I think they both realised after a while how well the arrangement suited me. But for a while, of course, it had also suited them. Now both women were growing impatient with the situation while I used it to turn out one book after another, putting off the moment when I would have to make a choice. Moll was ultimately the worst off out of our particular threesome. My guilt shifted its focus from Helena to her.

'You love us both, don't you?' Moll said sweetly one evening over supper in our Alsacia rooms. I think she was genuinely trying to empathise with me, to put herself in my shoes. As unexpected tears came into my eyes, she reached a hand to hold mine.

Molly wasn't weak. She only liked to play at being pliable. Even convincing herself sometimes that she was helpless. Passive-aggressive? She was certainly argumentative. I felt a certain jealousy, too. No matter how much I asked, she would never tell me who her 'cavalier' was, though I was pretty sure he lived in the Alsacia. She found my moments of jealousy ludicrous, and I was forced to admit some of my attitudes were hard to maintain in the Sanctuary. The place had no evident reason to be where it was, almost 'outside time'. In moments of depression Molly thought the Sanctuary had a way of taking your years so that you woke up one morning and found yourself too old to pursue any of your ambitions. So when I talked of leaving the Alsacia, she thought she might come with me. I think now she believed it was the right thing to do, a sign of maturity. But I really didn't want my 'fantasy' life in the Alsacia and my 'real' life beyond ever to meet. We began to have arguments in which she accused me of being ashamed of her. What had actually happened was that I grew increasingly suspicious of her histrionics. The arguments worsened. She knew very well that I wasn't ashamed of her and that I merely wanted to keep my two lives separate. I told her that if I left Alsacia I would, for the moment, have to go alone. It made sense. To take Moll with me would simply complicate matters.

One night, after a frustratingly circular argument, I did just what I'd threatened. Taking almost nothing with me, leaving a note that offered little but reassurance, I walked to the gates and stepped through them, not certain what would happen when I did so. On one level I knew what I did was cowardly.

I had no intention of leaving for long but somehow the days passed more rapidly in Ladbroke Grove than I anticipated. I had expected a cool reception from Helena. Instead, she was glad to see me. She said I was more relaxed, more my old self. The retreat had done me good. Maybe I should make a regular thing of it? I was calmer, more mature. To me she seemed warmer, less critical. The agitated nervousness which almost always plagued her had subsided. Our lovemaking was wonderful. We both agreed we were falling in love all over again.

So much for altruism, I thought. I really was falling in love with Helena and she with me. I hadn't told her about Moll. Moll, it's true, never left my thoughts. I frequently felt ashamed of myself. But I couldn't get over the simple pleasure of ordinary life, taking the girls out to the park, writing at my familiar desk, going shopping in Portobello market, the pictures at the International Film Theatre, meals at the Windmill. All so happily, comfortably, normal. The Alsacia became something of a dream again. A country I knew and loved but had no urge to visit. At least for a while.

The raven, Sam, returned one afternoon in early September, soon after the kids finished their summer holidays from St James's Norland, a local Church of England school with a good reputation. Most of the children there either went to the Fox school or on to Holland Park Comprehensive. Ours wanted to go to Holland Park which at that time was considered a good school to get into and a flagship of the comprehensive system. Sally and Kitty had made huge strides in their primary school. We were all upstairs in the big office-cum-living room at Ladbroke Grove. Helena's louche friend Marge was telling Sally and Kitty how much she and other girls from Godolphin & Latymer had envied Holland Park where they were rumoured to use drugs, drink and enjoy sex as much as they liked. Helena and I were desperately trying to divert Marge but she was hard to stop at full throttle.

As the girls told a story of one of their friends' older brothers who had been drunk in class, I recognised a pair of sparkling black eyes glaring through the big bay windows of my office, staring at me with an expression of weary discontent. They belonged to that sarcastic raven who made me so uneasy. Clearly he was hoping to be let in. When the girls had skipped back out to the gardens followed by Marge and Helena I went and slid open the sash window. 'So what's up?' I asked, a little brusquely.

He strutted in and stood on my little Olympia electric, his claws rustling on the sheet of paper I had recently wound in. 'Altruism?' he said.

'Don't you start,' I said. 'I'm doing my best.' I felt wretched. I hadn't heard a word from Moll. I had been relieved at first but now I was worrying a little. Had he brought a message, perhaps? By the way he cast his eye about I suspected he was looking for food. 'I was under the impression that we had an agreement,' he said, scoping our cat Tom who had just strolled up and was looking at him with mild curiosity. For Tom any animal who managed to make it into our apartment was by definition a guest, one of us, and so should be treated with politeness and generosity. Had he been able, Tom would have offered Sam a cup of tea and a plate of seedcake. Sam wasn't our first visitor to be accepted by him. There had been mice, a young rat, several blackbirds and wrens, not to mention an Old English sheepdog, which had been neurotic before it arrived and had lasted a week or two before we were forced to return him to his breeder. Sam nodded at Tom who left as soon as it became clear there was no food. 'My hope was that you would take my advice for a bit. I imagined that you understood how useful I could be to you in guiding you between the worlds…'

'Not *my* understanding, Sam.' I resented this intrusion and his general presumption about our relationship. 'I still plan to see Molly. I haven't *abandoned* her! I go back and forth between here and the Alsacia pretty much as I please. I have friends there, just as I have here. But my children have to come first.'

'It's the Chevalier. He begs for your company. For dinner.' Sometimes I forgot how Sam seemed able to read my mind. 'And that of your sweet lady Molly, of course. He was asking after you both. He suggests Friday or Saturday.'

'It'll have to be Friday,' I said. 'I promised to take the kids out on Saturday night.'

'Gotcha,' said Sam, by way of understanding. 'Good luck with the deadline.' He hopped up onto the back of the sofa then to the open window and flew east on his strong wings. Was that him cawing into the early-autumn air? Announcing his credentials to his fellows? Or mocking them?

When later I asked Moll if she was familiar with Sam, she gave an evasive answer. She seemed happy to see me. She didn't ask me to stay the night.

I had still not told Helena about Molly. Did it matter so long as Helena believed the 'retreat' had made me a better person? There seemed no point. Especially if I *was* a better person. Everybody won. I planned to make trips to the Sanctuary on a fairly regular basis. And if Molly wasn't prepared to accept the arrangement I proposed, so much for that. I would still go. I had even wondered about taking my kids there. The girls expressed cautious agreement but Helena wouldn't let me, even though she didn't believe the place existed. She knew my 'retreat' had to be fairly close. She had ruled out Kings Hall and decided I had been staying at the Mill, a posh reconstructed windmill only a few miles away, in Tufnell Hill where our drummer Tubby Ollis lived permanently. I could cycle the distance easily. Helena identified it with a delusion I controlled most of the time. She had decided I visited some posh loony bin like the Priory but preferred to call the mysterious place a 'writer's retreat'. That's what she told the neighbours. Knowing I could always find relief at Alsacia from the Whispering Swarm made it considerably easier to bear. Easier to work, too. I could anticipate visiting the Sanctuary, rest from the Swarm and, feeling restored, return to work. I could even go back briefly, as an experiment. Sam's invitation came at a great time!

So I told Helena I needed to go into retreat for another spell. And off I went!

I found it a huge relief to leave the Swarm outside those gates. I had scarcely realised how loud it had become! Prince Rupert, 'the Chevalier', proved a great host and that first dinner was wonderful, even though I wished Helena could be enjoying it too. There was no denying it. I loved them both. But meanwhile Molly was hugely pleased to see me! Apparently she held no grudge.

The prince had travelled everywhere across Europe, Asia and the Caribbean. He had even been to East Africa. What he called 'Far Egypt' or 'Far India'. He had wonders to show from all these places. I didn't think he was lying. How he covered so much distance baffled me. As on most other subjects, he never gave a satisfactory answer, always promising me a big revelation in the near future. He did it with every question. I had almost given up believing him. Debonair, tall and courtly as usual, he again seemed to have aged a little more than we had. He and Boye had grown older at about the same pace. And yet I had last seen him only a few weeks earlier. I murmured this to Moll as the prince led us downstairs to the public rooms, where our friends waited for us. She preferred not to hear me. I began to feel like some morbid bugger who was always going on about death.

All the prince's dinner guests, Moll, Duval, Jemmy Hind, Nick Nevison, the other 'giant' in our company, the four Musketeers, Prince Rupert and myself were soon sitting comfortably in the snug of The Swan With Two Necks, enjoying shants of the best porter in the world. Mrs Juniper Toom, the publican's wife, brought us food. She was tickled, she said, at serving four of the tallest trenchermen in the civilised

world. The cheerful, elegant prince rocked back on his chair, strok-
ing the dog with one hand, running his fingers through his own curling, dark brown shoulder-length locks and fully at ease in our company.
He travelled between Bavaria and France, between Venice, the 'Near
Indies' or 'Far Egypt' and China. He had explored the American interior. He had met tribes of fully formed tiny men in 'Far Egypt', living above the source of the Nile. A similar tribe had been found beside
the Niagara River in America.

'The Africans are the oldest created race,' he said, 'yet wonderfully
childlike and only three feet tall. The others, the Pukwudgie, did not
come from America originally, but also from Africa. They had tribal
memories of Adam and Eve. Some say they are our ancestors. Who
would believe our antecedents were small and black!' If he invented
some adventures I didn't care a bit. I might be listening to one of my
favourite old fantasy writers telling a tall tale. He spoke of a thinking
machine called the Grand Turk, which could play chess like a genius; of
flying in a balloon to Mirenburg; of serving beyond the Mountains
of the Moon in the army of Prester John, the great Christian emperor.
Doing battle against the great pagan kings of Congo.

I had the impression I was at table with Baron Münchhausen himself!

'Prester John lives even now?' I was delighted, astonished, dis-
believing.

Prince Rupert laughed, pulling on his Van Dyke beard as if to test
his own reality. 'It depends on what you mean by "now",' he said and
told a story about encountering coiling monsters in a fog off the coast
of Scotland, of tall sea-caves and sleeping dragons. But long before
Molly and I left to head back to our cosy little flat, he murmured
to me, promising that he would talk to me again soon. 'Moll tells
us you're a very curious gentleman!' He winked. 'Maybe now's the
time to ask me those questions you had and discover if I have the
answers.'

'I'll take your grace up on that.' It was the nearest thing to a promise I'd had from him. I was surprised by this sudden offer. Was he truly
ready with answers?

'I was beginning to assume, sir, that your secrets, like those of the
abbot, were not for general consumption. That you were putting me
off, as kindly as you could.'

He understood this to be the sarcastic challenge it was not. He smiled up into my eyes. 'There are no "kept secrets" here, lad. Just revelations for which you're not yet ready. What you call my "secrets" are our only currency, by which we and all we cherish survive. The means by which we maintain our pacts and treaties.'

'You'll explain to me how you and I can meet here yet come from centuries apart?'

'To be sure. I remember my promises. That's why I sent Sam to see you! An old friend has brought the remaining parts of my new astrological machine. Certain precise work had to be completed in Amsteldorp by the best Arab and Jewish craftsmen from Constantinople and Damascus. To specifications given them by myself and Dr Dee. The sage is over one hundred years of age, living in the Amsteli Palace, worshipping Bacchus as he once worshipped the mighty Gloriana.' He gestured. 'No friend, I'd agree, to the Stuart cause. Architect of his mistress's circle of intellectual paganism. No wonder the pope dubbed her The Great Sorceress.'

'You knew Dr Dee, the alchemist?'

'Non-believer though he be, we are good friends.' Prince Rupert rocked with reminiscent laughter. 'He still lives, over there in the Low Countries! A healthy old man. Still investigating the natural world and communing with the supernatural! He claims he cannot die, for his soul is not his own to give up, but I'd say that's no more than a way he has of explaining his longevity.'

'Well, I envy you his acquaintance, your grace.'

He grinned and sent his shant to Juniper for fresh ale. 'Young as you are, I know you're a man of the world like me, a philosopher who lusts after knowledge as do I, needing to satisfy a curiosity never understood by most of these happy louts! We need you for your size and skills. The monks, however, have a great hope that you are the youth they have been waiting for, who will represent their cause when the final moment comes. They fear for all their treasures. Indeed their great Treasure. So many seek it who are careless of its metaphysical significance and could easily damage it.'

'You know what it is, this Treasure?'

'I believe I do. That Treasure was entrusted into their care many centuries ago when terror and blood flowed through London's streets like rain after a storm. I have heard the stories. Shameful days for Christian folk. I am not sure if our consciences have the strength to stand the burden. So our minds banish the memory. But the monks are creatures of great resilience of soul and physical courage. They'll reveal the nature of their Treasure when they're ready. Discretion is the mark of a true friend, not so Maur's spawn?' This was one of his nicknames for me. I had learned that St Maur was a lesser-known French saint whom it amused him to consider my father. Maurice was the name of his late brother. Moore-cocke was another Norman and Anglo-Saxon hybrid. 'You'll keep a secret? Already, I'm told, the rumours spread like ripples in a pond. We must make more ripples, confuse the Lord Protector further. Happily we deal with men who would simplify the world to suit their own imaginings rather than expand their own imagination to take in the world's wonders! I intend to save the king, as our Moll has doubtless told you.'

'She has not.' I glanced at her. She looked down. He seemed pleased by her discretion. He continued, smiling.

'And my discoveries will ensure his safety until the people call for him again. Twelve days hence, we know, he will be escorted from Whitehall and led to the block by the Four Tall Men of Kent where his head will be struck from his body in an unholy act of regicide. *Save that it will not be Charles Stuart they slay!* The king will be aboard a waiting brigantine on his way to Holland and from there to France, protected by Duval and the Musketeers!'

It sounded a wonderful adventure. Like something by Dumas! I was immediately excited. I could have written the script myself. I could see the chagrin of the 'Four Tall Men of Kent', whoever they were. I visualised the laughing triumph of the Cavaliers as they carried King Charles off up the river to the open sea while the thwarted redcoats gnashed their teeth and shook their fists. I told him what a tremendous escapade it sounded. He slapped his knee and roared his pleasure.

'The instrument I have waited for all these years, without which the rest of my plan can scarce succeed, is with us at last, here in the Alsacia. That instrument is the finest of its kind – rivalled only by the great devices of ancient China and Greece. Oh, you'll marvel at my engines and my instruments, young sir! They are capable of the subtlest measurements and predictions. All made from honest observation and exploring of the Greater Heavens and beyond. My machine is the culmination of my own heavenly explorations!'

I said nothing to spoil the excitement of Prince Rupert, who rattled on with his usual enthusiasm. I did not expect too much. I had already seen the abbot's fantastic machine! I knew how simple most instruments of his day were.

When I was ready to go back to Ladbroke Grove, Prince Rupert bowed very low to us. I believe I detected something in his manner towards Moll and wondered again if he was her 'cavalier'. With elaborate French elegance he kissed Moll's hand, his brown eyes looking up from beneath pale lashes and causing her to blush. Duval turned to his friend, the gigantic Jemmy Hind, admonishing him to be at Moll's service. I joked about it when I said goodbye to her but for some reason she lost her temper with me. I suspected then that Duval, after all, was her mysterious cavalier. I hinted at it but she wouldn't say what was wrong. This was as bad as trying to deal with Helena in one of her moods.

The upper deck of the Number 15 bus was deserted when I boarded. For some reason, I realised, I was close to crying. What was in me which made women behave the same?

Helena was glad to see me when I got home. But she didn't like the way I made love that night. In the following days, I must admit, I was short with her and irritated by her attempts to find out what was wrong. I was, of course, thinking of Molly. It was as if she imprisoned herself in her femininity and didn't like it all that much.

But, of course, the obvious answer to my unease never once occurred to me. If asked I would have said I had never been happier or better balanced. Why shouldn't I be happy? I had the ideal writer's life. 'Every writer needs two spouses,' Allard always joked. 'That way they can share the strain!' I should be grateful. I had a wife, children and a mistress. For the most part everyone else seemed happy too. That was a relief.

CHAPTER TWENTY-FIVE

THE CHINESE AGENT

I WAS STILL worried about the whispering. I went for tests to several neurologists and at last got a diagnosis: *tinnitus*, which can take many forms. But why did it clear up completely the moment I entered the Alsacia?

Superficially at any rate, Helena and I became good friends again. The girls were happy sharing jokes about me behind my back. They took a little pleasure in it. They wanted to share power. I honestly enjoyed their jokes. They bonded against me, especially when I was getting too big for my boots or when I went mad with some piece of work I was doing. I began to believe that it was possible for grown people to get along together without dislike or bitterness. This was the falling zenith of hippy Notting Hill. 1968. The bankers and lawyers and stockbrokers were already moving in. Soon we would be told that money didn't grow on trees and we should maximise our assets, with our beautiful gardens and lovely old Victorian houses. Housing committees. Gardens committees. Goodbye Piccadilly, Farewell Leicester Square; hello America; goodbye North Ken, and the traders in Portobello jacked up their prices and off we went on the gentrification waltz.

For a few short years, before we realised it was too late to defend our heritage and our homeland against bobos and toffs, yuppies, nimbys and *colons*, we had some very good times. Maybe ten or fifteen years. Sweet times. The girls and I did almost everything together. Rainy weekends were galleries and exhibitions or the Disney cinema in St Martin's Lane.

It was their girlhood. I was happy for them. They began to grow up. There were also gigs to go to. The Move, the Allday Suckers, The Chargers were still performing locally, and I was writing for them all, even the Suckers. We taped some great recordings around that time, many of which are long lost. St Anselms Church Hall had been re-named The Golden Calf. The vicar didn't seem to mind. He had most of the local Hells Angels as his congregation. Wonderful jam sessions, making up the words as we went along. Great instrumental solos. My girls became a bit blasé about backstage visits and famous players.

Apart from hassles from a determinedly anti-counterculture bunch of rozzers, who were forever trying to cut off our power, we did some great sessions culminating with a famously disorganised concert fea-turing the Dead Legends (as they called us at the beginning) includ-ing Pete Pavli on bass and cello, Martin Stone and Paul Kossoff on guitars, me on banjo, Tubby Ollis on drums, Simon 'the Power' Pow-ell on fiddle, Arthur Brown and Jon Trux, also on guitars. Helena was determined to stay at home and chat with her girlfriends, so I took the girls. We'd drawn quite a crowd but the wind was making it dif-ficult for Arthur to light his hat. The first casualty was Kossoff, who went to sleep, snuggled up with his Strat behind the stacks before we ever began. The second was Trux, who lost his guitar and ambled off to find it. The third was Simon Powell, whose wife turned up unex-pectedly and chased him and his girlfriend off the stage. They were last seen disappearing up Latimer Road. Arthur still couldn't get his hat to light. I was laughing so hard I fell through the stage and busted my banjo and then I heard Trux shout out. He'd found his guitar. Then he slumped in on top of me. By that time all of those still awake and present began to laugh along with us and that was the end of The Portobello Mushroom Band, as they now called us. We got enthusi-astic applause from a bunch of French students, who thought it was all part of the act, and asked where we were appearing next. We told them the Hackney Empire. Anything was possible. In those days.

My girls had a great time in general but were utterly contemptu-ous of the quality of the entertainment, catcalling from the audience,

'Get off! Old hippy farts!' And I refused to be overwhelmed by the half-heard words, the murmured tones of the Whispering Swarm, increasingly insistent, increasingly threatening. When Helena came home from the comforts and cunning of her Ladbroke Grove kitchen séance I was lying in bed with wax in my ears, moaning and begging for it to stop. She thought I had missed her and reassured me.

A couple of mornings later, when I was reading over the previous day's work, I answered a knock and the front door was suddenly full of purple-and-white Ronno'noms, a Scientology breakaway cult that had the advantage of being known more for its flashy colours than its philosophy. They called it 'Scientific Spiritualism'. I told them to kindly bugger off, and for a second I thought I heard the Swarm buzzing into the distance. But it wouldn't go. Neither would the ronnies. The Swarm filled my head like angry bees. I was furious. I lost it, told the ronnies to fuck off. I wondered if these bouts came with depression. Helena and I had just read about the death of Baggy Tyler, for years the Fix's head roadie. That same night Smiling Mike tried to climb the wall of the *Frendz* office building in Portobello Road because he needed somewhere to sleep off a long acid trip. He fell backwards halfway up and was impaled on the area railings. Dead when they found him. As if in sympathy the Swarm went away again and I prayed it would stay away.

I was almost thirty and I was ready to retire.

The books got hacked out and supported the magazine which was breaking even with reduced pages. Early in 1969, I passed the *New Worlds* reins to Charlie Ratz, Graham Sharp and Graham Blount. They had all been contributors and worked as professional journalists. I called them my triumvirate but wasn't surprised when only Ratzo wound up as editor. I was never as well-trained as Ratzo but he had no idea how I ran the magazine or worked out how a story fitted or kept the finances going. He thought I was incompetent. Actually, he thought everyone else was incompetent.

I'd supported my ideas by writing a lot of honest adventure fiction as well as a few decent comedies. I had established a modest space for the kind of fiction I liked to write and read. I'd put a few new guns in the literary arsenal. I'd helped in the process of reuniting literary and popular fiction, which followed in the wake of new vocabularies for music and painting.

We were an active part of the zeitgeist. When I was twenty-five it was literary suicide to mention an enthusiasm for Mervyn Peake, and most critics ignored him. Literary careerists avoided Peake, Firbank and others. Not many read the French absurdists and existentialists. Few were fond of Philip K. Dick or Allard. The same was true of a number of other writers, painters and composers. Now Peake and visionaries like him are known to every educated household. Culturally, we were a little ahead of the '60s. Jack Allard and others were with me. But it was surprising how relatively few we were and we were not all artists and intellectuals. Scientists, painters, sculptors, philosophers, journalists and all sorts of people were fired up by what we were doing. During the few months I was in Sweden, through a mutual enthusiasm for Peake, I met my friend Dave Harvey. He wrote one of our best editorials as well as fiction. Most of us were were doing something interesting in the arts, academies and sciences and had a taste for certain kinds of visionary work.

I had the good fortune to be part of a generation which knew intense early experience followed by material success. We got there as much through our enthusiasms as our ambitions. We did it to popular music by The Beatles and The Who, to movies by all the great survivors as well as brilliant newcomers. Bergman. Fellini. Truffaut. The Italian Americans. A growing availability of music by Schoenberg, Ives, Messiaen and others. Steve Reich. Philip Glass. Bacon. Hamilton. Warhol. Paolozzi. Rothko. All those painters and sculptors. Coming together with everyone else.

The sciences were bursting with new ideas and applications. At a time when few of us thought about how to miniaturise computers, we worked out some of the strangest ways of miniaturising notional environments via computers. We created the RPG. We were pretty much a perfect team. Everyone pooled their best. We never thought in terms of intellectual property, just controlling our copyrights enough to get a reasonable income. The '60s and even the '70s were a tremendous time to be in London. Sex, drugs, rock and roll. We saw generous hearts exploited by greed. They say it wasn't really like that. They weren't there. It was a buzz. We mixed not only with talented contemporaries but people of previous generations we admired.

We experimented with sex. Sex without consequence. The notion of a sexually transmitted worldwide epidemic had occurred only to SF writers and even those thought they were inventing metaphors. We were all enjoying ourselves a lot just then. My life was a cloud of good things. I had never dreamed of success or had unsatisfied sexual frustrations! All the good things of the world were coming my way. I was starting to take them for granted. Whole bins full of loonies and colonies of hippies bought and read my work. Life would have been pretty perfect if it weren't for the whispering voices in my head – insistent, irresistible voices sounding alien words. Strange, unfamiliar vowels in no known language. They did not seem to threaten, yet I found them threatening. Tinnitus might be blamed but I began to go mad wondering if I could perhaps trace the languages and learn them. Were they warning me? Were they coming up from my unconscious? If so, what did they represent? Now I had to take the supernatural into account, too. I was no puritan, but experience had taught me there were real consequences to actions and that wishing for something didn't make it happen. Was I warning myself of consequences to a lifestyle that wasn't costing me very much at all? When I said there was always a victim in a threesome, I hadn't thought one would be me.

About a year after that brief return to the Alsacia there came a knock at the front door. Helena was downstairs with her friend Jenny so I went to answer. Standing there was a tall Chinese man in a dark blue uniform with gold buttons and trim who took off his matching cap, bowed and said:

'Mr Moorcock?'

'Yes – I –'

'A car for you.' He spoke perfect Oxford English without affectation or mockery, though I thought at first he said 'I care for you'.

'I'm sorry?'

'You'll need a small bag.'

'Um… ' I looked past him at the street.

Where the tourist buses usually stopped now lounged a long green Lagonda. I knew where she came from. But oh, what a beautiful machine! She might have been driven out of the factory that day. No wonder they called them classics. She was as English as they made them, down to the particular rake of her mudguards, the long, tapering boot, the arrogant tilt of her bonnet. Just enough deco to emphasise her elegance. I had ridden in some sweet, famous cars but she was the best.

In a bit of a daze I packed a few things. As soon as I'd told Helena, I was off in the green Lagonda with a warm wind in my hair. Suddenly I was the happiest man in the world. I felt intensely secure and privileged. I had no intention of staying long at the Sanctuary. I'd begun to take so many things for granted. I lived in the world of the beautiful people. I had a hat with feathers in it, just like the Cavaliers. My hair was long, my beard trim. I had big boots and belts and fancy silk jackets. I had a Rickenbacker twelve-string. I had a beautiful partner who rolled expert joints and cared for me as tenderly as she cared for a beloved pet. And if I felt euphoric in that Lagonda, I had grown habitually used to luxurious cars, a certain amount of euphoria, and I knew in my bones that soon I would not be bothered by the Swarm until I rode back in that beautiful leather upholstery, a liveried chauffeur bringing me home.

'May I ask who sent you?' I asked from the back seat, leaning forward and talking to the bloke in uniform. 'Was it Father Grammaticus?'

'The car belongs to Mrs Melody, sir.' Although very formal, the dignified chauffeur spoke English with patient grace. 'The lady's mother.'

'Mother?' I was more than curious. 'The lady?'

The driver was very forthcoming. 'So I believe, sir. She married a man called Melody. An anglicisation, of course. It's Persian. He was in furs. Jewish, I think. Or a Copt, maybe. She met him in San Francisco. I hardly know him. I, by the way, am Prince Lu Wing.'

I added under my breath, 'Prince Lu Wing? I thought they'd abolished aristocracy in China.' The name was curiously familiar.

I knew next to nothing of Chinese dynasties and aristocracy except that Fu Manchu had planned to re-establish his family on the throne of China. Maybe this guy was from Taiwan or Macao or one of those other disputed bits of China? I had almost certainly read his name somewhere. It was just as likely to have been in an old *Detective Weekly* from the '30s – *The Terror of the Tongs*.

I had known Rolls-Royces, Bentleys, Daimlers, Bristols, Mercedes, Jaguars, Duesenbergs, as well as my own wonderful Nash. I loved big high-performance cars and enjoyed every possible form of modern transport, including airships, seaplanes and gyrocopters, and had been stoned in most of them, but I'd known nothing quite as comfortable as that relatively short run in the dark green Lagonda. The car got a lot of attention as, glittering enamel and brass, she swung out up Ladbroke Grove, paused at the lights and accelerated up Holland Park Avenue and Bayswater Road. We purred down Park Lane like the King of Wonderland. I felt like waving to the people we passed. I rolled a joint and was beautifully stoned by the time, ladylike in her dark green livery, she sashayed into the Strand, flew along Fleet Street and, finally, swept down to Carmelite Inn Chambers, through the gates to stop at last just outside The Swan With Two Necks.

It had been a wonderful ride! I was content to luxuriate in that powerful atmosphere of leather and oil. Then Prince Lu Wing opened the door for me and I stepped down into the inn's courtyard strewn with straw and horse droppings. In my bell-bottoms and five-inch heels, my patchwork coat of many colours, I picked my way to a small door on the southern side which led along a passage to a snug private bar where an astonishing-looking woman stood waiting for me.

I could not believe that this was Moll's mother smiling up at me. The woman was short, well figured, dark and lush, with full, bright red lips. Her curved peacock eyes were exotically emphasised with kohl. Her black hair dripped in thick glossy waves around her bare brown neck. Mrs Melody wore a cape of red plush, a full-bosomed grey silk blouse. She drank with relish from a two-pint pewter shant almost half her size. Her wide, oval face was jovial as she exchanged a joke with Joey Cornwall, now a serving barman. He winked back as he bent under the counter. The woman spread her arms. Arriving behind me, after a moment's hesitation, Molly walked into them. Then she turned and kissed me lightly on the lips before returning to her mother's embrace.

'Hello, darling.' Molly's mother hugged her, kissing her on both cheeks. Her voice was husky with the hint of what was probably an American accent. She stared directly and frankly into my face. Unexpectedly I felt a guilty frisson of desire. She turned to Moll with a challenging smile. 'And this is your young man, is it?'

Those fascinating eyes! Wise, knowing, tolerant, with perhaps a hint of ironic malice. Sexuality that was almost greed. Her figure, though tiny, was full and lush and her subtle scent reminded me of every woman I had ever desired. I had never before been much attracted to women of exotic appearance. I could not say how I might have behaved if circumstances had been different. Short as she was, she gave the impression of substance. Her sense of fashion was all her own, seemingly drawn from several eras. She wore a wide-brimmed feathered Gainsborough hat. Like mine, it rivalled those of the Musketeers. Her grey blouse was edged scarlet under a small purple bolero-style jacket. Her skirt was deep blue and flared just below the knee. Her black-and-red shoes had very high heels, bringing her head just about up to my shoulder. She wore several rings, oddly cut and with large diamonds, emeralds, sapphires and rubies. Her gold, Egyptianate necklace fell in three long loops, spaced by small oblongs of lacquered platinum. It seemed ancient and might have been some ancestral badge of rank.

I could easily have taken her for one of those beautiful but cruel priestesses, the kind of woman found in the novels of H. Rider Haggard or Edgar Rice Burroughs. You saw her in illustrations, frequently with a long sacrificial knife raised high above the breast of some titled English hero. You were well off as long as she liked you. She bore almost no physical resemblance to her daughter yet she had a shared quality with Molly I instinctively recognised. Her exotic taste went well with her dark, olive skin. Her eyes were oval, deep brown, almost black, slightly oriental. Her dramatically curving crimson lips were like fresh, warm blood. Although not conventionally pretty, Mrs Melody had a lush warmth and a flirtatious manner which seemed genuinely unconscious.

I was a bit confused by the instant sexual attraction I felt for Mrs Melody and glanced at Molly, who was plainly displeased. Maybe I was not the first man to find Mrs Melody as desirable as her daughter? In spite of their subtle similarities it was hard to believe that this woman really was Molly's mum. Molly was about five foot six and slim and increasingly dressing down as I dressed up, disdaining the flower-child Laura Ashley fringes and big lashes which were a poor alternative.

I could tell Molly dared me to make a pass at her ma. It was a relief to have such a firm incentive to stay on the straight and narrow.

Claude Duval made a dramatic entrance from the common room. In all his silks and extravagant linen, his long fair hair and beard glinting in the light, he had a slightly sinister look and broke my mood, exclaiming his delighted surprise. This was a beloved old friend. 'Ah!'

He bowed to kiss Mrs Melody's hand and murmured something in French I could not catch. They were about the same height, both in heels. She responded with a throaty chuckle suggesting a private joke between them. Obviously they had a history. Duval, well mannered as ever, greeted Molly with an even deeper bow, a less lingering kiss on her hand. He clapped my shoulder with almost painful bonhomie, and ordered fresh drinks from Joey who appeared to be enjoying the situation as he pumped ale, poured wine and spirits and all the while hummed some current tune to himself. It was usually a variant of 'Tom, Tom, the Piper's Son'.

Duval and Mrs Melody spoke of cities whose names all sounded exotic to me, of events which had taken place years before. Then their tone became more urgent as they talked about 'the Treasure', 'the African', 'High India' and 'our good friend'. Molly doubtless knew what they were saying. Some kind of Thieves' Cant? She did not tell me.

Then Lu Wing entered, no longer in chauffeur's uniform but wearing a high-buttoned, deep blue silk tunic, an entourage of smooth, modern men of south China at his heels, ready, I heard him say, to do any further work required of them. The conversation turned to a more distant moment when his father died and he would claim the crown of the Wing emirates, to rule over a subcontinent and its colonies again. Sending his men off, he said, upon their errands and to visit their many relatives in Limehouse, Lu Wing leaned against the bar, as relaxed as he had probably been during his student days at Oxford.

'Thanks for the lift,' I said.

'Would you have come, otherwise?'

'I don't know.'

'Prince Rupert would have been disappointed. His Persian Cosmo-labe is assembled. It was why I brought you. I believe you expressed a desire to see it.'

I had almost forgotten. Now I felt a sudden buzz of fresh curiosity.

In the brass behind Lu Wing I caught a reflected glimpse of Molly wearing an expression I did not recognise.

CHAPTER TWENTY-SIX

THE MYSTERIES

IN A LONG, deep cellar I had previously known nothing about, squeezing past stacked kegs and spare pumps and all the accumulated paraphernalia of a busy old pub, we found Prince Rupert of the Rhine. His handsome features were given an almost demonic glow in the light from the single oil lamp held by his servant. Wearing a white smock, he bent over part of some large apparatus of astonishing complexity. While it followed a design similar to the machine once shown me by the abbot, it otherwise bore only a passing resemblance to any instrument I had seen, even at Greenwich Observatory. I had almost forgotten the abbot's Cosmolabe. The whole experience felt like a dream. I remembered the slender wires of copper, gold and silver, the globes of different sizes, the handfuls of tiny jewels which might be planets, even galaxies. Again, I looked at the thing and marvelled. A model not of the solar system but of something greater, extending across more dimensions than three. What could it possibly represent?

His servant now went around the cellar igniting flambeaux. Their light skipped and flickered on the walls, casting vast shadows. The prince resembled triumphant Satan as silently he pointed out features of the tall, impossibly intricate object in brass, platinum, gold and precious gems. The thing could have been spun by an inspired spider. Mrs Melody was revealed on the other side of it, staring from dark gold-flecked eyes as if in fear. Molly continued to show a certain wariness of her mother and placed herself between Prince Rupert and Prince Lu Wing while, a little embarrassed, I went to stand next to Mrs Melody. I feared I might be affected by her powerful sexuality. My attention, however, was soon completely absorbed by that astonishing machine. Prince Rupert was delighted by our responses. 'I am awaiting the boy with the remaining piece,' he told us. 'Joey will bring him down.' He was in a state of heightened excitement. His eyes burned like coals, reflecting the unstable light of the flambeaux. This, he muttered, was the culmination of all he'd lived and worked for. 'My Cosmolabe! More and less representing worlds physical and metaphysical! Radiant Time, my good friends! You, young Master Maur's Cocke, are already familiar with the mysteries it manipulates and the rarified reasoning it represents!'

Like the one Father Grammaticus had shown me already, the instrument or machine – I hardly knew how to describe it – was not a representation of our planetary system at all. The memories blazed back into my mind. Until now all orreries, even those showing far stars, had made our sun the centre. Attached to nearly invisible wires I saw clusters of tiny pearls, jade and diamonds. All reflected the restless light of the fiery torches. I imagined each jewel represented not a world, but a galaxy. These in turn had shadows of different colours. Auras. Between all these there circled wide bands of gold and brass imprinted with enamelled black figures and between these ran thousands of fine silver wires forming impossibly intricate webs. 'Undiscovered territories to wear the English crown. New worlds.'

'The gateway to Heaven?' He didn't hear her.

'Once he regains the crown, the king has promised money for continuing experiments.'

There was stillness in my head. No voices. No murmuring. Only now did I realise how free I could be from the Whispering Swarm. Was this what sent those sounds out to me? And silenced them, too? The constant movement of the machine threatened to hypnotise me. I imagined I could hear music, the deep notes of a cello changing as the ghostly lines of the web shivered and shifted in the light of massive candles. The bright tiny drops fell through the golden strands like tears. It drew me further in. I stepped close, then felt a hand on my shoulder. Duval drew me back a pace and winked. I heard voices coming from the passage leading into the cellar and then Joey Cornwall and a much smaller figure entered. A dwarf, I thought at first. No. A small boy.

'Good! You've brought me your uncle's piece, have you, lad?' Prince Rupert stretched his hand towards a boy, not much more than six or seven, who stood beside Joey. The boy's eyes were wide. He clutched a box in his long-fingered hands.

'Yes, your worship.'

'At last! Providence be praised!'

'My uncle sends his respects, sir,' fluted the lad. 'Coming out of Water Lane, sir, I saw...'

'Yes, indeed. A wonderful artefact. Only Mr Tompion himself could make it!'

'Sir?' the boy piped again, his wondering eyes still on the hypnotic machine. 'I saw, coming down Water Lane...' His voice trailed a little nervously as Prince Rupert still ignored him, tearing off the paper covering a beautiful wooden box.

'Good. Very good.' He opened the box carefully and looked into it with reverence. 'Excellent!'

'I saw 'em, sir!'

'I'm glad you did, Tom.' Prince Rupert clearly meant to silence the boy. He wanted no interruption. 'Your uncle's a clever man!'

As we all stared intently, the prince turned and very gently took from the box what looked like a copper sphere, about twice the size of a cricket ball. He crossed quickly to one of the dancing torches, fished a taper from his pocket and ignited it. Then, holding the taper in his teeth, he carefully opened a tiny door in the ball. Removing the burning taper from his mouth he inserted it into the ball which immediately began to emit vivid chemical light. This light was far brighter than that of the torches. The ball was some kind of dark lantern. The light only shone from one side. Prince Rupert crossed the cellar's flagstones to his Cosmolabe. With the sphere in his hand he reached deep into that complex arrangement of wires, rods and metal bands. When he withdrew his arm, I saw he had suspended the thing at the very centre, probably from a prepared wire hanging from one of the curved overhead brass rods. Half the ball was a deep, matt black, while the other hemisphere poured out light, illuminating the side it faced. I had no idea how the thing was made to work. I would say it was almost a yin and yang symbol. Was it meant to represent the moon? Too bright.

"'Tis complete! Now my model truly represents all Creation!' Prince Rupert clapped his hands. 'Absorbing light on one side, emitting light on the other. The fundamental model of our Creator's cosmos! The birth and death of the universe! Over and over, ad infinitum. Ad infinitum, ladies and gentlemen. Here is a model of *Eternity*!'

'What's that? The sun?' Molly frowned uncertainly. She broke a bit of ice. We all smiled.

I knew that strange sphere could not represent the sun. But I had seen nothing like it anywhere. What it measured and mapped was something far too vast for my inexperienced mind to contemplate. It spoke suddenly to me and its voice was cold and clear. 'There is no virtue rewarded unless by chance, for without any doubt the universe does play dice and has a very refined sense of irony.' Prince Rupert's voice? Lu Wing's? We were all gathered there now, observing the bizarre instrument murmuring and humming to itself. I had it in my mind for a moment that I was hearing all the voices of the Swarm.

Moll leaned to peer at the sphere with its dark absorbing aura on one side, brilliant rays of light pouring out on the other. For one awful moment I was afraid it would draw her in. 'Not the sun?'

Prince Rupert roared. 'The sun! Nothing so prosaic, Mistress Moll! No – 'tis our mighty master, Time.' He stalked around its perimeter, amazed by his own creation.

'Time represented as – what, a dimension of space?' Prince Lu Wing's mouth widened in a smile. 'You are audacious, my dear Rupert. What? Does each soul construct its own universe after all?'

I was surprised. I loved a good metaphysical SF writer, like Barry Bayley or Phil Dick. I still took *New Scientist*, *Nature* and *Scientific American* regularly. But I couldn't see how that object blazing over half the machine's hemispheres represented time, in all its abstraction. Prince Rupert's tone became more eager as he addressed that odd gathering of savants and adventurers. He grinned. He patted the head of little Tom as he continued. Tom's face had lost none of its urgency, though by now he was in awe of the prince's strange 'engine'.

'Most philosophers see time as a line disappearing into infinity, past, present, future.' Prince Rupert's eager features burned with extraordinary intensity in the red dancing light of the brands. 'Others have it as a circle, which is much the same thing, except theoretically you return to the beginning and start all over again. All representations of time are some variation on this simple idea. But the truth is time *radiates,* just as light does. Let the physical world be thought a dimension of time! Once this is understood much becomes clear. There are codes to be read by instinct, ciphers and maps which can only be absorbed through the skin. Only the human soul can cross from one beam to the next and to many others, interacting with beings whose entire history is subtly, or sometimes radically, different. Even natural rays have differences, one from another. A "star" like the one at the centre of our machine both absorbs and emits light.'

Tom stretched, as if to touch the thing. Absently, the prince pressed his hand away. 'Time is Creation. Space is time. What makes time our master is our inability to imagine it. My machine helps us in that respect, though I did not design it for the purpose. What is it, boy?' Young Tom Tompion was tugging at his coat. 'Your uncle will be paid, of course.'

'Yes, sir. Thank you, sir. But 'tis the redcoats, sir. I saw them in Fleet Street.'

'And fine they looked, I'm sure.'

I heard Mrs Melody's husky, rich tones from the other side of the instrument I could only think of as some sort of super-orrery. 'Really, your highness is an astonishing philosopher. Such a complex model. And what are those vibrating strings? A map? The silver roads some of our kind use, are said to walk?'

'Aye. 'Tis one of their representations. Yet also it shows how the Creator drinks light and dark and all matter, and at the same moment remakes them.'

'So what is this dark side of your sphere?' asked Mrs Melody. 'And why does it seem black enough to darken the cosmos? It drinks light, eh? Are these the Realms of Evil? While the hemisphere of light represents Good?'

'Chaos and Law,' agreed Prince Rupert. 'As in your own religion, Freni, dear. As we understand the laws with which God governs us.'

I recognised the name Freni as Persian. I'd done a little research into Zoroastrianism when writing *The Greater Conqueror* about Al-

THE WHISPERING SWARM • 247

exander. To be specific Freni was the name of one of Zoroaster's daughters and it took little knowledge of comparative religions to work out what Mrs Melody's faith was and how cheerfully she had adapted it to modern life, to a world where a dove-seller's shop lay next to the Xerox dealership and a halal butcher's to a video store. I had enjoyed plenty of these sights in my few trips to the Middle East and Maghreb. Why I always found that world attractive is at once obvious and subtle, a particularly interesting form of time travel. And was Lu Wing a Buddhist? Were we gathered as representatives of various religions? But no. There were too many of one belief, too few of another. Who was writing this novel?

'The balance of Light and Dark,' I began but his response was impatient.

'To a degree, to a degree. Balance. Balance. I suppose so.' I don't think I'd offered anything original to anyone but myself. His reply was a bit condescending. Like Hinduism, Zoroastrianism predicted many of our contemporary scientific ideas. There was an aesthetic to the belief system which appealed to the physicist. I heard a distant noise, nothing I was familiar with. A vehicle of some kind going over a street. Or maybe the Tube below? The heavy silver-and-brass machine shook like a delicate Christmas tree. The thing made you sensitive to every sensation.

'Sir!'

'I have the money, Tom, thrice over. And you *shall* have it. Wait, that's all I beg of thee. A few moments, lad.'

While young Tom Tompion chomped at the bit and waited out his miserable enforced silence, Prince Rupert lifted his head to chant in what I took to be Hebrew or Arabic. Evidently a quotation which only Mrs Melody and Lu Wing understood. After a while he continued in French. '*Out there in those spaces between the worlds, those shadowed spaces, is another kind of matter which some call "cosmic storm clouds" and others name Antimatter or Dark Matter, which is the opposite of our own and different in every respect, the Ultimate Anti-Cosmos lurking within their environment just as ours lurks within theirs. Travelling in apparently opposite directions. In Balance, these two forces also echo a human ideal, a happy mean, constant life, but in Opposition they come to Non-Existence. Non-Existence is not exactly a loss of consciousness. Consciousness without effect is the soul's worst hell. To watch and do nothing. Nothing at all. For all eternity.'*

Prince Rupert muttered something to himself in some sort of German dialect but continued in familiar English: 'In this curious pantomime with such high stakes, Glum Matter and Gaudy Time share between them, Rhyme for Rhyme, Creation's Secrets, Thine and Mine. Expand that to one hemisphere at odds with another and you have this model. Two interdependent philosophies whose adherents believe the other the epitome of evil.' He sighed. 'Thus the civil war is always the easiest choice as well as so rarely the last resort. War in Heaven reflects the internal battles of the human mind and is represented on Earth through familiar strife!'

I was used to the scholar prince's musings and the idiosyncratic nature of his mental associations, yet at that moment, as he gesticulated, he seemed more than half mad. Several of his friends in the room tried to disguise their concern for him. Was Prince Rupert excited by the completion of a great astrological device or was he simply raving, unable to distinguish truth from fancy? While a prisoner in Germany he had studied for years with some of the greatest alchemists of the time, including Dee. The texts he revisited would have been profound and obscure. He was familiar with all the wisdom of his own world as well as some elements of the future! Perhaps in a limited way he travelled in time as well as space. I had already noted how he occasionally let slip his knowledge of worlds so ancient they possessed languages and sciences only a rare few could understand. I remembered his references to Mu-Ooria, a world hidden under ground. I therefore gave him the benefit of the doubt and listened carefully.

I have forgotten many things in my life, perhaps because I needed to, but I can never forget that séance with Prince Rupert's Cosmolabe. I was in the presence of authentic genius. An historic moment. If Isaac Newton, that great man on the cusp of the Age of Alchemy and the Age of Science, was the father of modern physics, what was Rupert? Had Prince Rupert's main written works still been available to the public, he would today be regarded at very least as Newton's equal. For a man of such great talents, he, like so many of his clan, never did have much in the way of good luck.

Using his sword as a pointer, Prince Rupert continued to instruct us. '*See how the dark side of the sphere appears to absorb Light and Matter and how the light side invigorates all that its brilliance touches! This is how gravity sustains her tyranny over existence. The great Darkness draws even Light to itself. Then, under intense gravity, matter is first compacted to an astonishing density and then bursts! Emitting Light and Matter and all you see, emitting weaker and weaker gravity until it reaches a moment of complete dissipation and so diffuse it is drawn back into the Darkness to begin its Voyage over again.*'

'Both Creator and Created.' Mrs Melody was lost in thought. 'Is this what you are modelling for us, your highness? The Zoroastrian cosmos?'

'No, indeed, *madonna*. The Cosmolabe descries a cosmos common to all religions and sciences. Good and Evil, too, are represented. Law and Chaos...'

'Sir! Your Majesty!' squeaked Tom.

'Highness, boy,' corrected the prince absently. 'This process is repeated down the aeons – a kind of tide, absorbing and erupting. We have quested after such an engine for ever, of course. Modern philosophers seek the secret of perpetual motion as their ancestors sought to make gold. Well, I have the formula and I have built a model. And it is so much more! So much more!'

'But, your grace –'

By now I was not the only one paying closer attention to young Tom Tompion's urgent tugging and bleating than to the prince's wonderful machine. We all felt a tremor shake the cellar, causing the slender strings and shards to skip and twirl. Then came what was almost certainly the sound of a distant blast. And at last the prince was shaken from his euphoric address. Almost at once we heard a terrible underground booming. Long, rolling and massive, the noises suggested that some monster, powerful enough to walk through walls, was advancing upon us. The Cosmolabe shifted and swivelled. Prince Rupert stretched a hand towards it and hesitated.

Joey reappeared, galloping down the shaky stair. Near the bottom he paused dramatically to point behind him. 'Gentlemen – ladies – I beg your indulgence – but I regret to say we're *invaded*! Love and Clitch brought the Intelligencer General. No doubt about it because I already heard his terrible monstrous tromblon Old Thunder explode twice.

Twice, sir! That opened our gates. That's Jake Nixer. He's in, sir, on all sides, or nearly. He's placed spies here long since, that's evident. And they've let him in. No question. This is long planned, sir, and us not a wit in apprehension of it!'

'Find one who'll sally out, Joe, to parley terms. See if the Roundheads will agree swords and edged weapons but no guns. Because of the ladies,' commanded Prince Rupert. 'Civilians. At least clear the town.' He assumed command naturally. He was a great general. Cromwell would have lost some crucial battles had the prince been in command.

'They care nothing for the innocent or they would not use gunpowder on our cellars and conduits.' Prince Rupert spoke in the cold tones I had learned to associate with deep anger.

Up he climbed, his dog Boye at his heels, until he reached the top of the staircase where ginger-haired, tiny Sebastian Toom, the freckled landlord and part-owner of the Swan, waited, handing out weapons to those requiring them. His own favoured shotgun, big enough to bring down an elephant if filled with sufficient powder, stood against the wall. With a small charge the weapon was merely a threat. But a large charge threw steel balls and nails to pierce ancient oak. Further along the passage, near the outer door, I saw a wounded man. Perhaps he had brought the first news of the invasion. He was slowly employing a well-used, scabbarded, basket-hilted broadsword to get to his feet. As his head turned into the light I recognised my saviour from the altercation at the gates, when Love and Clitch had earlier accosted me.

Prince Rupert pushed passed the man, taking a glance at the wound. 'A scratch, sir, though nobly gotten.'

'A scratch, your worship, true. Not one I sought when I left my door this morning,' declared the man with a lopsided grin. He spoke in that same north-eastern brogue. 'This way, I am permitted a short sabbatical on which to contemplate the nature of human causes and why fools are prepared to die for them.' The unwitting messenger began to stand, panting a little. 'Assuming I live.' Seeing the ladies, he took off his hat and bowed as best he could, his dark chestnut curls swinging. 'Captain James St Claire, at your service.' Standing, he was scarcely taller than Mr Toom. Handsome, saturnine, a little plump. 'I am upon a mission to discover a means of reaching –'

'You are a soldier, sir?' said the prince.

'I've had a little experience at soldiering, sir. Enough to dislike the trade pretty heartily.'

'Are you game for another campaign?'

'Is there money in it?'

'Not a sou.'

'Then I'll not break the habits of a lifetime. And if we fight red-coats with purses for prizes, so much the better. 'Tis another habit I'd rather keep.'

'I'm here to recruit men to a noble cause.' Prince Rupert struck a pose which doubtless meant much to soldiers on the battlefield, but precious little in the confines of a passage in a public house. Even Mrs Melody exchanged a fleeting smile with Prince Lu Wing.

'Pah! There's no such thing!' St Claire, the wounded cynic, hob-bled after us. 'Why fight for so little advantage?'

'Honour's dead when a dream goes sour,' said Toom, the dwarfish publican, letting the trapdoor fall and hefting his great four-barrelled shotgun onto his shoulder.

'We'll challenge 'em to swords, but have firearms ready.'

'Why so little trust?' said Mrs Melody, producing a substantial twin-barrelled revolver from her bag.

'*Experience*.' I heard an echo of sadness in Lu Wing's old-fashioned French.

'Madame DeVere would call us fatalists for parleying terms so soon.'

'Fantasts, too, for thinking we can win.'

'Madame DeVere had a different agenda.'

'She'd know what hand to play.'

I was intrigued, as usual, by their speaking of someone I didn't know.

Another throaty boom which rocked the room and threatened the balance of The Swan With Two Necks. Pieces of rotten brick and mor-tar fell on our heads and shoulders. Fortunately they were compara-tively small. I remembered the street bomb shelters set up in Brookgate when I was little. They were no more secure than houses. People were buried in the basements of buildings all over Clerkenwell and Holborn. I began to shiver. I was disgusted with myself. How could I be fright-ened by nothing more than an unpleasant recollection? I caught myself addressing the deity I swore not to believe in.

Then came a monstrous roar which deafened us all and brought down whole sheets of lath and plaster onto our heads. Outside, slates from the roof crashed into the street. 'Bah! The cunning brute awaited a time when his spies tell him we're disposed elsewhere. And we are indeed sore underman'd.' Prince Rupert reached beneath a seat and brought out a small chest which, he said, insured us some sort of passage out of this hellish pit of sedition and blasphemy should God prove to be of the Parliamentary cause that day. With it beneath his cloak, he strolled for the door, taking one last, agonised glimpse over his shoulder.

As we inched along the passage I heard little Tom Tompion's voice piping after us. 'I told you there was soldiers, masters.'

Carrying my weapons, which I barely knew how to use, I was a somewhat reluctant volunteer, wondering how I had been so swiftly caught up in the madness. Through the different bars of the tavern, we rapidly gathered what forces we could, until we stood ready within the inn, panting like feral dogs, peering through bottle-green windows, just in time to see Messrs Love and Clitch rounding the corner leading a small force of well-disciplined troopers uniformed in broad red-and-white-striped wool shirts, long leather waistcoats, steel helmets, breastplates, greaves and boots. 'Intelligence men,' murmured Sebastian Toom with an oath. 'Their thrice-damned general can't be far behind.' These hard-looking special soldiers were armed with pikes, bowstaves and muskets. Over their shoulders were slung quivers of arrows or bandoliers of charges. At their belts were basket-hilted longswords. Their appearance was in considerable contrast to the rather ragged, uncertain and leaderless citizens of the Alsacia who faced them.

Still another tremendous *boom-boom-boom* in rapid succession followed by an alarming clatter from below. Prince Rupert cursed like a Billingsgate fishwife, then paused to doff his mighty hat, muttering an apology to the ladies.

'There's a damned informer somewhere amongst us!' swore Prince Rupert, increasing his pace. 'Maybe more than one, as you say, Toom. Waiting until our attention – and forces – were concentrated elsewhere.'

There came a great thump through the inside walls. Missing by inches, more bricks and plaster crashed at our feet. The very ground felt unstable. A crack appeared in the brick floor and ran all the way to the other wall. I called out for people to test where they trod. Now we feared death from below as well as above. But so far Prince Rupert's Cosmolabe remained unharmed. Voices now called orders out there. Bullying, military bellows. Having filled up the public bar we crept softly to a door looking onto the square. 'Gunpowder! Stripecoats!' Lu Wing sniffed. 'And my fighters all gone to Limehouse!'

'And my musketeers abroad!' Prince Rupert groaned despairingly, fearing for his Cosmolabe. Then he looked up and ahead as a deep-throated boom sounded from the west. 'What gun was that, Joey? What I think?'

'That was Old Thunder's tune i'truth, my lord.' Joey spoke in some awe. 'A hand cannon!' He looked from face to face. 'Few attract her anger, sirs, and retire unwounded at least. A blunderbuss such as is used at sea. That's Thunder. 'Tis the fine Prussian tromblon carried by Jake Nixer, our new Intelligencer General. He has warrants to pass where he pleases!'

'And has gold to pay a few traitors,' swore Mrs Melody, waving her double-barrelled pistol. 'The swine are coming through the cellars. Which means they have charts showing the Alsacia at her deepest. A whole nest of traitors, I'd say.' She had pushed her way to the front and flung open the door. 'This is dangerous. Dangerous. Look! They have every street and alley covered. Save what we guard with our traditions and our ranks so thin.' The Alsacians defending us were scarcely enough to call a line. Their weapons looked clean and oiled, however, which suggested they anticipated attack.

'Everywhere but the abbey. No doubt they could find no connecting cellars.'

I turned to look behind me and to my utter astonishment saw a row of wealthy young Orthodox Jews, with heavy black beards, in black mediaeval kaftans and tall astrakhan hats hurrying through the door into the abbey. They looked at us in some concern but didn't stop to help. Then they were gone. The door closed swiftly behind them. I had never before seen Orthodox Jews in the Sanctuary. I thought I remembered that all Jews were still banished from London at that time. Those were not evidently contemporary Jews, either. They looked more like people I had seen in ghetto engravings from Venice. Contemporaries of Prince Rupert? But, if so, Cromwell would not yet have invited the Jews back to England. Another damned hallucination? Or was this the only sanctuary Jews could seek and hope to be safe in times still close to the late Middle Ages? I was going to have to see a doctor. An optician at the very least.

Hallucination or not, I was scarcely unprepared. I had a big basket-hilted cutlass in my right hand, two pistols in my belt and one more in my left hand, hastily issued by Toom from that secret arsenal disguised as a wine cupboard. All of us, men and women, were similarly armed. But I doubted anyone carried a gun as powerful as Nixer's Old Thunder, rattling roofs and windows in the distance. No doubt he set it off to frighten us.

Still the Intelligencer General had not made an appearance. Hard-faced, disciplined veterans of a score of great battles, slowly the stripe-coats began to converge on three sides of the square. They all wore the jerkins and homespun woollen shirts and plain armour of the new Parliamentary police. Some wore helmets and others, mostly musket-men, wore felt hats with the front brim pinned to the crown. We had fallen back so we were defending both the inn, the abbey and the narrow street behind. The soldiers marched in strict order, halberdiers in front, archers behind, swordsmen and musketeers between them. We were one thin, overstretched line, even when a few more from the inn came to join us.

The Roundhead ranks parted and through them strode that short bantam of a man in a badly fitting red leather jerkin and a russet shirt. He had small, pale eyes, close together over a sharp nose. His cheeks were discoloured and puffy and his face was set in deep, neurotic lines. On his head he wore an iron war hat; a steel breastplate protected his chest and he had the woollen britches of a common foot soldier. Cradled in his arms he carried a massive long-barrelled, trumpet-shaped gun. This was Nixer's feared tromblon, Old Thunder. Resting on a scrawny turkey's neck, Nixer's gaunt Kentish face had deep-set eye-sockets with such dark hollows they reminded me of a skull's. His thin lips twisted in a smile and his fingers were like tentacles, curling around that long, heavy gun. Sharp little pale blue eyes, heavy, hooded lids and twin red spots on his cheeks spoke of an obsessive disposition if not outright madness. His famous tromblon boasted a hard-wood monopod to help balance it while firing. I had never seen such a beautifully finished weapon in silver, copper and brass, blackened from recent firing around the wide mouth and well-crafted locks.

Nixer's only other weapons were a long dirk and a big plain pistol at his belt. He had a slightly stiff and awkward manner and bristled with simple-minded self-righteousness. Self-importance personified. I'd heard he was a furious shiresman, a small Kentish farmer convinced that any city was a sinkhole of sin where Satan was openly worshipped. If so, then London would take a lot of cleansing. His unblinking eyes surveyed the defenders and came to rest on me.

Corporal Love brought his lugubrious, horsey face down to the level of Nixer's head and murmured something while the Intelligencer continued to gaze steadily in my direction. His unblinking eyes gave me the creeps.

Colonel Clitch had disappeared. For all I knew he was already blowing roads under ground into our houses.

'If you've come for my machine, Jake Nixer,' shouts tall Prince Rupert, stripping off his white smock to reveal all his silks, satins, lace and rings, with his long curling brown hair running over his lapels and shoulders, a long horse pistol in one hand and in the other a longsword. 'You'll best know, fool, that your damned unsubtle cannon and your kegs of gunpowder threaten the scientific work of decades! Gone in a moment. You shall suffer for your fanatic religiosity. That machine was built by the most skilled craftsmen of the Occident and Orient, the combined wisdom of centuries. Inspired by our Creator himself! 'Tis a sublime engine for cultivated men but it baffles the foolish whose only thought is to destroy it. With such an instrument we might truly still change the world and bring about Paradise on Earth!'

'You speak in lies and mysteries, Sir Sorcerer. Blasphemies, too, Master Stuart, I do believe.'

'Have the goodness, knave, to address me by my God-granted title. There is precious little Stuart in my veins, but plenty in my heart and in my brain. I speak God's honest truth. The truth of our invention remains undisputed. Last I saw her she was being rained on by brick and rendering. What d'ye think drove us up to confront ye?'

'You would divert my attention from the abbey. But I believe I am thoroughly wise to your devil's tricks, brother...'

'Wiser than I, sir! What other Treasure would we have?'

Nixer sneered with a practised ease. 'Men, you all know the plan,' he called out to his soldiers. 'We'll kneel and rise, likely to give us the advantage again.' He seemed to stare directly at me. 'Advance upon the abbey! Let's take it back in Christ's name!' He raised his right hand and the archers drew arrows from their quivers.

'Strategy which won us Agincourt!' called Prince Rupert with a broad grin. 'But can she win two centuries on?' He put his hands on his hips and laughed his mockery. 'You forget, Mr Nixer, that I have made something of a study of strategy.'

'We'll have an answer for thee soon enough, Master Stuart. There's still time for you all to join your kinsman and master on the block. Traitor to God and traitor to our country,' sneered Jake. 'We'll find much evidence to prove it when this midden falls to our cause!' Nixer was all strutting confidence and gamecock twitching of his long neck, like a self-righteous rooster. His discoloured cheeks burned bright and crazy. His nasty little eyes glittered with malice. 'Satan, son of the morning, is ever alert for new ways to trick us. That Treasure be the property of the people and I claim it in Parliament's name. We'll discover where it's hidden, never fear, for only thee, Rupert Stuart, know the veraciousness of that, I think!' He spoke in that stiff, pompous, semi-literate way common to most Low Church clergy, adding: 'When I see it,' as if he belatedly found a missing clause.

'If I could de-convolute thy sentences, man, I'd know whether I agreed with you and could offer you honest parley. Whatever it is you bray in your donkey speech, like old Bottom the Weaver in the play, we demand you lay down your arms, for you come illegally to a place of holy sanctuary.'

'Play, is it? Ha! O, Corruption! O, Disgust and Misery!' Jake Nixer had learned his rhetoric well. 'You speak of Paradise. Let me tell thee that hellfire shall come to this place this day and it shall burn as if it were kindling in the dry heat of summer. Our holy places and the Church's shall not fall to God's enemies, nor shall the Just perish!'

'Poppycock!' English slang in a familiar French accent. The mellifluous voice of Captain Claude Duval rang out across the square. 'The old laws of London are on our side! The good old laws of the ancient Christians from the time of Joseph's landing. And before that, from the time of the pagan kings of Troy. Law upon law to keep Englishmen forever free and give example to the world! I am a student of history. So believe me, *messieurs*, I know of what I speak!' All ready for battle, Duval rode his lovely sorrel mare, Petite Marie, which he stabled next to his lodgings, Mistress Spott's in nearby Carmelite Yard. Mistress Spott's sister Persephone looked after his other wants.

There came a pause. None of us had expected this.

In a moment, Claude Duval went into action. Complaining at his galliard's interruption and roaring a series of French curses, many concerning the fate of his liver, he tapped Petite Marie into a gallop. He came on quickly behind the redcoat troops, running one unprepared archer into the next, startling some and shoving others to the side as, with powder and flints and ramrods, musketeers sought to prepare their weapons. His pistols in his hands, his reins looped around his saddle-bow, Duval steered his lovely mount with his knees and filled the air with muffled curses. 'Name of a dog, these cowardly reversos in their depressing clothes shall pollute our thoroughfares no longer!'

I found myself grinning at this glorious rhetoric even as the soldiers lifted their bulky muskets. Beside me, Moll laughed openly. 'Duval always said he was prepared for just such an eventuality as this.' Her eyes shone and she applauded him vigorously. Then I guessed that Duval was perhaps her 'cavalier', the older man who had seduced the strange girl fresh from college. The man whom she still refused to name. Who could *not* love Duval? He had saved us all. Women keep secrets much less ostentatiously than men.

Duval was a wonderful rider, perhaps the first skill required of a professional highwayman. He cut a dashing figure with his long auburn hair streaming in the wind, topped by a dark blue befeathered hat. He wore a fine navy blue silk frock coat, his pale blue waistcoat and stockings all lace-trimmed. The incongruous, almost comical, aspect of his outfit was that he still had on his dancing shoes. The black leather pumps looked dainty in his heavy military stirrups, at odds with a massive cavalry sabre clattering at his saddle. Three Roundheads were alert enough to shoot an arrow into his left greave and try to engage him with their pikes. Two caught the force of his pistols. He drew his sword and dispatched the third. Then he was off, Petite Marie carrying him at a lick down another street. Ducking to avoid the overhanging walls and signs, laughing as he went, he left behind him a bunch of disoriented soldiers who no longer knew which way to expect the next attack –

– allowing Prince Rupert to lead his brightly dressed raggle-taggle army in a charge against the Parliamentarians. At his command our pistols and muskets blazed all together so that happily I never knew if I drew the blood of men I actually admired. My political sympathies were never Royalist, though romantically I enjoyed their dash. Like Confederates in the American War, they were the defeated past and a worse tyranny followed them. In this situation I had no choice save to side with the king's men. All my declared friends were for the Stuarts and my enemies represented Cromwell. I knew Clitch, Love and others to be turncoats of the most despicable kind. They had none of the best Parliamentarians' simple sense of fair play. A dangerous fanatic Jake Nixer might be, but he was driven by his convictions. There was something congenial about most of the Cavaliers. I couldn't help liking them. What's more, it is hard to see the viewpoint of the man who makes your blood run cold as he leers at you and fingers a massive, much-polished knife.

So rapid was our rush that the astonished Nixer had no time to reload his tromblon and fell back, letting the thing swing behind him on a great leather strap. He drew his broad-bladed sword. Unexpectedly outmanoeuvred, his archers and musketeers were unable to make use of their weapons and the Alsacians were good, it soon proved, at close fighting. Many more were moving in from the backstreets to catch the soldiers in a perfect pincer movement.

Once I let off my 'barker' I fell back. I had no taste or talent for hand-to-hand combat. To be honest, I took no pleasure in any kind of fighting, except as sport. I prefer my antagonisms kept to the archery field or the debating stage. I come from a long line of cowards.

I had to admit I felt the camaraderie. Standing shoulder to shoulder with Prince Rupert, on the other hand, and soon Moll Midnight and Mother Melody, the elegant Lu Wing and young Joey Cornwall, I almost enjoyed myself. In our exotic clothes we were a most mismatched group of individuals. Every one of my comrades clearly relished the skilful business of taking life. Their faces were flushed. Their eyes sparkled. They fought side by side like old comrades. They were ecstatic. They had new blood in their veins. I fell back as they led a little group deep into the Roundhead ranks fighting with swords and only a few pikes and pistols. I saw Moll suddenly stagger, her body blocked from my sight by Sebastian Toom's small ferocious figure. Forgetting my own uselessness, I took a grip on my cutlass and ran into the main press, cutting and defending, fighting my way to Moll's side as, gathering her strength, she continued to drive the redcoats back towards the gates. My love for her somehow gave me physical courage. I took a firmer grip on my massive cutlass and pressed forward ready to do the unthinkable if her life were threatened.

Discharging my other gun at an attacker, I reached her. Moll's wounded thigh wasn't serious but it looked as if Joey Cornwall's was. He lay twisted on his back, the flesh of his face pressed to one side by the cobbles, while blood oozed in a slow, steady stream from his mouth. He bore a jagged wound in his side. I was almost frozen by the sight but thought of Moll's safety kept me going. She had tripped, she said. Somehow I helped her get Joey back to the local doctors. They had set up a field hospital in the public bar and they were doing their best with very little. Gin was the main anaesthetic.

Those of us who were able returned to help push into the Roundhead ranks. Having expected an easy victory, the Commonwealth troops were demoralised. To my surprise, they did not concentrate their forces on the tavern's basement. The abbey was their goal. Though doubtless well indoctrinated into the nature of the Papist Beast, many had remained uncertain whether they desecrated holy ground or not, a question of great importance to such decent, upright men, volunteers in the service of their religion and respectful of Christ, if not their fellow Christians.

Eventually scowling Nixer called an order to retreat. He demanded that we let them drag their dead and wounded with them which, with great gravity, we permitted. I have since seen men wounded in grisly ways yet it surprised me even at the time why red-stained shirts and shallow cuts to face and hands seemed the most serious signs of brutal slash and thrust. The bearers came up and the bodies of the dead were arranged on stretchers. In a moment or two, led by their officers, they had marched from the square. In the silence, we counted our own losses.

CHAPTER TWENTY-SEVEN

COUNTING LOSSES

VERY FEW OF our men were seriously wounded and not one, it seemed, was dead. Even poor Joey Cornwall was able to walk without support, that great gash no longer bleeding. I was amazed people had not expired from the ferocious thrusts they had received from pikes or bayonets. Indeed, bandages very soon hid the wounds and few seemed seriously hurt. When I mentioned this to Prince Rupert, he laughed and reminded me that we fought to preserve the world's most ancient traditions, 'as well as the sacred ground of this great, old abbey. This is where miracles are made.'

As the silence faded and we realised that we had actually fought and defeated a larger, better armed force, I heard Father Grammaticus's voice behind me offering up a short unfamiliar prayer in what I guessed was Latin.

Beside me, suddenly, Friar Isidore materialised. 'There is too much pain in the world. They seek to remedy that but, sadly, they only increase it. They see their salvation in simplicity and purification, but the world is not simple. Nor is it easily purified. God made it complex and mysterious. They want to obey man's rules, not God's.'

I acknowledged that he spoke even if I didn't entirely understand him.

'They sought their simplified salvation through our Treasure, which they planned to steal. We were prepared to hold our ground, in spite of the danger.' I thought I heard an unseemly, slightly spiteful note in his otherwise gentle tones. 'But our prayers were answered. You fought a brave battle.'

I said I found it sad that Christian fought Christian. He agreed with me, vigorously shaking his head. 'Isn't that so! Sometimes I wonder why we threw in our lot with them.'

It seemed to me he excluded himself from his judgement. Surely a Christian monk had to feel empathy? Did he mean that the order was not actually Christian? He was decidedly melancholy, I thought, but in a way that set him apart from the rest of us.

Prince Rupert congratulated Duval on his tactics. 'You always claimed it was common sense to keep mistress and steed separate from one's quarters. The worst would have come if Nixer had not been so considerately overconfident. As is often the case, the battle was won not by the perspicacity of the conquerors, but by the errors of the conquered. We had to make sure he did not reload and fire his Old Thunder! His men were leaderless while he spoke. Show me a zealot who can resist making a speech and I'll show you a dead one.'

Now I shook Captain Duval's hand. In truth, he had saved lives on both sides. The Roundheads seemed grateful for Prince Rupert's courtesies. I knew he was simply behaving according to his sense of honour. Only later would he come to understand that not all of these up-and-coming creeds fought by the same rules of chivalry. And so Jake Nixer and his bombast, his lickspittles and Old Thunder retreated down the ratholes they had made, dragging their wounded with them, and our citizens set to rebuilding and blocking new walls as fast as they could as if they feared they might let some further evil in.

Once Prince Rupert was certain his wounded friends were safe he took a few of us with him to the cellar. The way through was blocked by fallen rubble and we turned back. We had to think carefully before we went back in there. We needed expert engineers to prop it all up. To move stones at random would risk bringing the whole thing down onto the cellar and smashing for ever Prince Rupert's incredible and intriguing super-orrery. As it was, we had no idea how much of the strange machine was intact. I had the impression he had worked on the thing for months.

As if in answer there came a rumbling and a shifting from below and we knew we heard more of the caverns settling, doubtless threatening any contents not already damaged.

'It can be repaired. It can be built again.' The prince was reassuring himself. He shook his head. 'Now we need your help more than ever, Master Michael. Will you not join our cause?'

Regretfully, I lowered my head. 'I have responsibilities,' I told him. 'Another cause, if you like.'

Molly touched his arm to comfort him, but he displayed an uncharacteristic reserve, nodding and patting her hand, telling her everything was splendid.

I saw the monks returning in twos and threes through the door into their abbey. Were those mysterious Jews still there? Had they been prepared to pick up arms if we seemed to be losing? I doubted it. The monks were the strangest Christians I knew! What was their purpose here? It had to be something particular. Had they been founded solely to protect that weird fish chalice, that beautiful, ancient cup used on their altar and thought by gossiping locals to possess magical powers? Their Treasure. The true object of Nixer's attack?

That last incident made me consider seriously what I was doing in the Sanctuary. I hated unanswered questions. I was sleepwalking through my life. I was missing my children pretty painfully. I saw them fairly regularly, but rarely casually. One thing that bit of violent adventure had confirmed: I could not risk my children becoming fatherless as a result of my own curiosity and relish for adventure. I disapproved of men who did that. I shared this view with Jack Allard. I had already bought far too much life insurance because of the way I chose to live. Unable to support his family, my hero Mervyn Peake was confined to hospital with Parkinson's. Other friends had died young, leaving spouses and children with next to nothing. I had seen the wives and children of other divorces and deaths having to struggle. At the moment my money was allowing me to stop time and enjoy the benefits of what amounted to a harem. It couldn't last. My girls came first.

Typical of the English petits bourgeois, I was raised with few moral boundaries in my life. 'Keep your nose clean and stay out of trouble' was the profoundest advice I got from my relatives. As a young man, therefore, I had to create some kind of morality for my-

self and I did this mostly through reading, especially the French existentialists and anarchists like Kropotkin. Kropotkinism gave me a
useful moral code by which to make ordinary decisions. Of course, I
never thought of passing on my ideas as moral wisdom. You had to
follow your instincts. And mine were to be there at my kids' disposal.
I wasn't at all alone in this. We were fathers of our times. In that sense
the cycle of life seemed to follow a pretty ordinary course. Much as I
hated the yuppy middle-class liberals moving into the old neighbour-
hoods, I still missed the cycle of normal bourgeois life. Every street
and house reminded me of some event that had happened in my past.
Brookgate was falling almost daily to the developers but the Grove
still seemed firmly in the hands of working and creative people. We
now know it was an illusion. We hadn't realised what liars our representatives were, how quietly companies were buying flats in the area.
Arts execs and their businessmen and politician friends learned how
convenient for work old Brookgate and Ladbroke Grove, with their
trees and parks, could be. But at that point, the areas still held much
of their familiar shabby atmosphere. I valued the area as I valued my
kids' childhood and I knew I should take advantage of it all before
the neighbourhood disappeared and the girls grew up.

I'd had enough melodrama. What on earth was I doing risking my
life playing at soldiers? I was sick of all those unanswered questions.
I wanted to get back to reality. I felt helpless, ineffective, and I knew
I could be of little help in Alsacia.

'Will you stay?' Molly asked when we were alone. 'I think Prince
Rupert needs your help.' She seemed unusually vulnerable and it was
almost impossible for me to resist her. Helena wasn't expecting me
back for at least a day or two. The wound Moll had sustained, which
I had thought so bad, was no more than a scrape. I was relieved she
didn't need me. 'Please,' she said. 'I love you with all my heart and
soul.'

I badly wanted to see my children and close friends again. I had
no solutions. I told Molly I was going back to the Grove. I promised
I would be back soon to see her. I loved her. But at that moment, I
just wanted to go home.

CHAPTER TWENTY-EIGHT

MY INDUCTIONS

I WENT BACK to Ladbroke Grove. I couldn't come up with a convincing explanation for what I had witnessed at the Alsacia. I told Helena I was having a bit of a struggle as I sat there in bed with her. She wore a demure white nightie and seemed in a great mood as we sipped our cocoa and watched TV. She didn't ask how things had been at the retreat, assuming I referred to my latest book. She thought I didn't want to talk about it. She seemed content. We were a settled domestic couple again. I sighed with relief.

Helena rarely said it but I supposed she loved me. What did that really mean? Like so many women she was turned on by power. She couldn't help herself. And I had the most power of anyone currently available to her. Maybe, too, I was simply her type. Our chemistry worked. The random elements which we translate into love and desire mystify us precisely because beauty has no universal standards. For most of my life I thought of myself as homely if not downright ugly but no woman I took up with – and they were all pretty good-looking – ever thought of me like that. Helena and Molly were both beauties of very different types. I don't look bad in those early pictures. Video from my twenties shows me as an aggressive, articulate, self-confident, much-travelled man of letters and the world.

On occasion both Helena and Molly loved to be my ally. What drove women to fight for men with everything they had? Not many men typically did that for women. All those novels and studies never solved the puzzle. Chemistry alone did not explain it.

I knew Molly expected me eventually to divorce Helena. I had a practical reason for being reluctant to do that. I didn't want to risk disinheriting my children. I wasn't sure I wanted a divorce at all. You don't think much in terms of death when you're that age but the episode with Nixer and his men had made me consider it. Something else worried me. When I first met Moll she had appeared a self-confident young woman. Since then she seemed to grow dissatisfied and hesitant, unsure of herself. Was that my fault? Or was Molly hiding something? Maybe another lover who was making her miserable? Or secrets I had not even guessed at? I worried about it. Why had she changed? Had I let her down? I certainly felt a passion for her I did not feel for Helena. But then my love for Helena was also of a different nature.

So I returned to the Alsacia and proposed to Moll that we keep going as we had done. Of course I coated the pill a bit. Nothing was altogether real. I was confident we could conquer what our parents called Common Sense. Those were the days. The golden dream of the endless '60s. We lived a far sweeter dream than anything which followed. It took a lot of energy and willpower, maintaining so many illusions. But we had a lot of energy and I had a lot of willpower. We enjoyed a very energetic few years. Working, fucking, playing so much more determinedly than any predecessors.

Reasonably, I expected Moll to object but she said that seemed fair. I did need to see my children. She liked what she called 'playing house' with me. If Helena didn't object, why should she? This response startled me a little. I still wondered if Moll were living the childhood she'd never had, though with someone more congenial than her lost father. I joked that the reason I felt so tired and old sometimes was because she was going through a difficult phase. One day, I added, she'd grow up and leave home. Perhaps she exchanged sweet dreams for my energy. It gave me a buzz when she bit my neck. I'm not saying our private world was entirely dull.

As I saw it, I was doing my best by everyone. Because of Kropotkin, my granny and my Uncle Fred, freedom was something I took seriously. It would be years before I learned that not everyone talking about freedom wants the same thing.

Moll was, she said, mine. She didn't want any more freedom than she had. I wasn't altogether comfortable with that! What do you do when someone tells you they don't really want freedom? Try to get comfortable with the idea? I'm pretty sure what my granny would have said.

And how do you deal with a constant murmuring in your head day in and day out? Anticipating it. Wondering sometimes what you could do to stop those voices, that Swarm? Because it only really went away, of course, in the Alsacia. Outside it got a little louder all the time.

At first the Swarm grew louder as the day went on, getting worse in the evening. Then it seemed worse at dawn and then increasingly at night. I began to think I would never escape from it. Unless, of course, I gave in and took my whole family back to that damned haven for the hopelessly romantic and emotionally cowardly, where the impulsive point of a poignard could determine if your children grew up with two birth parents or none.

With its violence and uncertainties, the Alsacia really was no place to raise children. I knew by then why parents with young families chose not to live there. Yet even now the place both pushed and pulled me. Ironically, while I lived in the Sanctuary, I often felt safer than in Kensington, where I hardly need worry about anything but the odd deadline. I relished the silence. While I was away from the Alsacia I knew nothing but a sense of loss and the urgent voices of the Swarm. Did the Swarm call me back or was it warning me away? Or telling me something totally different? Why did it never manifest itself in Alsacia? Was I protected from it or was it demanding my return? Or was the Swarm really nothing more than a form of tinnitus? I had long since given up attempts to talk about this with Helena. When I tried to discuss it with Molly, she said she had no interest in theoretical physics.

The fact was I knew of no way of stopping the Swarm or even regulating its volume. I could usually disguise my responses if I was in public when its voice grew impossible to ignore. I could pretend to function as normal. The Swarm rarely raised itself above a loud murmuring. Needless to say, resisting that sound, acting a part, sometimes made me impatient and short-tempered. There were some days, especially when I did not have the company of my kids, when I really did think of going away. Life became too difficult. I profoundly believed suicide to be a selfish act and never seriously contemplated it. In the past I'd always found distraction in passion, gossip, fantasy and research. My curiosity could be satisfied as much by some new revelation in science as by what someone told me in bed. All narrative. All grist for the mill.

Hopping between a variety of lovers was no longer really an option. I received nothing from it except discomfort. On the plus side you picked up a lot of good stories, sometimes at the expense of your friends. On the minus side it was a strain trying to remember names and addresses, let alone all the rest. And most people are conventional. Boring, even. Deeply predictable. I'd tried every other strategy but the fact was I couldn't hold work together unless my life was orderly and without deception. To work well I needed a routine. Adventures were experienced before and after a book. Only rarely did I allow anyone to interrupt. That was how it was. I warned Molly, as I had warned everyone else, that life with writers was worse than boring, even when you were one yourself. Moll seemed to think that reasonable and didn't mind much even when the sex got fairly routine. In the main she enjoyed a life given to creativity. She had a fine draughtswoman's eye and was a good painter. Her taste frequently echoed mine. We enjoyed many of the same things in poetry and painting. With her youth and enthusiasm she gave me a great deal. We laughed together a lot. She seemed as happy and content as I was. She loved me, she said. I loved her. I wrote love letters on her skin in Magic Marker. She didn't have to write back, but she did. She had proven her love. That had impressed me. And I had obviously proven my love for her. So that was okay. Emotional life in balance. Good. We were safe enough for a little rock and roll.

I think we were all doing our best. I might have been better if the Whispering Swarm had allowed me a few more days and nights off, just a few extra hours to think, but I gave my children a pretty secure life. They needed all the stability and clarity and loving I could give. In spite of the noise and the mysteries, the books got written. Sometimes I caught the Swarm's rhythm, almost like liturgical singing, and wrote along with it. When I appeared on stage I made up chants and songs incorporating the Swarm. If I told the kids a story I could sometimes include the murmuring. I think after a while the rhythm of the Swarm actually defined my style.

Those were in my defiant days. In my relatively few depressed days I couldn't get off my backside. I just sat in my favourite easy chair with my head full of voices while I smoked and wouldn't respond to food or entertainment. I demanded peace and quiet from people who were already creeping around me. They had no wish to antagonise me. I was the breadwinner and I was barking.

Slowly I began turning into a tyrant. I knew it, of course, subconsciously. I wasn't behaving according to my own ideals. If I took a step back, I could see I was becoming a bit of a monster. My old friends didn't come round as much as usual. Sad at being unable to see my children casually I had without noticing sidestepped into genuine melancholy.

At about this time, and not merely as a matter of pride, Helena began to think in terms of strategy. She probably suspected I wasn't alone in my retreat. She had seemed reconciled to this while it gave her some peace from my worst outbursts. Increasingly, I was reluctant to return to the Alsacia, even though it meant relief from the Whispering Swarm. The old me was coming back. And Helena wanted the old me back. And maybe a bit more besides. At that time I saw none of this. I thought everyone in the harem was happy.

We should have known better, but Moll was that much younger and made me younger, too, somehow. Helena didn't believe in altruism, not really, because, she reasoned, all men were unreliable on some level. If it weren't for lust and romance no sane woman would ever cloud her brain long enough to reproduce.

So far, however, we were both reluctant to bring matters to any sort of head. Our arrangement gave us all a little breathing space. That summer, Helena took the girls to stay in Devon with her friend Di. I went off to the Alsacia, glad to be free, if only for a little while, of the Whispering Swarm.

CHAPTER TWENTY-NINE

MRS MELODY

THEN, ONE MORNING, there came a knock at the chamber door and there she stood, beaming like the sun and smelling like Kew Gardens, her carpet bag apparently of the same dark material as her long overcoat. A huge, white, knitted tam-o'-shanter sat on her expertly hennaed curls. Her outfit would look eccentric to any age. I had answered her knock because Molly was downstairs practising on the piano in the private bar. 'Blimey!' I said.

'So this is the romantic slum you live in.' She stared past my shoulder with approval. 'Exactly where I'd shack up with Chopin, if I'd had the chance.'

'Oh, God,' said Molly, coming up from downstairs.

'Darling, I'm taking you and your young man to lunch.'

We went to the Cheddar-in-Chancery because Mrs Melody wanted some 'good old-fashioned English food'. I wouldn't have seen that as a recommendation in the 1960s, although in the nineteenth century English food had been generally thought better than French. Rules and the Cheddar were our nearest posh restaurants in those days. The Cheddar's proprietor had a penchant for collecting monkeys. They wore nappies and were chained to stands but could deliver a vicious bite if you got close enough. The food was always reasonable and the wine list well above its station. The place was popular with theatrical people. There were Italian *commedia* Harlequin, Pierrot and

Columbine murals all over the place and we generally got a great table because I had been going there since I was seventeen. Apparently they knew Mrs Melody, too. They treated her with the same pleasure with which they treated me and anyone who happened to be with me. She acted as if she were taking favourite children out for a feed at the school tuck shop. I apologised for not inviting her to stay as long as she liked because we had no spare room. She took it like a sport. She smiled carefully. She said it was her fault. 'I'll make it up to you, I promise, darling.' She spoke of a trip she was making to the Holy Land. She would stay in London, camping on 'that horrible sofa' of ours. She would be no trouble and she would be flying to New York tomorrow. After that she was going to Jerusalem. She shepherded us up the stairs to the restaurant's 'private' floor.

Descending just as we ascended, a handsome older man in an expensive silk suit recognised Mrs Melody and, with a delighted smile, came towards her. 'My dear Freni!' She was a little disconcerted by this. She smiled sweetly and tried to get away from him as gracefully as possible. She seemed relieved he was leaving. She made telephoning gestures at him before he left. She laughed about it at the table.

'He doesn't have my number. What would it matter if he did?'

'He's very good-looking. An old boyfriend?' I asked.

'Oh, not even that.' She offered her daughter a passing frown as if asking why I was so inquisitive.

I apologised, explaining myself with a joke. 'I'm a novelist, you know. We always ask too many questions.'

I already knew her first name, though I still called her Mrs Melody. 'Wasn't Freni one of the three Zoroastrian muses?' I lit her cigarette for her. I was genuinely curious. Zoroastrianism seemed such an exotic, romantic and actually rather attractive religion. Had her parents followed the old Persian faith? Many still did in some parts of India and the Middle East. 'I suppose your own mother and father –?'

She showed a hint of irritation and made an evasive remark. 'Michael, could you order another bottle of that delicious claret?' She ate and drank with great relish, having at least one bottle of the '57 St Émilion to herself and treating us to another.

I tried to catch the waiter's eye. 'Which one?' I asked. 'Painting? Sculpture? Or oratory?'

She knew what I meant and laughed in spite of herself. 'Astronomy,' she said.

Molly broke in, an odd look in her eyes. 'Didn't I tell you?'

'What?'

'Mum's a famous astronomer.'

That was a rather big bit of one's mother's CV to leave out. I flashed a question at Moll.

'In Iran,' said Mrs Melody. 'I know the shah isn't popular with young people, but it's my native country. And my job does give me certain visiting privileges at Cambridge.' She looked up at me from under long lashes, her expression mildly sardonic.

If she expected me to challenge her, I couldn't. What I knew about astronomy filled a page and a half or so in *The New Scientist*. Try as I might, I had developed no interest in the heavens. I fell asleep during a press showing of *2001* and Arthur Clarke, with whom I saw it, wasn't a bit offended. He told me how much money it had earned in Chicago in its first week. Ever since then, any giant spaceship which takes for ever to cross the screen during the credits for whatever protracted space opera it is has sent me off to the Land of Nod in an instant. I really didn't like space. Space bored me. Space was a distraction. Cute robots left me cold and they'd never duelled with light sabres better than in *Planet Stories*, the greatest of all the 1950s science fiction pulps. Time, however, was an entirely different mess of fish. Past, present and future in any order related closely to human affairs. Life is short but it needn't be dull. *And then you die.* Maybe a few times. Space just confirmed how insignificant you were. Or not. I don't care if I'm a specimen and some superior intelligence is observing this solar system through a microscope. But Freni Melody made it interesting. 'We are rare in having the power to observe our environment as well as living in it.'

I laughed. 'If I knew I had a cosmic audience, I'd clown it up a bit. I love the stage.'

'You do? So do I. I started going to plays early, when matinées were dirt cheap.' Mrs Melody was returning to a safe enthusiasm.

'I would have been an actor if I hadn't been a writer and a musician. At least an actor can see the type of audience they're working for. Writers have no real idea of their readers. The book just goes out there and whether anyone else is interested is frequently a matter of speculation.'

'You poor thing.' She was mocking. 'We astronomers know nothing of such problems.'

While I was trying to put that together, she changed the subject again, giving as an example yet another wonderful anecdote of her girlhood in Iran.

Soon I was in no doubt about who was the superior storyteller. Freni Melody was a genius at laying out a narrative. And what amazing stories they were! It was obvious that Molly laughed at her mum's tales in spite of herself. She had obviously heard many of them before. I saw her then as a little girl, begging her mother to tell one of her stories, and I fell in love with her again.

In that state I was impervious to Mrs Melody's charm. At any other time I had to make a huge moral effort not to embrace her. An effort flattering to nobody, I suspect, but some lunatic Puritan. I was discovering how that mysterious and attractive woman could confuse me very easily.

By now we were choosing dessert and Mrs Melody asked suddenly, thinking of an invitation she'd received for when she would be in New York, why Thanksgiving wasn't celebrated in the UK. Because it best illustrated the subject in a nutshell and offered a fairly good joke, I told her how some years earlier my friend Polly Zee, who was a guest at the big Thanksgiving dinner Helena and I regularly gave our American friends in England, asked why we British were celebrating Thanksgiving, since, after all, it was to commemorate the first harvest and the Puritans' safe arrival on American soil. 'Well,' I said, quick as a flash, 'you're thanking God for the Puritans' arriving – and we're thanking God they left.'

Mrs Melody loved that. Her laughter was heartfelt. She had always thought, she said, that it was no surprise that after the Indians had offered them squash, the Puritans persecuted them. I hated squash, too. Had she ever been persecuted?, I asked.

'Of course,' she said. 'They tried to make me a Catholic for years, my dear. That's the dark side of the Emerald Isle, eh? At that damned convent. I followed my father's advice. I ignored what didn't interest me and took from them what did interest me. By my second year at St

Bridie's the nuns believed me some kind of reincarnated pagan, possibly even a demon. They tried to beat the devil out of me. Because my parents said they were not Moslems, the nuns always thought they were Persian Christians who had somehow been used by Satan to give birth to me. I was sympathetic to their delusions. What decent person could not be? And they hated that, too. Their guilt and their superstitions didn't interest me.' Her crimson mouth yawned with laughter.

'When did you first discover the Sanctuary?' I asked, bold enough in my cups and hoping she was drunk enough to answer.

'Oh, I think I've always known about it. Haven't you?'

Somehow this wrong-footed me. 'Well, not always.'

'Oh, I think so.' She smiled into my eyes. 'I think you know a great deal, Michael. The mind is a kind of maze, isn't it? Sometimes it's possible to get lost in it. That's what's tricky about memory. Am I right?'

And that was how she blocked my line of inquiry. Moll didn't try to rescue me. Was this a familiar tactic of her mother's? If so, it worked to enforce my silence on the subject of the Sanctuary.

Although her plane did not leave until the afternoon, Freni Melody left in the morning. She had to make some phone calls to Iran, she said, and of course that wasn't possible from the Alsacia. The shah would not be deposed until 1979. His secret police watched her and were more or less of the same stripe as secret police worldwide, that is, highly suspicious because not very bright. She was on first-name terms with some of them. When she returned from the Holy Land, Freni went off to have an open affair with Billy Alford, her opposite number in Cambridge. Molly had been told all the details and some of the most sensational stories had been passed on to me as pillow talk. Freni told her daughter, for instance, how Alford had 'taken her' astride the casing of his gigantic optics. She judged an astronomer, she boasted, by the size of his telescope. In formal astrophysics, they would co-write a couple of papers in *Nature*, early steps towards modern string theory. She had supplied the abbot with a good deal of the detail for his Cosmolabe.

Years later I had the chance to ask Alford what he thought of string theory. Some still believed it a pseudoscience along with climate change indicators and such. Only in the twenty-first century did people start to take it seriously. The SF magazines had been warning about climate change since the '50s. Alford had laughed. Most of his ideas, he said, had come from Mrs Melody. 'She had a brilliant, if somewhat erratic, mind. She's the only astrophysicist I ever knew who believed in what I can only call magic!'

I wonder if he had meant her interest in the tarot. She had read both of us our cards the night she left and then, frowning and smiling, had refused to tell us what they told her. She was not so much troubled as puzzled by what she read. Every time I tried to find out what she had seen in the tarot deck she laughed. But she did leave a beautiful new pack for me as a parting gift.

Before the green Lagonda arrived to take her to the airport, Freni give me a quiet hint of what to expect of her daughter. 'Every woman dreams of a life which never came and never could have come,' she said as Molly prepared breakfast. 'Old flame dreams. We all had "what might have been" locked into our brain patterns. Men dream of possible futures, women of impossible pasts. When we grow older we realise what a disgusting weakness it is to harbour such infantile desires and what damage it does. You must expect at some point a period of turmoil. You, surely, have read her tarot? But if you really desire her, you will be at her service in a moment. If not, let her fly free. She can be as capricious as she is steady, as romantic as she is practical. And for all she seems mature, she is not skilled at bedroom diplomacy. She was born under Virgo and her moral conscience is developed in spite of herself. She struggles against her own nature. If she wants to move, she will find an excuse to make you the villain, be sure of that. "Beware the Crisis Maker!" as the tarot tells us. But who's to say that day will ever come? You have your own fate to follow, of course. You have three children?'

'Two.'

'Believe me, I mean to make no threats. I wish only to help you. I'll do a close reading for you, if you like, before I go.'

She never did find time to give me that last tarot reading. Astonished by her speech, I had avoided her. I could read the cards, of course, as I had learned from my Auntie Ethel and my gypsy babysitters. They said I had a talent, but I was convinced my own tarot stuff would seem amateurish to Mrs M. I didn't question her further. Some of what she said completely mystified me. I didn't take it very seriously. Not seriously enough in some ways. I thought I could resist Mrs Melody's mind games. But I came to realise, not without a good deal of admiration, that she had me completely outplayed. This woman was an expert at backgammon and chess. She played them to the highest mark and entirely for pleasure. I learned that lesson more than once.

I should have preferred to remain friends with Mrs Melody. I was never her enemy and I did not think she was mine. Yet somehow I felt she was not on my side. She was on no-one's side except her own. She was good-humoured, kind-hearted and exceptionally gifted, but self-sacrifice was not one of her most obvious characteristics.

To me, Molly hardly resembled her mother at all, except she sometimes seemed a bit judgemental. She told me that Freni Melody was also a September birthday, a Virgo, like Helena, Sally and Kitty. They all had quite a lot to say about what was wrong with the world, though Molly rarely let herself express such judgements in public. This made Mrs Melody all the more intriguing to me.

The night after she left for New York, I asked so many questions about her that Molly became impatient with me. 'You sound as if you're in love with my mother rather than me. Well, she isn't having you. And if you ever...'

But threats of that kind were not really in her nature and she never did say what she'd do to me. In the end, I suppose it was just as well I didn't know what was coming. That made it an infinitely more painful revenge than any I could have anticipated.

I became anxious to return to Ladbroke Grove. Something Mrs Melody had said had made me uncomfortable. I reminded myself that the Sanctuary offered me a kind of holiday, a release from those constantly whispering voices. I was really growing weary of mysteries and I suspected Freni Melody had tried to warn me about her daughter. I wasn't sure what. I was in love with Molly, but I loved Helena in that deeper way that comes from sharing children and domestic life. I longed to see Sally and Kitty. After I finished my latest fantasy novel, I told Molly I needed a break to see the kids. She accepted this, even seemed solicitous. She told me to take my time. I was a little uncertain of this, wondering if she was hiding her emotions, but she reassured me. 'I want you to go on loving me,' she said, 'not come to resent me. Freedom means a lot to both of us.' She seemed so ready to accept my leaving that I wondered if for some reason she was actually glad to see the back of me.

The Swarm seemed worse than the last time I had been home. Of course it was impossible to ignore, though I really had forgotten how beautiful Helena could look. She seemed pleased to see me and her lovemaking was wonderful. As before, she said that my 'retreat' had done me good and that I was my old self again. But the Whispering Swarm was almost unbearable. I could barely ignore it for seconds at a time. I was glad I had met many of my most pressing deadlines. I had a lot of them. I was writing about six books a year then, and also editing, writing short stories and doing the odd local gig on stage with the Deep Fix, just to keep my hand in.

An old friend, the actor Jon Finch, looked me up. We had met at a poker school we both belonged to when he was in the SAS and I worked for Fleetway. Jon would later play Jerry Cornelius in the *Final Programme* movie. He had a job in the West End revival of *Richard II*. After a bit of soul-searching I told him what was happening to me. I'm not sure if he believed me, but he suggested trying something which had helped him get rid of migraines. Together we visited the more upscale of Notting Dale's two opium dens, run not by sinister Fu Manchu types plotting to take over the Western world but by a couple of gay guys who were similar in looks and both called Charles. Strictly speaking they were This Charles and That Charles. A third, known as The Other Charles, had disappeared years ago, back to Kingston with a schoolmaster. Helped by two assistants, the remaining Charleses ran a very decent premises up behind Porchester Road Baths. Nothing nasty and sinister. A long way from the Limehouse of Thomas Burke and *Broken Blossoms*. The premises had been a hairdresser's and was still disguised using the old fittings in each cubicle where you lay down on fresh white linen and your pipes were prepared by two extremely pleasant Korean girls, dressed vaguely as geishas.

Within moments, just as in one of Burke's stories, May, my girl for the evening, came into the cubicle and began to cook for me. On a small table she spread the layout; lit the lamp, dug out the treacly hop from the *toey* and held it against the flame. It bubbled merrily, and the air slowly filled with sweetness. Holding the bamboo pipe in one hand, she scraped the bowl with a *yen-shi-gow* and kneaded the brown clot with the *yen-hok*. Slowly it changed colour as the gases escaped. Then she broke a piece in her finger, and dropped it into the bowl. She handed the stem to me. I took deep puffs and relaxed as the Swarm slipped a little further into the background. Could I hear words suddenly?

I think Jon left early. He was a drinker rather than a drugger and this was just something he was doing to help me. I needed more than one pipe to send me into the land of dreams. I felt an almost unbearable need to escape back into my old life when my simple enthusiasms had been Edgar Rice Burroughs, *Planet Stories* and P.G. Wodehouse, before I had met Friar Isidore what seemed centuries later. I yearned to be transplanted to a red planet where the world was forever in an English summer and giant green men rode over endless ochre deserts searching for a stolen cow creamer. And that was the tenor of my early dreams as I directed myself back to childhood, an engrossing book, an apple and perhaps some pop. Staying with my dad's relatives in the country. The scent of pines and roses, of rich red earth fallen away from the deep roots of oaks, elms and pines. The faint, pleasant smell of my dog Brandy as I cycled with him in the basket on my handlebars along the quiet streets of Brookgate on an early-closing day when not even a delivery van disturbed that peace.

Before I knew it, I was dropping deeper and deeper into an appalling depression as I fell from the bike and we turned and I was back in the street, near a patch of waste ground, a bomb site, and I had lost Brandy. I remembered the moment well. I had lost him for ever. I never found him. Almost the worst moment of my childhood. This dream wasn't going too well.

Like the opium eater himself, the resident genius of Hookem House, I seemed to roam a deserted Brookgate for ten thousand years before I understood that Brandy had been swallowed by a sewer linking to Alsacia. When I got into the sewer I heard the echoes of the Swarm, far away. But, distant as it was, it didn't offer much relief. I could hear the rush of my own blood. Was that the only escape? To return to the Alsacia?

Hearing Brandy's distant, hopeful bark, I awoke long enough to take another pipe and do all I could to get my dog out of that sewer, which turned into a tunnel, which opened into a wide, tall cavern where high brass boats sailed beneath blazing, roaring copper skies on bright indigo water which merged with the haze of the heavens and sped to spill over the edge of the world. Soon the boats were transformed into gigantic peacocks whose metal wings and enamelled fans clashed in time to a distant waltz-tune and I recognised it as one of my own from the Deep Fix gigs. *Began to swim in thick smoke tasting of chocolate from which glorious strawberry-coloured cities loomed and the Swarm was reduced to no more than the sound of a distant ocean. Lavender and lemon and the little chocolatier on the corner of Brook Lane and Fox Alley playing a tune on a tin whistle, doing a jig outside his shop while Claude Duval looked on and applauded. And over the fast-rushing Fleet was the great bridge of red iron, with its muses of the arts and sciences which had been a fermenting image in my mind as I danced one by one with those Graecian ladies, those lovely, wise ladies in their chitons and scarves and then I dreamed of fire and learning to inhale the smoke so that the pain should go as soon as it could.*

Or so I hoped.

So I hoped.

Jolie dansez, Mike, mon mari, she said. Kiss me sweetheart. Laissez les bon temps roulez.

Where was I now? What did she want?

My memories were locked in a sturdy box with straps. I smelled the box and began trying to open it. My licences were there. All my licences! Without them, I was nameless. I had no position.

And all the while the rise and fall of the Whispering Swarm. Not once, in my many attempts, had I completely escaped it. I'd had every kind of test, of course, but I knew that, since I was completely free of it when I entered the Alsacia, none of the wilder ideas of specialists, including psychiatrists, made much sense. Menacing, threatening to destroy everything I loved, everything I needed to keep myself focused and sane, it was relentless. I did not fear insanity the way a character in Poe or Lovecraft feared it, but there was an element in my family history I did not find entirely attractive. I had a barmy cousin in Amsterdam. I had a few eccentric relatives who were not, as we used to say, the full florin. Some had the odd paranoid delusion. We

all found them fairly funny, especially if the relative believed themselves to be some famous person being victimised by a shadowy power.
My grandfather's brother Alf believed Lord Nelson hadn't died at
Trafalgar but was being hunted by French secret agents in the pay of
the Bonapartistes. The very banality of such delusions shamed me. I
would have felt laughably stupid if I emerged from a similar situation to be told that I thought I was Sherlock Holmes or at least that
Holmes was on my trail. Admittedly, it would take a real brain of
Holmes's fictional brilliance to find a way of ridding me of the Swarm.
The Sanctuary had mastered me. Only by choosing to live out my life
within its confines would I ever know any real peace. And that peace,
of course, was meaningless without my children and the company of
those I cared for.

Like opium, marijuana and acid helped me a bit, as did coke, but
I stopped short at heroin. Of course I was offered it often enough and
took the odd snort, but it always left me feeling like crap and never
completely covered up the noise of the Swarm. I could understand
how people got to be junkies. I didn't want to be dependent on drugs,
whether booze or dope. People always had such pathetic rationales,
usually to do with the quality of whatever it was they were hooked
on. Bill Baker, my boss at Sexton Blake, used to blame his blackouts
on drinking the wrong beer or mixing wine and whisky.

Drugs failing to drown out the sound of the Swarm, my despair
passed and for a time at least I resolved to live with it, just as Smetana,
for instance, lived the majority of his life forced to hear a perpetual
A-flat while he composed his lovely music. But Smetana was a genius.
I was only a working writer trying to reconcile a variety of old forms
with a version of a new one. So, soon after I got back to Ladbroke
Grove, inspired by my enthusiasm for the English Romantics, I took
to hiking in the Dales and the Lakes whenever I got the chance. I had
never had much interest in the countryside but I almost immediately
fell in love with the wild, mainly unpopulated fells, where you could
frequently walk all day without seeing anything much bigger than a
sheep. The Whispering Swarm remained with me but was somehow
less intrusive, and I got great relief from those walks.

CHAPTER THIRTY

ENGLISH DIVERSIONS

MOLLY WAS, OF course, still in my thoughts, but I was very glad to be home. The girls were wonderful and I never tired of outings with them. It was also a pleasure to see old friends. My memory, never great at the best of times, seemed to be improving.

I understand how you might like to play down what some might see as a nerdier or less respectable past, but in my case at least I had to hang on tight to my memories or I'd forget them completely. I kept the tarot pack Mrs M. had left with me. I used the cards to remember. Somehow, by association, the cards really did help me remember things fairly accurately. Naturally, in the pub or at a dinner party, you might exaggerate a little if you were telling a good anecdote or making a point, but you didn't deny it when your wife or friends contradicted you. Not if you wanted to keep your grip on reality.

I remember, during a time I was working under a variety of pseudonyms in the mid-'60s, Helena warned me I'd wake up one morning and beg her to tell me who I was. And, she said with an evil grin, she'd refuse. Because of my situation I was terrified of losing the truth, of persisting and insisting on a lie or a false memory. My mum had grown infamous for her lies and inventions. Because my mum was such a mythologiser and had embarrassed me as a kid when I realised she was telling obvious porkies, I think I understood how the family had lost respect for her. I couldn't bear that happening to me. I was convinced that you learn by remembering. Of course I didn't mind polishing a good anecdote now and again, but I knew what I was doing. A narrative was all the better for the number of other narratives it carried. I never resisted being called on an exaggeration and I particularly valued close friends and partners to remind me if I got something wrong. But my more mythologically inclined friends made me uncomfortable. I suppose they found it a form of self-protection.

What amazed me was the vehemence with which people sometimes defended their new personae and histories. One, who periodically rewrote at least half his life as an ongoing project, frequently accused me of myth-making when my version of events differed from his but seemed to be shared by the majority. People like him reminded me of my mother. They believed firmly in their refreshed identities. One of them took to yelling at old friends whose memories didn't match his. He fell out with almost everyone, including his relatives. He clung fiercely to his re-created self. I cared for him and hated when he raged. He persuaded his new girlfriend of all his reinventions and she was malleable enough to accept the story when it changed, even if she were the subject. Some women are better at that sort of thing. They can transform before your eyes. You could say that generation was trained to it. The truth was important to me. I was pretty obsessive about it, doing all I could to never lie to my children, to teach them to respect truth, honesty and the other simple virtues.

I also did everything I could to give my daughters the egalitarian principles of my mother and her mother. I used to tell people who wanted my endless patronage as an editor, 'Don't expect me to be a father figure. I'm not even that to my own kids.'

I told the girls they were going to school for their own benefit, not that of the teachers, and they were to take the information, not the opinions, of those in authority. I did my best to teach them self-worth. I tried hard to make sure they didn't blame themselves for any problems in our marriage. I loved them with all my heart. I sometimes wonder if they were the real objects of rivalry when it came to my affections. I was never short of love. Later, even my ex-wives came to believe I needed two women to love as well as to spell one another, I suspect, when I was maniacally working. It must have been horrible. Once focused on a literary book's subject I never let it go and I talked on and on about it. The genre books were written so quickly, you might not have noticed.

The books were, it was true, beginning to take me longer to do. The generic books took me three days. If I tried anything else, it might be around two weeks. In 1969, after I'd handed *New Worlds* over to 'the triumvirate', I produced the second Cornelius novel in four episodes, as they were appearing in the magazine. *Gloriana* would take the longest time ever, at six weeks, but that would be years later. Maybe it was the adrenaline? I was never violent but I could get really crazy with anxiety. You need a strong woman for that, even to stand it for three or four years. By then you should have it under control. Looking back, I've never envied those women. It's no surprise that Elric, my earliest successful fictional character, was some kind of monster. Of course, romantic women go in for a certain sort of monster. They think they can tame us the way Fay Wray tamed Kong.

I'm probably being a bit melodramatic, but I speak from the perspective of age. When young we lived fast, dramatic lives, all of us, no matter how many children we had. Our experience showed that the world was improving and would continue to improve if we were prepared to make a bit of an effort. We were living in the fast lane. Sex and drugs and rock and roll. When we talk about those days now, people think we're exaggerating or else we were exceptional or perverted or nuts. It was the norm among the young romantics of Britain, especially in Ladbroke Grove. We were high on ideas and the arts, especially music. We were building the new Jerusalem. When the Stones did 'Sympathy for the Devil', the Royal Albert Hall sold out on the choral version of Schoenberg's *Moses und Aron*. A year or two earlier, Schoenberg concerts played to tiny audiences. Public taste improved enormously and with it a demand for ambitious popular fiction, painting and sculpture. Right up to the moment Margaret Thatcher went to ask the Queen about forming a government, there was reason to believe we were bumping forward. We certainly didn't need the dire scare stories of these new Tories who produced a way, in common with Ronald Reagan, of tricking us into a short-term gain with 'deregulation', starting the snowball that would roll 99 per cent of us downhill. Maybe there's an alternative world where the counterculture actually gained authority.

All of us involved in that odd threesome must have found our situation satisfying enough or we wouldn't have gone on with it. If it hadn't been for the Whispering Swarm I would have been enormously content. I think the Swarm distracted me more than I realised. I can't believe that my ego was so enlarged I entertained only the faintest notion of Moll's hiding deeper motives for being with me. To me love was love. I was very simple. It had, of course, crossed my mind that she didn't want to be left alone in the Alsacia, probably because she didn't want to be with her old lover, Duval or Turpin or whichever Cavalier it was.

I remained unjealous, trusting. Whenever I was in the area I did my best to drop by. I think she was able to leave the Alsacia but I was not sure when. I was so secure in my sense that my love was reciprocated that I forged cheerfully ahead, making all the decisions, because she said that was what she wanted. But I suppose I didn't listen very well. Was I totally self-deluded? I do miss those years when, maybe at others' expense, I was sublimely self-confident.

There are DVDs of me performing or giving interviews. I'm utterly fearless, horribly arrogant and aggressive. That's when I think I can see what they saw. Helena said I was always one to make a decision, even when no decision was possible. Uncertain people were attracted to my certainty. And there were a lot of uncertain young women about in those days. Some of them were talented but needed to learn self-confidence. I tried to get them work. I couldn't, in those days, conceive of anyone having talent and not wanting to earn money with it. I had spent most of my professional life as a writer. I had no conception of the amateur or the talented dabbler. I now realise I might have pushed one or two of them where they didn't want to go. Too much responsibility. Some women and men really did just want to look after someone. Preferably someone interesting.

Even when I wasn't nuts I didn't slow down much. Holidays were usually spent doing something, going somewhere. I was no good at simply lying on a beach. Christina Mackenzie, with whom I had a brief affair, told me I had an unsleeping brain. Was she right? Actually,

I almost never dreamed. I said I sold my dreams before I went to bed. And I didn't go in for fantasy much, either. Helena said I would never stop writing. I was compelled to do it. I wasn't sure. I found it a lot easier to work with a band than on my own. I had no desire to be a front man, in spite of the accident that gave me a good voice. On stage I was a natural sideman, playing rhythm guitar while the blokes who liked the attention bent all the flashy notes up the back end of the neck. I loved being on stage, working with others. I loved performing, particularly when we actually did well. But it really was for the pure pleasure of making music. Helena did something for my ego when she said she'd forgotten how good sex could get without tricks. Maybe those multiple orgasms compensated for my many shortcomings which she was happy to list on other occasions. When I needed it I always had the Sanctuary, where I could write escapist fiction without feeling I should be doing something better with my time. In the outside world this went against my own work ethic.

By 1969 I had everything in some sort of balance. Two lives, two wives, two children, two careers. The arrangement seemed to suit everyone. In spite of the stress, with the magazine undergoing various assaults, I remember those years with great pleasure. I anticipated an old age in which we took care of one another, shared jokes and memories, and became almost the same person, our experiences and memories entwined. I loved seeing both Helena and Molly, as well as the children, grow. I know. I know. Of course I didn't anticipate what would actually happen. Not me who said I didn't believe in magic?

Helena still refused to hear anything I tried to tell her about the Alsacia. Why did the Swarm stop whenever I was in the Alsacia? Did the Sanctuary actually call me back? A kind of Lorelei? By April 1969 it had grown so loud I definitely wasn't sure it was just tinnitus. I had to go to the doctor and make up a story about anxieties and symptoms like a migraine. But he gave me nothing strong enough to silence the Swarm. The downer, of course, just made me sleepy. I began to wonder if the Swarm could be escaped by putting a few thousand miles between us.

Helena thought we needed a break. The girls were now old enough to leave with my mum who was eager to have them to herself for a bit. Helena had never been to the United States and I wanted to see my editors. In particular I also had to find a former writing partner and get our manuscript back. In 1968 a bright young American, Bob Soulis, began collaborating on a book about pop culture with me. An emergency at home in New York meant Bob had to leave, taking the only manuscript with him. For some time he had dropped out of sight and I began to despair of seeing our book again. Then he wrote out of the blue. Damon Knight and his wife, Kate Wilhelm, had gone to Oregon to see two of their children and Bob had been asked to housesit for them. I must have known Bob better than they did. But Bob was going to be in Milford, Pennsylvania, for three months in the summer and suggested I come over to discuss what we were going to do with the book. To be honest, all I wanted was the bugger back so I could finish it and not be asked about it whenever I saw Livia Gollancz, who had commissioned it. Why, I proposed, didn't Helena and I go over, stay in New York, explore a few other parts of the Northeast and get hold of the manuscript?

We decided to fly on a three-week return. Our first transatlantic plane trip together! Helena was already in love with America and didn't share the anti-Americanism which had become epidemic since the country's involvement in Vietnam. So I dashed to the Alsacia to tell Moll I had to be in New York on business. She suggested I look up her mother. Mrs Melody was there all year.

CHAPTER THIRTY-ONE

AMERICAN DIVERSIONS

OUR TRIP WOULD prove unexpectedly tiring. Somewhere between October 1967 and May 1969, America had discovered sex. Our first clue to this was being met at the Gramercy Park Hotel, Manhattan, by Rex Fisch.

Rex had left England in a sober suit, a shirt, a tie and a neat haircut. He arrived outside our hotel lobby in tiny black leather shorts and a studded bolero jacket, astride his monster twin-cam 1100cc BMW bike. All six feet two inches of him. As he swung off his bike and flounced towards us I knew the sight would never leave my memory. Only Rex could mince under the weight of that many metal studs. He clearly intended to shock us, but of course we had trouble not smiling. We would have enjoyed ourselves in New York the more if Rex hadn't begun showing signs of what would become one of his periodic attacks of paranoia.

I insisted on taking Helena to Saks Fifth Avenue and Bloomingdale's where she reluctantly bought some beautiful clothes. We went up to the top of the Empire State Building and we took a boat ride around the island. Rex, dressed a little less like a Village Person, introduced us to some great restaurants. We went to the MoMA and the Strand bookstore. We enjoyed the Gramercy Park Hotel, which was at the height of her run-down glory and one of the cheapest, funkiest hotels in Manhattan. I preferred it by far to the Chelsea where Mrs Melody was staying. I had no intention of looking up Moll's mother! We found Port Authority Bus Terminal and off we went to Milford, where Bob awaited us. The bus was already packed so I sat down near the front and Helena took a seat near the back, causing sardonic comment from black passengers. Helena, with her posh English accent, still understood all that was being said and blithely ignored it until a black lady told off the men and made room for me. The law had changed but the culture hadn't. That would take a few more years.

We stayed at a creaking old Victorian four-decker mansion in what was then a near-deserted Pennsylvania town marked for flooding as a reservoir. The cabbie who drove us up there was so scared when he saw the house he gave us about five seconds to leave the taxi before he took off at speed. It did look a bit like the house in *Psycho*. I, of course, had been there before, but I hadn't arrived at night. Bob, skinny and neurotically stooped as ever, now wore a fashionable Zapata moustache. His eyes intense, he led us up to the third floor along creaking hallways and groaning stairs. I was already fond of the house but it freaked out some guests, including Bob's new girlfriend and her friend. Bob's wife and small son had been staying in the house for some time. They both had a strange, distant look. Helena and I soon realised that Bob had gone barking barmy. Not only had he invited another woman to stay, but he was already hitting on her friend.

After our first uncomfortable night and what was for most of us an awkward breakfast, we went to visit Rex and Jim Stefanopolis, who had recently rented a house nearby. Rex hadn't told us they were breaking up. So Rex decided to return with us to Bob's. We got back that afternoon to find even more people arriving. I was reminded of the opening act of a musical comedy. Bob had also given open invitations to a bunch of the most neurotic would-be writers and artists in the nation. They usually drifted in on Friday and stayed through to the following Monday. The exchanges of bodily fluids were so complex that Rex at one point joked that Jackie Kennedy was the father of his child. Avoiding advances from all sides exhausted us, but Rex was in his element, swanning about like a villainous Disney great white, sporting vast, grinning teeth. He would have had those gnashers filed if he hadn't been such a sissy about visiting the dentist.

The relationship complications lasted days and weeks, even months in some cases, feeding the gossip machines of New York, Paris, California and London. Apocryphal stories recycled for years, few of them as sensational as the truth. Helena's main complaint about our stay in the Delaware Valley was that she could never get into the toilet alone. When she did make it, there was usually someone there, hanging from the ceiling in a bizarre state of dress. If we hadn't already reached a sort of equilibrium that year we might have enjoyed it a little more. But we wanted to be together.

We couldn't have left anyway. Neither of us had a valid driving licence and there was some sort of transport strike. We were stranded in an amateur performance of *The Rocky Horror Picture Show* without the music or the jokes. Mostly they wanted advice – or that was how it started. Now, tell me Michael, should I fuck Buck and chuck Huck and should I only suck Chuck or should I settle down and get stuck with all of them? Anyway, how are *you* fixed for now? We only had to sit in that one set, the kitchen, from which led a double staircase, until the next lugubrious guest would come down after a row or in search of water and almost immediately propose to you. What's more, most of the proposers were pretty unattractive. So we were stranded there until a train reached Milford one Monday afternoon, signalling its imminent arrival from the bridge and causing us to flee down the hill to the station not caring what we left behind. Until then we'd had very little sleep. They'd given up invading our bed early on the second Friday evening, so that wasn't much of an issue during the last week or so. The worst thing was definitely the endless gossip and analysis. You couldn't get yourself a bowl of cornflakes without some bunch or other wanting to promote their own gloomy Aquarian wisdom. By that Monday I was pretty sure Andy Warhol was hidden somewhere directing it all. Script by Feydeau on acid. The ultimate boring formulae, twice as boring as any previous piece of boring cinema.

We realised that we had stumbled on a significant moment in American history: the Age of the Orgasm. Relativity prefigured relativism and here we were. The right to come led our sexual fashions. Helena and I stumbled on a key moment in America's public sexual experiment. In a couple of years the United States had gone culturally from low-contrast black and white to vibrant colour. We wished them well but now the buggers, like teenagers, wanted to tell the world what it already knew.

The Swarm had never ceased, even in America, but I had been able to ignore it better. We were knackered by the time we got back to Blighty, but were probably happier together than we had ever been. We had never been so thoroughly affectionate about our marriage. Everyone was delighted to see us back and of course we had brought all kinds of stuff for the girls. My mum said they'd all had a wonderful time. The girls had thoroughly enjoyed the visit from their auntie.

Auntie? We were puzzled. I had no brothers or sisters. Helena had one brother and a great-aunt. When we asked more my mum became a bit vague.

Did this auntie have a name?

Funny name, my mum said, beginning to look uncertain. Reeny? Ferny? Something like that. The girls were safe and evidently unharmed. Where had the lady taken them? Helena asked coolly.

'It was like a really old bit of London,' Sally told us. 'Like a country village.'

Helena frowned. She was furious with my mother. Mum was normally never short of common sense. How could she allow her own grandchildren to go off with a stranger? Could the girls remember anything else?

It soon became clear to me that Freni Melody had turned up while we were away and somehow persuaded my mother to let her take my children to Alsacia where they had met Molly and some of the other inhabitants of the Sanctuary. Helena decided they had been to somewhere like Lewes or one of the other towns around London that still had the characteristics of an older settlement, but the more I listened, the angrier I got. My mum was close to tears. She kept apologising. 'I don't know what got into me. It's as if she hypnotised me! How could I let them go off like that? Honestly, I feel I'm losing my head!'

'Well,' said Helena sharply. 'I suppose there was no harm done.'

Both Mum and I knew Helena would never again leave the girls in her sole care. Helena thought one of my 'hippie friends' had been responsible. She had always been mildly unhappy about my taking the children to gigs. Guessing the truth, I was much angrier than she was. Next day, saying I had to see an editor, I took a taxi to Carmelite Inn Chambers.

CHAPTER THIRTY-TWO

ROLLING IN THE RUINS

AND SO I went back to the Alsacia. It was a sunny Saturday afternoon, when the Fleet Street area was pretty much deserted. I half expected the gates to be hidden from me again. But there they were! Slowly, with growing uncertainty, I pushed open the heavy old creaking oak. When the gap was wide enough to admit me I slipped through.

After a moment or two my sense of anticipation left me. I stared in horror at the scene. Perhaps a bomb had hit the Sanctuary. A bomb of modern proportions. Like something from my own childhood. Everywhere I looked buildings were blackened and spoiled. Houses and shops were rubble. The Swan With Two Necks had come under heavy cannon-fire, with the whole of its front destroyed. The south wing, where I had lived with Molly, had partially collapsed. Furniture, decorations, a long bar on the ground floor and a good part of the stables were all half-demolished. I clambered through a gap in the wall. This was like the Blitz. The place was evidently looted of all valuables. I stopped. I bent down and picked up a piece of blood-stained silk. What remained of the wall behind me bore a great splash of dried blood. People had died here. People I had known and cared for. One of the women I had loved. Shot, stabbed and dragged away, living or dead, to suffer further indignity, sorrow and pain. Thank

God there had been so few children here! Now, again, I understood the wisdom of the Alsacia's inhabitants.

'Nixer!'

Turning, I saw that the abbey was also blackened. Her stained glass gaped with wounds, her vines and bricks were filthy with soot. I saw nothing alive. Previously furious with Molly and her mother, I now feared for their safety. I ran towards the abbey door. It was locked and barred. Sealed from within. Perhaps the monks refused to open their doors expecting further assault? I beat as hard as I could with the iron knocker on that old timber but nobody answered. The air itself was dead. I heard nothing, not even the scuttling of a rat or the rustle of a pigeon in the guttering. The Swarm, however, had completely gone from my head, as if rewarding me for my return. At that moment I hated the Alsacia. The stink of burnt timber and blackened stonework infected the air. There was no easy way to tell when the Sanctuary had been raided. The ruins could be a year or more old.

'I shouldn't have left.' I was angry. How could this have happened? Too much loose talk? Too much coming and going? Maybe the Alsacia couldn't sustain the whole thing on its remaining energy. 'Is everyone dead?' I spoke aloud against the dreadful silence. I regretted ever coming here, ever meeting Molly and the rest. And my grieving was still mixed with anger. What might my girls have seen if Mrs Melody brought them here while the place sustained the attack? I picked my way over the ruins. There were no corpses. No body parts. A relief. The door of the abbey was shut. Had Nixer's Roundheads taken everything, including the corpses?

The only habitable building left was the abbey. Fighting had gone on around it, but whoever defended the monks had fought a hard battle. Every shrub was trampled down and musket balls had made heavy indentations in the masonry. But still no bodies.

There was nothing else to do. Returning to the abbey, I lifted up the big, blackened knocker and hammered on the door. I'd break in if I had to! In the silence not even a bird called and the echo of the knocker was very loud.

At that moment I heard someone behind me. I turned, yearning for a pistol.

'Who could by industrious valour climb, to ruin that great work of time, and cast the kingdoms old into another mould…? You must be sorry not to find your friends here. And all this destruction! Rehearsing the End of the World, perhaps?'

I looked back and saw a smiling Captain James St Claire, the swarthy, brown-eyed soldier who had saved me from the Roundhead thief-takers and joined in that earlier fight at the inn. A bit of a mystery. Now unwounded, he stood leaning on a wall just across from the abbey. What was he babbling? Some seventeenth-century play? He was dressed much the same as when I had first seen him, though he had added a few bright pheasant feathers to his hat. This shaded his face at an angle and made me wonder if he were perhaps a survivor from some battle of the border. The Scots were as divided amongst themselves as the English. This man's accent was educated, from the north-east. Durham, maybe? As before, his long, basket-hilted sword was scabbarded at his side. He had pistols and a big sheathed knife in his belt. He reminded me of a man just back from a long journey through dangerous country. He did not seem to have found much plunder. He had the bearing of a soldier in some defeated cause. Part of the army Cromwell had finally scattered for good?

'Did you see any of this?' I asked.

He shook his head. 'I've learned little more than you. I came here looking for Prince Rupert, to offer help dragging his Cosmolabe from the rubble and repairing it.'

'But you disappeared after the fight,' I said. 'Where did you go?'

'I had some urgent business elsewhere. As now. War's made rogues and liars of us all.' He bowed his head. 'I've seen savagery in these days, but never a whole town destroyed and its inhabitants with it.' He looked up suddenly. 'I've left my horse outside. She'll be agitated. I should be going.' His brogue was deeper, as if he anticipated seeing his home. He took off his feathered bonnet and bowed again. Then he said: 'If you do not ride the silver roads, I would suggest you wait until – ah!' He saw something behind me. I heard a noise from inside. I glimpsed a pair of dark eyes looking through the little window in the door. Then, squeaking, the bolts were drawn back.

'Silver roads?'

The door opened. Friar Isidore was there, smiling shyly. 'I had hoped you would come. If only to reassure us of your safety. Would you like some tea?'

He spoke directly to me. I turned. James St Claire had gone. Back to his horse?

'Oh, what the hell!' I said to myself, accepting Isidore's invitation. And I followed him through the door of the abbey.

CHAPTER THIRTY-THREE

DICING WITH THE DEITY

FRIAR ISIDORE TOOK me back through the darkened passage into the chapel and the abbot's room. Was the old man expecting me? His features were a little drawn but hadn't aged. His pale fingers emerged from his sleeves. He gestured for us to sit down. As Friar Isidore poured freshly brewed tea, Father Grammaticus offered teacakes and crumpets. I remembered those English school stories, where heroic boys had tea with the headmaster. *Stalky & Co.* meets *Mr Chips*. The abbot asked after my health. How was I 'making progress' in the 'outside world'? He seemed surprised when I mentioned my children. Hadn't Mrs Melody brought them here?

In spite of my anger I was concerned for Molly and the others. What had happened to the Alsacia?

'Oh, it's of no concern, my boy. Time's rays, you know. The Cosmolabe. Really, it will all be put to rights.'

I was baffled. 'What has happened to Molly? Captain Turpin? Captain Duval? Prince Rupert and the rest?'

'There was an attack on the abbey. Captain Nixer's hatred of us is unreasoning. He calls us papists and other dangerous names. He believes we hide a great fortune in gold and gems. We were in some danger here, but the worst was averted. I am certain that no friend was harmed. They will all rejoin us here soon.'

'But what happened, Father Abbot? There were people living here! At The Swan With Two Necks. What of them?

'We grew spiritually weak. We let the men of violence break through. Of course, they never truly harm the abbey. Or, I should say, they have not harmed us yet. We were expecting an attack. Their soldiers failed to breach the abbey.'

Was it Nixer and his Roundheads again?'

'No doubt.'

'They took prisoners, I suppose?' I felt some hope. 'There were no dead that I saw.'

'We did all we could to resist them in our own ways. But many defended the Swan until the soldiers killed them.'

'Don't you know why there aren't any remains? Why everyone has disappeared?' Frightened, I was unnaturally aggressive.

'Remains? They hid themselves, I suppose.' The abbot smiled somewhat vaguely.

'Turpin, Duval and the rest? My Molly? Her mother? How? Where?'

The abbot shook his head, smiling gently. 'Some of us seek to choose our own destinies. Some of us insist on attempting to control that destiny. Not all chose to be here. Your friends are their own masters.'

'But they followed the prince,' I said. 'You know that. They defended the abbey, Father! I saw the evidence. The rubble.'

'Oh, no, my boy. We gave them sanctuary.'

'You let them be wounded, killed, abducted!'

The abbot was surprised. 'Of course not. You forget what this place is. Within the Sanctuary they are immune to mortal wounds. As they are to ordinary mortality. Here, as I'm sure you know, our longevity is that of the earliest prophets.'

'You control such things?' I could not believe I understood him.

'We do our best.' Exchanging a look of troubled amusement with Friar Isidore, the abbot settled more comfortably into his chair. 'You have seen the wonderful things we have done to protect the meaning and spirit of Holy Sanctuary. In Alsacia, thanks to our prayers and our learned wisdom, we have created a place where people, in lives of quiet contemplation, can study and learn to help their fellows.'

'I do understand that, Father. I do *not* understand how an enemy can get in and do the damage I saw. Who did this? Our friends are all gone! Was everyone taken prisoner? You can't leave me with so many questions unanswered. Where's your Christian charity?'

The abbot was shocked. 'Master Michael. I thought you knew we are an ancient order. We studied in time-begrimed Ur and survived the rise and fall of empires. We are at least as old as Persia. We came to Carmel long before Christ. Yet we acknowledge Christ, as we acknowledge all true prophets. But we have gained knowledge which Christians fear and call the Dark Arts!' He smiled. 'We have been hated by so many – so many... yet we continue to serve God and mankind and keep our word as best we can. As an adept, you must know –'

'Adept? I'm a writer, that's all. I'm not even religious, Father. I am concerned for my friends! Do you not take vows? I understood the Carmelites to be a Christian order!'

'Indeed they are, to the world at large. Our abbey never claimed to be simply Christian. Here, we retained our old practices, neither denying the divinity of Jesus Christ nor the wisdom of his message. We also acknowledge Abraham and Mohammed. We accept the teachings of Buddha and Confucius, of Shinto and Hindu and Jain, of Jat and Copt and Catholic and all our worlds' spiritual beliefs. That which divides mankind must be that which unites it. We acknowledge all faiths.'

'But you let people think you are Christians!'

'In these parts, anyone wearing habits such as ours is taken for a Christian.'

'So you are liars and hypocrites?'

'Is it not better to love God than merely to fear or worship Him? Jesus Christ taught that. We keep our knowledge secret. We live as Christians but tell no lies to protect ourselves. Since we all believe in the same ideals, we are saddened at the way the love of God is recruited in a hatred of others.'

'I saw Hasidic Jews visiting you,' I told him. 'Do they think you are Jews?'

'No.' The abbot made a sign. Friar Isidore refreshed our tea, offering chocolate digestives and Fig Newtons. 'No. They came to see our Treasure.'

'The Fish Chalice?'

He chuckled. 'Is that what you call it?' His grey eyes met mine suddenly. 'It is not the Holy Grail, my boy.' He smiled at my astonishment. 'I know your obsessions!' His expression was one of innocent delight. 'I am sure one or two of the Grail myths come partly from our chalice. We've enjoyed our stewardship for more than two thousand years, first in Palestine, then in England and France. Our fellow Carmelites gradually allowed themselves to come under the discipline of Rome. While embracing our stewardship and our guardianship, we continued to draw strength from all metaphysical ideas.'

Suddenly, he grew extremely sober. 'My boy, you are a natural psychic, as you no doubt know. And you come from a line of adepts, carriers of the old knowledge. That is how you always find us. You would not be here otherwise.'

I was confused. 'What about the prince? Was he also psychic?'

'Indeed. Psychics and changelings can come and go.'

'Changelings?'

The majority of Alsacia's children have your gift. But they find themselves unable to live ambiguous lives.'

I was increasingly impatient. 'What on earth happened out there?' He was trying to distract me. 'Was the Sanctuary breached by enemies hunting for your so-called Treasure? Are these enemies no longer ruled by any decent code of conduct? By law? Or God? Or honour, if you like?'

'Or chivalry? Another ideal we so rarely live up to.' Friar Isidore shook his ancient head. 'That is why some of us become friars, to study the old wisdom and counter the powers of the material world. These include statesmanship, speech, singing and, sometimes, swordsmanship. "*Touché!*" Thus you acknowledge your opponent's successful lunge.' And he pantomimed, with sudden humour, a passage of blades.

Reluctantly deciding that the old man was at least partly senile, I tried again: 'But why are they *all* gone and their houses left to fall into ruin?'

'An anomaly, I suppose. But they are safe enough, I'm sure. Not every brane is under our control.'

I turned to Friar Isidore. 'Do you know who or what set the houses on fire?'

He replied promptly. 'Our enemies! Of course! I thought we explained! Those who would steal our Treasure. God again provided a miracle.'

I was incredulous. 'But I saw the ruins. The blood. People died out there. Some were my good friends. I loved one of them.'

The abbot grew serious. 'Heaven protects its own. That is a constant.'

'A constant? What's a constant, exactly?'

Father Grammaticus frowned. 'We must get some more teacakes. I see you are enjoying them.'

I had been eating almost compulsively. I often did when I was nervous. I could eat a dozen doughnuts just waiting to board a plane. I began to apologise, but now both monks were smiling.

'We have plenty of teacakes,' said Father Grammaticus.

And then I wondered if perhaps they *had* slipped something into the buns. Weren't we reprising *Alice*? It reminded me of a mad hatter's tea party we'd done for school. I was certainly having trouble understanding the conversation.

'Where did they go? Out into Cromwell's London?' I grew increasingly baffled. I imagined a wheel with certain defined stops, each a different alternative to our own world.

Father Grammaticus sighed and lowered his eyes. I could tell the monks would not be any more forthcoming.

'Perhaps we could continue this conversation later?' I began to rise. I needed to return to Helena and the girls. They would be concerned and I was vaguely worried for them.

'That will be delightful.' The abbot got up slowly. Brother Isidore was already on his feet. 'You have a fine, enquiring mind, young man. I am so glad you are here to help us.'

I wondered if I should ask exactly how I was helping, but I wanted to get out of there. They wouldn't tell me where Moll was, so I would find her for myself. Meanwhile I needed to reassure myself that my children and my wife were all right.

Brother Isidore took me to the abbey's outer entrance. 'It was a great pleasure to see you. And you have made the abbot so happy.' He opened the door.

I walked out into a cold evening. The stink of burnt wood and stone had disappeared, replaced with sweet smoke softening the clean, frosty snap of the air. Every building was as fresh as my first sight of it. A horse and cart went by in the crowded street. I caught the stench of the open sewers. I heard human voices, a cock crowing, dogs barking. I looked back to ask the friar what on earth had happened but he had already closed the door.

The whole of Alsacia was exactly as I remembered it! People strolled the narrow bustling streets. Huxters argued. Lovers met and parted. They bought and they sold. They gossiped and laughed. The air was rich with the scent of life. I could smell food cooking. The Swan With Two Necks spilled over with customers, and her stables were busy with ostlers tending the usual horses. A muted babble came from her bars. I knew now what it meant to feel your head swim. Which had been the illusion? Could it be both?

I needed a drink. I headed for the Swan.

The warmth of the Sanctuary immediately embraced and comforted me. Those familiar smells and noises were like a drug. The day was as cold here as outside, but the temperature was somehow different. I inhaled the farmyard smells of a London where people rode horses and raised animals for meat, milk or fur. I heard the clop of horseshoes striking cobblestones, the clucking of chickens, the hissing of geese. Voices were raised in cheerful conversation. Someone shouted an insult from a top-floor window. The clatter of looms. A chiming clock. The clanging of cookware. Honking donkeys, bleating goats. The evidence of all those animals was left on the same cobblestones. Not all crap was good for the garden!

I hesitated. I wasn't sure I should go to the Swan. If my friends weren't there I should feel compelled to look for them. And where would that be? I collected myself and made my decision. I needed that inn, the very opposite of the abbey's austerity. Surely, any answers I found there would be more direct. There, too, I'd find some cheerful company, perhaps even some explanation. I decided to follow my impulses and hope my friends could lead me to a deeper understanding of the part of London time forgot. I wanted the warmth and friendship of The Swan With Two Necks. I opened the doors of the saloon bar and, my spirits improving in anticipation of all the comradeship I was about to enjoy, stepped over the threshold.

The place was crowded. The first man I recognised was big Nick

Nevison, a smile fading on his broad, good-humoured face. Then I saw Moll's curls falling down her lovely neck and back as it arched under the kiss of a Cavalier whose surprised eyes suddenly met mine.

Mrs Melody saw me before anyone else did and swiftly made a path in my direction as Molly turned and pushed away from her Cavalier.

'Michael! *My dear*!'

As only she could, she swept towards me. 'My darling. How lovely. And the only person here who could possibly help me.'

But I felt physically sick. I couldn't stop it. I stood there while men I believed to be comrades greeted me as heartily as they had no doubt greeted my betrayers. Molly had been first to say she loved me. I had based everything else on that. I reciprocated her feelings. And I had acted accordingly. She clearly used me, manipulated me. Lied to me. I had been naïve.

I controlled my expression. I knew how the people there they expected one of their company to behave. I did my best to show no emotion. I bowed to Mrs Melody and bid everyone else good evening. I was still furious at Moll's mother for bringing my children to this dangerous place, but I now had unusual control of my emotions. 'Certainly, Mrs Melody. What can I do for you?'

'Would you be kind enough escort me to the main gate. I have a taxi coming.'

Although Mrs Melody had conspired in my deception, it was impossible for me to refuse her request. Men of my generation were brought up to respond as I did. I bowed and smiled my farewells, especially to Moll, standing almost comically with her mouth open. The man behind her was, of course, Prince Rupert of the Rhine, inclining his head in response to my bow. Then I gave Mrs Melody my arm, bowed good evening to everyone in general, turned on my heel and escorted her from the inn.

Outside, in the bustle of the day, Mrs Melody spoke quietly. 'She had no intention of deceiving you, Michael. She was flirting, that's all. I was supposed to meet most of the others in Oxford, but it became impossible. Nixer brought his mad Puritans. They could not leave the Alsacia undefended. It is our last meeting before circumstances alter for us. You do understand. She has always followed her heart rather than her head. I brought Molly. She wanted to see her –'

302 • MICHAEL MOORCOCK

'Please, Mrs Melody! If you don't mind, I'd rather you said nothing. This should be between Molly and myself. At the moment I'd like to mention the matter of your taking my children from their home without troubling to ask me about it. And what on earth possessed you to bring them here? Especially if you anticipated an attack!'

I don't think she expected that. Her face carried a dozen expressions in a moment. One of them was pure fear. Helena had always told me that when I thought I was controlling my temper I was usually glowing like a red-hot poker. 'I –'

'Neither you nor Molly must ever do anything remotely like that again. I was going to ask why you chose to do it, but now I can say something simpler. I don't want to see either of you again. *Both of you will stay away from Ladbroke Grove. You will leave my children alone!*'

I had rarely seen anyone so placatory. I was almost embarrassed for her. 'She was innocent of any intention to upset you, Michael, I promise. It was my idea. I thought that, as your future wife, Molly should begin seeing Sally and Kitty.'

'My future *wife*?' Now I made an even greater effort of self-control. 'I hardly think that is likely, Mrs Melody. I wish never to see either you, your daughter, or, for that matter, Prince Rupert, again.'

Mrs Melody fell silent. We reached the gates. Because it was autumn the light was rapidly fading. A taxi dropping someone off on the other side of the little square came at my hailing it. I said goodnight to her as she climbed into the passenger seats. She avoided my eye. She gave an address in Bloomsbury. The taxi moved off and disappeared out of Carmelite Inn. I did not imagine I would ever see her again. I still felt sick, a little dazed. I couldn't return home just yet. I had far too much to absorb!

After a few moments I pushed open the gates and squeezed back into the Sanctuary. I wanted to be sure that I had actually seen what I thought. I glanced towards the Swan. There it was, as I had always known it. You could hear the boisterous arguments, the bawdy snatches of song, the gusting laughter. I smelled the beer, heard the horses and ostlers in the stables. Someone rolled a beer barrel up a ramp. A long-established place with familiar customers. At least three centuries old. Yet not long before I had seen it a wasteland with every sign that invaders had brutally killed, maimed, raped and kidnapped, doubtless into slavery, every man, woman or child. Even the elderly had not been spared. Nixer's men had laid waste to the Swan and the rest of the town all the way down to the foggy river. I was in an agony of self-hatred and loss. All that wonderful equilibrium. Molly happy. Her mother apparently happy. Helena happy. The children happy. No boat needed rocking. No china shop foresaw a bull. And Mrs Melody, for surprising and inexplicable reasons of her own, had charged into this perfectly balanced world, where everyone got the best from me and what they needed from me, and she had destroyed the balance. She was like the worst kind of villainess in my books. Insensate wickedness personified! That was how I felt, together with several other sometimes contradictory emotions and rationales. The Sanctuary had given me Molly. It now took her away.

I couldn't miss all the ironies involved. I had deceived Helena and then been deceived in turn. I was raging against Molly, her mother and myself. I even threw in a bit of anger at Helena. If she hadn't been such a sneering rationalist I would have been there with her and never been involved with Molly. I felt very self-pitying. I thought of all the gifts they had received, all the encouragement, all the reassurances, thus putting a price on what had originally been a bit of ordinary generosity. And I was in a melancholy state, of course. I felt numb from head to foot. I was sleepwalking through a nightmare. I could see the symmetry of my situation and felt an ironic sense of conclusion. Wasn't it what I had done to Helena? Didn't I deserve it? But of course the mood was not to last long. Eventually the pain would come. And with it the lugubrious self-pity we so despise in others.

I wanted to go for a walk and think things over. I was very shaky. As I wandered down towards Blackfriars, near the river, another idea began to form. There might be a silver lining to this cloud, perhaps one Mrs Melody had anticipated.

By the time it was twilight I found myself at the Monument, one of London's particular collection of phallic erections. A distinctly late seventeenth-century style, by Wren. Built not long after the time Nixer and his men had destroyed the Alsacia. Another thought likely to give me a headache. I tried to shake the thought free. So now, in the sunset, I walked up Fleet Street and Queen Victoria Street, past Southwark Bridge and London Bridge, until I could raise my head and stare at the Monument itself, outlined against a deepening dark blue moonlit sky.

I was fond of the Monument. It wasn't unique in its basics. I didn't know a capital without their Cleopatra's needles or proud towers. Before 1960 or so, few public buildings, even Downing Street and Westminster Cathedral, had guards to stop you going in, no railings protecting them from the people. A stern sign was enough to scare away vagrants. They usually read simply NO LOITERING. Sometimes you might find one ordinary copper on duty but they were generally tolerant enough, depending on how you were dressed. I don't even remember how or when all that security stuff started. Then, suddenly, it became routine to see British cops with sub-machine guns.

The Monument was one of my favourite retreats. Tourism brought a constant daily march of visitors up and down its 311 steps and eventually it was locked up at night. Built as symbolic thanks when almost the entire population of the city survived the Great Fire of London, it had some over-the-top allegorical imagery, much of it serving to remind us that a benificent king had seen fit to restore his capital with all the genius of Wren and Portland stone, to endure against all the future fires that threatened her. Wingèd Time with the help of his servants Science, Architecture and Liberty lifted battle-weary London from the ruins of the fire, pointing to Peace and Plenty who, thanks to Industry and consequent Prosperity, lay in the future. As a boy I had first been attracted to the dragons, one of which represented the city. But the whole tableau, showing the king and his brother rebuilding and defending the capital, was as fascinating to me as any comic book. I had a similar love for the Albert Memorial.

I wanted no company then, except the ghosts of my ancestors. Many believed the fire had cleared away the plague, too. It certainly gave architects like Wren and Hawksmoor a chance to build some impressive stuff.

The door opened when I turned the handle. The steps were narrow and steep. It took a while to climb them. I still felt shaky. And then I looked out over the panorama of night-time London with Tower Bridge and the rest in one direction and Whitehall in the other. Out of the rubble of the war's great firestorms, the city was coming back to life. Massive, perhaps, and ugly, the new architecture reassured us that we were able to put up strong buildings to resist whatever an enemy air force could bring against us. *Fortress London!* We had to look A-bomb proof. Simple psychology at work, of course. That brutalism made us feel powerful again. The city had not yet been fuelled by Thatcher's fast-fix, get-rich-quick schemes which would characterise the '80s, nor the wonderful grandiosity of buildings erected to display the power and taste of nations and businesses who were beginning to own more of London than we did. The council flats weren't improved. All she did was get local authorities to clad them in jollier colours. Smoke used to be the sign of industry. Now, with mirrors, it is the sign of political spin.

The foundation of the new postwar London was Hope. A determination to resist Tyranny in whatever form it came. Who remembers? Standing at the railings of the column, I found it a bit easier to believe our sustaining myth. How Evil Incarnate determined to destroy us; how a beneficent God had protected us.

I enjoyed the moment. The Blitz and the Battle of Britain were the closest most of us would come to a proud myth based almost wholly on truth. A benign God was going a bit too far for me! I was a secular rationalist from a family of atheists. Almost everyone I knew was an atheist. I was an Enlightenment man, through and through. My world had its roots in the late eighteenth century. Tom Paine was my guy. The evidence tended to be for a malignant rather than a benign God.

Then I turned towards where I knew the Alsacia to be. I again tried to clear my head. What had I seen? Where had I been? From here I could see over a large part of the city and nowhere was there a trace of Alsacia. I could go mad trying to explain everything. I could stay sane by accepting the supernatural's existance. It felt like a betrayal of all I'd been taught. But if I did accept the supernatural I could at least begin to think.

Whose side were the monks really on? What had happened to my friends in the Alsacia? All that devastation! A pretty traumatic night for me. Had I witnessed a miracle or an illusion? Depression settled as I walked back down the circular staircase. I had probably witnessed an authentic miracle, but my girlfriend had taken up with her old lover. Not much compensation, really.

With a thin drizzle falling, I walked to where I could get a bus. I had hardly thought of Helena and considered my original reason for visiting the Alsacia. I had told Helena I would sort it out. How would I explain what had happened? Well, first there was a mistress and her mother... For some considerable time now I have not been going to a retreat but have been living with a lady...

I decided that it was in everyone's interest that I said as little as possible. I could make a fresh start and put Molly, her mother, her lover and the Alsacia behind me. I walked up to the bus stop. The new electric street lights formed pools of pale gold. The high surrounding buildings took on a denser, sharper darkness. They retained that ultra-solidity they sometimes had when you dropped LSD. This time I couldn't put it all down to a couple of old monks slipping hallucinogens into my tea. Nonetheless, I remember thinking how like a trip some aspects of the experience were. Were those mysterious clerics creating an illusion shared by all inhabitants of the Sanctuary? It felt like something out of Phil Dick. What had I been drawn into?

No TV programme or film came close to creating the reality of what I'd seen. I knew, of course, what war-ruined buildings looked like. But I also knew in my bones that I had witnessed something supernatural. Something dangerously powerful and capable of terrifying acts of destruction and creativity. A lot worse than a few 'redcoats' making a raid. The English Civil War was the bloodiest in our history, when we lost a higher percentage of our population than during the First and Second World Wars. I could believe such destruction and bloodshed had taken place. I could not understand how the evidence could so easily vanish. And the dead restored.

I got to the stop just in time to catch the 15a. I went to the top deck and lit a cigarette. The bus turned up Farringdon Road. We passed Fleetway House. Much of my income still came from there. To me even that building had begun to look like a kind of temple. Until yesterday I had never for a moment believed in the existence of a deity. I had known my own visions were a trick of the mind. I had been certain the Alsacia had a scientific basis. But now I had witnessed an extraordinary resurrection! Surely I had to accept the existence of God! The alternative was madness. Again I shivered in my boots at the implications of what I'd recently witnessed.

I fell into a light sleep until a couple of happy drunks came aboard.

Slowly, a whisper began to sound in my head. The Swarm had returned. For a while it had left me alone! I sighed. For a moment I had thought my acceptance of God had been rewarded.

When I got to my stop my legs were weak. I steadied myself on the seats as I rose to go downstairs, gripped the rails from stairs to platform and staggered off onto the pavement. Nobody bothered me. I was just an early drunk going home. It was cold. Even though I had only a few steps to go to my front door, I turned up the collar of my black car coat.

As I put my key in the lock my lips began to move. I wasn't sure at first what I was doing. Then I realised what it was.

I was praying for the safety of my immortal soul.

BOOK THREE

*Two thousand, three hundred and thirty-six years ago –
that was when the light of the great prophet Zoroaster
went out and his wisdom committed to the memories of
twelve disciples who turned it into writings. Thus twelve
sacred books were made which together are called The
Raghabesta and it is the secret history of Zoroaster and
the story of each of the twelve who are represented second
by six, third by three, who are the holy carriers of the
thirteenth book – the so-called 'lost' Avesta – which tells
of the life of Zoroaster and reveals the place where Ahura
Mazda created the first* Homo sapiens. *Much truth and
wisdom is revealed in that book.*

– Jason Cartwell,
My Persian Nights

CHAPTER THIRTY-FOUR

THE ABSENCE OF MEMORY

I FELT THE Swarm grow louder, threatening. I didn't care. I determined to forget Molly and never revisit the Alsacia, even in my imagination. I was well aware of the ironies of being a writer of fantasy and what I was experiencing now. My misery was real enough. What had just happened? The emotional impact was hardly bearable. I wanted to talk about my confusion. Who might understand? My mum? Helena? Barry, in Telford, was too far away and wasn't on the phone. I couldn't think of a single soul I could confide in. Most of my closest friends were out of London. The core members of the Fix were off playing with other bands or doing session work. Besides, I had few male friends with whom I could talk about my confusion, even if they were around.

I had seen the dead come back to life. I had said that a single miracle might convince me of the existence of God. If so, there might be a point to learning His purpose, or at least finding out if He had one. *A decision even when no decision could be made.* Meanwhile I needed to spend much more time on the important business of my own ego. I was wallowing in self-pity, having been deceived by the woman with whom I was deceiving my wife.

I put a good face on it when I got back. Our daughters were already in bed, so couldn't contradict anything. I was sure Sally and Kitty wouldn't remember if they had seen Mrs Melody before or not.

Luckily, Helena was still a little euphoric from the trip and didn't blame me that time for having acid-freak friends.

We went to bed. Helena said something felt odd about my love-making.

The majority of my friends, when I raised the subject of God, found my new interest disturbing. Some, of course, thought that I'd fallen for a line from some guru and found religion in a sugar cube. At least, said Pete Taylor, I wasn't going off to India or somewhere. I'd stopped telling him that I didn't have to go to India. The Sanctuary was only a short ride away on the Number 15 bus.

Of course, I would never set foot in the place again. My heart was broken. I felt as if everyone there had conspired in its breaking. In other words, I was still refining my self-pity. Meanwhile I was suddenly forced to consider the existence of a supernatural world ruled by a Supreme Being. In Alsacia, at least, magic was real. The prospect scared me. Writing that stuff was one thing. It offered great images, metaphors, symbols, narrative devices of all kinds. But in no way did I believe in it. I didn't even have an interest in 'world building' or any of the other escapist pleasures. I had read and written fantasy as I'd enjoyed Freud and Jung, during a reading frenzy which included Camus and Vian. Logically, distant worlds, somehow parallel to our own, were fiction. Nothing else. I made my living writing that stuff. I never believed it. I knew how easy it was to invent.

Not any more.

Then there were the inhabitants of the Sanctuary: people with all the usual plans, hopes, ambitions, schemes. Real people who smelled and felt and sounded and had the inner lives of real people. Real people who ate and drank, belched, farted, shouted and laughed and told you jokes, shared a common frustration and gesticulated around you, oblivious of your mental world as you were of theirs. Real enough, I was bound to accept. Though they didn't appear to be defeated by death. And then I had to believe that the abbey, which I had assumed to be full of decent old gents belonging to a benevolent Christian order, was nothing of the sort. Instead it contained a bunch of *magi* or even *magicians* who protected the Sanctuary by spectacular supernatural spells and might or might not be benign. Whatever their identity, it was obvious they were capable of astonishing powers while possibly controlling the lives and destinies of hundreds, even thousands in the Alsacia. And they protected a living cup I had called the Fish Chalice, as well as a mysterious 'Treasure' that the bad guys, the Puritans, were after! And that was my *simplified* version of where I stood intellectually at that moment.

I really wish I had never spoken to Friar Isidore. This blurring of the borders between reality and fantasy was beginning to make my head ache and the Whispering Swarm had become the soundtrack to my bafflement. I knew a lot of writers would have been envious of my discovery of the Alsacia. They couldn't imagine anything like it.

It was pretty weird. I could really only talk about it with Helena and Helena didn't accept that the Alsacia and its inhabitants were real. Barry was stuck for ever in Telford, a miserable monochrome town insulting the name of a great Victorian engineer and rationalist! Barry was about the only man on the planet who would take me seriously. He was very spiritual. He had been meditating long before the coming of the Age of Aquarius. He just sat there and *thought*. But Barry was hours away and busy with his dying father, so I wrote him a letter and asked when he was coming to London next. Meanwhile, I was on my own.

I wasn't happy about the situation. I had seen Alsacia as a kind of physical phenomenon; something science could explain. I was ready for any argument that would convince me I was delusional, but somehow I could only believe what the monks believed, even if I put the arguments in more modern terms.

I did a lot of reading about miracles and faith and those who had believed in God. I read books which discussed the 'Perennial Philosophy', as Huxley called it. He thought all religions had beliefs and myths in common and one system borrowed from or lent to another. I really hoped to find a rational argument to explain the Alsacia and everything I had witnessed. After a few weeks of extended discussions with Barry at long distance, reversing the charges from his pub, I was still little the wiser.

Helena could tell there was something on my mind but I don't think she wanted to ask what was wrong. The more sympathetic she was, the more guilt I felt, and the guiltier I got, the more uncharacteristic my behaviour. She was genuinely worried by what she considered my delusions. However, when I tried to tell her the problem, her response was that I should seek professional help.

I tried a different strategy. One afternoon, I said I was trying to think through some theological ideas for a story about life after death. If the dead could rise living from their graves, did that prove the existence of a higher being? Not necessarily, I supposed, but the question was a complex one. Beneath this, of course, I grieved for Moll and what we had enjoyed together. 'What do you think?'

Helena looked up from her desk. 'I suppose, if you make it complex.' She pursed her lips. 'You should really not be doing all that pot, Mike. Either that or stop agonising about those old questions. I thought you'd written one of the definitive stories on the subject! Aren't you a person of rare goodness and sanity?' She was mocking me, quoting some newspaper review of *Behold the Man*. In it a character went back in time looking for faith and found it in an unusual way. I cringed. Maybe I was just getting simple-minded?

Perhaps it was good that my metaphysical dark night of the soul obscured my continuing obsession with Molly and her betrayal. Though everything in me longed to confront her, I refused to go back to the Alsacia. From time to time, I'd worked for *Bible Story Weekly*. Every man jack on the paper, including the vicar who was our titular editor, was an atheist. In researching articles, talking to clerics and discussing Christian sects, I'd developed a healthy wariness of religions which characteristically broke down into warring sub-sects. Visionary politics. Primitive power stuff. Leader of the pack.

I tried talking to Barmy Felicity. That beautiful, acid-burned woman had once studied religion in Spain. I understood she was raised a Catholic. She told me that 'everything is connected' and half the time seemed to be quoting ideas I'd made up for stories that had somehow filtered into popular mythology. She told me about Other Worlds and astral projections and advised me, 'Stay true to yourself, Mike.' I told her I'd do my best. I couldn't stop obsessing about Moll. Not just her betrayal but everything she had told me. Some of what she said had never really added up. Sometimes she seemed to have been in two places at once.

Was time travel part of this new equation? I had refused to look at the Alsacia with that in mind because I could see no way it was possible, given the constants. I was a lazy thinker, preferring to enjoy life and not brood about it any more than I had to. I had never much cared where we were from or where we were going. Instinctively I always avoided listening to preachers, teachers, evangelists.

Beyond Alsacia, the constant presence of the Whispering Swarm made serious thinking difficult. Maybe I should have spent more time learning mental discipline. Could the noises be a wholly psychological phenomenon? Would I have been better off simply giving in to the Swarm and letting it call me back? Should I have settled down and learned all I could about the place?

But how well was my own memory working? Was I actually experiencing psychotic episodes? I had to test myself somehow. I would start writing everything down. I could check on myself. I remembered the first big fight in the square and how Joey had appeared badly wounded. And Moll, too. I had gone crazy when I saw her hurt. But, by the time I got her out of danger, the wound was nearly gone. I began to wonder if they all weren't some sort of time-travellers. It might have been easier for me to believe if they were zooming around in time machines! Or that I was barmy.

That was the irony of course. I made a decent living writing quite convincingly about all kinds of supernatural beings. Gods and devils, immortals and the living dead were familiar grist for my mill. I could easily imagine a dozen different kinds of time travel in an hour. As far as pseudo-psychic powers went, I wasn't just pretty handy with a tarot deck: I had seen all those visions as a kid, including Jesus and the Virgin Mary when I had a fever. I pretty much took the odd saint for granted. I had always had perfectly good rational reasons for their visitations. The Jesus and Mary had been classic versions, straight out of their steel engravings in Victorian bibles. Mary, in an elaborate crown and brocade robes, had topped, on one occasion, an entire choir of angels soaring up from the end of my bed into a scintillating sky where the ceiling should have been.

I had seen Sir Francis Drake or Sir Walter Raleigh or both, I wasn't sure. I was fairly familiar with a few other miscellaneous famous figures from history who had hovered over my bed when I was ill. They arrived mostly in glorious technicolour. I had read the tarot

316 • MICHAEL MOORCOCK

and predicted the future. But when it came to it, I could not suspend disbelief for a moment, even when I was seven. I just didn't think I was experiencing anything more than an hallucination. I knew they were projections of my own imagination. I had never had a problem with them. I thought everyone could do it. My imagination was just a bit more elaborate than most. Possibly the surprises and the stress of recent times were getting to me. I knew without a shade of doubt that my 'visions' were projections of my own psyche.

Almost every SF or fantasy writer I knew was a total sceptic and embarrassed by people's assumptions that we were into flying saucers and all that stuff. People in pubs would try to share their barmy beliefs but it was hard for me to be polite. I was only likely to be persuaded by a huge amount of sustaining evidence.

Unfortunately, I now had that evidence and I was doing everything I could to understand it. The dead had been brought back to life, all their material possessions, animals and buildings restored. The monks had expected it. That was why they hadn't cared. Maybe I should accept that if there were, for instance, people who could receive mortal blows and recover from them more or less immediately, then other miracles had to be true.

But I wasn't happy about it! I had spent years developing a personal morality influenced by contemporary existentialists. When it came to thinking things through, Sartre and Camus were my models. My own mantra had gone 'I was not, I am, I will not be'. It had suited me to accept the fact that when we died, we died and that was that. To some it was a rather bleak way of seeing the world. To me it meant I lived knowing I only had one crack at existing. Obeying certain moral and emotional imperatives, I was determined to make the most of my one crack! That was the rock I'd given myself to stand on. But now there was a strong chance I possessed a soul and had misunderstood the fundamental nature of the world. I might be the subject of a higher power and if so it was probably my moral duty (or even a matter of survival) to determine what that power wanted from me and live accordingly. I was only a free agent in a limited sense. I felt I was being dragged back into the Middle Ages!

Admittedly, I also picked up the occasional work by a well-known

sceptic. I hoped to discover an argument to shore up my failing athe-
ism. None had my experience. I had to decide which modern thinker
best suited me. The atheists, after all, hadn't experienced an authentic
miracle. As an ex-rationalist Huxley had most to say to me. I had not
yet found a Jesuit, as Helena joked. She was amused by my research. Whenever she walked along Victoria Street she half expected
to see me strolling out of Westminster Cathedral arm in arm with
some red-hatted cardinal. My own mum's profound thought on the
matter that there 'had to be something' didn't help me much. I'd
talked to every believer I could find, but the truth was I didn't know
too many. For a while I had corresponded with a nun in Pennsylvania. She had read *Behold the Man* and liked it. She had insisted that
it was not anti-religious, which it wasn't intended to be. She then
added that I was the most 'spiritual' layman she knew. I didn't like to
tell her my intention was to write about demagogues and how they
were created by public desire. A number of people, mostly in Texas,
didn't share Sister Marie-Louise's judgement. They offered to send
me to meet my maker with help from Mr Smith and Mr Wesson.

There was no doubt about it, I had to get back to the Alsacia as
soon as I could and try to talk to the abbot. Maybe the old man would
answer any direct questions. I put this in a letter to Barry.

Barry wasn't sure.

'You don't want to open a healing wound,' he wrote.

'Is that what you think?' I asked.

He was clearly distracted by his other problems. 'I've got a feeling
it's just not a good idea now.'

I thought I understood. 'I have to go back,' I said, 'I'm having all
kinds of crazy anxiety dreams. And the Swarm –?'

'Please yourself,' wrote Barry. 'I'm sorry I can't go with you.'

And so, after debating this for some time, and not that long after I
had sworn never to return, I decided to go to the abbey, avoid the
rest of the town, and ask questions for myself. It was stupid. I had
never felt sicker.

The sharp air smelled good as I left the flat. I had almost abandoned my plan and went, instead, into the gardens to smoke a joint,
sit on a bench and think it all through. But I had thought about it as
much as I could. I liked to work out ideas through action and writing.

I needed more information. I needed to get down to the Alsacia and confront Father Grammaticus. I know I should have told Helena, but I couldn't stand another argument. I thought it important to preserve the domestic harmony we had taken so long to achieve. I shouldn't have even considered visiting the abbot. I should have just strolled into the gardens to enjoy the season. But I didn't go into the square and sit on a bench and take pleasure in the autumn trees. I turned right and I headed for the 15 bus stop. I was still looking back and wondering about the square when the Routemaster turned up, shivering and purring. I collected myself and made a decision. I set foot on the platform and swung myself aboard the bus full of cool determination and a ridiculous sense of destiny.

I got off in Fleet Street at the Law Courts, still enjoying the mellow fruitfulness, if not the gathering mist no doubt coming off the river. I wasn't sure how I would feel, especially if they denied anything had happened, as I feared Moll would. But my intention wasn't to see Moll. I needed the abbot's advice.

The mist was at its thickest in Whitefriars Yard as I cut through into Carmelite Inn. That orderly square of railed Georgian buildings of uniform size and design held in the heavy fog which the yellow gaslight scarcely penetrated. I headed for where I knew the gate should be. For a moment I thought I heard my name being called. The Whispering Swarm grew suddenly agitated. I slowed. I thought I caught words. Screams. Warnings. Should I continue or go back? Then, at last, I found the entrance. The Swarm's voice had dwindled. Turning the old iron handle, I pushed the left-hand gate slowly open until, with a low note of protest, it gaped wide enough to admit me. As I slipped through I heard a voice I recognised. A low, delighted chuckle. Colonel Clitch, I was sure. Cursing myself for an idiot, I stepped backwards. I knew I should have gone home. Only now did I think clearly of the children and how they would be affected if I died and never returned. I felt the flat of a sword on my back, restraining me. I saw a face leering out of the thickening fog and my heart sank. I thought I heard the Swarm falling away on a distant jeering note.

Corporal Love's cadaverous pale head was split by a great, yawning grin. His own basket-hilted cutlass was in his right hand, the point almost under my nose. His black broadcloth coat, like his linen, was stained with food and drink. He put out a strong, musty odour, like sweaty feet. Could this be a dead man raised from his coffin? Next hot, alcoholic breath bathed my face. I drew back in disgust, recognising Colonel Clitch, the other Cromwellian irregular, a leering grin on his gaunt features, his head surrounded by a halo of dirty red hair.

'Good evening, officers.' I spoke rather feebly. 'A cold night to be abroad...' Attempting to push the unyielding steel from my chest, I backed against the other sword.

'Oh, indeed it is, master,' said Colonel Clitch, his voice soft and sharp at the same time. The steel caressed my spine. 'Been out for a jaunt in the City, have we? Carrying messages for traitors?'

'Stealing from honest folks, is it?' came Love's unwelcome lilt.

'I just got off the bus,' I said, 'and am on my way home. As you can see, I am unarmed. I have no goods on me, stolen or otherwise. I am going about my honest business. So if you will excuse me, gentlemen –'

'Where did you hide the tools of your trade, you cunning rogue?' demanded Corporal Love.

'And your ill-gotten gains?' added Colonel Clitch.

I made to push past them. I was genuinely angry. My heart was thumping. The residents of the Alsacia might somehow be invulnerable to sword blades and pistol shots, but I certainly wasn't. Love's sword point was almost touching my upper lip and Clitch had slowly turned his own blade so that its edge pressed into my back. I wondered if I could throw up on them before they stabbed me.

'Off to keep an appointment with others of his devilish ilk I've no doubt,' declared the Welsh Puritan with a sniff.

Then I risked being sliced by Clitch's sword and stepped back into it, making him move, as I'd hoped, rather than wound me. I was again at the opening of the big gate and took another step towards it. I stumbled and nearly fell but in another second I stood on the far side in what I hoped was safety. I looked around. All I could see was thicker fog and not a single light cutting it. I was almost overcome by a sickening stench. I took two or three more backward steps. Suddenly flickering orange light cut through the fog. Clitch and Love, the latter raising a lantern, moved towards me.

I felt as if I were in Limbo, neither in my familiar world nor another. The cold cut into me. I saw silvery streaks shimmer and vanish in the fog. Roads? I remembered the two Cosmolabes. My pewter breath blended with the grey fog and made it thicker. I couldn't believe my bad luck. I had a sense of leaving solid earth behind me.

'How now, my young Moabite,' gloated Clitch. 'Do you fear justice? Could it be that you are guilty of all we suspect?'

'I'm guilty of nothing. I've given you two carrion birds too much of my time!' I had nowhere to go yet my danger made me more aggressive. I had little to lose. I wondered what my chances were of getting free and again hiding myself in the fog. I was probably in Whitefriars Yard. I might just be able to get back to the bus stop.

'Methinks we'll put you and your lies before a magistrate.' Clitch laughed unpleasantly. He was echoed by Love's disgusting snigger. The two closed in. Love's bony fingers grasped my arm but I shook him off. He seized me again, intending to bind me, I think. I resisted, careless of their weapons, and in struggling found my hand against the grip of a big pistol. Without thinking I tugged the firearm out of Love's belt and shoved the barrel into his ribs. He let me go in an instant, shouting a warning to Clitch.

I turned slowly to face him, cocking the pistol and holding it as steady as I could. The thing was huge, cumbersome and untrustworthy. They both heard me pull back the hammer. Covering them, I continued to retreat. 'Stand where you are, both of you!' I wanted to put plenty of darkness between us as quickly as possible. Then I tripped on an unexpected kerb and almost fell. The gun went off with a terrific noise. I had no idea where I was going but I still hoped I was somewhere I would eventually recognise. The mist had a strange heaviness to it. Breathing the icy stuff was difficult. Surely it wasn't hallucinogenic gas? The stench of gunpowder filled the air. I turned the weapon in my hand so that I could use it as a club if I got the opportunity.

Then I was distracted by a strong, sweet scent. I could not place it. I glimpsed a cloaked outline slipping past me. Someone I also should have known. Not one of my attackers but a woman, maybe? Then she was gone. She had distracted me. I had not escaped.

I heard a sound behind me, lost my footing, tripped again and fell off balance. I hit my leg on what was probably an iron bollard and went down. Even as I scrambled back up, having lost the gun, and limped off on my bruised leg I heard another curse. Had my inadvertent shot hit one of them? It would be my bad luck if I had compounded my alleged crimes.

Then I heard a voice on my right. 'Here, lad, to me.'

I recognised the speaker. Holding my arms outstretched, I walked very carefully towards the sound of his voice. He suddenly took shape on my left, a stocky, solid figure in a camelard. His wide-leaf hat with a fine burst of pheasant feathers in it. 'Good evening to you, Master Moorcock.' I felt him press a heavy sword into my hand. 'And how fareth thou this evening?'

From out of the fog, Captain St Claire offered me a thin, sardonic smile. 'Take care, sir. A serpent creeps towards thee!'

As I whirled, the captain in turn accepted an attack from the left. Clitch, a heavy-breathing lummox, thrust at him again. Meanwhile I engaged Love, marked out for me in the gloom by the excessive pallor of his skin.

I heard him gasp as my first lunge appeared to take him in the hat. When I withdrew my sword, I was off balance again. I cursed myself for my clumsiness. I had indeed spiked his headgear. As I shook my blade to free it, I saw him, crouching as if to spring, outlined against the fog. He jumped high, like a toad, his sword hissing past my face. My advantage and disadvantage when fighting these people was that everyone was so much shorter than I. I must have seemed a Porthos to their D'Artagnans! But Love was my first hopping opponent.

I think they mistook a tyro's unearned confidence for skill, for they engaged me almost reluctantly – first Clitch, whom St Claire took over. I now faced Love, whose second pistol was caught up in that red sash. Failing to drag his barker free, the Welshman spat an insult. Still cursing, he turned and sloped off into the dark. Meanwhile, through the silver-streaked fog, I heard the sound of blades meeting and occasionally saw the outlines of St Claire and Clitch, both evidently seasoned and economical swordsmen, continuing their fight until Clitch appeared to flee. St Claire put his back towards me and discharged his pistol over the head of his escaping opponent.

Replacing the barker in his sash, he reached towards me and

accepted his sword back, sheathing it on his right while his own sword was scabbarded on the left. Next, he removed his hat, inspected the lie of its feathers, brushed it a little and placed it back on his dark, shoulder-length hair.

He grinned suddenly. 'Well, 'tis an happy coincident, young sir. 'Tis lucky for us your swordsmanship is good, if a little unseasoned.'

I could think of nothing to say to him. Again, the brown-eyed northener had saved my liberty, perhaps even my life. I reached out my hand and he shook it, still a little amused. 'Well, sir, I guess ye'll want to be continuing on your way so I'll bid thee goodnight.'

'I'm obliged to you, sir,' I said. Jackdaw that I am I heard myself imitating his speech patterns. I had a habit of doing that. My daughter Kitty was also able to pick up accents and speech rhythms. 'I'm a little turned about. Could you give me an idea where the gates to Alsacia can be found?'

Laughing, St Claire, whose forehead was on a level with my shoulder, took my arm and stepped confidently into the fog.

'Where are we now, Captain St Claire?' I asked. His answer surprised me.

'What year is it? Why, it's the year of our Lord 1648, young sir, and Parliament is victorious.'

I was surprised by his answer, not so much by the date as the form of his reply. He had thought I meant which year, rather than which place! Hardly the mind-set of a late Renaissance man.

'What year might it be in the Alsacia?' I asked him.

He hesitated as if he were chewing over a riddle. 'The same. Oh, I know that you and your familiars travel the moonbeam roads. Be assured of this certainty – everywhere in Earth, Heaven and Hell, it is yet the twelfth day in the month of October in the year of our Lord 1648. Cromwell rules England. Parliament and justice have prevailed!'

'You sound like a Parliament's man,' I said

'I am indeed, though a thoughtful one since the king is so ill used. Fool that he is, like all Stuarts, possessing a taste for the bottle and more arrogance than sense, he persists in betraying his word and making war on his own subjects. He honestly believes he's God's chosen. And I choose not to question God. Yet there's still some hope of his finding nobility and sanity within that sea of hard-headedness, self-doubt and boyish need he calls a mind, but I fear it will not be. A hard-head he'll remain until the conversion of the Jews!'

'A great speech for a Parliamenter,' I said. 'You did say you were *for* Cromwell?'

'To my bootstraps. I respect the right of sanctuary, however, and let God alone judge those who seek it. But I'm not for imprisoning nor murdering the king. Or commoners. I fear the wretched anarchy such deeds will bring.' Using a scabbarded sword he felt ahead of us, leading me with one hand until he struck wood with an encouraging thump. 'Alsacia,' he said. He opened the gate and brought us into the Sanctuary. Captain St Claire was a godly soldier. Could I ever learn from him what kind of illusion the Alsacia was and how it was created? Could I learn whether God existed? And could I get someone from this world to take pity on me, explain what was happening? Prince Rupert had spoken a little of the logic by which the many worlds of his universe made their way through the heavens, but not enough to help me understand it and follow the logic of its existence. Today I intended to find out more, even if what I learned killed me or turned me mad! I looked to Captain St Claire. I owed him a favour. I could not do him the discourtesy of not offering him a drink.

'Let me buy you a shant,' I insisted, 'since you saved my life.'

'Your life is worth a shant of ale, eh?' He was amused. 'Well, I've known several who value their souls at less! But,' a flash of intuition, 'your business is with the abbey, no?' His dark, intelligent eyes looked firmly into mine as if he reminded me of my purpose. 'Perhaps we'll meet for a drink another time.'

I smiled and thanked him. As before, he strolled with me up to the abbey doors and then turned to leave. 'I'll wish you good evening, Master Moorcock, and trust we'll meet again soon.'

We shook hands. After he had disappeared back into the fog I turned to knock on the heavy oak door of the abbey. All I heard was echoing silence.

I knocked again. There was still no answer. I looked back towards the Swan but saw little activity. Was the entire place deserted? Again, I resisted an impulse to get a drink at the tavern. I knew it would be a mistake. I sensed a sinister, sentient quality to the fog. It curled like a snake, thicker mist against lighter. Sparks of silver fire flickered within it. It was impossible to distinguish the nature of the shapes or the sparks. Unarmed as I was, I thought it was time I got out of the Sanctuary.

Disappointed and nervous, I headed for the gate again and eventually found it. I was frightened. The whole place was dead and seemed filled with the dead. By the time I eventually found Carmelite Inn Chambers and almost fell through the gate into it, stumbling and running up towards Fleet Street, I had just managed to recover myself, but I didn't look back.

I boarded a late bus to Ladbroke Grove. Nobody was on the top deck until we got to Charing Cross. After that I shared the ride with two Irish drunks singing a chaotic medley of sentimental music-hall ditties about Killarney or hard Republican songs about Kevin Barry. I knew many of them. I had learned them when busking in Irish pubs from Notting Hill to Kilburn. I didn't mind the distraction a bit. I joined in where I could. 'As down the glen one Easter...'

When I stumbled into the flat at about ten thirty that evening, I found it fuller than I had expected.

Helena had been worried sick. She was afraid that I'd been in a fight or worse. No real harm done. Except all the harm in the world. The beginning of the end. Mrs Melody was there. Before she left for Oxford with her daughter she had come, she said, to apologise.

CHAPTER THIRTY-FIVE

ANOTHER FINE CHRISTMAS

For a couple of weeks after I had moved out of the family flat, I recorded a few new tracks with the band. It helped distract me, but my heart wasn't in it. I tried to talk to Pete about what had happened with Moll but since he had just split up with a girlfriend of some years, he had other problems. So I kept it all to myself and talked instead about whether miracles could happen without the existence of God. Was there a school of philosophy which proposed such a thing? Everyone apart from Pete was either totally sceptical or so far gone into Sufism that I couldn't understand them. If it hadn't been for the Swarm constantly reminding me of its presence, I might have put Alsacia out of my head completely.

I had sublet a room across the road in a big flat rented by *New Worlds'* advertising manager, Lizzy Mitchum, and her husband, Mick, who did light-shows. Lizzy was fond of the girls and didn't mind them visiting or even staying occasionally. Every day I got up, went across the road, encountered a monosyllabic Helena, and walked Sally and Kitty to school. Every day, whenever I could, I picked them up from school and took them home.

Helena had hardly spoken to me since Mrs Melody had visited to 'apologise' for taking the girls out to see her daughter. She hadn't realised, she insisted, that I had yet to tell Helena about Molly. Her daughter understood I was getting a divorce. I had been totally pissed off by Mrs Melody's aggression. How did she think she was helping her daughter? By forcing my hand? I really meant it. The threat of reality, perhaps never seeing Helena or the girls again, brought me to my senses. I was never going to see Molly again. Pretending to be placatory, she talked about her poor daughter in tears with a broken heart. Not the Moll Midnight I knew!

She was acting. I now knew Mrs Melody had left the Alsacia shortly after I arrived and was distracted by Clitch and Love. I even suspected her of paying the pair to keep me busy while she went to Ladbroke Grove. I had recognised her perfume as she slipped past me. I, of course, was impotently furious. She had deliberately destroyed the equilibrium of my life. Somehow, she had known I was visiting the Alsacia. While I was busy she had taken her chance to blow the whistle! Though I had warned her to stay away from my family, she had deliberately thrown a spanner in the emotional works. She had intended to force me back together with Molly. I was having none of it. In front of Helena I told Mrs Melody unequivocally that I was never returning to the Alsacia. I had no intention of seeing her or her daughter again.

It was off my chest, in the open, and at least I didn't have to lie any more. Of course, this hadn't stopped Helena from telling me to pack my bags. We hadn't talked much since and she was pretty grim. At least she wasn't keeping the children away from me, even if she shut me up every time I tried to explain everything to her. In the end there wasn't an awful lot to say. I didn't have a moral leg to stand on. She said I only made myself sound more feeble.

I stopped after a while. There was no point in beginning with a story she refused to believe. On the other hand, if the Alsacia didn't exist, how had I managed to have an affair there? Helena wouldn't talk about that, either.

The children now needed a lot of my attention. They were slightly puzzled by my moving across the street but, since their own lives weren't changed, accepted it as one of those inexplicable things adults did. They had developed distinct personalities and preferences. Sally was a natural vegetarian. Kitty loved meat. Sally was a confronter. Kitty did her best to negotiate. There was no serious rivalry between them and they bonded on almost every occasion. I loved seeing their complex personalities growing. I was very proud of them. They were a pleasure to be with because they were so curious. I was consoled by their general joy in living, their excitement of discovery. They wouldn't always be enthusiastic about going to a museum or an exhibition, but usually they would be drawn in by a new painter or an old bit of natural history. They enjoyed visiting working artists.

My sculptor friend Eduardo Paolozzi was always welcoming when we visited his studio. Some of his big metal pieces were shown at his Mayfair gallery, the Hayward. He encouraged the girls to drop by and climb all over them. Even when one was installed at the Tate he told the guards to let the kids alone. He was a sweet man in those days. They loved visiting his screen printer where all that pure, vivid colour was splashed everywhere, the prints coming to life under the rollers. As little girls Sally and Kitty saw a lot of the pop artists as well as those Beat writers, like Bill Burroughs, whom I still knew and, of course, the *New Worlds* contributors. They met Angus Wilson, Doris Lessing, Arthur C. Clarke. They went to a lot of exhibitions, openings, launches. They were extremely well socialised. People said they were like Victorian children. True, they did a few things Victorian children were allowed to do, such as drink small amounts of beer and wine with meals, and a few things that were unheard of by Victorians. You really could take them anywhere. We went pretty much everywhere together when they were small. They were never what my mum would condemn as 'precocious'. Used to going to theatres and restaurants, they always behaved well. They knew backstage etiquette. They had pets, went out with their friends from school, most of whom had interesting parents, enjoyed sleepovers and other fun. Quarrelled about what TV to watch. All agreed on *Doctor Who*. We played elaborate games for which we produced costumes, made pictures or wrote proclamations. We also played games out of the big Victorian toy box I had picked up in Portobello Road. A lot of our projects were developed from what we discovered there. Like me they had grown up enjoying the pleasures of several generations.

We probably saw a few too many Disney movies, but we also went to the National Film Theatre and other places to see silent films. They sat rapt through two and a half hours of Douglas Fairbanks spectaculars like *The Black Pirate* or *The Gaucho*. He wasn't a great actor, but he was an excellent cloak-and-dagger performer in his own right, could flash a devilish smile. His son was better in talkies and was superb in *The Prisoner of Zenda* with Ronald Colman.

I had enjoyed the old prewar story papers from the years before I was born. Now my children went to see black-and-white silent epics with title cards and piano accompaniment. In the cinema I would see other parents trying to control much older kids through *Robin Hood*, starring Fairbanks Sr. It did have some early longueurs, but my kids sat entranced, knowing how to watch. You grow greedy for such memories, for the experiences of earlier generations. I hoped I was teaching important lessons, widening their range of pleasure. Experience and a broad vocabulary always seemed worth cultivating.

After a month of exile I tried to open negotiations with Helena about coming back or at least talking. In spite of my passionate denials, she was convinced I was still seeing Molly and she wouldn't allow me to raise the topic. How could I blame her? I still felt the pain of Molly's betrayal. I had trusted her, as Helena had trusted me, so I knew exactly how my wife was feeling. I was in a moral limbo, horribly frustrated by the situation, and with no intention of taking up with Molly again. I wanted my family life back and absolutely nothing more. I wrote Helena letters promising this. I did get a response eventually. 'Don't waste your time,' said Helena. 'I always knew you would do this.'

As Christmas came round I recalled an idea I had planned earlier to save everyone stress. It would not involve Helena having to cook for me if I wanted to spend the holiday with the children. The Christmas at the Café Royal idea originally occurred when I realised we *all* needed a break from preparing the season's rituals. Recent events aside, the idea was still a good one. I proposed to take us all out for Christmas lunch at the Café Royal. And I thought I'd invite Pete Pavli since he'd just split up with Fiona and we were a bit top-heavy with women. The girls were old enough to enjoy the change and I was pretty sure Helena's mother would love it. Mrs Denham would be frustrated from expressing her firm ideas about how, what, when and why her daughter was cooking. Mrs Denham took the rituals seriously, down to watching (and criticising) the Queen's Speech which Helena and I tried to avoid. My mum didn't actually get on with the others much but agreed. So I booked us a big table, decided the wines, agreed to the menu and looked forward to a good time, at least for a few hours, where everyone could sit back and relax without worrying about what was due to go in and come out of the oven when.

Even when Helena asked if Molly and her mother were coming I didn't rise to the bait. I hadn't contacted them, nor did I plan to contact them. Seeing a way of avoiding a lot of holiday awkwardness, Helena agreed. So early Christmas morning saw me climbing into a posh scarlet-and-white Santa suit and whiskers from Harrods, haring across Ladbroke Grove with a sackful of good stuff and ho-ho-hoing like buggery as I distributed presents to everyone. In the taxis I'd booked, we all bundled off to Regent Street late on Christmas morning. Dashing through the near-deserted streets, we arrived at the Café Royal in time for a lunch which, if not up to home-made, was pretty splendid, enjoyed by all, especially a bunch of carol-singing waiters. Champagne sparkled, claret gushed. The other diners were mainly rather sad American couples who were only too happy to join in a day with kids, confusion, carols, paper hats and plenty of high-class presents bursting from the crackers. I sat on one side of Mrs D. and Pete sat on the other. Our job was to jolly the lady up and keep her from discovering fresh seasonal sins in her daughter. This gave me a good view of the man lunching alone across the aisle who was clearly trying to work out our relationships. I felt we should do our best to put on a good show for him.

That year I saw the fault lines in our family life as clearly as I ever had. Nonetheless, I was determined to make this as jolly, glittery, plush, traditional and memorable a Christmas festival as it was possible to enjoy. Thankfully, everyone was equally sporting and had fun. Even Mrs D., taking her cue from my mum, put on the elaborate, sturdy paper hats and comic masks and pulled the enormous crackers and read out the witty mottoes and marvelled at the glorious gifts. Even Pete, not a natural diplomat, did his best to charm Mrs D., who knew what he was up to but acquiesced to be charmed anyway.

It was dark when we left the restaurant. The taxis were waiting for us. My mum and Mrs D. went home on their own. Helena, the girls and I all rode in the same cab to Ladbroke Grove. Helena invited me to stay the night.

'I'm not saying this changes anything,' she said.

CHAPTER THIRTY-SIX

STOLEN BREATH

Pᴇᴛᴇ Pᴀᴠʟɪ sᴛᴀʏᴇᴅ on our couch and was still there for a bit on Boxing Day. Back across the road I told him what had happened and asked him what he thought it meant. 'Probably means she's going to divorce you,' he said with that deadpan look which had got him flattened more than once. But I had a feeling he was right. I was beginning to think Helena had her eye on someone else.

We smoked some dope and went over a couple of numbers. He had a habit of composing tunes that were almost unsingable and required some serious vocal gymnastics. I could make the range but came out sounding like a second-rate operatic tenor. The times had made us overconfident. We were slowly realising that the pop world wasn't ready for Schoenberg-inspired rock songs. We had a gig at Dingwalls in a few days. I decided to focus on that. Nothing too fancy. We'd keep it simple. No messing about with weird key changes and time signatures. Like most of my friends, Pete was a natural sceptic. He had been in two of the most infamous stoner bands of all time – High Tide and the Third Ear – and was no longer inclined to speculate about God and the universe. Dope inspired him merely to suggest we find something to eat. We got our rehearsals done and staggered round to the Mountain Grill Café in Portobello Road for a fry-up.

The gig went pretty well. We didn't perform any new stuff because

Adrian Shaw, our bass player, hadn't had a chance to learn it. He'd been on holiday in Wales.

I met an old friend at Dingwalls, Lou Willis. A friend of Christina's. A beautiful natural-blonde, peaches-and-cream Welsh girl. She had just broken up with her bloke, Tank, a talented loony who mainly did session drums. She was one of the most beautiful women I'd ever known and I'd fancied her for years. We had never been lovers, mostly because our periods of promiscuity never coincided. Now Lou felt like going home with me. I knew in my bones it wasn't quite right. But I was curious. She knew Helena slightly. Had Helena told her I was fair game? In which case Helena really did have plans for seeing someone else. If I slept with Lou I'd probably find out. But it seemed wrong in so many ways. Unsporting! Ridiculous! In the end Lou came round for some coffee and we had one of those conversations about how stupid it would be for us to sleep together. I did my best not to let her perfume distract me, but was about to make some tea when she remembered that I'd once read the tarot cards. Did I still do that?

I should have kept to my decision to put the cards away for good. I'd sworn never to drag them out again. But reading them would keep my other pledge and distract my mind from sex. First I did a simple three-card spread – past, present and future – which I placed at the centre around which I made other spreads, gypsy-style or, as my Auntie Bridge used to say 'Mitcham fashion', for the gypsies had many ways of reading the cards. *Wands. Nines and eights with twelve as the signifier and myself as the Fool.* I began to lay out the next spread, letting my head get into it, setting my mind free to range over what someone had called the psychosphere, to interpret what the cards were telling me. *Swords. Twelves and tens with nine as the signifier, Helena as the Queen.*

My personal card, the Fool, turned up in all three first hands. This was important news to a tarot reader. The card was identified with the reader, with myself. The Fool was God's own, whose intuitions were interpreted through the wisdom of the cards. Lou was leaning closer and I knew the part the cards might play no matter what they actually said. It might have ended up in the usual way if Helena hadn't rung from across the road to know if I was okay. I heard someone grumbling in the background, then Helena put the kids on and we had one of those conversations you have when you don't really have a lot to talk about. Had Helena seen Lou come back with me? I asked her to phone me later. After another half hour or so, Lou laid her dope and some rolling papers on the edge of the table, then kissed me lightly on the cheek before going down to the kitchen to make the tea.

The tarot cards were still on the low marble table. I turned the middle card. The Lovers. That would have done the trick. I hardly looked at the other cards as I wondered what I should do. Lou came back with the tea. Suddenly I was explaining my situation to her.

When I had finished Lou smiled quietly as she rolled another joint. 'Are you sure she's really telling you everything?' Her perfume had started to work on me, mingling perfectly with the hash. I said nothing. I don't think I wanted to know. I've often wondered how my life would have panned out if Lou and I had made love that night. Maybe spent the next few days together. I knew ahead of time how bad it would make me feel, of course.

Lou was so incredibly lovely. I didn't know what it was about her that moved me most. Her beautiful, soft skin, her long lashes, all complemented her beauty. Lou and I could easily have fallen in love over time, but we didn't have any time. If we had made love that night, Lou would have told me some more about what she guessed Helena was thinking. But Helena phoned back. Lou went home. I asked Helena if she'd mind me coming over.

She didn't think it was a good idea.

I tried to persuade her. I needed her company. I needed her solace.

Again she refused. She had other plans.

Other plans? What could be more important? I was so used to having my own way that I hadn't expected a refusal. Sometimes I had to fight a little to get what I wanted, but I always got it. Sons of single mothers generally have that advantage. Helena never accused me, but to my own astonishment, I behaved like a spoiled boy. Stoned, lonely and brooding, I determined that Helena didn't want or deserve my loyalty. How could she pretend she loved me, I asked irrationally, and refuse me her time? She was no better than Molly. Well, if she felt like that, I needed to take action. I had become a monster of self-pity. Molly and her ma were in Oxford. The whispering grew unbearably loud. It made thought impossible. I was going mad with the noise. I was out of control and had to get away.

I was already packing a few things and leaving. In the street I looked for a taxi. I had made a lot of decisions for Helena's sake. Not any more! I was furious. I was like a baby robbed of its milk. I'd turned down going to bed with Lou, a girl I'd been attracted to for years, on her behalf! I hailed a taxi and got in. Still stoned, I told the cabbie to drop me off at the top of Fleet Street.

Looking back at my decisions and behaviour of that time I am not at all proud of myself. The irony only later hit me. No doubt Helena thought it should have been the iron. It didn't occur to me how childish I was in rationalising my behaviour. Not then.

I left the taxi at the Law Courts. Before I crossed the street I hesitated. I decided I needed to have something to eat at Mick's. So I walked up in the general direction of St Paul's.

I doubt if that favourite Fleet Street all-night greasy spoon is still there. Mick's was a regular hangout for newspaper people – printers and journos – who worked the night shift. It was an ordinary caff where you could get typical meals. Comfort food. I ordered up sausage, egg and chips twice with a mug and two slices. Bromide or something in the tea made the brew unrecognisable as any drink known to man. The legend was Mick slipped the stuff in his brass urns for the same reason they did in prisons. To keep things calm. He got a lot of drunks in at night. They said Mick learned the trick as a canteen trusty in his first British POW camp. He did well in the system. By the time the war was over he had saved enough to send home for his whole family. Mick and Mrs Mick knew me from when I'd been a steady customer, so we had a chat and a gossip. I thought the papers moving would be disastrous for his business but Mick said it had actually improved, thanks to the renovations going on everywhere around us. 'We get a lot of men who work on the sites. What happens when they finish, I'm not sure. We might have to go a bit upmarket.' I hardly recognised some of the shops or even the pubs. Floral baskets. Window boxes. They'd be putting beehives in their backyards next.

The entire press exodus to Canary Wharf wouldn't be for another couple of decades or so but Fleet Street was already dying. Where the great rotary presses had thundered night and day, where copy boys rushed galley proofs from office to office, where delivery vans screamed in and out of their bays bearing the first edition or the third edition or the tenth edition, bringing the sports results faster than the BBC could broadcast them, everything took place at a more sedate speed. The Street of Ink, the Street of Shame, where tabloids vied to produce the most scandalous stories, was on its way to becoming the Street of Sobriety. The coarse vibrancy, the louche airs and graces, the pepped-up urgency of the place was fading. At least one old-fashioned pub had already become a wine bar. Maybe the boozers and cigar smokers would go somewhere else? It was hard to imagine where.

When I got into the side streets I didn't feel so bad. Things here had hardly changed. I even heard the occasional comforting whirr of a modern offset machine.

Mick's comfort food wasn't enough to stop me heading for the Sanctuary. I was still stoned. And yet the closer I got to Carmelite Inn Chambers, the more I wondered if I wasn't making a serious mistake. Should I have studied those tarot spreads more carefully? Something made me take them seriously. I now felt as if I had a bunch of maps in my head. I could visualise a sort of complex cat's cradle of silvery lines, like a sort of super spaghetti-junction. I was supposed to be the Fool, but what kind of fool? I thought about the other spreads I had laid out. I remembered a preponderance of Water cards including Cups and the Hanged Man. Wands and other Water cards, too, but very few Earth and Air cards, suggesting to me at any rate that I was allowing my emotions to rule my actions. There had been only complications ahead. I had not studied the spreads sufficiently. My anger against Helena had been brief and was already dissipating. It wasn't actually directed at Helena or Molly or even her mother. I was disgusted with myself. I would put the cards away for ever. I no longer had the discipline needed to read them. Not, of course, that I really believed in them.

Then I arrived at Carmelite Inn. The evening was a fine one. The sun had yet to set. Overhead, the sky was growing gradually darker. The Inn was still unlit. The lamplighter hadn't arrived on his bicycle. Very few windows were not dark. The place had that familiar hushed quality I had come to value in the city at weekends. Before I reached the gates I hesitated, enjoying the sense of solitude. Was I doing the right thing? I began to turn back.

Behind me now a fog appeared to be forming. I thought of Clitch and Love. Were they, I wondered again, in Mrs Melody's pay and not Cromwell's men at all? I was unwilling to endure another encounter with that pair.

I took a very deep breath and, putting out my hands, pushed open the gates of Alsacia. For a strange moment the sound of the Swarm grew to a shriek in my head. I cried out in pain. Once inside the mollified Swarm would surely stop. Was the Alsacia rejecting me? Or warning me? My movements became urgent. The Swarm subsided. Through the falling darkness I saw shivering lines of silver light, waves of colour. Series of numbers formed within my head. Pictures of tarot cards. I stepped involuntarily this way and that, in the movements of a dance. The silver network of threads remained in my head. Somewhere I heard a high, lilting flute. Duval?

I was feeling pretty bad by now. Was I still worrying about that apparent miracle of resuscitation? I was more confused than I could remember. Surely some greater power wasn't playing with my mind, interfering in my life? For the first time since I was a child I no longer felt in control of events. I was almost in shock!

As best I could I pulled myself together. I relaxed and steadied my nerves. I was determined to keep an open mind and stay focused on the question in hand. I headed first for the abbey. There was just a chance the abbot could enlighten me. Could any of the monks help? I was burdened by too many mysteries. Too many ambiguities. A writer actually trying to examine social ambiguities can be driven mad by immediate uncertainties in the surrounding world. Ambiguity certainly messed up my ability to work.

Was Alsacia a big lie? A scientific anomaly? If an illusion, what kind was it? Did anyone know its real history? How was it created? Would I find proof God actually existed? Could I get someone to sympathise with me? After the abbey I would visit The Swan With Two Necks. I wanted to see Prince Rupert. He was bound to be back. I became angry again with Moll and Mrs Melody for their conniving. I felt no malice towards the prince. He was probably the only person who could actually answer my questions.

If I found Prince Rupert at the Swan I was now determined to accept his request and help him rescue his king. That way I would at

336 • MICHAEL MOORCOCK

least make my life worthwhile. Of course, I knew the plan wouldn't work. History was clear. The king had died on the scaffold. By now, however, I was so irrationally upset with Helena I was willing to risk my liberty or even my life in order to get some questions answered. With those answers I might at last persuade Helena I had been telling the truth.

Most of the time.

CHAPTER THIRTY-SEVEN

NATURAL PHILOSOPHY AT THE ABBEY

WHEN I REACHED the abbey's heavy oaken door, I realised the monks might be at their evening prayers or doing any number of monkish things with which they routinely filled their time. But they were probably not going to allow me to disturb them even if they were engaged in something. So I lifted the lion's head and let it fall a couple of times. If nobody answered I would go to the Swan.

Silence.

I knocked twice more.

A few minutes passed. At length the little door in the grille opened. Dark eyes peered through. The door squeaked back a few inches. A monk I knew as Friar Eldred stood there. In his hand he held a beautifully burnished fencing foil, its guard bright with Moorish enamelwork. I was surprised. 'Are you expecting an attack?'

He smiled. 'We always expect that, Master Michael, but today we were merely at our practice.' He stepped back to let me in. 'Should the abbey ever be forced to defend herself again.'

I thought this was almost charming, coming from a middle-aged monk.

'Friar Isidore has talked about how he knew you were one of those who might ultimately help us.' Friar Eldred put his foil behind his back.

'So I'm famous,' I said. 'Well, Brother, I am very confused just now. I need to speak to someone, preferably the abbot.'

'Wait here and I will see.' Friar Eldred led me straight into the cool, dimly lit chapel. I sat down in a pew, looking around me at the ancient stained glass and the Latin memorials chiselled into the walls and floors. At some time kings and queens had come here to pray with the monks and demonstrate their piety. Now the altar was empty of furniture. I wondered where they kept the Fish Chalice, which I thought of as a living thing.

Eventually, Brother Eldred reappeared and I followed him to the abbot's study. The large room was less austere than I remembered. Grammaticus, that extraordinarily ancient yet vital man, sat on my right at the great desk which, it seemed so long ago, he had turned into a complex orrery. I sat across from him in a chair beside the fire and talked while he remained at his desk. His pale grey eyes seemed amused as I told him of my concerns, leading to the discovery a short time ago of Molly in the arms of a man I had come to imagine my mentor, and whom I now guessed to be her original lover. I'd anticipated her taking up with a man closer to her own age; not returning with someone older than me.

I told him how I was so certain I'd found my heart's desire, how everything in her corresponded to the woman I had dreamed about since I was a boy. I really had seen her in my dreams. I recalled one dream where I had rescued her from my own Viking kin! The image of us escaping together in a small boat was always with me. It wasn't the sex or her looks; it was all these things and more. It was the *sense* of her I loved. I recalled Proust writing of Swann being in love with a woman who was neither his type nor did she attract him. Love at the deepest level? Then how was it that I still profoundly loved Helena?

'We do not own another by virtue of our passion's measure,' said Grammaticus. 'Your pain will grow worse before it passes. It affects the mind and spirit. I suffered such pain twice before joining this order.'

It hadn't occurred to me that such spiritual men might have had material lives before becoming monks. So I had after all chosen the right person to ask for advice.

'I gather you cannot take pleasure in your partner's pleasure.'

I know now he was deliberately goading me. Of course I could take pleasure in giving pleasure. In fact I was sometimes accused of caring about that too much. But he continued in this vein. My heart was beating faster. He asked me again how I felt and seemed satisfied when I said: 'I could be in shock. I'm numb. Numb in almost every way. Were you trying to anger me? Frighten me?'

'To a degree.'

'I told you. I don't feel anything.'

Again, he smiled. 'And the man?'

'Prince Rupert? I can't imagine betraying anyone so badly!'

And to my utter surprise I burst into tears.

He was direct in his kindly response. I suspect he had intended to make me cry, to release my emotions. He left his desk and came to pat my shoulder. He rang a bell and when a monk appeared, told him to fetch a pot of Darjeeling. I forget the words he used but his voice comforted me. I felt considerably better by the time the tea arrived. Indeed, within a few minutes I was so cheerful I wondered again if Father Grammaticus had slipped something into my drink.

I said rather lamely, 'She really is the girl of my dreams!'

'Sometimes,' he said, 'we are permitted such dreams. Sometimes we are lucky enough to find a person who seems to step from our dreams. Who says they want to spend their life with us.' He told me of a girl he had known in Crete who was his 'dream woman'. She was pledged to another man, whom she loved. Yet she had fallen in love with Grammaticus. For a few days they had experienced a passion which seemed bound to last all their lives. They planned to be together for ever. She went to tell her fiancé. And never returned. 'She realised, I am sure, that our dreams were impossible. She didn't have it in her to hurt the other man. It was as well she cut things off before they developed.'

I thought of the cards I had played for Lou and myself. The Lovers. The other cards came back to me. Knight, Queen, King of Swords. I saw them more clearly. They had almost all been trumps and the Fool had been dominant. That was me and no mistake. Now I recalled what the cards had been telling me. Because of my confusion, I had let myself think I was laying out cards for Lou and myself. But those cards were really for me and Molly. The story was a warning.

I tried to check myself. I was giving in thoroughly to superstition and fantasy. I told him how, since the time I was able to read, I had looked for escape through fiction and make-believe worlds. I invented stories for my friends to act out. I had my mother's gift for fantasy. I was popular at school because of my creative skill. I had almost been expelled more than once because I distracted the other children with tall tales. From the age of eight I had filled magazines with my own writing and drawing. My first magazine was done when I was nine.

Father Grammaticus spoke without malice. 'She's had to create a good counter-narrative. A story strong enough to allow her to take independent action. She probably told herself that she was strengthening your union. Are you familiar with that logic?'

Of course I was. I had used it myself! Had she really convinced herself that a fling with her 'cavalier' would make our relationship stronger? Had she begun to slip into a darkness running with spilled blood and bitter tears? Unfamiliar waters? No doubt all she'd wanted was a brief affair. Some test. Then the narrative she created had grown more aggressive. 'Look to your cards. Have you confused the Fool with the Knight?'

Slowly a void was opening within me. I filled it with physical pain which nothing could ease. His questions were not comforting! They sent my mind in all directions. I wasn't sure what Father Grammaticus was doing. 'Why do you ask?'

'We have to find the place of maximum virtue,' he replied. 'Find that centre of balance in yourself, and you will learn how to control time. In controlling time you control memory. Time and Memory are the names of silver roads. I think it might be the right moment to mention the larger design.'

I began to think that there were too many abstracts in this. Father Grammaticus now sounded like any other spiritualist quack with a vocabulary at odds with common reality. My impulse was to ignore him completely. I needed more tangible ideas.

'This feels like betrayal,' I said, 'and reminds me of other betrayals.'

'Who betrayed you?'

'Certainly not my mum or any of my other relatives. I'm not really sure. Molly once accused me of being genuinely altruistic. I have a sort of insane loyalty to my friends. It goes beyond common sense sometimes. She can't accept altruism as being anything but naïve. The nearest she gets to it is the concept of enlightened self-interest. You know, Disraeli's two nations and so on.'

'Isaac D'Israeli?'

'Benjamin, his son. Isaac died sometime in the 1840s. The direct line died out. Benjamin's sisters married, I think.'

'The son became a Christian? Not so? I might have known the father...'

'To have known him you'd be a hundred and twenty now at least!'

'I have a very strong constitution.'

He was joking. But here was something else at once baffling and obvious. I was on the point of taking myself off to the Bin to be committed. But, from what I had seen of friends in the Bin, there wasn't a lot of curing going on. They just filled people up with Largactil so that they were sluggish and lost the will to do anything but kill themselves. 'I suppose you've been watching the Shangri-La story a time too many!'

The joke fell flat. Clearly the old abbot had never heard of *Lost Horizon*. He smiled at me, mildly puzzled. I gave up trying to tell him who Ronald Colman or James Hilton were. I simply said: 'Family tradition says Dizzy was our ancestor.' I preferred this topic to that of Molly, my inconstant love.

'And a fine man, too, no doubt. I think I see a resemblance. He visited us several times. Curious to see our Treasure.'

I thought for a moment he was going to reveal the nature of their Treasure. Instead he said: 'If it comforts you, I can find the old records...'

'That's all right, Father Grammaticus. We appear to be at cross purposes.'

'Your feelings are not unusual.' He shrugged. 'You love your wife. She's your children's mother. You want her to be happy. Your instincts and your reason tell you that what Molly and you were doing will lead to unhappiness. Anticipating a general misery, you now intend to forget it by sacrificing your other responsibilities to help Prince Rupert and his friends rescue the king from the axe.'

I said nothing. He smiled gently. 'Perhaps she merely needed to know if she is still in love with him. It is not uncommon. He might have proved a disappointment. Has she said anything to you?'

'She never talked about him much. Obviously she didn't want me to guess who he was. I've done the same to Helena.'

'And perhaps for the same reasons.'

'That could be self-indulgence, not a virtue.'

I think he agreed. 'You are not thinking clearly, young man. Could you spare a few days to stay with us at the abbey?'

What was he offering? The idea was suddenly very attractive. I nodded. 'Thank you.' I didn't actually care if they slipped me something in my tea.

The abbot leaned forward. 'What does the number nine mean to you?'

'Nothing in particular.' I was flippant in the face of his obvious seriousness.

'Do you think it has strength?'

I looked up into his deep, grey eyes. He was leaning forward with an expression of extraordinary intensity. Half out of his chair, he listened eagerly to my response. Like so many of Rupert's contemporaries, he was as interested in numerology, astrology, graphology and alchemy as in the true sciences.

'Strength? Well, yes. Nine *is* a strong number.' I was surprised.

'Strong numbers are important to us. Nine is a complex number, too. Nine strands. They bind together the so-called Nine Planes of Existence. Nine offers six and twelve and twelve is the strongest number. Nine plus one is the leader and his heroes. Twelve plus one is the number of greatest strength. Christ and his disciples.'

'Is this numerology? I've never...'

'Not the kind employed by charlatans. Understand the fundamentals. Reason. Reproduction. Regeneration. We speak of numerical resources. Like music. We order our minds with numbers. Numbers are narrative. Music. Painting. How we order the world is as important as ordering itself.

'All order is an act of imagination. To imagine that the numbers have power irrespective of what we give them is probably folly. The act of ordering is a quality of all forms of intelligence, whether animal, vegetable or mineral. Reproduction is fundamental to nature. Numbering is part of the act of reproduction. The mathematics of similarity. Numbers bring order to chaos, far more than words can, and give us control over it. They allow us understanding, to visualise. Once you can number the silver roads and hear their music, then you can walk them.'

I was scarcely following him. Yet his voice carried a strange reassurance which went beyond his reasoning. I thought of the cards, both the regular deck and the tarot. All the ways of reading them. And reading them depended on our ordering our minds. We had to run 'in tune' with the numbers and symbols they revealed. I couldn't play a guitar until I'd tried it. Silver strings. I think Father Grammaticus was trying to help me isolate my grief, to take a kind of ownership which might even help me control my pain. I was returning to the discipline of my boyhood when I learned how to channel my migraines. I no longer had to lie in a darkened room while waves of agony zigzagged different colours across the spectrum. I had ascribed numbers and names and other qualities to the colours and shapes. Some I revisualised as easily defeated creatures. This allowed me greater control over them. But before I could reject a migraine, I first had to relax. Relaxing could become a near impossibility when the pain grew too intense.

'*Our number is nine.*' Father Grammaticus's voice was sharp and distant. '*Your number is nine. Three times three. Complete. Three into three. Three and three is thirty three. Eleven and one. One here is the rogue number. It is the hinderer of success. Four is the strongest combination. One here increases the strength. Four plus four plus one. Four times three plus one.*'

'She told me eight,' I remembered suddenly. What had Moll said? 'She insisted that eight was the strong number. I remember. That number would protect us and bring us success.'

'She is poorly informed. Eight can be strong. But there are nine planes.'

'Nine planets?'

'If you prefer. That, however, suggests a simplification. *Nine worlds. Nine personae. Nine names. Nine rules to preserve the worlds. Nine stages of existence. All divides and multiplies by nine. Nine by nine and twelve by three, these decide our history. First we hear and then we find. Nine by six and twelve by nine, these our movements do define. Twelve is the web and twelve the node. How an adept finds the silver roads.*'

He seemed to be breaking into rhyme. I was struggling. 'Nine what –?' I thought nine drinks might help the pain go away. But I was terrible at burying my troubles with drugs. Christina said I could never let anything just go. Analysis and understanding were part of my trade. Simple mathematics gave me form. 'Nine – bowling pins? I'm serious. I'm looking for it – then I can look for a metaphor. Nine monks…?' This was still baffling me. 'Nine will take the pain away?'

'No. But it will help you take control of the pain.'

'Nine trumps?'

'Ah, now you are referring to your own discipline, not mine. Threes and twelves. The Fool.'

My aunt had told me: 'You can't just be the Fool or say you're the Fool. You have to become the Fool.' She meant the tarot, of course. The Fool is instinctive wisdom, God's fool. The Jinglecap, as I'd called him in an early poem about myself. *He will dance for you, not well, but with vigour.* Pierrot. Identifying with the Fool of the tarot was an indication of what I'd like to be, not what I was. My character Jerry Cornelius as Pierrot. Before he becomes Harlequin, the street smart, the cynical. Yet at the same time both Helena and Molly had identified me with the Fool. They never could make up their minds about me. '*The Fool is the piper leading the band,*' I said. He looked at me and chuckled.

'Perhaps? Perhaps that's the secret whose answer we all seek. Peering into the fog.' In front of me a patch of dark grey mist had formed. As I stared into it I heard the abbot's gentle, rhythmic voice.

'*Think of nines and threes and twelves. Think of the cards with those numbers. Think of the Fool. The child rides from the sun. The wheel turns. Nine Swords pierce the hanged man. Nine Wands support him. His queen is the Queen of Pentacles. See her?*'

It was coming back to me. My queen was the Queen of the Moon. My king was the King of Swords. My knight was the Green Knight. I was consumed by memories of that first séance with the abbot. His Cosmolabe. It was still there. He had no need to show it to me. Was this astonishing concoction of alchemy and misguided cosmic theory actually created to reach deep into my inner self? Had I needed to believe I owned a soul before I could see it at all?

If I had been asked how I felt at that moment, I should have said my heart was broken. My heart and my sense of self. I was lost within my own mind. His vision did nothing to stop my sadness. I tried to break the connection by imagining the tarot deck. How could I escape? All I saw in my mind's eye were the cards. The Swords and the Cups, the Wands and the Pentacles became webs and rods and planets and suns whirling before my eyes.

I still heard Father Grammaticus's faraway voice speaking to me. *Radiant Time*, he said. *The Black or Second Aether. A greater darkness lies within the familiar darkness of the void.* 'Here the black sun sits, drawing us all into its insatiable orbit. But on the other side of that sun are the anti-worlds thrown out by a blazing light bursting fresh. And so it turns, throughout Creation!' *There were so many kinds of light: crystalline, fiery, gaseous, sharp.* He passed his hands through the orrery again. I felt powerless to look at his face. *I saw the Queen of Pentacles dancing with the High Priestess and the Emperor dancing around the Sun. I saw the King, Queen and Knight of Swords form a circle. And in the middle of all was the Fool. The Fool, poor Pierrot, who had let his Columbine dance off with her Harlequin. The Knight in Green will lead you from the desert.*

Now it came to me. Suddenly the black energy pulsed and coiled between the stars. The silver threads arced and twisted making impossible connections. Heavy drops of blood fell like summer rain. Huge shadows spread to obscure a mass of suns. I was in agony. I screamed. My sickness had become an intense burning sensation. I did all I could to shrink it and rid myself of it. *Gravity is present but invisible, explained by the presence of identical worlds unseen by us. They nest, one inside the other, separated by density and mass. The only clue we have oftenstance is the Dark Flow!*

He was teaching me something. Was he hypnotising me? Is that what had happened the first time I met him? Was I learning what he wished me to learn? Should I have listened better? Perhaps if I had been in a different situation I would have done. The science involved was over my head! Was it time I turned to Harlequin in pursuit of my love? I was crying hard now. I gave no further attention to Father

Grammaticus. Silver roads? An illusion? Still crying I stood up. I shook my head to rid it of the images. I closed my eyes. Began to sway. My girls. How could I not think of them? I was tired of the pain, of the prospect of a future which no longer contained my girls. It felt like dying.

CHAPTER THIRTY-EIGHT

COMMITMENT

I SPENT THE night at the abbey. I slept fitfully, dreaming of Moll and Prince Rupert as Emperor and Empress in my old tarot deck. While my pain was still considerable I couldn't entirely blame them for what had happened. Rupert was an exceptionally interesting man. He was larger than life, intelligent, well mannered and funny. They made an extraordinary couple. Then why had she wanted to spend so much time with me? She said she loved me. About a hundred times. I'd had good reason to think she cared about me. Had she been setting me up, involving me in Rupert's plot to save the king? Well, she had succeeded. In the morning my head was surprisingly clear. During breakfast, which we all attended at dawn, I asked the abbot if his invitation were still open. I reminded him what he had said the previous evening.

Superficially I remembered very little of what Father Grammaticus had told me either the first time he had showed me his Cosmolabe or on the previous night. Yet it seemed to me I had absorbed the saliencies on a profound, subconscious level. I had heard a lot of weird cosmic notions in my time and his, though perhaps more complicated and elaborately supported, had to be among the weirdest. Barry Bayley had a fascination for barmy cosmic theories. He collected them the way some people accumulated incredibly bad records or movies. The weirder they were, the more they delighted him. But even Barry had never presented me with anything quite like this!

My scepticism was inclined to dismiss pretty much anything which didn't conform to conventional cosmological notions. Admittedly, I had learned nothing at school to explain my experience of the Alsacia. I decided that if I stayed there for a while, with no-one to distract me, I might be able to learn a bit more or at very least lose myself in my work.

This was not the first time my natural hard-headedness had led me to storm ahead with a plan into which someone was trying to manipulate me. I went back to Ladbroke Grove. I packed a bag and I told Helena I would be gone for a few days. She said she had no interest in my plans. I kissed the girls and said I should be back soon but if I was gone longer they were not to worry and were to be good and look after their mother.

I returned with the bag I'd packed. The abbot himself met me at the abbey.

I told Father Grammaticus that I remembered almost nothing of what he had said to me the previous evening.

'You need make no conscious effort,' he assured me. 'It is in you now. Yesterday, my main hope was to help you find peace and sleep. And, conversely, I did that by bringing out certain innate gifts you possess. Like his grace, you have a talent which I and most others lack. You will one day travel on the moonbeam roads, which I cannot do. Already you have an instinct for using those roads. I have had to learn patience and accept that I shall never see all you will see. Once I envied that talent. Now I understand what it costs. You are a natural adept. I was not conjured into existence. I have made my own journey and I have been given the lifetime I needed, indeed prayed for, to make it.'

'An adept? Is that to do with understanding the supernatural?' I had never knowingly travelled on what he called the moonbeam roads. I had only a hazy idea what he meant. In my semi-trance state I had seen those silvery strands branching away in all directions. I associated them with the abbot's notions of Radiant Time.

'As an adept you will gain direct knowledge of things I shall never experience.'

'The twentieth century?'

He smiled. 'Much more.'

'You spoke of Radiant Time. What is that?'

He raised his eyebrows to indicate that he might not be intelligent enough to know. 'To understand Radiant Time you must first know that Creation takes myriad disguises. Our Creator's mind is infinitely more complex and varied than any human mind imaginable. We use machines, made according to His wisdom, to measure, manipulate, imitate and survey His Creation. The key to much of this remains, of course, an understanding of Radiant Time.'

'It *must* have something to do with time travel!' I remembered that strange ride with Moll across the commons, when I had first met her. I had resisted so much memory. Now I was being forced to confront reality – and, for that matter, unreality.

'And that's why you were so glad to welcome me? Because I could come and go through the gate?'

'That, and your height.' Perhaps as a joke, he said this at a point when I ducked to avoid a particularly low ceiling. He, of course, was almost a foot shorter than me and, like a few in the Alsacia, found my height amusing. Sometimes I felt like Gulliver in Lilliput. 'Your broad back!' He reached up to clap me on it. For a moment I felt like a favourite horse.

We walked through the abbey to the cell they had allotted me. There had been no problem about finding me space. The abbey was built to accommodate many more monks than the current number. 'We are particularly suited for guests.' Grammaticus smiled, wished me a pleasant stay and went on his way.

By monkish standards this room was luxurious. The ceiling was a bit low but there was a washcloth, towels, a mirror, water jug and washbasin, two kinds of nineteenth-century soap, a packet of shampoo crystals, a shaving brush and a modern safety razor. The bed was surprisingly comfortable. I took off my clothes to stretch out on it, meaning to rest briefly. I fell asleep almost immediately and awoke feeling well rested and in much better spirits. I had brought a book with me – an early pocket edition of *Paradise Lost*, John Milton's extraordinary epic examining, among other things, faith itself. I had always loved it as I loved Bunyan's *The Pilgrim's Progress*, the first book I had bought with my own money because it contained a picture of a dragon. Thanks to Bunyan I had grown up believing that fiction should have at least two narratives, the surface story and the implied one. The faith of both writers had impressed but never converted me. It was their visionary intellect that inspired me. I was impressed by Milton's intelligence and talent but I was no further forward in understanding his God who was, surely, the ultimately sophisticated Protestant figure, allowing no other manifestation in its hierarchy. The freedom of choice he permitted his beloved Lucifer was precisely zero. Read that and you examine the American soul. Its great dilemma. Torn between seventeenth-century conservatives and eighteenth-century radicals. I made a couple of self-pitying notes in my diary. Then I washed as thoroughly as I could in the cold water.

As I got dressed I thought about Molly and her mother again. I was still astonished by the way Mrs Melody had deliberately revealed my relationship with her daughter to Helena. Feeling the anger returning, I did everything I could to concentrate on my new book. I was again wavering in my intention to throw in my lot with the Cavaliers. I couldn't hesitate any longer. I needed to find Prince Rupert and offer him my hand.

Telling a friar I hoped to be back in time for supper, I left the abbey and headed up towards the square. From The Swan With Two Necks spread warmth, light and cheerful noise. My spirits rose and I entered the saloon bar in some style. Prince Rupert and Claude Duval sat there, amongst their friends and followers. For a moment there was a pause. Then a cheer. Then a louder cheer as my friends greeted me. Good fellows all, willing to die for their cause and die again, especially brave because they never anticipated their own longevity. I was so glad to see them that I didn't care why this was happening or where. Rather than spoil the moment I pushed my way to the bar to order drinks.

I was too late, of course. Claude Duval was already buying the shants. Duval's close friend, the 'giant' Nick Nevison, a little shorter than myself, leaned on the bar and told some protracted tale of the open road. He was an untidy, good-humoured man with long, wild hair and an air of jovial patience. Frequently involved with Duval on various exploits riding the High Toby, his shorter partner, Jemmy Hind, was not with him. The majority of his listeners were Cavalier tobymen, sworn to rob the nouveaux riches so the vieux riches could be restored to the throne! A tale of sword and snobbery.

While I shared few of their ideals, I think I liked Duval and the rest because they remained contemptuous of people who gave up inconvenient ideals. In the solid reality of that bar I found it impossible to think as mature men and women were supposed to think. Gallant rogues representing justice against authority appealed to our common frustrations. Idealism and its goals had to be nurtured and celebrated. Justice was generally established in increments by one person at a time, one tear at a time, until drop by drop, cup by cup, bucket by bucket, river by river we had enough to make a lake and then an ocean. That was the optimism at the core of my existential understanding of the universe. I understood now that Molly had come to consider my ideals futile. She had turned into Helena. She probably thought I was naïve. I was never sure what brought on that cynicism. Perhaps she wanted to emulate her mother, having no ties to any individual? The fact was she wasn't there and I couldn't bring myself to ask after her.

Sitting at the head of a long trestle table, Prince Rupert told his audience of his adventures in what they called High India and what I suspected was actually East Africa. The prince talked of the fabled Prester Johannes who in two mighty battles defeated the Holy Kings of Congo. He spoke of adventures in the *Sa'Ha'Ra*, the desert land which possessed so much hidden history and wealth, of the tribes and creatures who lived there. These included the great Sun Eagle, Ta'a, which was captured by the Paladins of Chad and kept in a cage made of silver water.

As Prince Rupert finished his story the door opened and Captain St Claire stood there, a little hesitant. I was very glad to see him. He saluted me and sauntered in.

Welcoming Captain St Claire, Prince Rupert ordered him a shant of dark porter and called upon him to speak of his travels. The truth was the northerner did not take the same pleasure in telling as he did in listening. He stumbled and blushed his way through a tale of eating roasted rats in the West Indies but was relieved when he could finish and accept his shant. For a Parliament's man, St Claire was no thin-lip'd finger-wagger. Everyone enjoyed his company as much as I did. Later, I stood next to him near the back of the bar and asked him why he trusted me to keep his secret.

His answering smile was almost sweet. 'I trust you for more than that, Master Moorcock.'

I took this as a well-intentioned compliment and changed the subject. I wondered if he had ever visited the American mainland. He had. He knew Maracaibo, New York and Boston pretty well. He had unusual views on the subject of the West Indies, he said. But, in spite of my laughing insistence, he refused to elaborate.

Typically, the evening continued with everyone in splendid spirits. For a while I kept remembering Molly there but the shants helped me forget. These roisterers behaved like disciplined men familiar with death and warfare and took their leisure seriously. They told incredibly funny tales and for a short while I felt some of the old happiness come back, but soon my spirits began to sink. I didn't want to return to the abbey so, feeling as if I intruded. I sat in the shadows near the stairs.

At length, Prince Rupert came up to me and, looking away as if he spoke to himself, began a quiet soliloquy. 'Believe me, Master Michael, I've soldiered and explored all over the world, and I've loved. People and animals, the animate and inanimate, all have taught me a great deal. And I've learned best to recognise when I've become not merely a sharer of dreams but a dream in my own right. In short, I know when I have become a young woman's fantasy, and I have to say I was frightened by your Molly's greed for experiences we almost shared some years before. Of course, we have both changed. I know when I am just a good lover or when I am a cherished and idealised memory. I had little doubt I was a wonderful memory and must soon become a disappointing reality. I chose not to exploit that. Your finding us that night had the effect of slowing the inevitable, that was all. But I have to admit here a selfish reason which allowed her to stay. You know the plan we have discussed in the past concerning the king?'

I said that I did.

'She's important to that plan. We need a woman with us. One who can shoot and fence as well as flirt. Though let's hope none of us will be forced to draw a weapon.'

So that was it. One need was paramount. The king must be saved!

Even if I were not completely convinced by the prince's reasoning it was a comfort to believe him. By now I was glad of the respite. For all that I loved her, I wanted Molly out of the picture so I could think clearly and act according to my conscience rather than compromise with her needs.

It emerged that neither of us had seen Molly since that particular evening. I told him how her mother had called on my wife. He frowned a little, understanding the implications. 'Mrs Melody believes all reality's a mere dream,' he said. 'A familiar notion. We brood upon it when we're young. Even more so in the Orient. And what matters it? So it is a dream, in a way. God's perhaps? Or is that blaspheming? I'll ask the bishop when I see him!' He put his arm around my shoulders. 'Some think they'll find adventure here. Some –' he paused – 'hope to rekindle romance. Some seek sanctuary when that other world feels dull or too complicated or too dangerous. Here we can make the wildest plans. Reality is of a different order. Here we are safe from our enemies. And here we can plot impossible dreams and find distraction, adventure, even success of sorts.' He lowered his head and smiled. 'But there's more vexing you than a doxy who knows not her own mind.'

'Do you remember our fight at the inn?' I asked. 'When Nixer almost defeated us?'

'I do. We showed 'em our mettle! In the end they scampered off like rats from a terrier!'

'Do you recall, sir, another occasion when you were less successful?'

He frowned. Then laughed. 'Only in my nightmares!' He became a touch uneasy. 'Why?'

'I'm curious, that's all.' As I'd suspected, he did not remember clearly all that happened there. I said, 'I've made up my mind. I'm prepared to come in with you.'

He gasped involuntarily. He had not expected that! He put out his hand and gripped mine. 'You had lost us. And I thought we had lost you! We were unsure how to continue since Nixer and his men damaged parts of my great Cosmolabe which will take months to remake. As a result we conceived more direct plans. It involves courage, deception, effrontery, skill and manly self-possession. Only one who steps forward to volunteer those qualities in a wild and impossible cause need ask to be considered.' And he offered me a sudden boyish grin.

'How would I be of use to such a plan?' I had not expected to feel so elated. I had missed his friendship.

'You are tall, like myself, Porthos and Nick, and another tall man is needed. Also, you have the means to lead us home should we lose control.'

'So the abbot says, though I don't understand and can scarce believe it.'

'Think seriously on it, Master Moorcock. We cannot dare fail in our ambition. Would you let the king be killed?'

'Of course not!' That was an easy one. I was against all capital punishment. 'But I still don't understand...'

'Come with us. We can get there without your help. But we might not return unless you're there. It's dangerous. You know that? But if you're with us, we're *all* safer. You have skills – the abbot must have told you.'

'I'll come with you. I give you my word. But I really have no particular skills. There are a score here at least who would be of more use to you than I!'

'Oh, to be sure!' Prince Rupert laughed spontaneously. Rising, he slapped me on the back. 'Thank you, lad. Our venture promises success. Your nation will bless you.'

'My wife and children might not.'

And then we were done with it, in the fashion of his day, and even of my own in certain circles. Everything had been said. The subject was over.

CHAPTER THIRTY-NINE

KNOWING

MINUTES LATER THE doors of the bar opened and in strode Duval's friend Jemmy Hind. He was greeted with a cheer by the others as he stepped up to the counter. Inevitably his comrades wanted to know how he had fared.

From the capacious pockets of his greatcoat Jemmy brought out a hefty soft leather bag and tossed it on the bar. 'That'll pay for our ale tonight if it's the king's health we're drinking. And the rest's to pay for his health, if that's what's necessary to free him!'

Another cheer at this. Then Jemmy became the object of his friends' attention as he told a story of how he'd come by the private steamer on Hounslow Heath carrying two plump churchmen on their way to Southwark to give tithe to Cromwell. There it was. Gold, all of it. He joked of the run he'd given his pursuers. Jemmy was London born and bred and had lost them at Cheapside before doubling round and making his way here, where they dared not follow.

I began to feel overwhelmed. I had done what I intended and so got up, moving towards the door. I begged Captain St Claire's company back to the abbey. I did not expect too many answers to my other questions just yet, but I hoped he might be less cautious than Prince Rupert and his men. Not knowing what I was about to ask him, St Claire readily agreed. Once we walked towards the abbey, I asked: 'Can you tell me what lies beyond the Sanctuary's gates? You have come to my rescue there twice, so I thought you might have some idea. *Limbo*? Is that what it's called?'

St Claire had begun to chuckle. His large brown eyes sparkled. 'You wanted my company so you might put questions to me, eh?'

'I'm baffled, that's all. I'm mixed up in matters I really don't understand, captain.'

'And if it *were* Limbo, what was its nature? An *absence*, maybe, of matter and time?' His expression was almost challenging.

'Entropy? Is that what we're talking about?' This was an obsession of my day with the ongoing debate over the Big Bang theory. I hated the notion of entropy. All existence dissipating. Did the Alsacia actually lie at the heart of nothingness? I knew I had created my fictional 'multiverse' partly out of a distinct discomfort at the notion of empty space-time. I preferred a heavily populated cosmos. Even what the monks called dark clouds – perhaps the traces of unseen worlds – was actually matter, or possibly antimatter, though I had never heard of it outside the Alsacia. But Captain St Claire replied with studied charm. A charm which made me slightly uncomfortable.

'I'm a simple scholar and, perforce, a soldier,' he said. 'These are matters best discussed with clerks. And –' he paused at the abbey gates – 'here's the place to do it.' He grinned, saluted and was away before I could reply.

I got back to my cell, cleaned up and opened my notebook, jotting down what I remembered from that evening with the prince.

Then I heard a soft, almost hesitant knock. I opened the door. Brother Isidore stood there smiling his meek, uncertain smile. Supper was about to be served. If I wished to eat he would be glad to escort me to the dining hall. Surprisingly hungry, I let him lead me through the beautiful old building to the hall.

I was, as usual, impressed by the contrast between the monks and their surroundings. They were obviously poor and yet had an extraordinarily rich environment. I mentioned this as we filed through the chapel on our way to the dining hall. Friar Isidore told me I had as much right to ask the question as anyone, but he did not really answer.

Evidently the abbey's patrons had spent lavishly. There were almost no buildings like it left in the City. Few of our churches had survived the Blitz so well. Even St Paul's had emerged with some damage. Many of the older churches had been burned to the ground. The abbey, of course, was much earlier than St Paul's and had been built during the first flowering of the Gothic period. The style had fallen out of favour in the late Renaissance when many buildings, even churches, had been torn down and rebuilt in whatever was the current fashion of the day.

Brother Isidore called the style 'Frankish' but there was no doubting its origins. It was pure Gothic. The hammer-beam ceilings were elaborately painted and gilded, with the heavens a deep blue. The stars, in familiar constellations, were picked out in gold. The beams themselves were painted green and brown, suggesting the heavens held up by sheltering trees. The beautiful windows were of the finest stained glass, with rich emerald greens, deep vermilion reds, pulsing yellows and glowing indigo blues, either in complex abstract designs or illustrating a scene from the New Testament, most of which I recognised. Some weren't Christian images at all. The green marble in the frames was similar to that used on the altar, while others were gilded or painted in a lustrous colour.

In my early career I had done a series on the cathedrals of England for *Bible Story Weekly*. Much of my education came from researching a subject before I could write it up. All the abbey's features had evidently been endowed by a wealthy person at some stage in its history. Friar Isidore confirmed that Henry III and the Earl of Morn were their main benefactors. Often, too, money had been left them by men of science, including Francis Bacon. Dr Dee, it was said, had once worked closely with members of their order.

The order had renewed vows of poverty in the early seventeenth century. At that time James I, who for some reason favoured the 'Flete friars', had given the Alsacia its charter in perpetuity. Some said King James needed to show his piety and his support for the Church of England, particularly to members who made no claims on his tightly clasped purse. Others thought he had baser motives, including secretly paying for a house in 'Whitefriers' for a favourite associated with the stage. Few people believed that. James was not known for spending lavishly. No further money was settled on the abbey. The Carmelite vow of poverty meant they lived off local charity. They received increasing revenue from rents. They had briefly published a magazine, in hopes of paying for necessary repairs. Friar Isidore sighed with pleasure when he spoke of that, for the magazine had been the cause of our acquaintance. Ultimately failing to meet its costs, *The White Friar* had been discontinued.

I was given a place at the centre and on the right of the long table. As soon as we were all standing beside our assigned places the abbot spoke an unfamiliar prayer. Then he told the monks why I was there. He referred to me as Brother Michael, as if I had joined the order as a novice, and explained how I had come to them to help serve the Creator. I was a little surprised. I thought I had agreed to a somewhat hair-brained plan to rescue Charles I from the scaffold! I remembered almost nothing of what I'd said on the previous day. I was indeed tempted to stay. The food was superb, as was the wine. In a previous life our Friar Ambrose had been a first-class chef!

Even now I was so dog-tired I only wanted to sleep again. I asked if I might return to my cell. Drugged by good food, wine and company, I soon fell asleep. I realised I had lost any animosity towards Prince Rupert and Molly. My anger at Helena had already faded. It was too late now to go back on my decision. I had given my word to the prince.

As the days passed, the emotional pain occasionally returned, but someone was always there to keep me company. At one point Ambrose, a cheerful, pleasant-faced monk, a little younger than the others, casually asked if I had ever experienced a miracle. For the first time in my life I couldn't easily tell him I hadn't. I was still profoundly confused. I even felt my identity changing as I behaved in ways I might expect from others but not from myself. I had better control of my feelings. That didn't mean, of course, that I was wholly aware of my own motives or desires. Like many others, I was proud of my self-awareness. But of course because I understood one or two aspects of my interior world did not mean I knew everything there was to know. As the years went by I'd learn how a little self-knowledge could be a very dangerous thing.

CHAPTER FORTY

MELANCHOLY BABY

I COULD AT last think of Molly without feeling I was going crazy. I doubted Helena would ever forgive me. I now understood what a shock Mrs Melody's revelations had been to her. I felt numb. I wished her well. I shared my granny's sense of freedom. Wasn't the true test of love a willingness to have the other person do whatever they wished, whenever they wished? But shouldn't that be reciprocal?

I hoped to learn something else from the monks and their wise abbot, but I was still a little wary, not entirely sure of their motives.

There were just eight friars and the abbot. The monastery had been built for sixty or more. Each monk had a distinct personality and corresponding specific duties. Brother Balthazar ran the pharmacy and was their doctor. Brothers Isidore and Erasmus had worked on the magazine and now occupied the library. They devoted as much time to illuminating manuscripts as they had in the past. I spent long periods with them. I had a free run of the place. They had almost as many manuscripts as printed books. Brothers Theodore and Sholto looked after the large kitchen garden which was enclosed by the other buildings on the far side of the chapel and the cloisters. Brothers Aylwyn, Eldred and Ambrose were in charge of food preparation, housework and so on. I joined in their routines, some of which involved prayers in unfamiliar languages. A few were in Latin or Greek, others in Hebrew, though none of them seemed to involve a bible with which I was familiar. In spite of that, whenever I felt like it, I took part in their meetings and found the rhythms and rituals very comforting. Ultimately, however, I could not help becoming just a little bit bored and wanted to get back to the chaos of Ladbroke Grove just to be with the children.

I began to wonder if the Alsacia were some form of giant time machine, capable of visiting relatively few periods. Maybe in some sort of orbit. The orreries might actually navigate the whole thing. There was another mystery. All those people in the Alsacia were now of pretty much the same period. The first time I came, the people had belonged to at least three different centuries. Duval, for instance, was from the seventeenth, Turpin from the eighteenth and Cody from the nineteenth. Now everyone was dressed in seventeenth-century clothes. And there was no sign of Turpin and his contemporaries, nor of Cody, Carson and the rest. Nobody would tell me anything very revealing. Perhaps the Alsacia was a hub which somehow rotated according to different rules to the rest of the planet, stopping at different bits of London's past. Or maybe they were alternatives to history. My own historical past didn't contain big electric trams being robbed by highwaymen in cocked hats!

Now that my anger had subsided I was worrying about my family, of course. There was plenty of money due in for Helena and the kids. I always made sure of that. And if I died, they'd be well taken care of thanks to my obsessive buying of life insurance because I had seen so many authors' families ruined by premature death and illness. Even if they never found my body, my family would be fine.

Meanwhile, I had resolved, if everything worked out and I survived this adventure, to stop writing pulp fiction. My ambitions were being threatened by my own facility. I invented new formulae for pulp fiction with lazy ease when I could as readily be inventing new ways of looking at the world – or trying to. So I resolved to work out my Jerry Cornelius stories and a planned novel called *Breakfast in the Ruins*, which would mark the end of my pulp career and the beginning of serious ambition. I tried to take advantage of the peace and order at the abbey yet somehow I could only write Meg Midnight stuff! A bit of an irony. I decided I was forcing myself too hard. I should relax for a while and regroup.

I did make an effort, one evening, to drop in at the Swan, to meet my friends and share a shant of ale. Almost at once Prince Rupert stood up from a booth at the back of the saloon bar and waved me over. The crowd had fallen a little quieter. I pushed through it, shook his hand and sat down across from him. Not everyone had heard we had buried the hatchet. I knew there were eyes on us but none openly.

Prince Rupert asked after my health, I after his. He bought a round. I bought another. We discussed the health of various friends and acquaintances. He told a story of meeting Colonel Clitch and Corporal Love near the gates and how they had engaged him, how he had been forced to fight them again, aided in the end by Captain St Claire. I said that they probably hung about there all the time, hoping to catch the odd royalist alone. I told him my own experiences. But St Claire was a mystery. The prince had heard he wrote poetry, that he was hunted by redcoats for some Puritan transgression. He quoted Shakespeare, whom his uncle claimed to have seen in the flesh, performing at the Globe. He narrated a couple of good stories. And soon he was charming me again, though on a deeper level than St Claire. Since we were now allies it wasn't especially difficult for us to bond. Some people naturally strike alliances. Now I wondered: Had he from the start actually conspired with Friar Isidore and Father Grammaticus to hypnotise me? Was I now a character in someone else's fiction? The idea was too weird for me. But I was beginning to get used to weird.

Next, even as Prince Rupert drew me into his plot to rescue King Charles from the scaffold, Molly started writing me letters care of the abbey. She was coming back to the Alsacia. She could not keep away from me. She told me I mustn't believe what anyone else said about her. She would explain it all. We should meet, perhaps at the Swan. I was confused. If this was a cunning plan to embroil me in some complicated amour it was pretty pathetic. Her letters were full of contradiction and revisionism.

I met you on the rebound and you met me on the rebound, she wrote. *I'd just split up with you-know-who – my 'cavalier' – and you'd just split up with Helena.*

No I hadn't.

You talked me into living with you...

No I didn't.

... you asked me to marry you...

No I hadn't.

I fell in love with you slowly. But deeply. I love you so much. I want you to have the best of me.

I was prepared to let her rewrite her own history. Like so much she said, she addressed my pride. Most of it was sentimental nonsense. I was clinging as tightly as possible to my own reality, my memory. If I didn't I felt I was done for. Memory is the foundation of identity. Through our sense of identity, we act. We determine our moral judgements. We rewrite our own memories, of course, all the time. We create fresh narratives to use in our survival. We agree on fresh histories enabling us to take action. It is part of what makes us such flawed creatures. Creatures of narrative fiction creating cause and effect. In the main I was prepared to go along with my friends' versions of events even when our memories varied enormously. We are protagonists in our own novels.

I told Father Grammaticus about the letters. 'She must have sent fifty!'

He was a little surprised. 'I suspect she does loves you,' he said. 'Or you reflect something in herself that she loves. Why else would she not let you go? Money? You are not especially rich. Power? What else?' He cleared his throat and looked up at me, his eyes sparkling. 'Have you considered that you were meant to be together?'

'Not a day passes I do not think that,' I said. 'But I think the same of Helena. And she's my children's mother...' I could feel the tears returning to my eyes. Crocodile tears? I doubted every emotion.

'Our Creator might have chosen to bring you all together, perhaps.' I think he was teasing me a little.

I laughed, but decided to change the subject to something less personal. 'What part does God play in any of our petty schemes and ambitions? You must have thought about it, Father Abbot.'

'None,' he replied quickly.

'He plays *no* part?'

'For He has given us free will.'

'And if that free will results in our self-destruction?'

'So be it.'

'And so it hardly matters if God does or doesn't exist?'

'He has given us the means of achieving His plan for us. He will not help us should that plan go wrong after so many attempts. There is no beginning; no end. But He is a patient and a loving Creator.'

'Why should He care if we fail Him, if we fail to realise His plans for us?' I was uncomfortable with the idea of such total authority.

'I think He cares profoundly how we act. When we pray, He sometimes intervenes to help.'

'What is God, Father?'

'God is Nature. And all else is Nature, too. God is all we would become. That is why we must strive to know Him,' said Father Grammaticus.

'But why?'

The abbot lifted his ancient shoulders in a gentle shrug. 'Perhaps He's lonely?'

CHAPTER FORTY-ONE

PURITAN CLOTHING

MOLLY CONTINUED TO send letters. Several a day for a while. I was tempted to reply, then I was tempted not to read them. I was still very conflicted. Were all her preferred relationships with powerful older men? Had she only become attracted to me because of my power? I was only a few years older, of course, but I had known quite a bit of power for that time. When I first met her I had been a pretty powerful seventeen-year-old. Had that made me attractive to a girl with a mysterious father? That was when she was breaking up with a father figure. When she came to live with me was it because she had left him and didn't trust herself not to go back? She would have had to live alone. I remember the first time she told me she loved me. I had been so relieved. I could tell her I felt the same. Now, of course, I was pretty certain that she had never loved me much. In another letter she said how she had 'come to love' me. Which meant she had other motives for being with me initially. What had they been? And I thought *I* was confused!

I love you, she wrote. *I want to stay with you for ever and look after you. Iron your shirts, make your lunch…*

She'd got the wrong bloke, of course. I really did enjoy equality. I wanted her to fulfil herself, become the painter she could be. I had never felt such deep sadness. I should have known better. I had taken advantage of a girl looking for the unobtainable in an older man. My anger was being replaced with painful melancholy. And a sense that I had betrayed her. I had failed her. All that sadness. Nobody deserves to be lonely.

Not even God.

Next Mrs Melody wrote. I didn't know where they were living. Oxford? Obviously not in the Alsacia. She explained how Molly was impetuous and had always followed her heart. This seemed a little insensitive to me. She had moved in with Molly because the girl was in a bad way. She added that her daughter had health problems and could probably do with some money for private treatment. She really wanted me back with Molly!

I was tempted. I was so much missing female intimacy. I even considered seeing Lou. That wouldn't have been fair to anyone. I went up to see my mum occasionally, but there was so much that would have worried her it wasn't fair to tell her. Helena continued to be cold whenever I came to see the girls.

I reconciled myself to keeping my journal and spending my evenings at The Swan With Two Necks. I continued to meet Prince Rupert, Duval and the rest, as they plotted to change history. They had heard the Puritan spies asking questions about us all by name. We awaited our four collaborators from France. They had attempted unsuccessfully to recruit Cardinal Mazarin to the Royalist cause. He had no wish to openly support a Protestant king. While Mazarin was prepared to give secret help, it was not enough to save the king. We had to do that. He would send us the means of escape.

'In the event of our success, a Dutch brig captained by Master Sprye will wait above Blackfriars just off Flete Reach. Mazarin's prepared to give the king temporary shelter in France, as he now gives it to our Queen Henrietta Maria. But he'll not risk war with England. Not yet. He cannot be sure of his own Protestants.'

Then at last the news reached Alsacia from Whitehall: arrogantly the king refused to recognise the legitimacy of the court. He had been disdainful of all chances offered him to be exiled or reduced in rank or even to rule a land where Parliament's powers outweighed his own. He had refused the many attempts to offer clemency and had been sentenced to death for the crime of making war on his own subjects. Tyrannicide, they called it.

At this, Prince Rupert worked obsessively refining his plan. 'I refuse to let the king throw away his life and his crown.' Cromwell, now Lord Protector, had not set out with any intention of destroying the monarchy. As with most revolutions, this one had begun with a relatively modest demand which, on being refused, inflamed the tempers of the petitioners. Charles's willingness to make war on his own subjects had outraged many Parliamentarians, most of whom had begun as Royalists. The only atheist sitting at Westminster was imprisoned in the Tower for his sin! The king's stubborn folly had given a certain kind of inevitability to the trial. Now the verdict was issued. Charles Stuart, former king of England, Scotland and Ireland, had behaved with the arrogance of one who understood the court to be a farce. He, the king by right, ordained by God, was to die on the block at the end of the first month of 1649. No doubt some sort of witch-hunt would follow as Charles's followers were tracked down or chose exile.

Prince Charles, the king's heir, was in France with the rest of his family. Prince Rupert, whose superb generalship might have saved the day, had lost his king's favour through the political scheming of corrupt courtiers. He had elected to stay behind, nonetheless. He was considered the most dangerous single enemy still at large. Rupert remained highly popular with the commons. He was the only man capable of rallying the people to the House of Stuart. What was more, Rupert was a devout Protestant who had refused more than one opportunity to convert to Catholicism while a prisoner in Bohemia. People even talked of his replacing Charles on the throne. Rupert himself had no such plans. He did not consider himself a particularly suitable candidate and he had sworn an oath of fealty to the king in God's name. A man of principle, he could never in conscience betray Charles. Indeed, he was driven to making plans to save Charles and persuade him to accept exile while he, Rupert, dealt with Cromwell. The Puritans, who increasingly controlled Parliament, were determined to see the end of kings and the setting up of a republic, the Commonwealth of England. The Church and the nation would both be ruled by sober consortia.

'They can call England whatever they choose,' declared Prince Rupert that evening, 'but she shall always be a kingdom under the rule of God and I intend to maintain that condition!' His plan to snatch King Charles from the scaffold and carry him away to France seemed insane to me, but then daring plans often did seem crazy until they were successful. There would be eight of us under his leadership, together with our prisoner.

For some time Rupert and his men had held captive a well-known corrupt thief-taker, Jeremiah Jessup. With his beard and hair cut right and a little discreet makeup to hide the worst of his 'biber's bloom', he bore an uncanny resemblance to King Charles. Jessup had caused many unjust deaths and had preyed on the women and children whose spouses he had sent to their doom. The man had been drugged with drink and opium and persuaded that he was about to be crowned king of England on a special stage in Whitehall before the assembled folk of London. We would substitute Jessup for King Charles in the king's apartments in Whitehall, the only place the exchange could be made, because the guards at that point would be few. As well as the regular guard, its commander and a chaplain, the king would be flanked by four black-hooded executioners, so that none might know who struck off the king's head. Drawn from a foot regiment, the four executioners were all tall men, something over six feet. Now I knew the first reason for my recruitment.

While Jessup went to the scaffold, the king would be hurried back through old passageways known to a few members of the royal household. He would be smuggled down to the Whitehall steps and from there into a skiff waiting to take him to a Dutch brig commanded by the loyal royalist Captain Peter Sprye. I was promised I would not be chosen to swing the axe. We would disperse as soon as the deed was done and make our way back through an old passage to the river.

I felt Prince Rupert, if anyone, could pull the plan off. But now came another flaw which nobody had anticipated. Jemmy Hind returned from a scouting expedition with a dark look on his broad, usually cheerful Cockney face. Big, amiable Nick Nevison brightened at his friend's appearance, but Jemmy brought bad news. After greeting his large friend affectionately, he turned to the rest of us.

'The river,' he announced gloomily. 'We can't get a boat into Whitehall steps. 'Tis bitter cold out there. The watermen have given up trying to break the ice. She's freezing over.'

There was ice almost an inch thick all down the river from Lambeth to the Tower. Below London Bridge men were breaking it as it formed. 'There are a few channels through which you can take a barge or a rowing boat. But they're getting harder to negotiate with every passing hour.'

'The crowds will be too thick and we'll have no horses. We can't get all the way to Blackfriars by land,' Nick Nevison growled. He scratched his huge head. His hair was such a long tangle of curls that he could scarcely run his fingers through it.

Prince Rupert frowned. His eyes were almost closed as he considered this. 'You say the ice is thickening rapidly?'

'Almost faster than they can open it,' said Jemmy. 'Another few hours or so of that and they'll be forced to give up. Oldsters say it hasn't been this cold for a generation.'

'Then we'll have a clear road. Someone must get word to the brig. They must bring their longboat up to where the ice thins. Could that be Blackfriars Stairs?'

'The river's slowing all the way to London Bridge.' Jemmy gave his news gloomily. 'A day or two and even Blackfriars will be too thick. The brig's lying just below the Tower.'

The logistics were discussed at some length. Nick Nevison was considered a giant at six feet one inches. Being just above his height, I was tall enough to help Porthos and Prince Rupert carry Jessup. He was currently living in the Swan's ruined cellar, waited on by his 'subjects' keeping him happy with brandy and laudanum. Prince Rupert took me down there once, introducing me as the Archbishop of Canterbury. Jessup, a classic drunkard, with his red-veined face and bulbous nose, greeted me with a certain lordly hauteur. The Cosmolabe had been dismantled and was being reconstructed elsewhere.

My qualms about tricking a man into going to his own death were dismissed by the others. They all knew of women widowed and children orphaned and worse, all directly due to Jessup's murder of men bearing a passing likeness to someone wanted dead or alive. His bloody career in London had ended when the corrupt authorities were replaced by men appointed by Cromwell and directly answerable to the Protector. Privately I wondered if we were not simply using one murderer to save another, but I had learned to keep my republican mouth shut.

CHAPTER FORTY-TWO

COCKE O' THE HEAP

I REMAINED IN the Sanctuary for several weeks, hardly going out except to see my mum and the children. They were all used to my retreat, so didn't notice much different. I had seen nothing of Molly but her letters still came. I had become mixed up in an adventure I might have invented for Meg Midnight herself. I didn't really want to go with the rest but I had given my word. The Whispering Swarm was gone. Instead, my head filled with sets of numbers, tarot hands, geometric shapes, silvery wires. Madness. I remembered a neighbour across the street, a mathematician, had a nervous breakdown quoting nothing but numbers and equations. When I told them, Father Grammaticus and Prince Rupert were agreed that it was important I remember the numbers. When I asked why, they said something about sturdy backs and strong wills.

Four of our party had yet to arrive from France. They were, of course, D'Artagnan, Athos, Porthos and Aramis. Claude Duval, Nick Nevison, Jemmy Hind, myself and Prince Rupert were the others involved. That made nine of us. The abbot had been adamant that nine was the appropriate number. I could only guess why certain numbers were better than others. Oddly, I had always nursed a good deal of superstition around numbers. Mum did, too. She was born on Friday the 13th.

The king was to be beheaded the morning after next. The execution had to be done in public. Cromwell knew that. The Protector believed he had given King Charles every opportunity to live. That old Stuart arrogance and disdain had fuelled Charles's belief that he did not have to keep a word given under duress to a commoner. The king had made no attempt to defend himself against the charge of treason and had refused to accept the authority of the court. He had pushed all patience to the limit. The Stuarts seemed a fairly unintelligent clan with a strong will replacing any sense of strategy or, indeed, realism. At best they were amiable and at worst charmless, small-minded and vindictive. Charles believed God had chosen him to rule a united kingdom which cemented its bond in blood and treasure. Ironically, of course, Charles was the last absolute monarch. He caused two terrible civil wars. So many had died that even convinced monarchists thought he should be replaced while most Londoners supported Parliament. Yet there was little triumph among the winners and only lacklustre resistance among the defeated.

I found it hard to grasp that within a few hours I'd be present when Charles prepared for his death. I would even witness an execution. Admittedly, the executed man would be the contemptible Jessup, but I still had a strong sense of history being made, even changed. Unless this world suffered huge alterations, I would soon be present at one of those moments when history changed for ever.

Perhaps for this reason I decided to see my children again. If I were captured I had a fairly good idea that Cromwell would not be very forgiving. All my comrades in arms were far better trained and able to carry out Rupert's plan and probably had a good idea of the odds. Meanwhile I was still half dreaming, not entirely convinced anything was real.

I was about to inform Prince Rupert that I intended to go to Ladbroke Grove for a few hours when we heard a commotion outside and Nick Nevison came in, stooping under the doorway, his wide mouth open in a happy grin. 'They are here, sire! They've cut it a little fine and are seeing to their horses now.'

I looked enquiringly at Claude Duval. The Frenchman jumped up and grabbed my arm, dragging me with him. 'I think you already know who it is.'

We arrived in the inn's stableyard to find a man as tall and solid as

Nevison giving minute instructions to the ostler. Since he spoke exquisite French and the ostler spoke none, the man merely stood there smiling and nodding. The Cavalier was dressed in all the finery of a seventeenth-century dandy, with many-coloured ribbons, beautifully worked lace, silks and fine linen, his boots and belts of soft, gleaming leather, a great basket-hilted sword at his side, two massive pistols in his sash and a hat heavy with brightly dyed feathers. He was about as tall as me but much heavier and his long hair was arranged in greying curls about his neck. He remembered me and clapped me on the back, asking after my health and that 'mistress of yours'. M. Porthos du Vallon de Bracieux de Pierrefonds looked a little older than when I had last seen him but still radiated good will and conviviality. Emerging from the stables came three more Frenchmen, two of average height for those parts and another a good deal smaller. Against the rest of us D'Artagnan was virtually a midget, yet with a swagger, a definite air of self-regard and an indefinable elegance. Behind him came aquiline Athos, le Comte de la Fère, fastidiously aristocratic as ever and dressed with tasteful simplicity in black, and pale Aramis, Abbé d'Herblay, quietly amused, also in black but with the finest white lace at collar and cuff, a silver crucifix on his breast. An impressive display of several kinds of dandy and each one as brave a swordsman as ever lived.

Beside the Musketeers, I looked dowdy, even though I wore the finery associated with what they called the alternative society. I dressed, of course, in the style of my peers when we all had long hair and big hats. Scarves. Brocade, silk and velvet. Serious Frye boots. In contrast to both, Prince Rupert's clothes were well cut and of a more evidently military nature, from his red coat to his soft leather waistcoat worn, in the fashion of his time, almost to his knees, while Duval's dandyism was more restrained and practical. Nevison and Hind, though dressed well, wore more subdued clothes. All together, however, we made a pretty colourful crew.

We were so full of pleasure at seeing these old friends we paid no attention to the barking of Marjorie, Mr Toom's little fox terrier. I turned to see why the dog was making such a fuss and my heart sank. Jake Nixer stood there, just outside the courtyard, a detachment of Roundhead pikemen at his back, his weighty tromblon in his huge, scarred hands. He took a dark joy in the way he had surprised us.

'Thank you, gentlemen.' He addressed the Musketeers with a sarcastic sneer. 'I am obliged to you for opening the gate and saving us the trouble of blowing it down.'

'You have no right being here, Jake Nixer.' Claude Duval glowered. 'This is the Sanctuary of the White Friars where no human creature may be arrested unless it be for murder. The Alsacia is deemed holy ground by God and king. Now, take your men and leave.' He smiled broadly. 'Or I shall have the pleasure of trouncing you again.'

Nixer ignored the highwaymen and talked past us to the slightly bewildered musketeers. 'We have no quarrel with France, gentlemen. You may pass out of here without hindrance. These traitors are under arrest.'

The four newcomers seemed so uncomprehending that the Intelligencer General of London chose to repeat himself in awful French.

They continued to seem puzzled, but, shrugging, made for where their horses stood, still with their saddles on. They began apparently complicated adjustments to girth straps and stirrups. Then the stable doors opened again and the four strode out. Each man carried a short pole with a brass attachment, curved like Spanish bulls' horns, at the top. And each held in his other hand a heavy flintlock. As Nixer watched, dumbfounded, the four took their muskets and laid them over the brass rests, pointing directly at the Roundheads.

Lifting his Gascon chin, D'Artagnan addressed Nixer. 'Some would league me with your "traitors", m'sieur, since many in my native land still call Charles their king. But, that aside, I would remind you, m'sieur, that we four are all French musketeers. We are gentlemen, well trained and seasoned in the field. Because of your station we have forgiven your first transgression. However, you will continue your threats at your peril.'

Seething with rage Nixer made an involuntary movement with his tromblon. He raised his fearsome blunderbuss slowly, almost without thinking, his eyes fixed on me for no obvious reason.

And then Porthos walked past me. He strode directly up to where the Intelligencer General stood in the shadow of his own men's pikes. He reached out his hand in its beautifully embroidered glove, grasped the ornate blunderbuss and yanked it from Jake Nixer's hands, snapping the thong by which it was attached and hurling the thing disdainfully into a nearby midden pile.

'There is your cowardly instrument, m'sieur.' He pointed into the heap. 'You shall threaten no-one, I think, today!'

Now all my companions drew pistols and stood shoulder to shoulder. Nixer, maybe seeing me as his only unarmed opponent, darted a thin forefinger at me. 'You have chosen your friends badly, young sir. We are the masters now! In scarce thirty-six hours your foolish king will be kneeling before the block. Any attempt at rescue will be anticipated. The best of our New Model Army is prepared. My intention was to arrest you this evening. Since that's denied me, for I do not care to risk so many good men, I look forward to any traitorous folly you intend. We shall be prepared for your attack.'

He strutted over to the midden and ordered two of his men to lift the gun out with their pikes. It was covered in dung and straw. Holding it by the stock, Nixer reached into his pocket and withdrew a voluminous neckerchief, cleaning off the worst of the dung.

'Now there's a thought,' said Prince Rupert, laughing. 'A plot to rescue a king. A king rules by God's will, not man's. And as one dies another king lives, so we sing out "The King is dead. God save the King!"'

'That whelp shall never return to England and I have it on good authority he's unwelcome in France. Mazarin cannot afford a war with us. There is nowhere for young Stuart to hide. And you, Rupert of Rhineland, shall follow your uncle to the scaffold. Cromwell has signed the warrant. You shall be arrested and imprisoned as a rebel and a traitor's co-conspirator! You shall be charged with murder.' Jake Nixer hissed with rage.

He was forcing himself not to challenge our unexpected firepower. I looked directly into his mad black eyes and laughed, wondering if it was possible to give him a heart attack just by being amused at those apoplectic features. He glared on, fingering his massive blunderbuss so obviously that I knew what Freud would have thought.

Then Jake wheeled around and led his men through the gate, our mirth beating against his back. I knew he would never forgive me. I had made a very dangerous enemy.

I started a little as Porthos's great hand fell on my shoulder. 'He is not your friend, that one, I think.'

I nodded. Jake Nixer would kill me in a moment if he could.

Without really thinking I began to follow him. I wanted to shout some catcall at him, but I hadn't gone six paces before I felt Prince Rupert's hand on my arm. 'Very dangerous,' he said. 'Not the best moment to venture outside the Sanctuary.'

'Dangerous? Nixer just led a whole detachment of Roundheads through those gates! I have come and gone a dozen times!'

'Believe me. It is unwise of you, Master Moorcock. At present it's unsafe for any one of us to leave the Sanctuary by that gate.'

'Surely we'll be leaving by it?' I said. 'When we go to Whitehall?'

'We do not go that way to Whitehall. Spies will expect it.'

'There's another way?'

'On that day? Yes. We'll go by the river gate at Whitefriars Old Stairs. Then it should be open for twelve hours or more.'

He could tell that I was worried. I had to see my children. 'Fear not, lad. You'll be able to use the main gate soon enough.'

I was relieved to learn there was an alternative way into the Alsacia from the river, though I was familiar with the Thames. I couldn't remember any stairs down to it, as there were at Whitehall, say, or other parts along the embankment.

We agreed that Nixer was not going to receive his humiliation philosophically. He would not rest until he had killed us all.

I began to guess what real security the Sanctuary afforded its inhabitants. Did people think it impossible to die there? Did the inhabitants have an exceptionally long, even biblical life span? Did Prince Rupert hold me back from the main gate because he knew Nixer would be waiting to kill me once I crossed that threshold? Or was it something less readily definable? Something more dangerous? Possibly to do with the Second Aether, the dimensions in which the Sanctuary existed? If I went through the gate, would I find anything familiar on the other side?

It was dark by the time Prince Rupert judged it possible for me to leave through the gate. I found myself in Whitefriars Inn where lawyers and their staff came and went and the gas still warmed the grey, eighteenth-century stone. I hurried through the court and into Lower Temple Lane, cutting through the back ways until I got to Essex Street, finding a taxi almost as soon as I reached Aldwych.

There had been no time to phone Helena to tell her I was coming but I knew the kids would not be in bed for a while yet. I didn't think I'd be interrupting anything. It was a lovely, clear winter's evening. The stars could just be seen over the glare of my wonderful city. Again I wondered what on earth I was doing mixed up in a wild scheme, apparently three hundred years earlier, to rescue a king who, in my opinion, was guilty as charged. I knew what would happen to those who tried him. On the ascension of Charles II, those honest, conscientious men had been hanged, drawn and quartered, perhaps the cruellest, most painful and disgusting punishment ever devised, while Cromwell's body was dug up and his head displayed at Traitors' Gate. I was already behaving and thinking atypically and now I found it almost impossible to think in contemporary terms. I was caught up in the adventure. I had given my word and I was determined to go ahead with it.

I got out of the taxi in Ladbroke Grove. There was light in the windows of both floors. I rang the bell. I heard Helena's voice finishing some argument. She seemed pleased to see me when she opened the door, but she still said, 'Oh, hello, Mike. I'm sorry. I don't want you in.'

'I'm off on a job soon,' I told her. 'I just popped over to have a word with Sally and Kitty before I left. Is that okay?'

'They're at the pictures with my mum. They'll be here in an hour or two. What about this time tomorrow?' She seemed confused. Who was she with?

'I'll hang around at the pub until they're back.'

'Not tonight,' she said. She looked out of the door. 'Is Molly with you?'

Helena's face wasn't easy to read.

'Helena, I haven't seen Molly since that night. I really don't want to see her. I told her.'

'Not on my behalf, I hope. Because, if so, you'd better get back together.'

Was she just trying to hurt? I couldn't blame her. I had betrayed her. I had been foolish to come. 'Okay,' I said. 'I'll phone in a day or so. But if I don't get the chance...'

'Say hello to Mrs Melody,' Helena said, closing the door. Only then did I wonder if Molly's mother had paid Helena more than one visit recently. What had my wife been told? I had lied, of course, and understood her anger, but Mrs Melody could be adding fresh lies.

The night felt very cold as I crossed Ladbroke Grove and walked round to Elgin Crescent and the 15 stop. The voices of the Swarm grew in a kind of mocking crescendo. It became for a moment so intense I wanted to cover my ears and run screaming through the streets. I was lucky. A bus came along immediately. The Swarm subsided. I sat on top smoking and looking at the bright, electric streets. I would have to write to the kids. A letter would be best, anyway. I thought about where I'd be the morning after next when we made our attempt to rescue the king. I hardly noticed as we drove along Westbourne Grove, passed Paddington, drove the length of Praed Street with its sleazy hotels, porn bookstores and kinky knicker shops, down Edgware Road and Oxford Street, Regent Street, Strand, Aldwych, every stop with a memory. I began to wonder again if I was doing the right thing. I knew it wasn't the sane thing. But, if Helena was now stopping me seeing my kids, I didn't have much to live for. Should I get out of this thing, I'd spend all the time in the world making sure I saw them. We reached the Gothic revival towers of the Inns of Court.

My stop.

CHAPTER FORTY-THREE

PREPARING

I DISEMBARKED AND paused. The Whispering Swarm grew in sudden intensity. I could barely stand it. Yet I was still reluctant to return. It was fairly late but Fleet Street still had some offices working. I wondered if I shouldn't go up to Brookgate and talk to my mum. I decided against it. She would see my face and start asking questions and I didn't think I could bear the consequences.

I was hurting. A new kind of pain. I hadn't done any second-guessing but I knew, if I continued feeling like this, life would be intolerable. I certainly didn't judge Helena. And poor Molly didn't know what she wanted. All those intense love letters! I couldn't think about them. They had stabbed like a knife. I understood how she felt but I wasn't going to be her anchor any more. I still remembered that night I fell in love with her, when we had ridden out together to hold up the Hackney tram. The morning of 31 January, 1649, would be the day I cauterised my emotions and took a fresh look at my life. I had a priority: If I survived this one adventure I wouldn't allow any barrier between me and my children. I pulled myself together and took that familiar route down to Carmelite Inn Chambers, returning to the Alsacia, leaving my children and that terrible Swarm behind.

Brother Isidore came to see me in my cell. We had passed earlier in the corridor and I supposed he had noticed how I looked. 'Are you well, Brother Michael?'

I told him I was fine. I was beginning to think Prince Rupert's plan might just possibly work. But what if the Alsacia were attacked while we were away? It had struck me as a possible strategy for Nixer or someone to conceive. All they had to do was get the people they wanted out of the Sanctuary and into the world where they could be seriously harmed. I put this to Isidore who was reassuring. 'We are capable of defending the abbey or indeed the whole Sanctuary. We have done it before. It is not something we would volunteer to do, but if there was no recourse...'

'I'm not sure you could stand against the power of Jake Nixer's tromblon, not to mention his musketeers and pikemen,' I said.

'You must not concern yourself on our part, Michael. We follow the teachings of the great prophets. You will be risking much trying to help the king.'

'You think he should be saved?' I asked out of curiosity.

'Well, the man himself is perhaps not the most worthy to carry out God's will, while Oliver Cromwell is perhaps a better king...'

'He'll never be king, Brother. You know that as well as I do. I'm certain he feels he is holding the position for another. Perhaps he plans to bring back Charles's eldest son?'

'Not if he kills the lad's father. No, I feel the chance of compromise is gone. We now see a war between the old ways, in which I was brought up, and the new, which Cromwell himself can barely conceive.'

The birth pangs of democracy. 'You fear the future?'

'I welcome it.' He was emphatic. 'After all, you and I have both existed there. And here we are creating it. I would never have met you, remember?' He smiled. I was beginning to understand that these men were not simple, unworldly monks. In fact, I now wondered how much power they must wield and how sophisticated they actually were.

The next morning Prince Rupert called us all to meet at the Swan to go over the plans again. The king would be brought first to the Alsacia. 'There, we shall wait at the abbey until the Treasure is ready.

Then, together, we'll continue on with both king and Treasure to the river where we'll meet the boat sent by Sprye's brig.'

'The Treasure is being taken from the abbey?' I imagined he referred to the Fish Chalice. 'Do you know why?'

'It is part of the same business, Michael. It is all I can tell you.'

I was about to ask why when the door into the bar opened and there was Molly.

CHAPTER FORTY-FOUR

THE SHADOW OF THE SCAFFOLD

MOLLY CAME IN looking contrite and cute in a way she knew worked for her and which almost broke my heart again. I couldn't respond. Prince Rupert, perhaps on my behalf, was not pleasant.

'We're glad you've arrived at last, Molly.' His sarcasm was a bit schoolmasterly. 'Now here's our map. I want you to remind us what you do when you get to the old tunnel to St James's Palace.'

Her eyes went uncertainly from him to me. I wouldn't look at her.

She suspected she had lost us both. A familiar ending to a game playing both ends against the middle. Like many of us, I had once tried to keep two girls going without the other knowing. I wound up losing both. Long-term threesomes, as I'd noted, usually ended with someone feeling left out or hurt.

She sat with Nick and Porthos between us but I could still recognise her perfume. I'd bought her a bottle big enough for a lifetime's supply, after all. Shalimar by Guerlain.

I knew why Prince Rupert's plan required four giants. It would also be useful when it came to handling the unsavoury Jessup, still happily legless in the basement. Until we became headsmen, surely our height would make us stand out like Christmas trees at Ramadan. Prince Rupert reassured me. There was some slight danger but we would be bent while carrying Jessup. Having no warning of the rescue attempt, the king would prepare for his execution in St James's Palace. He would get dressed there, no doubt praying and so on, and concluding any outstanding affairs. Most of those in the rooms would be his own staff. From there he would walk under guard to the scaffold erected outside the Banqueting House at the Palace of Whitehall. I actually knew the Banqueting House, with its marvellous Rubens murals. The only important part of old Whitehall to survive the fire.

We would have to get into St James's. Molly would go ahead of us to open the secret south gate. The old passage ran from Whitehall Stairs at the river to St James's Palace. The passage had long been used by members of the royal family and household to come and go discreetly. This route might now be known to the Roundheads, who doubtless believed no-one but those under arrest or exiled were aware of it. This was not what concerned Prince Rupert. He had explored St James's Palace as a boy, and knew of several older abandoned tunnels. One was built by Henry VIII, another by Elizabeth. They led up from the river. Apparently Hampton Court had similar tunnels.

Cromwell was likely to put guards on permanent watch but Molly assured us she could deal with a soldier by whatever methods occurred to her at the time. She met neither Rupert's eye nor my own. The Palace of Whitehall itself was the largest in the world, a huge warren supporting every aspect of the royal entourage. A veritable Gormenghast, it sprawled over a huge acreage. The river, still wide and shallow here, in those days before embankments, was currently frozen solid. It came close enough to the palace's south side. There, we stood the greatest chance of all being discovered together.

'There will be Roundheads as thick as deer in the king's forest,' said Duval. After Rupert he had the closest familiarity with the royal compound.

'Where's the best place to bury a needle?' Prince Rupert asked.

Porthos brightened. 'With all the other needles.'

'Precisely, my friend. There will be so many troops drafted in from the provinces, we'll be less conspicuous by flaunting our disguise. We'll go with caution at first. As soon as we see Roundheads we'll assume military order and proceed as a party of musketeers.'

'Which essentially is what most of us are,' said Athos, almost to himself. Then he smiled his most charming smile around the table.

'As trained soldiers we'll excite almost no suspicion. If any of you knows not how to march and so on, follow the others.' He looked towards me. I hadn't told anyone about my two years in the ATC preparing for induction into the RAF. It was a bit like joining the reserve. I would have had an advantage if they hadn't abolished national service within a whisker of my eighteenth birthday. One of the great ironies of my life. Up to now, at least.

'I've had a little experience with a musket,' I said quietly. I didn't like to tell him that drill was about the best of that experience. The other experiences with loaded weapons had not gone well.

Once again we went over the plans.

The scaffold had been erected outside the Banqueting House, an independent building. Prince Rupert had lived at Whitehall until relieved by Charles of his generalship of the Royalist forces. He knew the palace probably better than anyone. I was impressed by the plans and pictures. Whitehall was virtually autonomous and run like a small town. Countless buildings housed the apartments of scores of servants, general staff and aristocrats attached to the king's entourage. Built up over five hundred years, it represented every style of architecture.

Rupert told us how we'd take the passage to St James's Palace, rescue the king, substitute Jessup, and send the king back the way we had come. Disguised as executioners, I and the other three would get him to the Banqueting House in Whitehall proper. One of us, probably Rupert, would cut off Jessup's unworthy head. We would then make our escape by another passage known only to Prince Rupert.

Whitehall consisted of the remains of King Harold's royal residence and the Norman redoubt of William the Conqueror, with additions by all the Lancastrian, Tudor and Stuart monarchs. Kings and queens, princes and princesses had been married here. Turrets, steeples, chimneys and battlements rose next to tall red-brick buildings reminding me of Hampton Court or the Bishop's Palace in Fulham. Portland stone sat beside parts of the original buildings faced in white ashlar and with grey slate-finished roofs. I could see from the prints that the place was a firetrap but, when I suggested a bit of diversionary pyromania to give us a better chance, Rupert frowned and rejected the idea. For added secrecy and as a courtesy to our allies, he continued in French, which, of course, we all understood.

'While we have to get in from the river by Whitehall Stairs, the old passage I spoke of runs from that to St James's. We'll leave by a more obscure passage. I discovered it as a boy and opened it up. Because I feared punishment, I hid what I had done. I'm reliably told that it has not been explored by Cromwell's people and can still be used. There will probably be one guard at the entrance to the first passage which will take us to the royal apartments where his grace will be prepared for his execution. From there, surrounded by his servants, courtiers and a guard of redcoats, he'll go to the Banqueting House. And from that to a specially prepared scaffold. With him will also be his chaplain, four masked executioners and the captain of the guard, probably Colonel Thomlinson, and soldiers guarding him. Once we have given Jessup's body up, we shall march off in the direction of Scotland Yard, in the eastern part of the palace.

'The scaffold itself will be surrounded by many pikemen, musketeers and mounted troopers, all there to keep back the crowd and deter any direct attempt to save the king. That's why our only chance to arrange the substitution will be after he takes his constitutional with his dogs in St James's park. We can't do it anywhere else. There will be too many soldiers guarding him. The execution is to be at ten in the morning. The king will be bathed and dressed and will take communion with his chaplain Dr Juxon. When we're in the passage we'll have to watch for more guards but there are not likely to be many. The passage leads directly into his bathroom. At any other point it will be impossible to undress the king and dress Master Jessup, so there it must be. The king's grooms of the bedchamber will be overpowered for their own good so they shall not be judged parties to our plan.'

'Will not Jessup's voice betray him?' Duval asked.

Prince Rupert had considered this.

'If his last pint of alcohol doesn't kill him, it'll numb his voice for a good while. Any odd behaviour on Jessup's part will be taken for the king's terror at his coming death. No doubt his gentlemen of the chamber will surround him. He will also have some of his own people there. Drums and fifes will accompany him. They'll walk to the Banqueting House. Outside the House is the scaffold erected between Whitehall Gate and the gate leading from St James's. So our plan, as prepared, is to overpower any guards within the rooms and, dressed as redcoats, as we shall be under our cloaks the whole morning, accompany "his majesty" to the Banqueting House and onto the scaffold erected outside. We'll need to take a prayer book to place in his hands. M'sieur Aramis, you shall be, if he won't agree, our Juxon. You have his build and general appearance. Meanwhile, Hyde will guide the king to the passage I'll show him on my map while Moll will be waiting. From there the king will be brought back to the Alsacia.'

To me the scheme still sounded impossible. Cromwell and his officers would surely anticipate every effort to rescue the king. And what if we got that far?

'Are any of us to remain behind once Jessup's dead?' I asked from curiosity.

'No. A rearguard is a luxury. Aramis, if disguised as the priest, will have to find his own way home. I'm anxious not to arouse suspicion. The tunnel is the best way out. Perhaps our greatest asset in that respect is Moll here.'

I looked up involuntarily. She was blushing, her own eyes downcast.

'Without you, Moll, we cannot get through the first gate and the passage into St James's Palace. Shall you have your pistol with you?'

'In my muff.' She held up her fur hand-warmer. 'Don't worry. I'll have as much insurance as I can carry.'

'So, while attention is on the king and the executioner holds up his head for the crowd to see, the others will head for deserted Scotland Yard and from there to Whitehall Stairs and the river.'

'Which is frozen fast as we now know.'

I had not known that the whole river was frozen. I raised my eyebrows. 'So no boat?'

'No boat, but a road. And a good diversion. The citizens of London prepare a voluntary Frost Fair! It takes advantage of the public holiday. We have some chance of mingling with the crowds on the ice. With the king, we shall make our way first to Whitefriars Stairs and thence to the safety of Alsacia. The last steps of our plan we'll execute at nightfall when the other passengers shall accompany his grace.'

'They'll guess what's happened and who's involved! You can be sure of that.' Slowly Aramis fingered the silver-and-ebony crucifix at his throat. He considered the plans and engravings laid out on the table. 'They will send men to our gates. Of that, I think, we can be certain.' The Abbé d'Herblay fingered his elegant beard, his beautiful features dark in thought. 'This M'sieur Cromwell is a good strategist, correct?' He reached out a gloved hand to turn the prints, which included Prince Rupert's own sketches of the palace's secret passages. 'He will have anticipated this business, perhaps?'

Prince Rupert nodded and smiled. 'Absolutely. There's little chance that he hasn't. He'd relish the opportunity to lay a trap for us. That would deliver to him several of his greatest enemies.'

'Particularly your highness.'

'Indeed, but even Mazarin would be unable to save you, gentlemen,' Rupert addressed the Musketeers. 'And, since most are commoners, save me, you risk hanging, drawing and quartering while I can expect the mercy of the axe. No doubt we shall be accused of attempting to save a traitor from his just deserts.'

Everyone laughed at this apart from Molly and myself.

After discussing further details, Athos raised a languid hand. 'How will you be certain, your highness, that Cromwell will allow this Frost Fair to take place? Did he not recently abolish Christmas?'

'Under pressure from his left wing, probably.' That was my contribution. Everyone but Moll looked at me blankly. 'His zealot Puritans,' I corrected myself. 'From all I've learned, Cromwell is not that much of a religious hypocrite.'

'Yet Puritans have his ear, I think,' said Aramis. 'Not so?'

'I suspect anything which distracts from the possibility of the people storming the scaffold will be welcome tomorrow,' Duval suggested. 'There are a good many Londoners who worship godless commerce better than their maker or His representative on Earth. They'll be in a celebratory mood. Possibly their last chance to rob honest folk. All the worst elements of the nation gather in London just as you find in Paris the most *parlement Frondeurs*.'

'May I ask what is your quarrel with *les Frondeurs*, m'sieur?' asked Aramis, frowning. He was himself a supporter of the aristocratic arm of that movement.

'None, m'sieur, at this moment. Forgive me if I inadvertently...'

But Athos was smiling now, as was Porthos. 'Who could guess our friend's allegiances? Come now, Aramis! Let's not quarrel over politics. All of us here have seen where such arguments lead, with friend fighting friend and all important matters diverted! Bad blood infects the entire being. No?'

With a small smile and a slight inclination of his head Aramis relaxed. 'I agree. The Frost Fair will suit us very well, assuming Cromwell allows it.'

'It has not been *dis*allowed,' said Jemmy, who had been going about the town learning what he could, 'and it was running earlier today when I walked beside the river with my lady. The people make merry and play at who knows what to take their thoughts away from the enormity of the act being done in their name. The Puritans allow it this once as it makes their work easier.'

It surprised me to know that some of us could come and go like that or, for that matter, had lady friends in seventeenth-century London. There was no real reason I should have been surprised, of course, since most of the people around the table were from that era. I should have been more surprised that I was one of the few who had gone to at least three different worlds pretty much at will.

Duval might well be a likely traveller between dimensions. A loyal Stuart supporter in the entourage of the Duke of Richmond, he had built himself a fine house in Wokingham, where my own Methodist weaver ancestors, down from Yorkshire, had settled. They remembered him in the village. That his exploits dated from Restoration times – the 1660s – was now a relatively minor issue for me. I had become used to meeting men and women representing different eras. Had it been seemly I could have quoted Duval's famous epitaph:

> *Here lies Du Vall:*
> *Reader, if male thou art,*
> *Look to thy purse;*
> *If female, to thy heart.*

If Dick Turpin, who lived a century or so later, could drink with Prince Rupert of the Rhine, then I should be surprised if Duval could not also be there. In one penny blood I'd read Duval, Turpin and Tom

King all met Bonnie Prince Charlie at Colloden and voyaged to America to battle redskins.

Popular fiction, of course, mixed up all kinds of dates. I had fleetingly seen Pecos Bill in the pub earlier. One of our companion publications when I was editing *Tarzan* had the legendary Texan as a contemporary of Calamity Jane, Davy Crockett and Buffalo Bill. Earlier myth cycles had Attila the Hun threatening the France of Charlemagne or King Arthur dealing with invading Saracens. I had come to accept that I had somehow slipped into a world where myth was being created and was real and active. Regular history was of relatively little consequence. Perhaps, after people like us had interfered with time and history frequently enough, there were worlds now where King Arthur actually did go man to man with his great, almost equally mythic enemy, Saladin! I hoped to learn a bit more of the truth behind this process later, if I had the chance. Naturally it had occurred to me also that the process might be a projection of my own mind. To keep sane, I had to believe the reality around me.

We spent another hour or two familiarising ourselves with the plans. The light had gone out of Moll's face, replaced by an unfamiliar heat. I had made up my mind to say nothing to her. I didn't want to do anything to jeopardise Prince Rupert's plot to save the king. As it was, I could imagine everything likely to go wrong. We could be arrested the moment we left Alsacia. Feeling a little as if I were already condemned, I ate a hearty lunch. There was a time when I couldn't board a plane until I had a large helping of steak and kidney pudding, apple pie and custard, and a bottle of decent claret inside me.

Molly was careful to keep clear of Prince Rupert. He seemed wholly uninterested in her. Was this acting on both their parts for my behalf? I refused to speculate. In Rupert's private room at the Swan we continued to debate our plans until I made my excuses. I was just beginning to understand the full import of what could happen if we were arrested. Guy Fawkes and Co. had discovered the folly of relying on tunnels. Very nasty. Barbaric. Feeling a little queasy, I left them all, slipped out of the gates and made my way up Shoe Lane into Farringdon Road and Brookgate.

I wanted to see my mum.

CHAPTER FORTY-FIVE

SETTING THE COMPASS

As soon as I was through the gates, the Swarm savagely assaulted me. I almost wept from the furious pain of it. Soon I was barely sane. I made a huge effort to relax. Mum would be bound to notice if I was tense. I invented a story about migraines and bad dreams. That would explain any anxiety she detected. I really did think I might never see her or my girls again. I'd written Sally and Kitty a letter which I'd leave with Mum. I'd thought enough about time paradoxes and the like to know that by tomorrow, even if we were successful, I might have vanished from the face of the earth.

Mum was in the living room, on the sofa watching TV. She turned it off when I walked in. 'Hello, love,' she said. 'Anything wrong? You look a bit peaky.'

'I'm all right,' I said. 'Shall I make a cup of tea?'

'If you like, love, though I haven't got any of that insipid stuff you drink.' She had it in her head that Assam had no body to it. She also hated tea bags. She had enjoyed a brand loyalty to Brooke Bond tea for as long as I remembered. I didn't mind. I was in the mood for a good old-fashioned cuppa. As the water boiled I called from the kitchen, 'I'm going to be gone a few days, Mum. I've got a job that'll take me out of town.'

'What? America again?'

I knew I wouldn't have much chance of being transported if I was caught but I said, 'That's right,' and got the teapot down. I fed off the comforting familiarity of the house and the little bit of yard outside backing onto St Odhran's graveyard. Very little had changed since I was a boy. The smell was the same. Comforting. She had got new furniture, carpets and wallpaper from time to time but they always seemed identical to the old.

'How's the girls?' she asked.

I said they were doing fine.

'And Helena?' asked Mum. 'Everything okay?'

'Not bad.' Waiting for the kettle to boil, I sat across from her on the other side of the fireplace.

She said nothing as she tidied up the coffee table. I could tell she was getting ready to listen.

In the state I was in, a little support from my mum was very welcome. I finished making the tea and found the McVitie's chocolate digestives. I put everything on a tray and took it in. She had the gas fire on full and it was a bit warm, but her overheated room, with its familiar photographs and knick-knacks, was comforting.

'I was thinking of telling Helena I'd take the children for a couple of days,' she said.

'She'd like that.'

'I haven't seen them since Christmas. It would be nice for me and would give her a break.'

'Smashing,' I said.

'You all right for money, love'? She was trying to find out what she sensed was wrong. I laughed.

'Honest, Mum! I'm rolling in it. I just sold a couple more novels in France.'

She didn't really approve of France. She thought I had to be writing something racy. But I think it was mostly because my dad had gone astray there.

'Well,' she said dubiously, 'you know best. How's Barry doing?'

Once again I thought she was stuck in her own little time warp. I reminded her that Barry was back in Shropshire these days. Telford. The ugliest settlement in England. She was fond of Barry but couldn't remember from one day to the next what I'd said about him. 'He's fine.'

'I bet he misses London!'

'Who wouldn't?' I said.

We agreed on that. Few Londoners could ever work out why someone would live anywhere else. At least until they were sixty-five and migrated south to the nearest bit of coast.

'Have you ever thought of leaving, love?' she asked me. I think she worried that we might move away from her. I told her I never wanted to live anywhere but London.

'Cockneys get sick out of the Smoke,' I said. She enjoyed that.

I stayed another hour or so. 'I've got to get up bright and early tomorrow morning,' I said.

'Look after yourself, love,' she said as I left. She blew me a worried kiss.

I walked back to the Sanctuary considering the next day's plan. Could we really convince the king's guard that Jessup was their man? It was very cold now. Too cold for snow. That would explain any bulky clothing, at least, but the day was likely to be bright. What on earth was I getting myself into? Did I really not care what happened? I rarely felt as powerless as I did then. Or as responsible for so many. The children and my mum would miss me if something happened. I wondered if Helena would care. Maybe she'd be relieved to see the last of me.

CHAPTER FORTY-SIX

SECRETS AND SURPRISES

I WENT BACK via Ludgate Circus. This part of the city was pretty dead at that time of night. The café across the road from the Old King Lud still had its lights on. I couldn't see any customers. The pubs were all full, of course. Many journalists were just starting the serious drinking of the evening. Later, they would stagger along to the expensive late-night chocolate shop near El Vino which did a thriving trade in their guilt, selling massive boxes to anyone who needed to take a peace offering home or had forgotten someone's birthday. In that profusion of grey office stone, undecorated sandwich shops and no-nonsense masculine chophouses, the place was as incongruous as a diamond in a bag of liquorice allsorts.

I turned off at Carmelite Street. The *News of the World* bloomed with yellow light, shadows came and went in the windows, but everything else, apart from the steadily throbbing printers, was dark. The streets grew even darker and narrower the closer I came to Carmelite Inn Chambers and the gates of the Sanctuary. The Whispering Swarm filled my head like a great gallery of quarrelling men and women, growing increasingly urgent the closer I got to the gates. The Alsacia was calling me home. I slipped through into welcome silence. I left the Swarm on the other side of the gate and crossed the square to have a quick drink in the Swan.

By now the tavern was quiet. There were only a few people there, most of them talking quietly in the booths, but I was glad to recognise that mass of dark auburn hair. Captain St Claire stood at the bar finishing a glass of brandy. His hat was set back on his head. He wore a suit of dark blue wool, linen shirt, a suède waistcoat to his knees, military-style overcoat hanging open, his belt and sword strap secured by heavy brass buckles, tall riding boots folded at the tops. Into a blue sash around his waist he had stuck his pistols. As usual he wore both a basket-hilted longsword and his shorter-bladed sword, one on the left, the other on the right. These days I recognised him as a professional soldier. Perhaps a Dutch mercenary. He might have fought on either side. Foot on the rail, he lifted a brandy glass to his lips.

He seemed pleased to see me. 'A cold night, Master Moorcock!' Would I care for a drink? I accepted a half-shant because I'd be going early to bed.

He said he'd join me in that for the same reason. When we had our pints we took them to the long, empty table opposite the bar.

'I hear the Thames has frozen,' I said. 'I've never seen that.'

'Nor I, until now. I grew up near the Humber and she did not freeze in my time. Of course, she's a faster-running river.' He was probably talking about a beautiful rural river and not the industrial one I knew.

'Is it true establishments of every kind are actually built on the ice?' I asked.

He laughed. 'Shopkeepers have set up tents and stalls in a long row from the Temple to Lambeth right across the river. I'm told the water's frozen all the way down to the bed. Boys pull carts with the wheels removed, sliding passengers across. The boatmen charge folk to walk the ice, since their livings are threatened. There are mummers acting plays pretending to tell the story of the king's trial, and sellers of hot codlings, sausages, meat pies and the like, taking every advantage for commerce. They allow it, of course, because it will distract the commons from any thought of rebellion against Cromwell. How can folk be blamed in these impoverished times?'

I heard a note of familiar disenchantment in his Humberside burr. 'You don't approve of commerce, Captain St Claire?'

'I'm not among those who say it's demeaning to practise trade. Men who affect disdain for merchants are mere hypocrites, since all depend upon trade. It's trade, not kings and their schemes, have made this land wealthy. For all we grumble, we're paying the lowest taxes in Christendom. That a man should make a fair profit for his efforts is only just. English cloth warms kings and commoners worldwide. But I share the general view condemning unfair profit at the expense of the hard-working weaver!'

I heard in his reply an argument still fuelling revolution.

'Neither am I of the Leveller persuasion,' St Claire insisted. 'But could not inherited wealth and excessive profits be examined by Parliament and a tax be implemented to spread wealth more justly? It is surely a sin in God's eye for the commonweal to let poor folk starve or afford no doctors for their ailments, no food for their children, no roof, no hearth to warm elderly bones. Perhaps the answer is to levy a tax on all to provide for all. Thus no citizen need go hungry or sick or unlettered. We could build more workhouses which do not separate families. Schools could be attached to them. Children could be educated to read and figure for themselves, read their Bibles and reckon their own accounts the better to practise intelligent frugality. These are not sinful ideas, I think, but truly Christian ones following the teachings of our Lord. Every right-thinking creature in this sad kingdom holds some version of these views.'

'So you *are* of the party that would execute the king and make commoners of all highborn lords and ladies?'

'I lean, it is true, towards support of the Puritan cause. I do not hold extreme versions of those views, though it is hard to disagree with folk who look to the Bible for their guide. Unjust tyrants are dealt with swiftly in the Old Testament. Psalm 149 admonishes us to bind our king with chains and his nobles with iron fetters. I believe God empowers us to curb the king and his Court. We must always be wary of popery in disguise. However, I do not believe we should do murder in the name of the Commonwealth.' He took a long pull of his pint and threw me a searching look as if he feared he had said too much. But I was simply relieved because it had begun to occur to me that Captain St Claire might be a Parliament's man searching for information. A spy, in other words. What they still called an intelligencer.

Then I remembered standing beside him as we met the aggression of Messrs Clitch and Love. I knew, somehow, that I could trust him with my life.

'Do you go tomorrow to witness the execution of the king?' I spoke as casually as I could. Most of London must have been asking that question. 'Or shall you take advantage of the public holiday to enjoy some other pursuit?'

He smiled a little unhappily. 'What else is more involving? But I'm told Whitehall and much of the City itself will be so packed with soldiery it will be impossible to do or witness anything. I pray that poor devil's soul goes quickly to its maker.'

'You're a praying man, Captain St Claire?'

'Aren't we all?'

I was amused. 'Not where I come from.'

'You come from a godless land indeed.'

'I think so,' I agreed. Here, almost everyone accepted the Bible as the last word on any argument, whether moral, legal or political. Many Puritans found in it a clear admonition to put the king on trial and to execute him. They did this reluctantly, but in God's name. My growing preparedness to believe in God's existence didn't extend to taking as true all the conflicting messages of a myth cycle to the letter. I found deism as close as I came to having a religion. I had that in common with many signers of the American Declaration. I was confused again. I knew I couldn't match Captain St Claire in any theological debate. I finished my pint and said that I was now ready for bed. 'Do you stay at the inn, Captain St Claire?'

'I have quarters not far from here.'

'Then I wish you goodnight and Godspeed!'

'And to you, Master Moorcock. I trust you will fare well tomorrow.'

I left him in a thoughtful mood. I knew how important God was to these people in determining actions or inspiring their best and bravest deeds. To understand their reasoning, I needed to understand their God. I thought Captain St Claire might be a good teacher. Meanwhile I'd read a bit more of Milton's *Paradise Lost* in the hope of interpreting the Cromwellian mind-set at its most brilliant. When I got back to my room I opened the book again. Milton seemed even more profound and complex than I had originally thought, but while I was impressed by his vision of God I still had no coherent ideas of my own. God was not necessarily benign. Indeed the majority of His supporters seemed to regard Him as entirely otherwise; a rather cruel and intolerant entity. In the Old Testament, God's smiting record bettered Hitler's. I was living at the end of a generally optimistic period when our efforts to introduce a little more justice in the world seemed to be paying off. A distinct plus for the Prince of Peace. But what if Jesus was just another guy who defied that terrible old tyrant of the Old Testament? Eventually, and still reading Milton, I fell into a deep sleep.

I awoke suddenly, too early. In case I went back to sleep again I prepared everything for the morning. I had a full suit of 'redcoat' clothes, including a breastplate specially altered to fit me, a musket which I knew to have a horrible kick if held in the hands, a monopod on which to rest the gun, a big, heavy straight sword and a holstered pistol, all part of a campaigning soldier's equipment. The monks would wake me at the proper hour. We had to be near the Privy Steps to St James's before dawn. I looked at my watch. Molly had been sent ahead to divert any guard. If more than one was on duty she must distract them until we arrived. I could attest to her flirting skills.

I wondered if I should pray. I had a strong sense of what she risked. How would I feel if Molly suddenly vanished from my life, killed by the ball from a Roundhead musket? All that relish for life snuffed out. I could not hate her when I thought of that.

I got up shivering and washed in cold water. I then donned the warm New Model Army uniform, including the standard-issue russet shirt that gave them the 'redcoat' sobriquet. Nick Nevison had once served in the army. He had shown me how to buckle all the little straps and buttons. Our uniforms had been accumulated over time from various sources, taken off soldiers or stolen from some quartermaster's store. I thought I could still smell the original owner of mine. The helmet came down low over my forehead and the straps of the breastplate chafed my shoulders and ribs, the knee-high boots were a bit tight as were the breeches, but the long waistcoat hid my obvious problem. My cell had only a small square of mirror but I imagined that I would pass as one of Cromwell's troopers.

After a little bread and wine for my breakfast I stepped out of the abbey's relative warmth into the invigorating bitterness of early morning. They waited for me. The cold made my teeth ache, my lungs felt filled with razor blades and my breath boiled into the faint orange glow of Prince Rupert's bull's-eye lantern which burned whale oil and could be adjusted fairly easily. None of the others had more than a couple of dark lanterns between them. We would need them for the tunnels.

We assembled in the courtyard of The Swan With Two Necks. Porthos, Nick and I pored over the map while Duval and Aramis went to fetch Master Jessup from his happy nest in the tavern's ruined basement. He was singing to himself as our friends handed him over and I took his arms, getting a good grip underneath while Porthos and Nevison took the feet. We would alternately change positions as we carried him. He said we were his bosom friends and tried unsuccessfully to remember a song until he relapsed into a mumble. We left the filth on his face and his hair tangled so he looked as little like the king as possible. We planned to clean him up before his big moment.

At Prince Rupert's signal we formed ranks around Jessup. Eight of us led by the prince as captain. Then, with Jessup bundled amongst us, we went marching, pretty smartly, following him down the serpentine streets of lower Alsacia above the river while the air grew colder still. I was glad of my leather gloves and the woollen socks inside my boots. I also had a cloak in which I could wrap myself if I needed it.

'Molly?' I asked the prince as we marched.

'Gone ahead as planned,' he said.

In spite of the warm clothing, I was still shivering. The dirty grey fog clung to every surface and made vision almost impossible. We had to stay close and hold our rank because we could not see beyond one man at the front and another at the rear.

We soon reached Whitefriars Old Stairs. At low tide the slimy wooden steps led to an equally treacherous set of planks forming a walk across the shingle. Now the frozen slippery stairs ended at uneven ice windswept into bumps and jagged ridges. I couldn't tell what lay ahead for any significant distance. Each man held on to the next man's musket. Led by Prince Rupert, we stumbled over the ice.

The air flickered and billowed and I found myself stepping a certain way, following threads of colour, murmuring to myself – *Five and four, follow the nines, sixes and threes, make the score; follow the Fool and the Hanging Man, first to the pool and the silver span* – and there was that mysterious Saracen knight, his face veiled, swathed in dark green, leading us out of the fog. I tried to speak to him but he didn't see us. I knew a moment of sudden, intense pain.

Quite suddenly the mist lifted. The Green Knight had vanished and we were in bright moonlight, able to see the stars in a clear, black sky. I now saw Prince Rupert pointing at an equally rickety set of steps. They led back off the ice and up an easy incline to the black silhouette of some three-storey, half-timbered buildings, a few with lights burning in their windows. Snow stood inches thick on old roofs. Smoke fluttered from leaning chimneys.

We crept up another plank walkway, dragging Jessup between us. The smell was horrible. We were very close to a sewage outlet. Then we were marching through the seventeenth-century streets like any other detachment of musketeers told to watch for the Commonwealth's enemies. If challenged we would explain our muffled prisoner as a captured thief. We might sport a greater preponderance of Van Dyke facial styles and long hair, including my own, but many in Cromwell's service wore exactly the same. If Jessup didn't accidentally betray us, we need not fear unwanted attention.

I had known we were to march at the double for some distance and was very glad now that we did. The cold still exhausted us. At length Prince Rupert made us pause and take a pull of brandy from his flask. Even out here I could still hear the Whispering Swarm. That constant chorus calling me back to the Alsacia.

Now, as we marched swiftly through the narrow, twisting streets, we saw trudging toward us another detachment of Parliamentary soldiers. My heart beat heavily as we drew closer. Suddenly Prince Rupert brought us to a halt and saluted the oncoming officer and his men. To disguise his aristocratic drawl, he spoke in a broad West Country accent.

'Officer of the Watch. How sayeth thou?'

'All's well, sir, God save us.'

From somewhere far off I thought I heard a roll of winter thunder.

The worst kind of storm, my mum always said. I was never sure why. Unless it was its rarity. She was given to hyperbole but winter storms over London really did scare her.

Once again, breath streaming, breastplates gleaming in that grey, clear hour before dawn, we nine, partials of Father Grammaticus's 'potent twelve', marched out of dense London lanes still primarily built of timber and into the wider streets approaching Whitehall, surrounded by her not-quite-sylvan groves and pastures where soldiers crowded thicker than flies on dung. Grave, saluting cavalry rode by. Infantry marched seven deep, their partisans, as that kind of broad-bladed weapon was called, at the slope. Muskets at the ready. Roundheads were everywhere. The cream of Cromwell's conquering crop were here to ensure the setting up and maintenance of his free citizens' commonweal. This acknowledged that 'the people are, under God, the original of all just power' and that the Commons Parliament represented the people who had 'the supreme power in the nation'. Nothing less than a modern republic.

We marched back to the river. One by one we slipped down a fairly steep bank, which stank ten times worse than the first, and reached a kind of raised stone jetty. Taking a careful look about him the prince reached to move a hidden lever revealing a grille, hinged and well kept. Someone had been charged to keep it in good order.

Moll peered out at us. Her eyes glittered with heat. I hadn't seen them like that for ages. That special orgasm. That lopsided smile which came afterwards. I felt a bit ill. In other circumstances I would have said she had just had violent sex. Was that how she distracted the guard?

As we filed through, Prince Rupert asked Moll, 'Was it hard to quell the guard?'

She made a small noise, shrugged and glanced over at a man sprawled inside the gate. 'It was easy once I'd exhausted all other routes.'

His throat had been expertly cut. He had died instantly, almost smiling.

And then I knew what Molly missed in me. *The darkness and danger*... Forbidden adventure. The excitement of jumping blind into mystery.

Killing the redcoat had quickened her blood. She had begun to look like her old self, the girl I thought I fell in love with. Moll Midnight, the laughing girl highway thief, 'for justice and the right', was back with a vengeance, a bloody razor hidden in her muff. I was glad when she slipped out of the tunnel, back up to the riverbank, and waved a swift goodbye. She went to prepare the way for the king. I was trembling. Moll's happy relish for fun had been replaced by that terrible fire in her eyes. Fuelled by something far stronger than cocaine or speed.

The tunnel was of brick and rubble supported by old wooden beams through which mud oozed. It was dark. I could easily imagine Elizabeth's lover hurrying up from the river to greet her. Perhaps the smell had not been quite as bad then! I was seriously afraid I'd slip on a patch of filth. With the supine Jeremiah Jessup held between us we continued to slither on through that horrible stuff. Twice we passed dilapidated entrances to other tunnels. I guessed anyone taking either of those risked the worst kind of death. My stomach recoiled just thinking about them. I was very glad our plan did not involve returning that way!

At long last we reached the end of the tunnel. Through a couple of peepholes we saw two Roundhead soldiers. They had their backs to a smaller man being helped into a second wool shirt and what might have been a second pair of drawers. From the others in attendance I guessed this to be Prince Rupert's Uncle Charles. The man in clerical black was doubtless Dr Juxon, the king's chaplain. Four or five gentlemen standing near the door were the king's courtiers. They would have to be isolated while we dealt with the guards. The last thing we wanted was panicking retainers.

Swords bared now, we crouched in the tunnel until the prince gave his signal. Then, when the guards seemed most relaxed, we threw open the secret door and poured into the room, stunning the Parliamentarians with the hilts of our swords and swiftly disarming them. With pistols at their heads they were bound and gagged while an astonished King Charles, drawing a long brocade dressing gown about him, glanced enquiringly at the clergyman and his courtiers as he collected himself and, in his slightly pinch-lipped, high-pitched tones, asked what in the name of Heaven was happening.

Sweeping off his helmet, Prince Rupert fell to one knee. 'We are here to take your grace to join his cousin of France until such time he chooses to return to reclaim his throne.' His language was awkwardly formal, especially given that Charles was his uncle.

'Rupert! Oh, how unkind we were to you, my darling! Of all those we did treat unjustly, you were the most loyal!' The king's large copper-coloured eyes held tears. For whom I was uncertain.

'Sire, this is our enemy, a foul murderer and thief who deserves death a hundred times. He will die in your grace's place. Be it God's will, none shall suspect the truth until we are well on our way to France, to be reunited with your grace's lady the queen and her children. Quickly, your grace. He must be dressed in your clothes!'

As he listened, the king's expression bore a mixture of gratitude, puzzlement, kindness, love and that hard-headedness which had rarely served him well. He shook his head reflectively. 'Our dear, sweet bonny nephew. It is too late, you see.' He smiled slowly, lifting a tired hand to his head. 'Too late for us to lodge any defence of our decisions. Too late to change certain actions which might have been better for our nation. Yet God guided me, of that I'm certain...' This last a failing murmur.

One of the king's courtiers, understanding the plan, stepped forward. 'Sire, since time is of the essence –'

'We will not be rushed any further into folly, Wisheart. Flattery and poor judgement have played too great a part in this business already.' There was a melancholy, wistful undertone to his words. He was quietly sorrowful. At that moment I saw an unexpected dignity in the king. I believe a sense of reality had at last come to him. His manner was reflectively sober, unlike the haughty defiance displayed at his trial. His affection for Rupert was genuine and touching. 'Had we not listened to the advice of others, 'tis certain our favourite general might now be standing beside his victorious king.' That strange, fluting voice took on its own gravity. 'Now we, who sought to lower that price like some Cheapside merchant, must pay the price of kingship. And die like a king.'

'Sire. Your grace blames himself too much.'

'We go to our deserts by God's will.'

'Sire! In all humility I am God's instrument, come to rescue your grace!'

A wan smile brightened the king's sadness for a moment. 'I face a saviour later today, who is the only saviour with the authority to save me.' And with that he reached forward, snatched up Prince Rupert's hand and kissed it. 'Tell our queen and her children how we died and how the people received our death. Only one other thing we ask, for we are the sum of such things. We live on as dust and memory. There is one thing I want you to promise to do, dear Rupert.'

'Ask me anything, your grace.'

The king inclined his head. For a long time he peered into his nephew's eyes as if seeking some unknowable truth. He made to speak, then changed his mind. He paused. His last word was whispered.

'*Remember.*'

Then he turned from us.

Prince Rupert made a gesture towards him.

The king signalled for his gentlemen to continue dressing him. He cleared his throat. He spoke briskly, even cheerfully. 'Well, well, *messieurs*, let's continue. We'll wear warm clothes and plenty of 'em, lest the people think we shiver from fear. Two sets of drawers should be enough.'

From back in the passage we heard voices. Had someone discovered the soldier with his throat cut?

This was an unexpected anticlimax! We stood there like fools, a pile of insensible redcoats at our feet. Rupert's sword dropped to his side. He could do nothing but obey his king. He stood up, bowed once then turned leaving Jessup where he lay. In a clear, decisive voice he called:

'King's men. Loyal Englishmen. Order arms.'

With something resembling military discipline we shouldered our muskets. Without any hesitation the prince gave a curt order and we wheeled left to face the interior of the palace. Then he led us out of the royal apartments into a corridor full of redcoats.

Again I learned a little of Rupert's qualities of leadership. Somehow he was able coolly to march us through that press of enemies, some of whom went ahead to push their fellows aside so that our way was made easier. I think many mistook us for the chosen headsmen because of our height. Not once were we stopped. A soldier, recognising Prince Rupert, began to speak, then shook his head, obviously telling himself he must be imagining the likeness.

At full march we reached the great doors into the courtyard. By then I had begun to feel sick. We pushed the doors open and, still in order, marched on to the next gates. Rupert, Nevison, Porthos and myself expected resistance as we threw our weight against them. They opened easily, almost throwing us off balance. Then, astonished at our prevailing good fortune, we stepped as confidently as possible into a street as packed with Parliamentarians as the palace.

To ensure no sudden onslaught of the mob, hundreds of soldiers lined the wide, tree-lined thoroughfare. They marched back and forth between St James's and Whitehall proper. As before, we were saluted but never challenged. When he could, Prince Rupert murmured to us, saying we were heading for Whitehall Stairs. We kept expecting to be stopped. I discovered later that we had the king himself to thank for this lack of pursuit. When asked where those who had tried to free him fled, he told them back into the tunnel. Our pursuers had turned and reversed their steps, probably taking one of the other horrible burrows we had seen on our way in. Not a fate I'd wish on anyone.

Now we marched through the London crowd itself. They had been walking the distance between the City proper and the palace. All in the hope of saying they had seen a man's head chopped off. Masses of people pressed towards a large gate on our right. More and more people were moving into that gate. I guessed that it led to the Banqueting House and the scaffold. I learned later that we had created a delay. The tunnels were being scoured by scores of soldiers, leaving fewer to guard other parts of the palace. Poor Charles must prepare himself again to make a dignified death.

The confusion meant that soldiers were less suspicious when they saw uniformed men they did not recognise. Prince Rupert's military experience was perfect for our deception. Another ten minutes and we were past the Horse Guard Yard and crossing over into Scotland Yard, the gates of which stood open, attended by a single soldier who saluted us as we marched through. It looked as if the staff had been dismissed or gone to watch history in the making. There was a bleak silence hanging over the vast palace. Blank stone and brick walls rose on all sides of us. We trod cobblestone courtyards, wood-paved pathways, wary of the oddly quiet atmosphere, wondering if we were marching into some sort of trap.

The big yards were haunted by the spirits of those who had worked in them. They had an abandoned air. Once they had supplied the sprawling palace with all its needs and kept or carried every kind of goods and provisions on every kind of errand. If it had not been for Rupert's intimate knowledge of the palace we would have been easily lost and doubtless captured simply on account of our uncertainty.

After a glance around him, the prince led us through a side door and into a wide room which stank of blood. I almost gagged on the smell but the others hardly noticed it. The long glass-roofed shed was hung with game of every kind, from great stags to rabbits, geese and pheasants to skylarks. The place was a deserted butchery, judging by the knives, saws and axes hanging from hooks over broad, shallow stone sinks. Rupert knew his way. He lead us out of the game store into a narrow, flagged passage. This finished in a short flight of stairs which we descended. We were in a dark hall hung with the skins, antlers and other remains of already eaten animals. The place reeked of old blood, fur and scraped hides. This part of the royal kitchens was where food was prepared for banquets. Normally, the prince told us, the whole area bustled with servants, most of whom Cromwell had given leave, dismissed or sent off to work in other parts of the city. I thought privately how so many dismissals would have added to the unemployment figures!

Royal Whitehall employed hundreds of servants for dozens of functions. All had to be fed, watered and sheltered somewhere. Now they were gone and the palace echoed with their ghosts. But, on the other hand, the halls and rooms were not defended. Few soldiers came and went here. 'Nobody expects an attack from the king's game pies,' murmured Prince Rupert, looking about him as if he wanted to sit down and eat one then and there. He took us up another flight of narrow, winding wooden stairs into a long gallery lit by small, high windows. The gallery ended in more stairs which took us to a set of sparsely furnished low-ceilinged rooms where servants and footmen dressed for work. Footmen's uniforms filled long wardrobes which Rupert opened and inspected. Almost at the last one he found what he was looking for – heavy winter cloaks of dark homespun. They had wide hoods like monks' habits.

'Get rid of your armour and wear these,' he told us in a low voice.

'Our redcoat garb's a liability now. They'll be looking for us.' He discovered some wide-brimmed hats. Dressed in these we resembled palmers or a group of countrymen. Prince Rupert explained our strange costume to us so that we had a cover story for the Roundheads. 'We are Puritan brothers, tin miners from near St Ives, in Cornwall. Up to see the execution of the king, if you're asked,' he told us. 'No need to say more. Few here know anything of the West Country so it's unlikely we'll be discovered.'

His ringlets were tied back under his hat, his beard roughened. We did our best to disguise our allegiances. Only the Musketeers had some trouble. My own hair was fine, straight and relatively short. I already looked like a Puritan.

I was glad to be out of the bulky armour. It had begun to rub in all kinds of tender spots. Wearing cloak and hat I felt almost normal and much warmer. We still had on the remains of the Parliamentary uniforms. If caught we would probably be charged as spies, but I was glad to risk it. We now had a better chance of mingling with the crowds. We had heard no church bells ringing. That told us the king remained alive. The time of execution was long past. Prince Rupert said we should wait a while. He was puzzled, uncertain. He perhaps realised how poorly, with unexpected delays, his original plan would have gone. The plot would have been discovered and we should have been captured, tortured and killed.

Suddenly, out in the alley, a group of troopers rode past. Rupert thought this over. 'Best hide until the coast is clearer. Their attention wanders for some reason.' He muttered something about 'cursed bad luck' as if he were angry at himself. Rupert ordered us up another two flights of increasingly narrow stairs until we reached a long, low gallery with rows of narrow beds. A servants' dormitory. I had never seen anything quite like it. It most closely resembled a hospital ward.

We sat down on some hard chairs at one end of the attic and drank a little sour wine Rupert found for us while discussing in whispers the king's decision to accept his fate.

'I can understand him, I think,' said Aramis. 'What gentleman would wish his last hours on earth to be represented by that wretch Jessup?'

Rupert agreed. 'He takes his kingly position seriously, even if we cannot always understand his interpretations. That office is more important than the individual. Charles is England and England is Charles. Or so we used to think. His grace could have ruled from France until another army was assembled but that would have made him all the more unpopular with his subjects. His queen's plotting with France has not been taken well. Our civil war has destroyed too much and too many. The people would have resisted his return.'

'But you were surprised by his decision?' I said.

'If I were not I should not have tried to free him,' Rupert said bitterly. 'His other decisions in the conduct of this business led me to assume he would elect to go. I respect him the more for recognising at last his duty to his nation. I think his trial sobered him. A little too late, perhaps.'

'Why did you try to rescue him if you feared the consequences?' I demanded to know. It seemed to me the prince had led us all on a very dangerous adventure for no great prize.

He guessed my thoughts. 'Why did you continue to help me?' he asked.

'Because –'

'Because you gave me your word. Just as I gave mine to the queen, perhaps rashly, that I would attempt to bring her husband to her if I possibly could. If he could not be saved, I should bring the news myself, together with words from his own lips. Now it is my duty to go back to her and tell her that the king made a good, dignified death and sent his last message to her and his children. *Remember.*'

'*Remember*,' murmured Duval. 'What better message?'

I personally thought it a little vague but it clearly meant more to them. I thought briefly about memory and history, the death of friendship, and I was seized with melancholy.

We found plenty to eat in one of the pantries. Porthos in particular was ravenous. He drank a flagon of Rhine wine and ate the best part of a cold rabbit, then a cooked chicken. His spirits and his bravado rose again. 'The Protestants might kill us soon,' he reasoned, 'and it is always better to meet one's maker in a contented frame of mind, with a full belly.'

All along Porthos had called our antagonists 'Protestants' and sometimes 'Huguenots'. Like many Catholics of his day, he believed we supported the 'high' church by being on the king's side. The politics were actually more complicated in England where there were almost as many Anglicans in favour of the king's executioners as there were Puritans who felt the king should be reprieved.

The trial had been clear to me. A king who makes war on his own subjects is a traitor to his nation. Once kings made war for a throne, but here for the first time in modern history Parliament, speaking for the people, defended itself against the crown. The trial had been a hard one to structure and had taken skilled lawyers a long time to formulate. Whomever next claimed the crown, a precedent had been established: those who defied the people's will also defied the nation. It was a radical idea, of course. The men who conceived it laid down a logic which would be echoed more than a hundred years later by the American Constitution. Duval and the Cavaliers, of course, merely wished the king's courage in accepting his fate to be widely known. It left the way open for his son's return.

After a couple of hours Prince Rupert looked out of a window at the weather. There were a few more clouds but the sun was still bright in a cold sky. A family of crows flew croaking overhead, and Nick Nevison grew unhappy. I think he saw the crows as an omen. For my part, I had made them a kind of personal totem.

CHAPTER FORTY-SEVEN

PURSUED BY PURITANS!

RUPERT THOUGHT WE'D be best advised to get back to the Alsacia by the river. 'We should continue on as countrymen up to witness the execution but frustrated by the crowds. We had best use the ice, the route with fewest redcoats. We can mingle with the common folk. With luck they'll still be looking for us in our soldiers' garb and we'll make easy progress.'

'And if we're caught?' broad-faced Jemmy Hind asked, his mouth gaping in an honest grin.

'They'll be unlikely to catch us all. Some of us will get through. It will be Sprye's duty to take the ship to Holland where a coach to France is waiting. Whichever of us reaches France must inform the queen of her husband's last words and stress how well his grace died and how many of his people mourned him, demanding a new Stuart. That will be my duty now, if I'm not captured. But if I'm caught my guess is they'll not search so hard for you. And so one of us is bound to get through.

'We'll head for Scotland Dock,' he continued. 'It's unlikely to be heavily guarded. And from there to the ice. Many people go in that direction now. The Puritans don't object to the Frost Fair today, but we'll not see another until a British king again sits on England's throne.'

We crept back down the stairs, pausing at every window to check for activity in the courtyards. Evidently, if Cromwell were to celebrate his triumph with a feast, this was not where it would take place. From what little I remembered of the period, Cromwell was anxious he not be regarded as the king's successor. Four or five years would pass before he made Whitehall his residence.

Aramis looked up suddenly. We heard a familiar sound from outside. Military harness clattered and iron-shod hoofs beat on cobbles. Peering carefully through a window we saw three horsemen ride into the quadrangle. Leaning from their horses, they were looking for a trail. Of course we had left one as far as the house, but it could easily have been made at a different time. We had deliberately walked where the most feet had turned the snow to slush.

And then one of the riders said something, pointing towards the roof. All three looked up at once, revealing their faces. I knew them well.

I was stunned. For a moment Colonel Clitch appeared to stare directly into my eyes. His bedraggled hair and beard looked as if they had been too long in the wash. His befeathered hat was pushed back from a face almost as mottled as his grease-stained jerkin. He rode a horse overeager to be on her way, which he had difficulty controlling. He was not a natural rider. On his left sat pinch-lipped, black-clad Love, also having difficulties with his horse, a black stallion too boisterous for him. Borrowed mounts, without a doubt. I heard his Welsh accent drifting up to where we crouched in hiding. I didn't catch his words.

The third man was plainly their leader. Though the Whispering Swarm still gabbled in my head, I heard my own gasp clearly enough. I fell back from the window, unable to speak. I doubted any judgement I ever possessed. I experienced feelings of sickening betrayal. How could it be true? The man was none other than that sympathetic and brave friend I first met at the inn. Whom I thought had saved my life! A play-actor. Worse!

Captain St Claire turned in his saddle to call instructions to a trooper who ran up behind him. 'We're to St James's for further orders. Look for men dressed as soldiers. Three or four very tall. They'll have a woman with them, maybe. Search both yards and the house if necessary. I'd guess they've horses and took the road. They're not the only traitors who plot to save the king! They'll try to get away overland.

Follow us to St James's when you're done. Send men to stand guard at all roads into the Alsacia.'

He *commanded* those bullies! Fresh fury filled me and I wanted nothing more than to confront St Claire. Of course that would have been folly and would endanger us all. I remembered all our friendly conversations, my confidences. I do not believe I had been especially indiscreet but clearly he had some clue to our whereabouts. I tried hard to recall what I had said. I knew for certain I had never made any direct reference to saving the king or indeed to our plans, which had not then involved Scotland Yard. Drinking at The Swan With Two Necks, the spy must have picked up a little information here, a little there, and passed it on to his masters. They had no doubt commissioned him to find and capture us. Prince Rupert would be a prize almost as valuable as the queen and young prince.

My anger threatened to choke me. St Claire, a spy! He had seemed so noble. So genuine. His own man. I had trusted him and liked him and confided in him. Some atavistic impulse overwhelmed me. I took my pistol from my sash. I prepared to fire it into the air to get his attention. I wanted to challenge him, fight him to the death. Then I felt a heavy, gloved hand on my right arm. A slight movement of his head, his eyes staring urgently into mine, and common sense prevailed. I heard St Claire give orders to search the area and to meet back there in a quarter of an hour. From their response he was a man of some authority in their ranks. I heard one of the others address him as 'Captain Marvell'. The spy had not even given me his real name. Ironically, 'Captain Marvel' had been my favourite US comic-book hero when I was a boy! We had divided passionately into Superman and Captain Marvel fans. I had always been in the minority.

'I know that name!' Prince Rupert signed for me to replace the pistol. 'Would that we'd known the face. That man Marvell is incorruptible.' We crept back downstairs. Prince Rupert took a key from its hook and locked the door. 'That will delay the troopers for a little while. We'll leave by the back. There's little time now.'

CHAPTER FORTY-EIGHT

A DEATH

THE AIR WAS growing colder as we emerged cautiously into the courtyard. Elegant Athos remarked on it, drawing his hooded cloak around him. 'The birds must be falling frozen from the branches.'

'The oracles predict the end of the world when King Charles dies,' said Jemmy Hind drolly. 'The Lord promised us no further destruction by water. So, mayhap it's His intention to freeze us and Hell at the same time? That's what my sweetheart, Judy, thinks...'

His words faded as we heard horses' hoofs. In my confusion I had hardly listened. Had Marvell, Clitch and Love returned? Then my heart sank, as riding round the corner, at a controlled canter, came a tightly grouped squad of cavalrymen in the full uniform of Cromwell's famous crack troopers. Troopers, known and feared for their godliness as much as their expert bravery in the field. They carried their helmets on their saddle pommels. All had very short hair. A Puritan zealot makes an excellent soldier. They're the men with very short haircuts. Those of us who wear our hair long haven't got a chance against them. Romans, Normans, Huns, Puritans, Iroquois, Zulu and no doubt many others never felt they could properly deal righteous death until sure of their short-back-and-sides. It's something about soldiering that makes you want to be certain you can, like buzzards, clean the blood off fast.

Prince Rupert saluted them, touching his hand to the brim of the wide hat shading his face. 'Go you with God, good soldiers,' he said, in that West Country accent of his.

'And may you do the same, sir,' the leading trooper returned the salute. He was only moderately suspicious. No doubt he had been told to look for us in New Model Army uniforms.

'Is Charles Stuart not yet gone to meet his maker?' Rupert enquired. 'Are we too late to witness that blessed event?'

'There's a delay, we're told. No executioner can now be found to do the deed. Some fear for their eternal souls. Others demand a higher fee! But I heard one had been found amongst the papists, whose souls are already damned.' The troopers behind him laughed at this. They were seasoned militia and familiar with death. They enjoyed a good black joke.

'May the necessary blow be struck soon,' said Nevison. They warmed to us then.

'Now, now,' said the captain, grinning.

'Go you to the City?' asked one of the horsemen.

'We go to look at the sights, sir. Thames River, so we've heard, is frozen solid,' said Rupert. 'Do you go that way?'

I feared for a second they would offer to escort us. But we were lucky. 'We go to strengthen the garrison,' the officer told us. 'Do you go by Thames River?'

We said that we did. 'Is there something we should know?' asked Prince Rupert.

'Only that the most ungodly merriment is practised there,' the leading trooper replied, 'with hucksters, mummers, bear-baiting, whores and every kind of frivolous temptation defying the edicts of the Lord. Vanity Fair, indeed! Night falls early and Satan rules it, methinks.'

'As he rules so much,' returned Rupert, which I thought was a reckless remark in those circumstances. 'For the last time.'

'You speak truth, brother,' said one of the other troopers. 'But the Lord of the Flies shall be banished from England from this day on. His servant in England goes to justice at last.'

'Thanks to our blessed general, I'm sure,' said Nick Nevison, 'and brave men like yourselves.'

'We do God's work, 'tis all,' said a thickset trooper at the rear. He spoke a little belligerently, a man wishing to reassure himself. 'As His will be done for ever from this moment on.'

'God speed you, captain,' declared Jemmy Hind in a moment of irony. 'May we soon restore the New Jerusalem in England. We'll hurry on to the execution in the hope we do not miss it.'

We all touched our hat brims as he rode past. Soon he was sure to run into Marvell and his men and exchange notes. We needed to get to the Thames and mingle with the crowds. With a parting courtesy the nearest trooper called out: 'If you venture on the ice be careful, brothers. She's mighty treacherous and London still abounds with rogues taking advantage of this noble day.'

We did not relax until the troopers turned the corner of a tall brick building and disappeared. A minute later I heard them talking to the trooper at the front door. However, they apparently did not stop. We hurried in the opposite direction and were relieved when we encountered no other soldiers. We were still in the palace grounds, passing every type of outbuilding. I began to smell something familiar and could not immediately place it. Then, entering a gate standing half-open, we saw stacked planks and heaps of golden sawdust. A wood-yard. Rich as a forest. Were we at last out of the palace grounds? I asked Prince Rupert. He shook his head. His smile was nostalgic. 'That yard is there to serve the palace,' he said. 'It was what I sought, for that's our route to Scotland Dock. And we must hope Mrs Chiffinch is no longer in residence.'

'Mrs Chiffinch?'

'I recall this timber yard is separated from the good woman's back door by a stand of willows. She was the king's nurse and confidante and so came by a grace and favour house when a relatively young woman. Mrs Chiffinch taught me all the secrets of the palace I did not discover for myself –'

'And about the king, too, no doubt,' said Porthos in a rare lapse of taste, and he blushed. Everyone overlooked this and soon we entered a neatly ordered collection of racks containing planks, arranged according to length and width. The building was open on three sides. A wide variety of carpenter's tools was arranged on one wall. Everything was ordered by type and size. It was one of the neatest work spaces I had ever seen.

'It is said the king laboured here himself in happier times,' Prince Rupert told us.

There were no carpenters there that day. As with almost everywhere else in Whitehall the normal occupants had disappeared. We did not go into the yard but took a narrow path around the building, walking on an incline covered in frozen snow. At the bottom of the incline a stand of willow trees, their bowed, leafless branches intertwined, was outlined against the warm bricks of a good-sized building. A red sun hanging in the slate-blue sky behind the house told us it was past noon. For some reason the king was still alive. No bells had rung all day.

'This is all Mrs Chiffinch's?' I peered down through the trees. 'A pretty good set of rooms.'

'She has a large family.' Prince Rupert led us forward. 'Now we'll see if the regicides have frightened them off.'

Slipping and sliding he began a descent of the slope towards the willows and the half-timbered house beyond.

Wrapping my cloak tightly around my chilling body, I followed him. The others scrambled behind me, running and sliding down the slope to the relative shelter of the willows. Anyone in the house who happened to glance in our direction would see nine suspicious-looking fellows in wide-brimmed countrymen's hats slithering and jumping down a snowy bank. We wore still a motley of robes underneath which were parts of Cromwellian uniforms. Roundheads would probably take us for deserters or spies. I hoped the house was still occupied by Royalists.

When we came close enough we saw that a note had been nailed to the varnished oak door. Dusting the snow from his clothes, Prince Rupert tore the paper off, reading it while we dug lumps of ice from our boots, knocked it off our backsides, and waited rather urgently for the door to be opened. I thought my own legs would snap clean off. When he had finished, Rupert passed the note to Nevison who gave it to me, knowing I could read:

'*Mr Coveney, We are visiting our aunt in the country. We shall be there for quite a while we do believe. Your svnt. Mrs Chuffingfinch.*'

'Chuffingfinch?'

'That's how she spells it. A harmless affectation. So, she's not here.'

Prince Rupert frowned. Then he reached to turn the door handle. It opened at once. The prince hurried us into the house and closed the door behind us. The house was cold but had a pleasant atmosphere.

'As I'd hoped.' Prince Rupert smiled reminiscently. 'I don't think she locked a door in all her life, sweet lady.' He paused and took a deep breath. 'Nor would she see the need. She's fled for fear of the anarchy. Now we have a chance to catch breath before we go another step. Here, follow me into this withdrawing room. See? Through the shutters. Look!'

We bent to peer at a vegetable garden under deep snow, a low wall, also thick with snow, and a stretch of cobblestones on which the snow had melted, having been in sunshine for part of the day. Beyond them lay a half-timbered three-storey building of dark red brick.

'That's the king's storehouse. Old Henry built it. It's not been filled since King James's time and Elizabeth was the last to make full use of it. Her pirate captains stacked it high for her. Beyond it is the Scotland Dock. Not guarded, by the look of it. Usually it would be impossible for us to get out that way. But of course with the river frozen over we can get down to it on foot.'

'Shouldn't we divide our ranks, sir?' Duval spoke with the experience of an old highwayman. 'Aren't we too many travelling together to be rural sightseers or visiting merchants? We all know where we go, I assume.'

'Back to the Alsacia I hope.' Jemmy winked.

'Aye.' Rupert agreed. 'My plan was to get us to Scotland Dock and then break up into two parties led by men who know the roads. Myself and the Musketeers make one party, Duval and the rest, the other. But first let's go over to the warehouse. From there you can see Scotland Dock. We should find at least one wooden ladder set in the brickwork down to the ice. We'll use the warehouse as cover and go two by two until it's reached.'

From somewhere in the distance behind us came what sounded like a roll of thunder.

'Drums,' said Prince Rupert snatching off his hat, 'they're taking him to the scaffold at last.'

There was talk of a king's twin. Jessup's sudden appearance and his resemblance to the king had frightened off the men who had originally volunteered as headsmen. They saw it as some sort of sign.

'As soon as his grace is executed there'll be a thousand more soldiers free to pursue us. We should make haste.' Duval prepared himself, wrapping his cloak about him. He wrenched open the door and ran for it.

'You'll follow, lad,' Prince Rupert murmured to me. 'Go now!'

I ran and slid over the treacherous snow and ice. I had no choice. I knew I was making a trail any pursuer could easily follow. But it was growing dark at last. Twilight softened the edges of the day. When I reached the comparative safety of the warehouse wall Duval peered cautiously down at the dock. 'Nothing there but fresh snow,' he said in relief. Within moments we were joined by Nevison and Hind. 'We're the first four. Let's make speed.'

'Should I blame my imagination or is it dangerously thin there?' I asked.

'It'll be thinner until we're closer to the city, where the water slows,' whispered Duval. 'Best go carefully until we near Temple Stairs. The river bends fair sharp at that point and you should see it easily. That's where the main Frost Fair's built.'

'I'm still surprised they let it run today,' I said. 'Those people seem to hate any sort of festival.'

Duval smiled. 'Puritans are hypocrites. They love Mammon better than God. They cannot admit it so are forever confused, thus forever insistent! I blame King James.'

'How are Puritans his fault?'

'He commissioned the Bible into English, so now any man can pick through it to find justification for his sins, whether it be murder, theft or adultery. Ordinary people are unqualified. True, the commandments of Moses are published there, but so are the deeds of earlier and later great prophets, giving other views, all of which they say come from God!'

'Are you an atheist, Captain Duval?' I was amused.

'On the contrary, sir, I am a good Catholic and oppose the dissemination of that holy book in the common tongue. This is the result. Chaos, sir! Any man may now give his own interpretation and, as we see, even do regicide in God's name.'

Jemmy, always laughing, snorted derision. 'As the pope has done for centuries, eh?'

With the sigh of a man weighed down by the words of fools, Duval ignored his friend. 'If we're separated, we make for Whitefriars Old Stairs and meet there. If there's a fog, we wait for Master Moorcock here to lead us through it.'

'What? I'm no expert in negotiating fog.'

'There are fogs and fogs. I'm told you can see the roads.'

I wasn't entirely sure what he meant. 'The roads?'

He became a little exasperated. 'The Roads Invisible! The Silver Roads!'

'I can see them and you cannot?' I was bewildered.

'Precisely,' said Nevison, seeking calm between us. 'You are blessed with what we used to call "witch-sight" in Kent when I was a lad. You can see what they call fairy pathways. Not so?'

'Possibly.' I was more than a little bit nervous now. 'Is that what they are?' Did he mean the familiar streets by which I reached the Alsacia from my world?

I was uneasy now that Prince Rupert no longer led us. Still, Duval was a resourceful man, no doubt even better at avoiding pursuers than the prince. I could have a worse captain.

We slung our muskets over our shoulders and prepared to follow Duval down the ladder. He called up softly, 'The ice is holding but it's a little thin. Be careful where you step.' He walked away from the ladder looking up at the steep sides of the dock. 'We'd best stay as wide apart as makes sense. My guess is the ice will improve for us in a matter of yards.'

Nevison went next and warily joined his leader on the ice. I followed. Jemmy was behind me.

As I reached the ice and walked cautiously towards Duval I heard voices above. A single pistol shot told me all I needed. We had been discovered!

A moment later Jemmy's body came hurtling down to smash on groaning ice which splintered at the edges. Duval crossed himself and quickly unslung his musket, dispensing with his monopod and firing from his hip upwards at the first Roundhead face that looked over. The man collapsed with a ball in him but did not fall. Duval was hissing orders, insisting we leave Jemmy for dead and escape. With some reluctance I obeyed. I wanted to vomit. Cheerful Jemmy was the first of our company actually to die. There was no doubt that here, unlike in the Alsacia, he was decidedly and horribly dead. In the fading light a great scarlet stain spread across the littered ice, and his head lay at a horrible angle.

Another soldier peered over the edge. Nevison shot this time and the head dropped back. I fumbled with the lock of my musket. Duval's hand pulled me faster. I heard a few more shots. Men talked urgently amongst themselves. I prayed that Prince Rupert himself wasn't dead.

CHAPTER FORTY-NINE

THE FALL OF THE AXE

THAT WAS MY first prayer addressed to a God I still barely believed in. The exhortation was certainly fervent. In another second I had turned and followed Duval out onto the ice, hoping Prince Rupert had detected the soldiers and hidden. The highwayman was expertly reloading his musket as he ran. Had he seen the prince? He shook his head.

I was anxious to put the big solid beams of the dock between myself and our pursuers. 'Jemmy's gone!' I told Nevison. My stomach was settling. Everything was frozen. Emotionally and physically. As was our world. On the day a tyrant was made answerable to his people, the world was set on a very different course. The idea of the modern democratic republic was born. I nearly died on the ice of the River Thames as a crimson sun dropped below the horizon and suddenly it grew very cold indeed.

A few stars now lit that sharp blue-black sky now invaded by roiling, ebony thunderclouds. Solid as slate, their blackness filled the horizon. Lightning silently flashed from sky to earth, from cloud to cloud. I heard a hurdy-gurdy. Fiddles. Drums. A fife. Singing. And still the Whispering Swarm. Lamps and rush brands and tar-sticks blazed along both banks of the river. To my right, near the Lambeth side, mummers wearing scarlet conical caps in mockery of the Spanish Inquisition roasted an ox. Judging by his still-blazing rags, they'd dressed the ox as a bishop before offering him to the flames. The Puritans and the common people shared many opinions. Thus it was easy for Parliament to forgive a pasquinade or two when the targets were so frequently the same.

So the fair flourished as in the distance Captain Marvell and his redcoats ran rapidly up from behind, the troopers more recognisable in their uniforms than we in our homespun. The world was transformed to lunar silver, bringing a certain light-headedness to London, even perhaps a sense of relief that the execution was done. Or did we simply witness bravado in the face of coming calamity?

As he turned his puzzled head to look at me, Duval was half-obscured by those strangely solid shadows created by heavy clouds drifting across the sinking sun. In spite of his mismatched collection of disguises he still managed to look like a true romantic swashbuckler, his hat pinned back and his hair blowing wild. Before him the Frost Fair came to life with its fluttering coloured lanterns and blazing torches guttering in the growling wind. At that moment the place seemed a paradise in which we might lose our pursuers. Save for the constant noise of the Whispering Swarm.

Then a bell began to toll.

The sound was taken up on both sides of the river. Every church bell in London swung to tell Christendom that the divine right of kings was challenged by the commons. From that moment no tyrant would sit so easily upon a throne.

I looked back. On the far bank driftwood and seacoal fuelled thousands of filthy fires lit against the cold. The night was murky as the wind tossed the heavy smoke back and forth. Demonic shapes writhed against the shadowed sky. Very dimly I made out the figures of three men, conventionally dressed in cloaks and broad-brimmed hats. They led a fairly large troop of redcoat infantry. Could they be St Claire-turned-Marvell and his two cronies? For a moment the wind brought a touch of sweetness from the fair. Duval and Nevison thumped on ahead of me. I hurried to catch up. We were down to two muskets. I was useless with mine; I gave it to Nevison.

Then the fair hit us, washing over us like a welcome wave. The smells alone made me feel drunk. No time to mourn Jemmy yet. In relief we revelled in the change, everyone plunging into that mélange of merrymaking. They seemed already aware how little there would be to be merry about in England for the next decade or so. To me this was a reasonable price to pay for Milton. Most artists are part-time Puritans no matter how many wives or lovers they discard on their selfish way through life. But these Puritans were of a rather narrow persuasion, substituting obstinacy for reason. For a while they prevailed. Their bullets had already killed one of us and could easily kill the others.

As the old king's reality gave way to a fledgeling democracy, I knew I experienced the last of London's mediaeval Frost Fairs. It embraced me with its hot, greasy sweet smells and its bright cheap colours. All around me Londoners restored their spirits and senses with rosewater ice and lavender tea or ginger. What remained of London's wealth was spread out before us. The stalls were piled with sweetmeats, sausages and pies of every kind. There were gaming rings and shellfish stands and stalls selling beer or hot wine. Pathways of ash and sawdust were ground into the ice. Here and there a boardwalk supported spectators at a bear-baiting or a cockfight or a group of mummers playing out the topic of the day. King Charles had lost his head to a repentant Cromwell and broadsheets were already being sung to the hornpipe and drum.

> *This day in sixteen forty nine*
> Cromwell *ended* Charles's *reign*
> *And* Citizens *now we all are named*
> *Since* Subject's *in the Royal Vein!*
> *And 'tis to his Eternal Shame*
> *That* Regicide *brings* Cromwell *Fame!*

I looked back. Here came the implacable Puritans with pikes and muskets at the ready, shouldering their way through the celebrants, and thus making better time than we could. We dared not risk a shot at them. The fair was full of children brought to take their parents' minds off an event they did not care to consider. A day to overawe and make one afraid. A day when responsibility passed from crown to commons. Never again would a British sovereign selfishly imperil their subjects or the security of their realm. The first steps to full adult suffrage had been taken. *Tyrannicide*: the precedent was now established in law. The stage was set. Even those active in securing it would hardly believe what they had created. Another fifty years and Newton would offer his wonderful unifying discoveries to make the modern world. A day to celebrate.

A battered old coach appeared from the Lambeth side, dragged from some scrapyard, daubed with yellow paint, its wheels replaced with planks, it was pulled by sliding boys, sharp nails sticking from their clogs. For a while the contraption hid the Puritans' side from ours, giving us a moment to regroup and catch our breath. The image of Jemmy falling face down in Scotland Dock came back to me and I smelled blood for a moment. Shock? Most likely it came from a slaughtered sheep whose brothers I could hear bleating wildly a few feet away. Another drum roll against the earlier rhythm and for a short while there was cacophony as we straightened up and continued our race through the fair.

We passed another stage where Italian comedians acted out the same scene, already titled *The Martyrdom of King Charles of England with Harlequin Cromwell, Columbine King Charles and Pierrot Executioner.* Another troupe of English mummers in motley pranced expertly across the frozen river, avoiding the hubbles of small hillocks in the ice. I was reminded of the famous Cornelius troupe from Notting Hill. They performed their version of the play for the first and last time. It would die with their company.

Little boys on wooden trays zipped past us to right and left; little girls whipped their parents' servants as, pretend horses, they galloped cheerfully along with the mob. The dark, distant clouds massed like a besieging army preparing a final overwhelming charge. I was filled with dread. The tolling bells might be booming a melancholy triumph for England. One implacable idea had met another. Past had clashed with future. The result had been the greatest bloodbath England ever knew in a millennium of warfare.

Charles was killed to ensure kings and queens would never again be responsible for setting common folk against one another. We passed from a virtual dictatorship to a democratic republic. Once we sampled it, we never lost the taste for it.

Mourning great-hearted Jemmy, I was filled with sadness. For a while my melancholy even made me forget my fear.

I saw a flame puff gold, briefly lighting the face of a redcoat musketeer. A ball rushed past me.

Someone cheered.

A new era came with the fall of the axe. The bells of the city continued slowly tolling, from Bow to Temple Bar; from the Old Bailey to St George's to St James's; to St Mary's to Shoreditch and St Odhran's. Mourning for a Stuart king. And even Cromwell not willing to stop them.

If God did in fact control our fate, then the pious Charles and the equally pious Cromwell should have been in no doubt as to God's opinion. And now, after so many English men, women and children had died in that bloody conflict, Cromwell was reconciled to this course of action. He knew it would cost him many moderates, even among his own generals, and possibly lose him the republic he came increasingly to wish for. So those bells did not simply ring for the death of an intemperate king, they rang for the death of Parliament's most cherished dream, which would have to go to colonial America and wait over a century to return to its roots. To England.

Another tremendous crack of lightning pierced the scene and seemed to threaten the end of the world, bringing everything to a sudden stillness. Even the bells stopped their relentless ringing. Silence.

There on the ice, hunted as we were, we stopped and took off our hats. We bowed to the memory of that poor, proud Stuart king. Had there been any sorrow in him for the thousands upon thousands killed, raped, impoverished by his insistence? And what had he meant when he asked us to 'remember'? Remember what? That he was an honourable man, in spite of his bad faith in reneging so frequently on his word to Parliamentarians who believed profoundly in keeping an oath given in God's name?

For a little while the soft, uncertain silence continued to fall across the fair. Few moved or spoke at that moment. Every small sound seemed like an offence. Then the bells began to ring again as if in a mingling of fear and joy as London wondered at the repercussions of its heavy deed.

Without thinking, I drew back into the crowd again. My calves ached horribly as my feet tried to keep their grip on the smeared filth of the ice. Distant reports of the muskets were drowned by the sound of another hurdy-gurdy, its handle turned by a man dressed as a some-what cankerous ape. A smaller ape danced on his shoulder. A couple of drunken merrymakers fell against me, apologising. I caught the smell of deliciously sweetened meat and hard-baked pies. All of it carried favourite memories of childhood, of my Uncle Alf taking us up to Hampstead Heath for the Whitsun fair or to Mitcham at Easter when we would stay at my Auntie Di's and buy fish and chips from the truck that followed the fairs when not serving holidaymakers at Butlin's. Tastiest fish and chips in the world. (He sieved the cooking fat to fuel the van so you could smell his coming and his going.) This seventeenth-century variety wasn't so different except the potato was not yet universal and fried trout and mackerel was sold with bread or pastry. The smells were similar. Fat. Flour. Sugar. The shrieks of pleasure were no different. The wailing overtired cries and quarrels were the same. Only the celebration itself was different.

Suddenly Nick, who was between Duval and me, grunted and went down onto the ice, apologising to us and struggling to rise. But he couldn't easily do it. He had turned his ankle. Using our muskets as a makeshift pair of crutches, he continued to hop as we kept pace with him. We could now hear the Puritan guns. But they were still too far away. Only a lucky shot would bring us down.

I hoped that the pursuit of our half of the party had succeeded in taking attention from Prince Rupert. Unless she had been recognised by someone, Moll should be home by now. I was despairing a little when Duval began cheering and tugging at me. He had spotted the Temple Stairs. Not far on from them was Whitefriars Old Stairs where with luck the Roundheads would be unable to follow. It seemed only misfortune could stop us.

At last I spotted the familiar stretch of shingle by which we had entered the city! Soon thin, grey fingers of fog drifted around us like a fisherman's net. At moments we could hardly see one another. Duval and Nevison began searching for an opening but I told them not to waste their time.

'There's only one way of leading us in and I'm not sure I can do it. Remain close to me.' I pulled my pistol from my sash and offered it butt first to Duval. Understanding what we must do, he took hold of it. Supporting Nevison he grasped the thing. 'On your lives, do not let go.' Followed by my friends, I had to dance somehow, or at least step the way we used to step as kids, following the figures of the reels and jigs geeky old Miss Mackintosh insisted we learn. And I had to sing. More a kind of calling, similar to vocalising I sometimes did on stage, echoing the harmonics of the guitars and keyboard. Very high. And I must remember the numbers, the figures of the tarot, the sight of the silver roads, like strings on an instrument, shivering and whimpering. All this is what Father Grammaticus had taught me, sowing the seeds in my brain as I sat hypnotised before his strange and elaborate orrery!

'They have us,' murmured Duval. 'Unless we can get deep into this sorcerous fog, we are lost.' He grinned at his own despair as his eyes grieved for Jemmy.

More musket balls whistled past us. Getting closer. My blood was crystal cold. We'd be dead or badly wounded if we remained there. I had to concentrate and do what Father Grammaticus had taught me in the visions he had induced. Use the tarot. The real. The imagined. Anything. I remembered his lessons. I had to find a focus – in my case the tarot. A goal – the Sanctuary. Marshal my powers and prepare myself mentally for the so-called moonbeam roads: those thin bands of silver, no thicker than a guitar string, which, once sighted and used by an adept, became a pathway. I had used them to get out onto the ice. I recalled clearly all Father Grammaticus had taught me: how to visualise the cards and the reality around me at the same time; how to find in the fog of my vision a slender string which became a narrow ribbon to be followed pulsing and curling into the darkness.

Between the stalls – eights and fours – avoiding the whores – fours and eights – the clouds roll black the raven caws – flapping canvas, eights and fours – threes and nines – dodging the law – the Fool, three staffs – the smell of ice – chestnuts and hot wine – kings and knaves – the Ace of Spades – scales and spears from the buccaneers – twelves and four for the scales of law – twos and eights don't hesitate to the nine of Fate don't deviate as the six and eight the queen shall take to the busiest road of the eight hundred and eight the heaviest weight of all the loads is the load we share on eighty-eight and here she rises like a vein under flesh to the flick of a thumb time enough to drive the needle in. I look I see clearly I see the moonbeam roads, I see everything at once. Everything. At once. To survive I must narrow that vision to sharp sharp focus, a thin silver rope on which to tread most carefully and now we're on the moonbeam road just for a minute. The Second Aether is open to us and so are all the worlds and places of the heart, deal another card and bile rises up but my friends are all through – threes and nines and Twelve of Cups – adieux adieux – four for the law adieux adieux – Play the Fool, Play the Fool; and Play the knave two by two and Harlequin the tale shall spin. Weary, we of the Eighth Degree, finding only the golden scale to bring down the fist of mail. Weary, weary, we of the Eighth Degree. Rhythm and the rhythm and the rhythm and the rhythm and the beautiful blues. Are we that part of God that grieves? That part of God Weeping as so much knowledge fills us. Skipping from stand to stand seeking to save so much. For how long? And for what? How we must sadden Him. The feeling is mutual. I resist the lure of fur and fang. God is good. God has a plan. God is merciful. God is divine. Find the knight and follow him. Find the knight that's all in green. Find the great Green Knight and follow him. Rose of all the Amazons, take us to High India.

Somehow all this was being dredged from my unconscious. There was just a chance that the whole adventure was taking place in my own mind, the events were so much like a bizarre dream. I saw a silvery ripple cross the unstable grey wall between us and Whitefriars Old Stairs. I had to get us where I hoped Marvell, Love and Clitch could not pass. The shadow of a rider in the mist. I strained my eyes to see. Nick did his best to stand on his sprained foot but his will wasn't enough. He staggered. He jerked again. I saw blood spread over his shirt from a wound in his side. A redcoat shot. Blood darkened the ice. Between us, Duval and I dragged Nevison. He was a heavy man but made no complaint. The Roundheads were rapidly gaining on us. I saw Marvell in the lead, yelling something to Clitch and Love. His arm around his friend, Duval tugged a big horse pistol from his belt and fired it at Marvell. He missed Marvell but took a redcoat soldier full between the eyes.

'I fear that's war,' said Duval with a shrug. We were both thinking of Jemmy. The Frenchman looked at me and grinned again. I saw little humour in that grin but there was passion. Fighting was what he loved. I could imagine him as a pretty implacable opponent. Thankfully, a daring ally.

Round and round me ethereal silver figures, the slightly sinister figures of the tarot, danced singing their silent song and clapping time with their soundless hands. In my mind's eye I tried to read them, discover their logic, order them and then I had done so. *I had done so.* The Whispering Swarm? Did I now visualise the Whispering Swarm? It was singing. It became a choir. *Nine by nine,* the strands curled together. *Twelve by twelve,* create the weather strong enough to carry us. Strong, strong enough. *Three by three.* A mounted knight reared his beautiful black Arab stallion directly in front of us, his chain mail glinting silver, his silk surcoat glistening jade, his tall lance flying the fluttering dark green banner of Islam! His spiked burnished helmet was inset with gold and shimmering emeralds, the leather of his horse's harness was stained the colour of grass, his eyes were a piercing green. A Saracen knight of the twelfth century in all his magnificence. He signalled to me with his mailed hand. His bearded face was partly obscured by the curtain of steel dropping on either side of his face. His deep green eyes glared into mine for an instant. Was he signalling? I knew that our only chance was to follow him.

Nevison was a heavy man. I had trouble helping Duval with his friend, who now and then uttered a grunt of pain. I met the Saracen's gaze and called out to him. My allies of the tarot swarmed around his horse. Nevison and Duval looked at me in surprise. They could not see what I saw. They thought me mad. Yet they trusted me enough to stay close beside me. I did all I could to visualise what I sought to find. Then that stallion stamped with his silver-shod hoof and the Green Knight pointed with the lance on which the emerald banner fluttered. One silver road was fractionally wider than the others. It shook and quivered but I was at last able to set foot on it.

A sudden fusillade sounded nearer and might easily have killed us if we had not kept close and acted together. I pulled them both with me. Neither man knew exactly what was happening but willingly trusted my judgement as they trusted Prince Rupert's. Duval and Nevison could not see the Green Knight, whom I followed with the same trust. My last sight of our pursuers was of Marvell's frowning gaze as the mist, now glowing a golden green, folded about us.

At that moment I hated Andrew Marvell. Who would have guessed him a mere sneaking meddlesome spy! He had tricked me into believing he was a friend, an ally. God knew how much information Marvell/St Claire had subtly milked from me in our conversations. Thanks to his coming to my aid more than once against Love and Clitch, I thought he was solidly on my side, shoulder to shoulder with us. But he had fought in those last battles of Alsacia only to gain our confidence and learn our plan.

What would have happened to us all if we were captured by him at Whitehall? At the very least we should have been racked and otherwise tortured to discover all the conspirators. We might have been burned alive! Or worse, hanged, drawn and quartered. What was left of us would have been buried in an unmarked grave. He knew the consequences and willingly condemned us to that horrible death.

I experienced a sensation of fierce cold, worse than anything I had known before. I was almost tempted to turn round and go back. Then we stepped through to the thinner mist following the road which widened to form something like a bridge.

For a moment silence fell. The Swarm muttered and mumbled. I caught a glimpse of the green-cloaked Saracen knight ahead of me. Was he real? An illusion? A projection? I heard the muffled sound of hoofs. What had Father Grammaticus said about the Second Aether? That it was dangerous to anyone not familiar with it. And familiarity with it sent you mad? The only safe way through was by a silver road. The silver roads crossed the Second Aether like paths through a swamp and if you fell off you'd be sucked into what the abbot called the Black Aether, which appeared to coexist with the Second. I knew that I confronted a whole new kind of physics. Grammaticus called it Natural Philosophy but some called it magic and it obeyed its own rules. I would need to understand those rules if I was going to survive for long!

The Whispering Swarm was suddenly gone. In its place, I saw a complex of silver roads on which I walked from world to world.

CHAPTER FIFTY

CONFERENCE

THE SLIME-GREEN MIST gave way to whatever filthy stuff filled
that part of Alsacia. We were still on the ice, still expecting a
musket ball to smash into our heads. We panted from the weight of
poor Nick Nevison doing his best to use a musket as a crutch.

For a moment the Green Knight was still there. Did he watch over
us? Then he faded. We paused, drew breath and continued on until
at last we had reached Whitefriars Old Stairs. The scarred, knotted,
half-rotten wood of the steps was slippery with greenish slime which
seemed to absorb the vanishing mist. The figures of the tarot had
also disappeared. I sent out silent thanks to the Saracen knight, whoever he was. But for him, we should all be dead or captured. But
what of Prince Rupert and the Musketeers? They had gone the other
route home. Had they been so lucky?

With considerable effort, we pushed and heaved our wounded friend
up onto the wooden pier and from there to damp cobblestones. There
was no-one visible on the quayside. Even Alsacia's strange watermen
disliked the river. But we carried Nevison a few yards further up a
steep, unlit cobbled street to a desolate public house with crumbling
timber beams, vine-stained slates, with flaking lath-and-plaster walls.
The battered board was weather-stained and its words were faint: The
Lost Apprentice. Inside, the bleak place was scarcely warmer than
outside. A few surly customers, drinking tin shants of thin ale beside

a guttering fire, looked at us warily. Not one offered to help. The sickly-seeming publican, a Mr Sam Sweetlick, from the notice over his door, forced himself to be friendly enough. He was probably glad of the custom. I ordered brandy and hoped Claude Duval or Nick, who was no longer groaning but had taken on an intense pallor, had money to pay for it.

We discovered Nick's wound was painful but relatively superficial we bound it up, left money on the bar and ventured out into the streets again. I had the overwhelming feeling that the people in The Lost Apprentice were half-dead, waiting for a boat across the Styx. We must have been a very strange-looking party, but they showed only a dull interest in us. Mr Sweetlick did make a half-hearted attempt to keep us at the bar for a further drink but nobody followed into the cold. I had the impression they never went out. Were these the undying damned of the Sanctuary?

In ten minutes we had reached familiar territory, the lively, bustling heart of the Alsacia. In another five minutes or so we at last saw our square, with the big, welcoming coaching inn on one side and the solid old stone abbey on the other. Wood-smoke, ornamented by glinting sparks, drifted up from the inn's big crooked chimneys. Had Prince Rupert been successful? It was our first question as friends and acquaintances gathered. Was the king safe? Who had died on the scaffold? Someone, they claimed, had heard the bells.

I could tell them very little. It wasn't my place. I looked impatiently for Rupert and the Musketeers.

'And the ravens came in. They perched on the roof of the abbey before they flew away!' Tiny, rotund Sebastian Toom brought in hot wine. We were glad of it and thanked him heartily. The unique chill down by the old stairs had woven itself into our bones. Was that stuff only a mixture of miscellaneous gases onto which I imposed my imaginings? To me, it was something almost intelligent and probably malevolent. I associated it with the Whispering Swarm.

'It's ravens flying south, I tells thee,' Mr Toom confided. 'That says good luck.'

On cue I heard a busy flapping. Out of the shadows my old friend Sam came to settle on his shoulder. The bird cocked his head with what I took to be a sardonic expression. Good luck for whom?

Sam looked at me and winked. Did anyone else there know he could talk?

Mrs Toom had made up her mind we had been starved on our mission. She and her servants came storming in carrying an extraordinary collection of dishes. The next thing we knew we were in a booth contemplating a hot steak-and-kidney pie 'dressed', as they liked to say there, in dumplings, carrots and runner beans. There were few meals better than Mrs Toom's pies but I had little appetite. Even Nevison, who could usually tackle a plate of food at any hour of the day, didn't do justice to his dinner. He had lost too much blood, he said. He needed to restore himself with black beer. And he ordered another shant of porter.

We all knew what the bells had meant. And, no doubt, the royal ravens knew, too. We hardly needed to talk about it. In spite of our attempt to save him, and due to his own by turns obstinate and mercurial nature, Charles I of England had met his end. He had believed so thoroughly in his own right to rule that he rejected all legal help. Refusing to accept the legitimacy of the court, he did not defend himself at his trial. Only at the last, when he understood his sentence, did he try to speak in his own defence. Yet, in the end, he might have been a fool, but he was never a coward. He went bravely enough to his death. He was martyred by a belief in God's justice common to both sides. I had to work hard to keep my mouth shut. An old-fashioned liberal republican to my bootstraps, I still felt sorry for the man, as did any number of his enemies.

On my mind, Marvell/St Claire's treachery now weighed heavier than Molly's. If anything stood to attack my thoroughly uncynical nature it was his actions! I had suffered betrayal upon betrayal. Marvell had hung around for months, collecting information, spying. He was nothing less than what his contemporaries called an intelligencer, as Christopher Marlowe had been known a century or so earlier. No wonder Marlowe had been murdered! I had liked and admired Marvell. I had seen him as someone to emulate. Now I knew him to be treacherous to the bone. No doubt he had told his Puritan masters all about me. They seemed to see me as a special enemy. I was fuming as I slowly forced myself to eat my steak-and-kidney pie. What was worse, my anger and disappointment did nothing to improve my appetite, either.

Yet, for fear of seeming ungrateful, I had managed to get most of the food down when the door of the saloon opened and in strode the very enemy of whom I had been thinking. He was flanked by his sneering Parliament men, Clitch and Love. All were a little dishevelled and out of breath. I guessed they had failed to follow us up from the ice and had entered through the main gates.

Did Marvell have the power to sense the hidden universe and lead others through it? Had they left their men out on the ice? These three, it seemed, also had the power to pass to some degree between one plane and another. Marvell must have been their guide. I already knew he was as capable as I was of stepping over dimensions where the Black Aether ran like a deadly tide. Perhaps I should have given that some thought earlier. The entrance they and Nixer had carved for themselves with the aid of various fifth columnists had been blocked off again. Only those with what Prince Rupert called my 'second sight' could get in.

I put my fork on my plate and wiped my knife before slipping it back in my belt. I pushed the remains of my dinner away. All three of us stared in silence at Marvell as he and the other two strode up to the bar and ordered rum. Toom began to fill three pots from the barrel, calling the price out very loudly, glancing from us to them and back again. 'Rum for honest men claiming sanctuary,' called Corporal Love, challenging us to honour the laws which preserved us all. Laws he had broken more than once and threatened to break again. For all that, I admired their courage in risking this venture into the enemy heartland.

'Rum for spies and traitors, Mr Toom,' I said. 'I'd be curious to see the nature of their silver. A little soiled and tarnished I would guess, like their consciences.'

Duval rose from our table as I did. Nick Nevison took a little longer to get up. He showed signs of a fever and his eyes carried a terrible grief. The realisation had struck him at last. His closest friend had died hours since at the hands of Roundheads.

'You have no business here,' I said. 'This inn only serves the brave and the bold and has no wish to make money from murderers and traitors.' Which caused Mr Toom a little embarrassment as he reached to take the pennies Captain Marvell had placed on the bar. With a shrug he left them there.

Marvell leaned back and took a pull of his rum, his eyes full of amused irony.

'Our business is with murderers and traitors indeed.' Colonel Clitch leaned against the bar and stuck his hand in his wide, green sash, staring in our direction. 'We learned today of a plot to save the condemned Charles Stuart from justice and so defy the law of England! One of your cut-throat rum pads was killed in the attempt. We come to arrest the remains of the band.'

'England's laws are her own,' I said. 'Not those of self-raised criminals and traitors who think they can play a cheap game with the crown of the Three Kingdoms.'

Colonel Clitch scratched his short red beard and offered us a crooked smile. 'We play no games here, gentlemen. We respect the laws of sanctuary. We come to arrest you. We have redcoated soldiers standing by who will burn down this whole town if she continues to defy the law of the land. We have a warrant to that effect.'

'Warrant? Let's see it!' Duval stretched out his gloved hand.

Corporal Love reached into his waistcoat. From an inside pocket he took out a thick, foolscap document which he proceeded to unfold and then began reading: 'Whereas the Crown of England by common consent now lies under the benign protection of General Cromwell...'

'Why, lads, he acts out some penny play like those we saw on the ice today as we strolled amongst the mummers!' called Duval. 'None can arrest another while in sanctuary. God's law trumps Man's. Is this a satire to regale us, Master Love? A moral to improve our consciences?'

Corporal Love had none of his master's self-control. 'No fiction. It has the support of several bishops. 'Tis a warrant. It removes the right of sanctuary. You are dead men, gentlemen. There remains but the ceremony to confirm it. Or shall you take your punishment here?'

'Here's a good enough place for you to try, gentlemen.' A fresh voice. A voice with authority. 'The right of sanctuary can only be established in God's name by the king and removed by God Himself. You come to us claiming to be protected against our blades by the laws of sanctuary, then you attempt to abolish those same laws and put us in custody!' Prince Rupert laughed with genuine amusement. 'Can you not see how you are situated, Mr Marvell?'

Marvell's smile was full of self-mockery. With an inclination of his head he acknowledged the prince's point.

Prince Rupert stood in the doorway, still in his mixture of borrowed clothing yet somehow managing to look elegant as he drew two massive pistols from his sash and pointed them in the general direction of the trio. 'Well now, shall you place your weapons where your money is? Or shall we fight? I'm confused.'

There was no doubt about it. If I cared for hero-worship, Prince Rupert of the Rhine would be the hero I worshipped.

Grinning, I stepped up with hands outstretched to collect their weapons. Marvell's men were baffled. I don't think they had expected to find so many of us still alive. They had planned to round up the rank and file, believing the ringleaders dead out there on the ice. Glancing at their leader for guidance, the two mercenaries hung on to their weapons. When he nodded to them to obey, they reluctantly disarmed. Only Marvell responded with good humour to Prince Rupert's logic. Wryly, he unbuckled his sword and laid it on the counter. He had no other weapons.

'Thank God you are safe!'

Moll's voice came from the stairs leading down into the bar. It was uncertain to whom she spoke. I looked up at her and might have gasped, she looked so beautiful. She stood there, freshly bathed and dressed and as lovely as ever. She looked directly at me. And for a moment I loved her more than I had ever loved her and wanted her more than I had ever known.

CHAPTER FIFTY-ONE

ALL FOR ONE...

PRINCE RUPERT'S ARRIVAL broke the tension. Now the place was all of a bustle. Some of our men were for binding the three Cromwellians; some Cavaliers wanted to kill, blind or otherwise maim them. Marvell and Co. deserved death, as far as Nevison was concerned, for Jemmy had been a true and loyal friend, but they had neither fired the bullet nor commanded it and had shown courage in coming here when so heavily outnumbered. Further, the laws of sanctuary had been invoked. Our argument over all this was to take some twists and turns, to be avoided altogether for a while as more shants were ordered up. But eventually the chivalry of the day prevailed. Marvell's courage had impressed us. We wondered what drove him.

I saw Moll go over to Rupert and speak a few words before pecking him on the cheek. My emotions again had the better of me. I hated her again. I recalled all I had given up to be with her. And I almost hated Rupert when he smiled at her, murmured a word, then disappeared to his rooms. As I watched him leave, I could only wonder what England would have become had Rupert and Thomas Fairfax remained in command respectively of the Cavaliers and Roundheads. Moll moved through the crowded tavern, heading for me. I should have turned my back on her but could not bring myself to do it. Then she stood looking up at me.

'I'll be waiting for you when you come back from Amsterdam,' she said quietly.

'Will you, Moll? Can I trust you?' My question was rhetorical.

'I promise. All I want is to look after you for the rest of your life.' Suddenly she reached up and kissed me lightly on the lips. 'I know that now.'

I remembered that ride across the heath, those wonderful weeks together, that intense period of loving and writing, our laughter, the pleasures we had learned. But I shook my head. 'I'm not going to Amsterdam,' I told her.

She wasn't listening. She turned to go back even as Duval approached me. He had heard what I said. 'Your help would be of great use to us, friend Michael,' he murmured. 'Our success would go a little way to avenging Jemmy's death.'

Of course I could not refuse. With a deep sigh, feeling everyone was working to persuade me against my own interests, I inclined my head. I had no choice, but I might yet compromise. 'Meanwhile, how shall we continue to give our friends sanctuary?' I asked.

Having spared their lives and most of their limbs, we appeared to be at stalemate with Marvell and his men. Should we deal with them simply as we had dealt with Nixer, and send them home with fleas in their ears? Should we believe them when they claimed reinforcements were coming? Probably not, we thought, or they would be here.

The prince was soon back. Now, with his own magnificent silver, gold and ebony pistols in his sash and delicate lace dripping at throat and wrist, Prince Rupert swung into the room. 'Oh, we have had a busy day –' He carried himself like a man trying to make the best of a disaster.

'Busy but unfulfilling, I would say,' said D'Artagnan.

'Fulfilling enough. We learned a fresh gavotte.' Before a grimly smiling Marvell and his glowering henchmen, Aramis began to dance. Stepping back and forth between one pool of light and another, he disturbed some of the other Cavaliers. Although I could not see what he imagined, I knew that he danced rather as I had danced, on silver roads above the running darkness. Perhaps Aramis had led Prince Rupert and his friends to safety, back to the Alsacia. The other musketeers were shouting for him to stop. He obeyed with a shrug, raised his eyebrows and sang in oddly accented English: 'Oh, we'll go ahuntin' a merry, merry buntin', we shall go ahuntin' all along the moonbeam roads. We'll go ahuntin' tonight.'

'That's a threat only made by those free to go about that Devil's world,' says Porthos, laughing without humour. And Aramis stopped.

Athos inclined his head a fraction, speaking with a quiet, sharp smile: 'For our pleasure, if you please, Mr Clitch. You, too, Mr Love. Shall you perform a measure with us? Or maybe the Great Galliard itself?'

The other musketeers seemed familiar with their friend's cryptic words and behaviour. Was he warming for a duel?

The conversation became obscure. Everything was conveyed by a hint and a gesture. A kind of rehearsal. I think it was intended to establish a certain atmosphere without recourse to weapons but I could hardly follow it, especially since some of it was in Latin. Jemmy Hind's name was mentioned once or twice. I felt sick when I remembered the sound of his body hitting the ice.

'Well, well, Mr Marvell now, is it? Did you enjoy your jaunt with Jack Frost? Like Captain St Claire's dabble in politics?' says the prince. 'It gives you a good living?'

'Poetry rarely pays well, my lord. One requires a patron.'

'So, sir, you're forced to earn a crust as Cromwell's creature, are you? Been so all along?'

'Cromwell's cause suits me well enough. I never told you otherwise. I'm my own man, your highness. I live and serve according to my conscience.'

Prince Rupert spoke with derision. 'Aye. I've encountered those consciences. They satisfy themselves by torturing priests, firing churches and looting the homes and fields of English yeomen.'

'Best not to talk of so many faults, my lord.' Marvell's voice was low as he leaned back on the bar eyeing his confiscated weapons and enjoying a pull of his shant. 'War makes barbarians of us all. Especially men of some wit who are forced to take up arms because others will not.'

Prince Rupert acknowledged this. There were many of us there who preferred the pleasures of peace.

'Christian men, attend thee!' Coarse, braying from the bar, a drunken

Love was a Love to be avoided, for alcohol was evidently not his friend. I was glad I had taken his pistol from him. 'Your treasure is the Commonwealth's now.'

We all seemed to be waiting for something. Had a bold attempt to arrest us been their real motive for coming here? Why did Marvell seem to show a keener interest in me than the rest of my companions? I felt time was running out. Were they hoping we'd bribe them with a treasure not ours to give?

'Now sirs,' said Prince Rupert, much enjoying the joke. 'What d'ye say we play some games and carouse a while longer, since you were so happy to make this day a public holiday, not yet a holy day?'

'That will come,' said Love, 'with the dawning of the millennium.'

'Hark!' said the feverish Nevison, recovered enough to sit up in a booth. 'There's a sound of fornication.' Pretending to a vision? 'Oh, lord! Get the women in. Up the drawbridge. Fool! Old fool! The enemy's here and not a single dancer for the crown.'

'We know you all took part in a plot to rescue a convicted murderer!' cursed Clitch as if hauling on that tiller would force the conversation back to what he understood.

My friends, of course, outnumbered Marvell and his pair of jacks-in-office. Their weapons piled on the bar, they sat there, sullen and defiant, sipping their rum. I didn't think them in danger. Molly was distracting herself with the flirtatious attentions of two other Cavaliers, but she kept glancing at me. My already damaged nerves weren't in great shape. I felt an almost unbearable pain in my chest. In spite of everything I was almost irresistibly drawn to her. Her beauty. Her fire. Her intelligence and daring. I longed for the old days back. She had the means to bring about their return. Could I just forget everything else and fall back into her arms? Never have to hear the Swarm again? How much longer could I stand the pain of staying away from her?

Prince Rupert ignored her, perhaps for my sake. Though now in his best clothes, he wore a broad black ribbon on his arm to mourn the death of his king. He scarcely said a word but clearly blamed himself for our failure to rescue the king, even if the king had refused rescue.

Remember!

I began to think I had no reason to stay there. Maybe I should return to the abbey and perhaps try to read one of my books? Later
perhaps I could ask Father Grammaticus to tell me more about the
silver roads, the bizarre mantra that came from nowhere, the Green
Knight, the black tides. All the mysteries.

In the end it was Molly who drove me out of the tavern. She threatened to break my heart all over again. I couldn't forget those love
letters she had so recently sent, promising to be a different woman for
me, a better and more constant lover, the woman I wanted her to be.
Strange promises. Some I longed to believe. Others mystified me. I
wanted so much to be there in our rooms together, experiencing that
idyll. I wanted my past back and my future restored. All she could offer was a compromised present. And I couldn't forget Helena and the
girls. One relationship made me weak. The other strengthened me.

I slipped out of the inn unnoticed and crossed the square. The
abbey was in darkness, but I knew there would be a gatekeeper. Almost as if he expected me, Friar Ambrose let me in. I offered him a
silent goodnight. To reach my room I had to go through the chapel.
Pushing the door to enter, I heard low voices and realised some kind
of service was in progress. All I caught was the term 'Ketchup Cove'
or something like it in a foreign language. Closing the chapel door
very quietly behind me I couldn't see very clearly. Billowing light, alternately pale and rich, raced to embrace me. I turned to run. I looked
towards the altar. The Fish Chalice writhed and flickered in its own
glorious, extraordinary light. That light passed out into the chapel
and back again, filling the place with soothing colours. The colours
shaded into the tones of the song performed by the congregation
singing gently in an unfamiliar language. I felt that the combination
should be addressed to an entirely new sensory organ.

Although I hadn't heard it when outside, all this music was measured by the tolling of a single, sonorous bell, deeper and richer in
tone than anything I had heard here in the past. Surely they were
mourning the king. There was nothing I could do now but join the
rest of that strange little congregation gathered in the abbey. To my
surprise, not all were monks. Where were the newcomers from? I saw
men with locks, thick black beards and long black kaftans. Although
I didn't recognise individuals I was sure they were the Orthodox Jews

I had seen earlier! They did not separate themselves from the monks but sat among them in no apparent order. Again I didn't know the language they used. Not Greek, Hebrew or Latin, it was probably Aramaic. I had learned a bit of Aramaic for my *Behold the Man* novel about a man looking for the historical Jesus in the Holy Land.

But then the language of their prayer changed, resembling the scraps of ancient Egyptian some radio linguist had spoken when I heard him trying to make a point about how the language must have sounded. Whatever it was they spoke it sounded closer to an African language than a European one. Perhaps Coptic?

One individual looked out of place. I was bewildered. There he sat as if in prayer, a figure I believed I had imagined! An armoured knight. His metal was Syrian or possibly Persian, of a kind I remembered from the Wallace Collection. His silks were all various shades of rich green and veiled his face so that all I made out were those expressionless eyes, so dark as to be almost black. On horseback he had led us along the silver roads. He had saved our lives.

Friar Theodore, the jolly, rotund monk who reminded me of Friar Tuck in the Robin Hood comics I used to write, saw me standing there and gestured for me to join them. Unable to refuse, I hesitantly went forward and sat in the pew furthest from the altar. Some of the monks and the Jews looked up. They smiled a welcome. The Green Knight turned, the veil falling away from his bearded face. I looked full into his intense dark eyes. He smiled. A substantial man. Then he looked back to the altar and bowed his covered head.

Though the Jews wore yarmulkes, the tonsured monks remained bareheaded. Breathing in the sweet incense, they were swaying in time to the bell. Why did they pray? To whom were they praying? Back and forth. *Jahweh. Jehova. Jahweh. Allah.* I recognised other names. *Abraham, Moses, Jesus, Mahomet.* I had never heard of Jews or Moslems praying in a Christian church together or Christians in a synagogue or a mosque. Only as my eyes grew accustomed to the dancing light did I see two more men partially obscured by an arch. Both had their heads covered, not by cowls or shawls, but by the Arab chequered keffiyeh headdress. They reminded me of Saudi princes Christina's stepmother used to have to her parties.

With no familiar imagery to help me I sat quietly amongst the worshippers, watching the radiant chalice and listening to that beautiful music. As the congregation began to sing, a wonderful feeling of pleasure suffused me. The air grew warmer. The voices rose and fell in superb, unforced harmony. The colours of the chalice grew deeper, more intense, then became pastel again. His expression ecstatic, the abbot didn't direct the service but remained among the worshippers. I was surprised by the clarity and complexity of the singing. As if they had rehearsed for years. Those old Greek chants which had been popular for a while in the 1960s were my only comparison. I had visited the big Greek Orthodox church in Bayswater more than once, just for the pleasure of the choral music and the impressive intensity of the service. This was even better. Sublime.

The chant rose to a climax and then subsided, resolved. I got up and began to leave, making for the far door which would open on the corridor leading to my cell. The door opened before I reached it. There in the shadows stood what I took at first for a child. I then realised I saw a tiny and very ancient man held firmly between Friar Sholto on one side and Friar Erasmus on the other. Although old men themselves, they looked young in comparison. He was tiny, scarcely more than four and a half feet tall. Dressed in a simple red, black and green robe, the ancient wore a yarmulke on his completely bald head. There was nothing else to indicate his religion or his race, unless it was the thin silver beard falling to his chest.

The old man's smile was utterly benign. I knew he had experienced all the world's pain and most of its pleasures. All his earthly experience had added to his great store of accumulated wisdom. He was unimaginably old. His almost invisible skin was mottled yellow, taut over his delicate bones. His costume looked almost mediaeval. He was even smaller than the others, most of whom were only an inch or two above five feet. Standing over him I felt like some Nordic explorer meeting pygmies for the first time. He was not actually supported by the monks but walked under his own volition. When he smiled up at me his deep blue eyes held a quality I could only describe as divine. Amiable, certainly, and full of wisdom, yet he had another aspect I had rarely seen before. I guessed Gandhi and similar people had the same charisma, an empathy with the whole world in its sorrowing.

Was this appearance illusory, just something I wanted so painfully to believe? I found it almost impossible not to be convinced by those eyes. I was not looking at some hyped-up preacher with a message of salvation for those who agreed with him. He had a quiet integrity about him, a calmness and a self-confidence I had never encountered before. He certainly didn't need to persuade me of his authority. Who was he? With his thin, frail appearance, his sunken eyes, I thought at once of a Holocaust survivor. Why on earth would he be here in what was at least nominally a Christian church?

As if he recognised my confusion, the old rabbi stepped forward and reached out to touch my hand. I felt a shock of something. I never did understand it, but his smile was full of humour, almost as if I had just told a joke he appreciated. I was pleased to see this. He had all the qualities people ascribed to their 'guru', whether it be the sad little Maharaj Ji or the jolly old gent The Beatles took up with. Yet I instinctively trusted him as I had never trusted anyone like him. I felt I was in the presence of something I could only describe as 'divine'. Instinctively I knew he would reject any attempt by me or anyone else to call him that.

The abbot came from the front of the chapel to introduce me to the old man. 'Master Moorcock of Brookgate, may I present Master Elias ben Moses, His Excellency the Chief Rabbi of London?'

I felt awkward. I didn't know how to address an ordinary rabbi, let alone the chief. I know my face was burning when I bowed and said: 'Master Elias, I'm glad to meet you, sir,' and felt a bit foolish.

He smiled. He put his hand out for me to shake. His fine, delicate fingers at once felt powerful and very fragile. I was overcome by a strange emotion which made me want to laugh and cry. His accent wasn't in any way foreign. It was old-fashioned like the abbot's. 'So ho – thou art the young fellow who comes to help us restore the balance of our lives!' He spoke in a light, vibrant, musical voice full of character. I, of course, hadn't the slightest idea what he was talking about. I was, however, utterly fascinated by him. I had never met anyone so evidently ancient. I felt his delicate hand settle on my arm as he led me along a passage and into a chamber filling up with the rest of the abbey's occupants.

The Chief Rabbi asked me to sit beside him. I was a little embarrassed by the honour. Arriving in some disorder, Prince Rupert was the next to appear. 'Marvell and his men sit like logs, refusing to leave the inn.' He was seated on the other side of the old man. Asked if his day had been good, the prince replied gravely that, with certain exceptions, to his surprise it had been. I knew he had not expected the king to reject his attempt at rescue. I also knew he grieved for our Jemmy. His old gravitas never failed him.

'You're glad that your kinsman lost his life?' One of the Jews had obviously heard the recent news. Had one of our company carried it here? St Claire? No!

'Of course not.' Prince Rupert's gaze was steady. 'I wish with all my heart that he had lived. And that some compromise could be established between church and state. I have to say, I had begun to hold a rather unhappy view of the king's character. In the end he died with dignity.'

'And how, your highness, was that death?' asked Friar Balthazar, his eyes twinkling as usual, no matter what the subject. I sometimes wondered what, if anything, he hid behind that expression.

'King Charles believed that he died, Friar, to save others. Therefore he at last displayed true Christian qualities. He allowed his own sacrifice in support of the common good. I think he came to understand his faults and realised that he was paying a fair price for his sins. He died humbly, before God.'

I confirmed what he said. 'The king could have saved his own head but believed in the end that his death as a man was justified. The office of king being what it was, he had already passed on his birthright to his son, who became king the moment Charles's head fell into the basket.'

'But you risked so much to save him, your highness,' said the abbot. 'You wanted him to live.'

'Of course I did, Father Abbot. He was my kinsman. I promised his wife that I would do all I could to save him. He released me from that vow while going to his death with such courage. I still serve the Crown. Tonight I leave for France so that I might swear my allegiance. Charles the Second is my king now.'

'So you believe, do you, Prince Rupert, that kings rule by divine right?' The old rabbi's voice was strangely vibrant, yet at the same time frail.

'I do, my lord. But I also believe in God's wisdom. I believe He moves mysteriously and deviously to accomplish His will. I believe that this land had indeed, as the Puritans insisted, become ruled by Satan. Our kingdom was given to self-indulgence, grown unjust. The king lost all regard for his people. King Charles *was* the Realm and God's representative. That is my belief. Now that he stands before his Creator, I suppose it is fair to say the nation has been reduced to anarchy. I hope, for the nation's sake, Oliver Cromwell will soon see fit to restore the monarchy, albeit one ordered by Parliament. Stability is what we crave now, your honour, and consistency. We are neither rich enough nor secure enough to continue with that bloody business which my uncle, in his obstinacy, would have prolonged. For a while he had forgotten the whole of his duty.'

The old man nodded his head. 'As have others, I believe. Think you Oliver will become our king?'

'It is one of the things I fear,' Prince Rupert replied, 'but if God wills it then let it be so. Unlike other usurpers Oliver is reluctant to take the throne. Or says he is. He has no right of inheritance, of course. He would rather a kind of Episcopal system of elected ministers. He denies any other ambition pretty fiercely, I gather. But in like vein Julius Caesar refused the laurel leaves of Rome only to wear them when the security of the realm was at stake. Sometimes we must accept that our Creator's will is stronger than a nation's.'

Everyone there agreed. Our conference was to discuss ongoing plans. I had now promised Duval I would help them, but I was also hatching a scheme of my own.

Master Elias, as Chief Rabbi of England, was to attend the Amsterdam conference which would be held in secret. He had waited decades for this. 'Once the Jews are admitted back into England, my great vow to remain in London until that time will be fulfilled. I shall no longer be needed here.' Apparently a number of *marranos* and others had resettled in England for some years; they were ostensibly Christians but practised in secret. Almost all were regular visitors to the abbey. The few remaining English Jews and their descendants, officially expelled from England by Edward I in 1290, had lived and attended synagogue here in secret for some three and a half centuries!

Now I was beginning to understand some of the things mystifying me at the Sanctuary! A rabbi by the name of Judah ben Har, scarcely older than me, very young and enthusiastic, told me how the time had come for Jews to petition Oliver Cromwell for the right to return openly, to practise their religion unhindered and continue their traditional trades, arts and services. Like many Puritans, Cromwell was known to favour the idea of admitting Jews and not merely for practical reasons. The Jews, as usurers and traders, brought greater flexibility to any economy. But more profoundly, the Protector identified with certain Old Testament teachings. They brought a religious scholarship and a rigorous intellectual tradition the country dearly needed after the prolonged and ruinous civil war. This idea sounded good to me. I asked Chief Rabbi Elias how long he had held his office. He was amused, knowing he would surprise me.

'About three hundred and fifty years,' he said. 'The former Chief Rabbi of London made me his successor. I became Chief Rabbi of England until such time as the edict should be revoked. As soon it shall be.'

In spite of everything else that had taken place, I still could not believe Master Elias was some four hundred years old! I looked from face to face. Not a man there, Christian or Jew, showed any surprise or incredulity. Why on earth did they come openly to London, albeit Alsacia? What went on here? Shangri-La, indeed!

I responded a little weakly. Some of the others laughed, enjoying my expression.

Just as I was coming to a grudging belief in the supernatural, every day brought some new test of my credulity! Now I was supposed to accept that the ancient Chief Rabbi at our table was only a bit younger than Methuselah! There was no question the rabbi was very old indeed; no question that he had an extraordinary charisma. He spoke almost in a whisper, yet his voice was thrilling. His accent was soft, even gentle; controlled and precise, as if he conserved his strength.

'You must remember, young sir, that I was from a very long-lived line even before I came to the Sanctuary.'

Did he mean that the Sanctuary had extended his life? I knew Alsacia somehow preserved life because I had seen that with my own eyes. Disturbingly, the dead might even be resurrected. But could the place actually prolong life? Hadn't Methuselah, Enoch, Noah and all those others in Genesis lived almost a thousand years? Abraham was ancient when he begat Isaac. Maybe there was something in the diet? I seemed to be getting even deeper into the swamp of gullibility, a growing belief in the supernatural. I was in a kind of fugue, I suppose, carried along by events possibly created by my own imagination. Because of my familiarity with drugs, my usual scepticism kept kicking in. In Notting Hill in the 1960s you had to develop a certain habit of mind or go crazy like one of those poor acid-burned freaks wandering up and down Portobello Road, their unblinking eyes glaring into some hellish private fantasy. I knew people whose brains had been wiped and replaced by a bunch of pretty pictures and the crazier aspects of the world's great religions.

I had to admit this old man was pretty convincing. That pale, yellow skin stretched over his bones was the thinnest ever seen, but it wasn't proof he was as old as he said he was. Were *all* these people perhaps delusional? Including me? I really didn't want to believe what my logic forced me to believe.

I asked the Chief Rabbi why he had chosen to stay in anti-Semitic London. He might have been better off going somewhere like Prague where there were active synagogues to support him. He didn't need to live in secrecy. I think he found my question a bit naïve. I had to bend forward a little to hear his response which was almost a whisper.

'My place was here. I was not the only Jew to disobey the king. Our duty was to remain here until called home. In truth there are fewer now than there used to be. But to them I have passed on my knowledge of the Torah. After the great concordance, I will discover the next stage of my journey. God can always use another rabbi somewhere.' And he smiled the sweetest smile I had ever seen.

I continued to be curious. 'Sir, have you always lived in London?'

'I was born in York but my parents moved soon to Leeds and from there to London. I went once to Lisbon. It was a common experience for Jews in my day to be like our nomad ancestors. We were forever pulling up stakes and moving on. But we made many friends among the English scholars.' He smiled toothlessly at me through his thin white beard. 'Fewer in the Lords or Commons. The English were not the first to persecute Jews. I gather your mother's family is Jewish. But you are not a Jew by religion?'

'I have no religion. No belief.'

He laughed. 'You have what my friends call the "second sight"? A Sufi? You are an adept. A magus. You can see the roads?'

'Does that involve belief in God?'

'I think you know that answer. If you believe in the supernatural you'd be wise to believe in God, but that's my opinion. I hope we can continue this conversation. It has been some time since I spoke with someone who found their faith.'

From respect, I didn't tell him I hadn't exactly lost my faith first. Logic brought me to the assumption God was likely to exist. I wasn't yet thirty, but speaking to a man allegedly born in the Middle Ages, who had lived through the Renaissance. Who even now was living in a time immediately before Newton! Newton, who practised alchemy, invented modern physics and had a profound belief in God. So a belief in materialism and science need not be incompatible with faith!

From across the table Friar Aylwyn asked me respectfully, 'Did you not believe in our common God, Master Moorcock? Were you an atheist?'

'I was until recently, Brother Aylwyn. Now I think you could fairly call me a fellow traveller...'

Master Elias smiled at this. 'Brother Aylwyn, do you think it right that we query our friend's beliefs when he supports ours with practical help?'

A little ashamed, Aylwyn murmured an apology. 'I have never known a man who did not believe,' he said.

'Perhaps you'd answer a couple of questions I have,' I said.

'Of course,' said Father Grammaticus from the head of the table.

'I don't understand how Christian monks and Jewish rabbis can work together so closely. And weren't there Moslems in the congregation earlier?'

This was an easy one for the abbot. 'We work together because we work for the Old Faith, which some call the Faith Undivided. We have no divisions concerning belief, but place value on our common un-

derstanding of God so that we may better do His will. We do not worship in the old, exclusive way. Only those uncertain of their beliefs
insist on a single ritual. You have attended our services, Master
Michael, and know we never refer to a specific prophet or embrace a
single religion. It helped us that to the outside world we seemed to be
following conventional Christianity. There were times, like now, when
everything for which we work might have been utterly destroyed. Our
fellow believers follow Islam, for instance, and others study the Hindu
sutras or Buddhism, Shinto and other great religions of the world. We
come together in secret to study all beliefs and take the best they offer. Once a faith becomes an organised religion it becomes a political
system. We are pledged not to one religion, but to the spiritual core
of all those religions, which agree on the profoundest levels.'

I have to admit I agreed strongly that organised religion was no
more than party politics. The spiritual aspect was always the first to
be abandoned. 'But why do you leave here now?'

'It is time I spoke in person to a number of colleagues. I have things
to discuss concerning our ultimate goals. The matter of High India,
for instance, where we shall travel when the great day comes. Then
there are the domestic issues. Some prepare to petition the Lord
Protector, Oliver Cromwell, for Jews to be allowed to live and trade
openly in England. We have every hope of success. In High India, the
conference will determine many other issues.'

Prince Rupert interjected. 'Sadly, however, certain enemies learned
of our intention. They are coarse, gullible people from all walks of
life who believe we conspire with foreign kings to assume their
power and steal their wealth. Cromwell's advisors want to turn him
against the Jews.'

'When we learned the king's ship was bound for Holland,' added
the abbot, 'we begged Prince Rupert to take Master Elias.'

'I had envisioned other circumstances than these.' The prince spoke
quietly. 'But it is my privilege, sir. The journey is dangerous for all.
Our Musketeers offer you protection. They return to "The Winters",
as their own particular sanctuary in Paris is called. Our ship already
waits in the Thames below the Tower. A Dutch brig, an English skip-
per and a mixed crew. She has an English name, I'm told. We must
hope the ice is still thin once London Bridge is passed. The brig'll

send a longboat for us. All must be done swiftly in darkness. She'll be stopped if our enemies have the chance.'

'But you believe Cromwell is likely to be sympathetic to your cause,' I said.

'Cromwell, yes. As far as he understands it. And the majority of Puritans, too. But there are others, Catholics or political Anglicans like Colonel Clitch and his creature Love. They would stop us at every turn. They have already poisoned the minds of many Parliamentarians against us...'

'I suppose you are selling your Treasure to help finance your other ventures?'

At this everyone began to laugh and I was baffled. Seeing my expression, Father Grammaticus apologised. 'I had forgotten not everyone knows the nature of the Treasure we have guarded here for some three hundred and fifty years.'

'Well guarded, too, in spite of many rumours down the centuries,' added Prince Rupert.

'It's very valuable, no doubt.'

'No doubt.' Father Grammaticus smiled. 'Though we'd judge your manners poor if you continued to use the term "it". I think it time I introduced our Treasure.' The abbot rose from his seat and bowed to the ancient Jew. 'Rabbi Elias here is our valued Treasure. We protect and defend him with every means available to us. We have no Treasure as valuable as Rabbi Elias!'

CHAPTER FIFTY-TWO

SOLDIERS AT THE GATES

'Now we are pledged to take this Treasure to Amsterdam,' said Prince Rupert. 'There I shall leave him when I travel to Paris to give my sad news to the queen and her family.'

'But why take me with you?' I asked.

'You are no longer safe in London. Both Nixer and Marvell know you. Duval and his men will return here to carry on the fight. And there is a big fight coming, believe me.'

I thought of the children. I simply couldn't go. I might never return. These assumptions had to be nipped in the bud.

Already Father Grammaticus was continuing. 'You possess the so-called witch-sight. You are one capable of seeing all there is to see in our crowded universe. It's in your blood, Michael.'

'Like an inherited disease?'

I had no particular wish to stay in London, since Helena had made it clear I had no home with her. I decided to keep my own counsel. I had told few about my family. If the situation changed, I would behave according to my instinct.

The conversation became a bit cryptic after that.

'You saw the prince's orrery,' I heard Friar Erasmus say. 'No dark matter or light can exist in the Grey Fees. That fog! I tell you it is godless Limbo, pure and simple. Without time, without physicality, without, we believe, any higher being of any kind.'

'Without hope, by the sound of it,' I said.

'We don't think so. Anything sent to Limbo or even coming into existence there returns as long as it obeys certain conditions.'

'No light can enter. No anti-light or dark aether can enter. It is only possible to leave!' said an older rabbi I had been told was Meinheer Uriah of Bruges.

They looked to the prince and the abbot for confirmation but all Prince Rupert would do was sit back in his chair and quote a piece of verse:

'All th'unruly hordes of heaven
Came in concourse to salvation
All the whispering swarm created
Call to thee in unison...'

I had never heard the verse before, but at the mention of a whispering swarm I grew alert. This was the first time I'd heard the phrase. Of course I applied it at once to my own experience and butted in somewhat rudely.

'I'm sorry, Prince Rupert,' I said, 'but did you say whispering swarm?'

'Oh, it's just a reference to the gossiping mob. A bit of verse by a common enemy!'

'I've heard that Swarm.' I was barely able to keep my trembling hands still. Was this a reference at last to some shared experience? 'I hear it almost every time I leave the Alsacia. What is it?'

The prince merely looked mildly embarrassed. 'It might be something of our enemy who sits drinking in the inn across the way.'

'Captain St Claire? He's still here?'

'Aye. His companions are nothing more than taproom bravos but Mr Andrew Marvell, as he's otherwise known, is a man of some gifts.'

I'd heard of Andrew Marvell, of course. A Cromwellian. That would explain his interest in the Alsacia and why he wanted to overhear Prince Rupert when he demonstrated his orrery. He certainly was not a common spy. He was an educated eye. A knowing ear. What else had I inadvertently told him? How much had he passed on to Cromwell and how much had he kept to himself?

'Marvell's surely an adept of some kind. He knows of the silver way.' Friar Balthazar frowned. 'And plans to betray us?'

'How could he betray us?' Rupert asked. 'What could he tell Cromwell which the Lord Protector does not already know? What could he show him that he would believe? Or condemn as Satan's illusion?'

'What does Cromwell know? More than we guessed?' The abbot smiled at the table in general, seeking to reassure us. 'He wants what we possess. I think he fears it. Or covets it. Or both.'

'You'll be able to tell when he makes his next assault,' said Rupert grimly. 'Perhaps you should all abandon this place and settle in some other?'

'Your royal highness forgets,' the abbot said, 'Cromwell has no personal knowledge of the Sanctuary. The Protector relies on the reports of creatures like Nixer, who has certain crude abilities. Nixer, Love and company fear what we hide and what we know. Most outsiders believe the Alsacia to be no more than a den of common thieves and renegade royalists. Cromwell would destroy us on principle. He's never seen us yet he allows Nixer and others to pursue their ends as part of a general policy to attack London's rookeries. Sadly, his natural instincts never let him believe in the Sanctuary for what we know it truly to be!'

I hoped then that he might expand a bit on what the Sanctuary actually was but Prince Rupert interrupted. He was still uncomfortable. He was lost in his own thoughts. 'A poet,' he murmured, 'and a swordsman. An intelligencer for Cromwell, too! That could be a dangerous mix. I saw such a creature in my last full reading.'

'Reading? You're familiar with the tarot, my lord?'

He shrugged. 'A little. I was thinking on how we are compromised. Can we be followed? If so, who would follow us?'

'I believe Captain Marvell is able to see and use the silver roads,' I said. 'Probably in a limited way.'

'Aye, 'tis possible. He's an alchemist of sorts, I hear, an adept and an Oxford scholar. What did he say to you, lad?'

'He spoke poetically. He talked about everywhere around us being deserts of vast eternity. I thought the vision a bit bleak.'

'Well, if he knows certain routes and is a good poet, he speaks truth of sorts,' said Master Elias. 'Poets can be seers. My great-uncle, for instance. If he's a genuine poet and no mere versifier, we should perhaps believe him. He has power. His words resonate. Magic and poetry are closely related. Yes, we must be very wary of your Mr Marvell. Where is he now?'

'We left him in the Swan,' said Prince Rupert, rising. 'Come, Master Moorcock. We must confront him, I think. It might be necessary to make him our permanent prisoner.'

Friar Erasmus looked up. 'Could that duty not be left to us?'

'There are three practised swordsmen there,' Prince Rupert warned him. 'My musketeers already await. No, Brother, I think we had best be on hand in case there is violence.'

Erasmus turned away with a faint smile. Prince Rupert's lips were pinched and his eyes narrowed. I had learned from this expression that he anticipated trouble but didn't know if he had the means to deal with it. He picked up his sword and pistols from where he had left them outside the dining room. I wished I had brought a weapon as we left the abbey. I took big strides to keep up with him.

'They are only three. They can't be much of a danger to us, surely?' I caught my breath.

'It depends on the men they have ready, what he knows, and if he knows what that means. I did not see him for an adept.' Prince Rupert reached the door of the Swan and paused. 'Don't let them suspect I am taking action against them,' he murmured. 'And stay clear, lad. You're keen but you're no swashbuckler.' With me behind him he pushed the door open, to step inside.

The place was very busy. I saw no sign of Marvell and his uncouth companions. We searched every possible part of the inn. But they had gone. When we found Mr Toom he told us they had abandoned their weapons. They remained piled on the bar where, as Toom pointed out, they could have retrieved them if they so wanted. They had left at least a half hour since. There was nothing we could do. Our plans were not clear even to the Musketeers. 'We had thought it your strategy to let them go,' said Athos. Duval had taken the injured Nevison into the saloon bar to separate him from the three interlopers. I was the sole person amongst our band Prince Rupert had taken into his confidence.

Again we all spoke in French.

'I supposed them trounced,' said Porthos. 'I did not understand they were in need of a further trouncing.'

'*Alors!*' Athos dabbed at one eye with a soft glove. 'I was for finishing them. Why did you not let me challenge them, Aramis? While they were here?'

'Because I understood we were not to indulge in brawling in an inn protected by the prince!' Aramis spoke with familiar dry wit. 'Believe me, your highness, we should have enjoyed nothing more than to engage your king's enemies. But I understood –'

'You were right. You were right.' The prince drew in a great breath and let it out again. 'Well, they're gone, maybe for reinforcements. I still don't fathom their game. My guess is that they suspect a plot by us to introduce more than one king's double. They were here to make certain they had indeed killed the king and not some second substitute. I doubt they'll be back before we leave. Marvell's to be feared but the other two are mere flotsam in his wake. Hurry. We must prepare. Gather here. This is the right moment to go. We'll take our charges to the ship as soon as we're all assembled.'

While he climbed stairs to his room I returned to the abbey and told them to prepare. Then I went to my cell. I got into some suitably warm clothes, wishing I, too, had a sword and pistols at my side, then returned to the chapel where several of the rabbis already waited. Soon the other travellers were gathered. Chief Rabbi Elias was the last to join the group of rabbis. Just as we prepared to set off for the Swan and meet Prince Rupert, an anxious monk ran in.

'I think we are attacked again, Father Abbot. Armed men at the main gates. About thirty or more led by that Mr Marvell we thought a friend. What shall we do?'

'Only one thing for it.' Father Grammaticus was grave. 'You, Brother Michael, make speed with Master Elias and our fellows. Tell Prince Rupert what has happened. We'll delay these others as best we can. We are all expert swordsmen and pistoleers when needed. Go – and may our Lord's grace go with you!'

Somehow I found myself outside the abbey helping six bearded Jewish rabbis bundle Master Elias, their Chief Rabbi, into a heavy sea-cloak and then get him into a sedan chair. I was tempted to pick the old man up bodily, since he seemed so light, but I was too respectful to suggest it. So we crept along at his speed, with many glances behind us, and reached the Swan just as we saw the gates of the Sanctuary swing open to reveal Messrs Marvell, Clitch and Love at the head of at least a score of heavily armed redcoat troopers.

We couldn't risk the Chief Rabbi being harmed. Rather than obeying our natural instincts, we turned for the Swan just as Prince Rupert, the four Musketeers and Claude Duval ran out with their scabbarded swords and sword belts still in their hands. The Frenchmen had their muskets on their backs. I was still unarmed. Seeing this, D'Artagnan darted back into the inn and re-emerged with one of the blades, a musket and a pistol surrendered by Marvell and Co. With him, struggling into his own harness, came Nick Nevison.

'What's the rush?' Nevison asked me, slipping his belt over his shoulder and settling his sword at his side. Then he saw them all slowly filing in through the big gate. 'Ha! Well, I've looked forward to dealing with them! We have you now, Mephistopheles!'

Duval growled. 'You're not well enough, Nick. Let them nurse you at the tavern!'

Nevison's glare of contempt silenced the rum-pad captain who shrugged and readied himself to run at the redcoats. Prince Rupert halted Duval. 'We need to make speed, old friend. Come, there'll be plenty of enemies to engage later. Our duty is to get our Treasure aboard Sprye's brig. Others will stop those lads!'

'Others?' Duval adjusted his hat. 'There's barely a dozen Cavaliers in the house and they're in poor condition for a fight.'

As if on cue the monks of Whitefriars Abbey appeared between us and the Roundheads. I thought at first I witnessed some kind of Gandhi-like demonstration. Then I noticed what the monks had in their hands. Forming a line between us and Marvell's men each monk flourished a large pistol in one fist and a heavy sword in the other.

'Those poor creatures are good as dead!' exclaimed Porthos.

'Make haste!' cried Rupert urgently. 'There really is little time. Marvell and his men got what they wanted from us. They know our plans!'

Abandoning the monks and hearing their first shots in defence of the Sanctuary we rushed down into the maze of streets where Whitefriars Old Stairs waited for us.

CHAPTER FIFTY-THREE

ACROSS THE ICE!

As we ran down to the river, the rabbis took turns to carry a sedan chair probably heavier than its occupant. I heard gunfire behind me, the urgent cries of battling men and the sound of metal striking metal as swords met pikes.

I still found it hard to accept that Marvell had been intriguing against us from the very first moment we'd met. We had bonded in our view of the world. He had seemed so generous, so friendly. I had been certain he liked me as much as I liked him. What other betrayals should I have anticipated? Moll's treachery still hurt worse but now, if I hated anyone, it was Marvell. Otherwise I was now thoroughly wrapped up in the adventure though I knew it to be very dangerous, even lethal. Should I, the father of two young children, risk my life so readily for what might be a delusion? Probably not, though I'd scarcely had much choice in the matter.

We armed those others who could use muskets. Prince Rupert, Rabbi Solomon, Duval and myself carried one as did Nevison who was defiant in his insistence on coming. Prince Rupert now laughed, accepting him. 'A limping Nevison is better than no Nevison,' he said. The Musketeers still carried their own guns. They had made Athos their captain. They had three big pistols each, giving us a fair amount of firepower. Most of the Jews were unfamiliar with any weapon.

Few sported as much as a sword. They stayed close to the sedan chair, as if to protect it with their bodies.

Now we were at the steps and descending very carefully, trying not to bump the chair on the slippery wood.

Once at the river the point of their choice of transport became clear. The thing had brass runners and could easily be pulled and pushed over the smoother ice. The surface varied widely. Whole stretches were as unruffled as an Olympic rink; other parts were covered in hubbles and knolls made by the cold and wind.

Carefully, we lowered the sedan chair onto the slippery planks leading away from the bank. I went ahead then, treading carefully through the darkness, following the rotting planks I had used earlier. Again fog rose up around me, clinging to my clothing, obscuring my vision, chilling my flesh. It almost felt as if solid bodies pressed against mine. Silvery threads tangled themselves in front of me, forming shapes, dissipating, muttering. I took as firm a grip as possible on the sword D'Artagnan had found for me and pushed on against the yielding fog. As before, I let the next man hang on to my musket and gingerly we moved forward. Shadows swam around us like ghosts.

Off in the distance the hazy light of the Frost Fair warmed the night. Here, we were hidden in darkness. We were a good-sized party consisting of the six rabbis and their Treasure, four musketeers, Nevison and myself. We would be easily recognised by anyone looking for us. Duval, Prince Rupert and Porthos led the rest. D'Artagnan, Aramis and Athos formed a useful rearguard. Their dark lanterns could be adjusted to make the smallest amount of light. With these they could only see or be seen for a short distance ahead.

At least for the moment we had outfoxed Marvell. He had expected us to leave by Carmelite Inn and planned to capture us all as we emerged beyond the gate. Did he know the nature of our Treasure? I felt oddly humble in the presence of the six young rabbis and the old man who claimed to be about the age of Methuselah. The rabbis clearly adored their chief and considered Prince Rupert to be a good friend. They probably weren't aware he had originally planned to bring King Charles with us or that they were almost incidental passengers.

The rabbis obviously considered him a hero. Scientist and explorer, experimenter and strategist, privateer, courtier and wit, he had everything he could have except luck in his choice of allies. Some had already schemed against him. That was why he had not lately commanded the king's forces. Cromwell respected his skill and his courage as a leader. He would have dearly loved to get his hands on the 'German prince'. Only Rupert could plan a successful uprising. If yet another royalist army was raised more than likely Prince Rupert would command it. Even now, as leader of our little band, Rupert instinctively knew our strengths and weaknesses.

The noise of the fair was distant now. But the church bells still boomed from Camden to Kennington. The continued tolling from the towers confirmed that Londoners now fully understood how the old world had died when King Charles's head was held up for all to see. A *traitor and a tyrant*. The only concession the Puritans made to the feelings of his family and followers was to let them stitch the head back on the body. In future, republicans would see this as Cromwell's first mistake.

The thunder and the lightning still roiled and flickered, signalling another storm marching to the Thames from the Medway. If the storm reached us it would be much harder to get Master Elias aboard the boat. The water was going to be rough. The ice would begin breaking up below London Bridge. We would be in danger of being crushed to death.

I kept looking back. The Musketeers signalled they saw no danger but I was certain the Puritans and their rather impure captains must have defeated the monks by now. I listened for sounds of their pursuit. Marvell knew we headed for the river but we couldn't be sure what bad information he had gleaned with the good. He might be searching for us between the Temple and Lambeth in the thick of the Frost Fair.

Every so often a squall swept up fragments of ice and flung them into our eyes. For a while we were doubly blind to what lay ahead. We needed to regroup. Turning, I counted our party. Six rabbis, one Chief Rabbi, four French musketeers, one Prince of the Blood, two highway robbers following one formerly sceptical, deeply conflicted journalist. I have to say it was no real contest: I didn't want to go to Amsterdam and discover the wonders of her secret city, or go to Paris before she had anything like her modern appearance. Paris of Notre

Dame and Quasimodo was full of tremendous wealth and obscene poverty. Out of it had come the likes of Molière, Racine, Corneille and that great creator of other worlds, Cyrano de Bergerac. But I was not going to cross a gulf of Black Aether with the chance of never seeing my children again, or, indeed, of being killed a couple of hundred years before my time!

And then I had led us through the silvery fog and we took tally of our numbers. Hearing no pursuit we judged it a good plan to rest for five minutes or so and renew our energy. Several of us had flasks and shared them generously. The rabbis appreciated the warmth the brandy brought them.

The old Chief Rabbi winked at me as he handed me back my flask. 'Nothing like strong grog to renew the spirits.'

I had brought the half pint of twenty-year-old Hine from home and was amused to hear it called 'grog'.

Then, as we pressed on past Blackfriars, with distant Southwark to our right, a stretch of deep darkness suddenly surrounded us. Hidden in the shadows we saw armoured horsemen at the trot on both banks, light glancing off their helmets, cutlasses and breastplates. Cromwellian cavalry, riding in good order, led a squadron of musketeers marching at the double. They couldn't see us, but they seemed to know where we went. Which meant we travelled as fast as we could towards confrontation with many well-trained soldiers whose leaders desired to stop us at all costs. They wanted Rupert but they might also want our Treasure – the old gentleman currently being slid across some fairly bumpy ice. Who knew what Cromwell and his advisors knew about the Alsacia? And the redcoats were led by Marvell. Whatever else did the poet-turned-soldier-turned-intelligencer know about the Sanctuary, the Chief Rabbi and the rest of us?

Mordecai, a round-faced, innocent young rabbi, had seen the horsemen, too. 'Do they mean to stop us reaching the ship, Master Michael?'

'That's their hope,' I said. 'My guess is their horses will be useless on the ice. They'll not have that advantage at least. Every man here is prepared for them.'

'Prepared, but no match.' With long fingers Rabbi Esau combed at his thick black beard. 'Think you, meinheer, that we could be in some danger of being slaughtered?' He spoke with the resigned irony of a man for whom calamity is constant. 'Might a little prayer perhaps be in order?'

'By all means,' I said. 'Anything is worth trying at this stage!' In the circumstances it seemed to me that this was not unrealistic. As the Jews prayed for us all, Prince Rupert, Duval, Nevison, the Musketeers and I discussed our strategy. We had few options. Six of us were experienced, capable soldiers, familiar with all our available weapons. One was an expert general. I had a little training. Rabbi Solomon could shoot the musket he carried. Looking ahead I saw the light grow brighter around London Bridge. I was not sure what that meant.

Prince Rupert and the other soldiers took stock. Snow still lay pretty thick on much of the ice. There were no stalls or tents there. Duval said the river flowed faster once past the bridge. About twenty narrow arches, necessary to hold the weight of so many buildings, slowed the water and allowed the ice to form, but once the Thames left London Bridge and continued on towards the Pool of London, where a good many great seagoing ships were anchored, the ice became thinner. Where it had frozen into heavier slabs, it tended to split apart and crash together again, forming miniature icebergs as hazardous to us as their larger relatives of the Arctic. We had no spyglass with us and so were unable to get a better picture of what we faced.

As we drew closer to the bridge we heard a gurning and groaning as huge pieces of colliding ice crashed together, threatening the sturdy stonework of the arches. Again I turned and begged the rabbis to say if they had any experience with any weapon!

Once again only Rabbi Solomon raised his hand, holding up his heavy flintlock musket. Like a number of other Jews he had fought with the Dutch against the Spanish and had risen in the ranks to captain his own men. 'I can handle all firearms and the sword', he said, grinning from his heavy beard with a certain boyish pride. Two of the others then chimed in to tell us they, after all, had some small experience with axes. So, somewhat sceptically, we dragged the remaining muskets from under the sedan chair and armed them. Duval muttered that we were wasting scarce powder. But Prince Rupert knew how best to keep up morale.

While the courage of these men was impressive, we were still vastly outnumbered, though the redcoat cavalrymen would have to dismount if they were to be any use against us on the ice.

Prince Rupert, used to mustering confidence in his troops, congratulated everyone on their bravery. He did not for a moment express his own understanding of our situation. But we had no choice. We had to keep going until we could rendezvous with Captain Sprye's boat, assuming that the ship herself had not been already captured or crushed.

There was now nothing for it but to press on towards London Bridge as the great winter storm, which some already said showed God's displeasure at Cromwell's deed, rolled rapidly nearer, seeming to follow the course of the river.

I felt there was something distinctly supernatural about that storm. I had witnessed weather as bad and at this time of year, but never in London. In England I'd known it only once, when I had celebrated my birthday in the Lakes on an evening excursion from Ingleton.

I found it difficult to keep my spirits up as I took my turn at pushing the sedan chair while trying to sound confident. At that moment we became aware of the tolling of a singular bell.

The deep-throated measured sound resonated slowly through the night and found an echo in my chest. I barely had time to reflect on the strangeness of this before London Bridge loomed out of the billowing blackness ahead of us.

Seen in reality, the architecture cramming the structure overhead was very impressive. Many houses backed directly out above the Thames. You could see tiny faces peering from candlelit windows. I could even hear the odd shout from above. Some buildings were of half-timbered brick, like much of the city, but most of them were made of stone like the bridge itself. I then realised that the source of the tolling bell was a church built in the middle of the bridge itself. We heard it clearly from below. Looking up I saw more figures peering down. I guessed they were not just idle sightseers. Luckily they were also not marksmen. Nobody shot at us as we came through, though a few odds and ends were thrown down on us. We slid, pushed and carried that old sedan chair and its precious human cargo under one of the arches nearer to the city side. I was pretty sure no regular soldiers saw us clearly. I heard voices overhead but the darkness made it impossible to make out any detail. The creaking and cracking of the ice not far downriver let us know that the river thawed there. Did I hear raised voices, too?

And then came a massive, deafening crash.

The Chief Rabbi uttered a high, surprised cry followed by a string of Hebrew I couldn't follow.

A monstrous flash of golden lightning burst over us. Instinctively I lifted my arm to protect my eyes. There came an unexpected pattering of ice which stopped almost instantly. I thought at first I heard broken glass. Another crash. Cold winter lightning. Underfoot I felt the ice shivering and above us I heard screams.

No doubt some of the people living on the bridge thought the whole structure was threatened. I must say I didn't blame them. My own dim memories of the V-bomb raids on London towards the end of World War II came suddenly into play. Chills shivered up and down my bones. Not for the first time I reflected on the terrible situation I was in. What on earth was I doing there? I had tried to save a king who was in my opinion guilty of his crimes. I was now helping a handful of European rabbis carry one of their elders to what we all supposed was a safer place for him. I wished I had read more of this period of history. It had never particularly engaged me until now. I preferred fictional accounts. At that moment, of course, it was too late to start wondering about steps down to the water from other parts of the bridge. We kept as low as we could. I remained watchful, searching for a way off the river which didn't involve moving closer to the bank on our left. If one existed, I couldn't see it.

Neither could I see Captain Marvell and his men. There was no sign of the redcoat cavalry we had seen earlier. Were they still riding along the bank? Perhaps they planned an ambush.

No ambush came. No shot was fired. We were increasingly nervous, expecting to see troopers in every shadow. I did hear a few rough voices calling from the top of the bridge. Some soldiers on the Tower side suddenly let off a musket fusillade until an urgent voice bawled at them to stop. So it was a trap of sorts, except they were as unsure of our position as we were of theirs. The guns had been aiming some distance behind us. If they thought we made slower progress, we had a slightly better chance of reaching our boat before they realised where we were. In a whisper I warned everyone to keep quiet. Prince Rupert confirmed this, murmuring into my ear: 'Here is the point, Master Moorcock, where we rely not on our own wits but upon the witlessness of our enemies.' He grinned and winked at me. 'Battles are never won by the strategists. They are always lost to he who makes the fewest mistakes.' And he grinned at me, a wild and reckless expression which immediately inspired me. I could see why his soldiers followed him so willingly. Death meant nothing when Rupert of the Rhine commanded the charge!

Another flash of lightning. A great clap of thunder. Almost on cue it began to hail. The hail at once turned to snow. Sheets of white whirled and hissed. The wind picked up the ice from the surface and flung it into our eyes and mouths, drawing blood as it struck exposed flesh. A deeper booming came from cannons positioned along the walls of the Tower on the riverside.

'The devils are trying to break up the ice! They plan to drown us in this freezing water!' Aramis wiped sleet from his eyes, glancing around him for a means of escape.

'They don't need to hit us, but they risk losing what they believe we carry.' Athos smiled that thin, grim smile of his. 'When, I wonder, will someone remind them that we carry treasure with us.'

Porthos and Duval laughed heartily at this and sure enough, after a minute or two, the cannonade stopped suddenly. What its purpose was, if not to drown us, I had no idea. Perhaps a commander of the Tower's guns had made a mistake, thinking he spotted a ship. Someone had clearly given the order to cease firing. At that moment an eery silence descended. I heard nothing but the wind whispering like distant surf.

Still unsure of ourselves, we crept across ice growing thinner and less safe with every step. Great massings of dark troubled clouds formed above us on all sides, as if we inched along the bottom of a gigantic well. Then, with a tremendous noise, like heavenly cannon-fire, the clouds split open. Lightning cracked down again with deafening strikes wherever it touched, illuminating vast pieces of jagged ice gathering like Titans to finish us off. For a minute or two, tired and terrified, we rested panting against stone piers. Then, with the next lull, we moved forward again.

There were no embankments as such running beside the river, so our pursuers were either on the shingle and mud of the bank or on the roads above them. Dimly, I saw the outlines of trees and buildings – a clump of poplars, a tall warehouse, a row of cottages. I smelled the filthy water and the snow. I heard horses trotting. A distant exchange of curses.

Suddenly the ice shifted underfoot. The movement felt like my feet being tugged from beneath me as I walked, except it was accompanied by the sound of fast running water! I recognised and feared that sound. I had once climbed a big glacier in Finland and experienced something similar. I'd heard a river directly below me and nothing but thin, creaking ice separating me from it. The difference being, of course, that then I was roped up to another climber and had no particular fear of dying. Prince Rupert called out a warning. Someone began to respond, then, with a yell, was suddenly silent.

'I have him. Give me a hand someone!' called Nevison. A bright yellow light appeared briefly. I started to go to help him. Then, from the left bank, came a sudden fusillade. I saw Prince Rupert and Nevison with a rabbi between them. On the prince's orders we moved further towards the centre of the river. Then I saw the Jew fall again and shout. A confused cry from Nevison. He and Prince Rupert bent to pull the rabbi up. It was round-faced young Mordecai. He struggled to rise, fell back and sprawled on black ice creaking alarmingly beneath him. I heard him call a prayer.

Flattening himself, Prince Rupert stretched out a hand to the rabbi. A flash of lightning. Then darkness. We were safer there, not just from the shifting ice but also from soldiers shooting at us from the bank. Another flash. Rupert had dragged Mordecai back to thicker ice. Acting on my own, I told the rabbis they must abandon the sedan chair. It was too easy a target. Athos and Porthos helped the Treasure out and Rabbi Solomon, one of the youngest and strongest, got the frail old man on his back. Porthos and I then gave the chair a massive push out to where the ice seemed thinnest. I hoped to draw any fire. Apparently, only one Puritan musketman detected it. A single shot rang out and I heard a ball tear through the chair's fabric. There was a loud crack. In an instant the chair began to sink. I yelled a warning and told the least warlike of the men to take turns carrying the Chief Rabbi on their backs, to keep as low a profile as possible. Then I gave a great yell, which echoed as I'd hoped, and gave no clear idea of where I was. But there were no more shots. I guessed the troopers had been cautioned to take care.

Again that quasi-silence engulfed us while the snow continued falling steadily. The sky grumbled and flickered, almost as though it were talking to itself.

Taking over from Solomon, tall, skeletal Rabbi Zachariah now had the Chief Rabbi in his arms, carrying the ancient man like a small child. In his heavy kaftan and tall hat he made an unlikely figure, praying audibly as he made his awkward way over the ice. The rest of us encircled him, ready to fire if he came under attack.

Another great roll of thunder shook the ice. The surface continued to move underfoot. I could hardly keep my balance. We were likely to be sitting ducks soon and Prince Rupert knew it. Almost desperately he peered this way and that, trying to see what surrounded us. We crept on. Where was the longboat supposed to meet us? Lightning flashed and snapped. Up on the left bank the crouching dark mass of the Bloody Tower was suddenly revealed, a massive, solid outline against the darkness, its battlements no doubt lined with Cromwell's musketmen. Then the prince at last saw something.

'A longboat, look. There!'

I saw an outline, rocking gently. I could just make out the shape of a big skiff moving at the edge of the ice. Then I spotted the light, dancing ahead of us like a will-o'-the-wisp. I was puzzled by this until I realised she was signalling. Rupert, an experienced seaman, knew exactly what was happening.

From what I saw, the longboat was in no way big enough to carry us all. The six rabbis, Master Elias and Prince Rupert were in most urgent need of escape. The rest of us could probably split up and find our own ways to safety. When I put this to him, Prince Rupert nodded briefly. He had a mission to accomplish, having given his word he would be first to tell the queen how her husband had died.

The prince made his way carefully to where Athos stood with his lantern ready. The Musketeer now lifted his lantern to shoulder height. Then he began to work the shutter, signalling to the boat. There came a long, pregnant pause. 'I can't risk widening the shutter,' Athos muttered.

We waited. Then, all at once, we saw a light flickering *behind* the longboat! It became almost immediately obvious to us that the ship was signalling back. I heard Prince Rupert murmur a brief prayer under his breath.

'It is dangerous for the brig to be anchored in midstream,' he said. 'The ice breaks up but floats downriver in large pieces. Any one of those slabs could hole a vessel. Look, see. That's our ship.' He pointed to a great black shape rearing out of the waters of the Thames. Then he turned. 'Let us get you into the skiff, your honour.' He reached out his arms to take Master Elias.

'Assuming the ice doesn't break her up or lift her,' said Prince Rupert, 'D'Artagnan and Athos, perhaps, could go with them, being the lightest. Then we'd have to hope the brig can afford to wait long enough for the skiff to return for us.'

Aramis was adamant. First the rabbis and their charge should go, together with Prince Rupert. 'You have your duty to the queen.' The rest of us would use muskets and pistols to hold the Roundheads at bay until the skiff came back.

As we argued we neared the edge of the ice. The skiff was a good-sized boat but she already held four or five sailors. At a pinch there was room for Prince Rupert and possibly all six rabbis and their charge. Those of us remaining were well armed with guns and swords and could hold off the Parliament soldiers if they advanced across the ice.

After a quick discussion we agreed. Duval stepped on the ice close to where the skiff waited and Prince Rupert called out urgently.

'Duval! Take care, man!'

We watched in horror as the ice slab sank down under his feet and flooded with water. He was as careless as he was courageous. 'You'll have to bring her in closer,' he called, his legs astraddle to balance himself.

The answer, a little muffled by the weather but amplified by a brass speaking horn, came in Dutch-accented English. 'We cannot draw any closer, meinheer. The ice is very treacherous. Those sharp edges already threaten to hole us. If you step in a fraction closer, however, it will press the ice down. Perhaps you can board that way.'

Duval and Prince Rupert thought this over until at length the Cavalier prince agreed. 'Throw us a rope, meinheer, at least!'

An acquiescent grunt. Then, out of the darkness whipped a heavy strand of rope. Almost toppling into the icy water, Duval made two unsuccessful attempts to catch it. On the third cast he fell, landed on one knee but caught it. He leaned back, using the rope to steady himself as he got up.

We all moved slowly and carefully as Duval backed towards us. Then we began to take our own places at the rope. Nevison, the last, wrapped it around his waist, using his weight where he now lacked strength. Duval's oldest lieutenant was showing weakness from the wound he'd received that afternoon. We got the line as straight as possible. Duval had shown how the rope could be used as a kind of rail, absorbing some of our weight. Rabbi Phineas would go first, with Master Elias on his back. Phineas was the smallest and lightest of them. He had the best chance of us all. He would not put as much weight on the ice and it was not as likely to sink under him.

Porthos and I now joined Nick Nevison. Together they gathered a few turns of the rope around their waists. Then they got as far back onto the solid ice as possible. At Prince Rupert's signal Phineas began to inch forward.

For a moment all was silent again. The thunder was a distant, threatening grumble. The snowfall was still light. We heard the slapping of water underfoot as the boat bumped against the great slab of ice on which we all stood. I knew if any one of us slipped into the water they would die almost instantly.

Now Phineas and Chief Rabbi Elias were a few feet away from the skiff. We watched intently as hand over hand the young man inched his burden over the ice.

Phineas was almost into the boat. Then we heard another sound. At a different time I might have dismissed it as the cackle of a wild duck. But Prince Rupert recognised it at once. 'Nixer!' he cried. 'That's his lunatic laughter! Where?'

Was Nixer aboard the Dutch ship?

'We've been tricked!' Porthos cursed. 'They have already taken the ship!' Had we indeed been outmanoeuvred by the Roundheads? I strained to peer through the falling snow. All I could see was the looming shadow of the Dutch brig. Who commanded her?

CHAPTER FIFTY-FOUR

REMEMBER!

Nixer showed his position in a very dramatic way. We heard splashing oars. Then a boat, rowed by redcoat troopers, appeared suddenly in a thin channel of black water running between us and firmer ice. The Puritan stood in the prow easily identified by his thin, cruel face. Lit from below by his lantern, the Intelligencer General's features had a demonic cast. Satan gloating at his harvest of souls!

As if confirming who it was advanced against us, I heard the bellow of Nixer's tromblon. Depending on its charge, one of the nastiest weapons of the time, the blunderbuss belched a massive charge of shot and small nails. We heard a wild shriek. Metal whistled past us on both sides. Suddenly somebody yelped with pain. Young Mordecai stumbled and went down. I watched in despair as his body slowly slipped from the ice and disappeared into the ebony water. Rabbi Uriah, horrified, dabbed at a wound on his cheek as Nevison scrambled upright on the unstable ice, trying to reach the downed Jew.

'It's Nixer, true enough.' Duval swore. He peered in the direction of the shot. Two big horse pistols appeared in his hands. He cocked them, aimed. But the Intelligencer was invisible again. 'Nixer, you murdering coward! Shooting at unarmed students and a frail old man!'

'Oh, 'tis *General* Nixer sure enough! Traitors! I have been expecting you!' The pipsqueak's jeer brayed out of the darkness. It could belong to no-one else but Cromwell's swaggering Intelligencer General. Anticipating our plans Nixer with his Old Thunder had been lying in wait for us. Foolishly we hadn't considered this strategy. His boat swung heavily in the current. Now I saw the Intelligencer General's ratlike features contort with glee in the light of his own lanterns. Reloading, he reached for his powder horn, turning his tromblon's muzzle up on its prow-mounted swivel.

'Did you think we'd so easily let a traitor escape our justice? Or let ill-gotten revenue escape our nation?' pomped out Nixer. I glimpsed him packing down his powder with his ramrod. Then he vanished in another patch of blackness.

'You'll not give English gold to Rome!' I heard him swear.

'You're under a misapprehension, Master Nixer,' called back a mocking Rupert. 'And an amusing one.' The prince could not help himself. He struck a brave pose and, when the boat swung into the lamplight again, studied the Intelligencer General as if he were especially disgusting vermin. 'But you'll not exert your new authority unless you put that vulgar thunderous blunderous toy of yours down and meet us with pistol and sword like a gentleman. Would you become a gentleman, sir? You must learn your manners, Mr Nixer, if you're to rise in King Oliver's new Court!'

'Bah! You don't understand, do you, "Rupert van Rijn"? You're as much a dullard as any other Stuart. Courts and kings have been abolished by Parliament. Like your foolish uncle's, yours will be the next head on the block. All your kind are peacock proud until persuaded by a sentence of death. Then I'll warrant you'll be spitting excuses all the way to the scaffold.' The prow of his boat rocked in the bleak water. Falling, Nixer reached hastily for the side.

Prince Rupert smiled as if at a poor joke. He began to turn away. Then Nixer, abandoning his tromblon for the moment, bent and brought up a musket. Grinning he aimed at Rupert, fired, missed and fell sprawling back into his boat. The ball had passed through the decoration of Rupert's hat. The prince's laughter was spontaneous. 'You owe me one bent ostrich feather, Mr Intelligencer!'

Nixer was growling with rage. He scrambled up. He frantically finished loading his big gun. Fixing it back on its swivel, he swung it towards us. A slow match began to spark. Behind him, a soldier, seeing his chance to kill one of us, lifted his musket. Before I realised what was going on, he had fired at Nick Nevison.

The ice began to flood under our feet. Nevison, already shin deep in water behind us, roared, a wounded and defiant lion. Unsteadily he brought up his own big barker and returned the Roundhead's fire. The redcoat threw up his arms, fell like a stone into the water and remained down. Duval, too, let off both his horse pistols and killed another soldier.

Our booted feet were up above the ankles in water. The huge slab rocked and jerked under our weight. We slid back and forth. We found it almost impossible to keep standing. We had to balance and pray the slab did not disintegrate beneath us.

The remaining rabbis were now all settled in the skiff. Prince Rupert stood guard over them, looking to where we had last seen Nixer. Master Elias sat in the middle, a tiny figure so light I thought he would float on the wind if the boat sank. His face was intent as he smiled back at me, lifting his hand. His voice, thin and high, sounded above the shrieking night as he called out: 'Quickly, Master Michael. We shall both go to High India when all shall be made clear! When the great time comes!'

Privately I wasn't sure the old man had the strength to get to Amsterdam, let alone 'High India'. I watched as the darkness folded around him. I regretted I had been allowed no more time with him.

I lifted my hand to wave goodbye. As I did so a great bolt of lightning smashed down upon the Tower. I fell backwards, just recovering myself. I thought for a moment the castle was totally destroyed. For an instant a light blazed out. I saw the brig herself then. She was anchored some yards downriver. She lay at the very edge of creaking and squealing ice. The ominous outlines of broken slabs loomed high over her decks. Seamen moved in the rigging, hurriedly unfurling her sails, ready to weigh anchor. No wonder they had shown such urgency! The sailors had every reason to be terrified. The ship was drifting dangerously near the slab on which we stood. Any one of the huge blocks of floating ice could hole her and sink her. She would go down like a stone in minutes. The captain and crew showed enormous courage by remaining in such treacherous water. Meanwhile, the rowers in the ship's boat urgently bent their backs, back and forth, like so many machines. The gap between the two narrowed. Our 'Treasure' was almost there.

Beside me, Nevison sighed. 'He, at least, will –'

A cannon sounded suddenly from the shore. A massive ball whistled through the night. I felt it go by. It fell with an explosive gasp into the water. The ice rocked wildly and the skiff almost capsized.

'They're done for,' muttered Nevison painfully, preparing his musket. 'Nixer's won.' But he was only expressing his fear. A moment later and the ship was hidden in darkness again.

Another great boom of thunder. This one was so loud I took it for more cannon-fire from the shore. Everything vibrated. The boom was followed by another burst of brilliant light. Then, to my complete astonishment, I saw the gold-painted name across the brig's swaying stern. A single admonition. *Remember*. I shuddered when I recognised it. The king's last word to Prince Rupert! How on earth could they have anticipated that? Or was the name of the ship just a coincidence? Or was there a secret to which I was not party? *REMEMBER*. An odd name for a ship, if so. We'd been told she was a Dutch brig. Certainly Amsterdam was her home port inscribed below her name. She was a good-looking vessel, probably refitted from one of the Royalist ships fled to Holland on the defeat of Charles at Worcester. I could now hear the voices of her crew. They were chiefly English. The mate was a West Countryman. Her captain a Yorkshireman.

REMEMBER.

For all its high-sounding resonance, I hadn't a notion what it actually signified.

Another loud report from Nixer's boat. We had almost forgotten him. I heard him cheer. Next there came a stifled gasp and something fell heavily against me. I tried to catch it. A body. A giant. Nick Nevison, down again.

Duval shouted 'Nick! *Mon ami*!' and ran towards us. I bent down, trying to help him. His face pale with pain, the giant highwayman lay on the drowning ice. He had lost his hat and his clothes were soaked. With my aid he struggled to his feet, swaying as the wild ice rocked under us.

'Nick!' Duval saw his friend trying to clamber upright. The rope he had wrapped around him now lay in coils below the water. 'Get up, man! You'll be drowned!'

Nevison clung to my arm. Dazed. He frowned. He stared around himself, as if he did not know where he was. He reached into his belt to tug free another pistol. Then, releasing his grip on me, he drew his sword.

'Nick! Get back!' Duval and Porthos tried to join us now. As the ice grew more treacherous, they inched their way towards their wounded friend. From the boat, Rupert looked anxiously behind.

The big ship swayed and groaned. I heard orders being shouted. As far as I could make out, the voices were mostly English.

With a loud clap, the unfurled sails smacked down. The wild wind snapped into them and they bulged at their rigging, straining like living creatures. I heard someone shout from the yardarm. The sailors were getting Master Elias and the others aboard the REMEMBER. But surely there was no hope for us. Buying as much time for our friends as we could we would have to stay and fight to the death. I thought of my children. How foolish I was to let myself be engaged in this adventure.

'Are you hit?' asked Aramis, seeing my expression. I shook my head. At that moment I was trembling with anger and despair, certain I would never see my children again. The anger was directed as much at myself as our enemies!

Another shot from Nixer's boat. It went harmlessly through the rigging.

Then, almost at once, the ship's longboat, having delivered her cargo, pushed back away from the brig. As the ice parted the daring oarsmen struggled to head for an ebony shard, a thin black channel of water. By remaining there the brig was in serious danger. So were we all. I could hear the ship's oaken timbers creaking. The pressure of the ice tested every plank in her.

Nixer was now preparing his gun to fire at me again. I was tired of accepting his attacks so passively! I raised my big flintlock and settled it on its rod. Aiming at him carefully, I pulled the trigger of the musket.

And fell back, deafened by the loud explosion!

The musket butt had slammed violently against my shoulder. I was sent staggering to the edge of the slab. Unwounded. As was the sniggering Nixer.

The boat pulled closer. The rat-faced Intelligencer General leered and slowly turned Old Thunder on me. As I stared into the tromblon's muzzle, I steadied myself with the spent musket and tried to tug out my pistol. I was a sitting duck. Looking into his wicked, triumphant face I could have been staring into the eyes of Lucifer himself. We both knew I was a dead man. Standing there, my legs far apart on the rocking ice, I prepared to make as good a show as possible when I went down.

Bang!

Shocked, I felt sick, knowing this was the end. I was filled with remorse. I had betrayed my children. It took some moments for me to realise the shot had come not from Nixer, but from the brig. The Intelligencer General snarled out my name, clutched at himself, glared around him, sputtered in pain and rage, then fell down in an untidy heap while his men tried to help him. Clearly believing him dead, Nixer's remaining redcoats turned their boat hastily. In confusion they headed back into the shadows of the Tower Hill shore. Meanwhile from all around me came a great cheer of victory. My friends were congratulating the marksman. He stood at the rail. For a moment his face was illuminated by a ship's lantern.

A little unsteadily, his free hand waving a greeting, Rabbi Solomon balanced himself at the rail brandishing the musket that had saved my life. That intellectual man of God was almost comically pleased with his prowess. With a grateful grin I saluted him. Then the ship turned at her anchor and he disappeared into darkness.

Now one of the brig's seamen brought the longboat in close to the ice. Watching from the brig Prince Rupert appeared again. He raised a melancholy hand, sweeping his hat from his head in an elegant bow, the kind of romantic gesture which made him such a popular field commander.

We were still in considerable danger. Duval and I picked up the rope while Porthos held the boat steady for the other musketeers. I wanted poor Nevison to go first but he refused. He was on his feet again. He held back with Duval, shaking his head. Then, carefully, while we held the boat as hard as we dared against the edge of the ice, the Musketeers got in. Porthos and D'Artagnan held their hands out to help us jump aboard. I signed to Duval, but he was looking back at Nevison. I knew he would not leave without his friend.

'I see them!' Voices bellowing in the distance.

Nevison collapsed suddenly onto the ice. I turned to look past him. Was he hit again? Duval tried to help the giant up. Who pursued us this time? Lanterns winked and blazed. Three figures in silhouette. And there they were: Captain Marvell and his grinning henchmen, Colonel Clitch and Corporal Love, marching relentlessly, leading a troop of infantry towards us. They had us cut off surely. Meanwhile, along a riverbank slowly being exposed as the tide went out, there rode a party of Parliamentary cavalry.

'There's no more time!' That Yorkshire accent from the ship. No doubt Captain Sprye. 'Make haste, gentlemen! We've the wind with us. We'll just make the tide if we don't run aground!'

At our urging the Musketeers settled into the boat. I could not go with them. Somehow I had to try to get back to my children or die in the attempt. I raised my hand in farewell to brave friends. Claude Duval got his arms under Nevison who gasped in long breaths, holding a neck cloth to his wound.

Duval helped Nevison up. 'You must go with them, Nick. They'll hang thee for sure. There'll be a doctor aboard the brig. Those Jews are famous healers.'

Pale, Nevison grinned his disdain for what he considered kind-hearted nonsense. 'I'm a Londoner, captain. And not able to swim.' He spread his hand, wincing. 'I've had a good life and enjoyed all the many pleasures of the senses, sir. So this could be the reckoning, eh? And if it's the price I pay for my misspent life, why then, by Heaven, I'll take two and a bargain it shall be.' He laughed over his pain. 'I've had a mighty good run with rum pads gay, full of fun and high adventure. Free tobymen my friends have been! Free of censure and free of fear.

'With Jemmy gone and General Cromwell ruling over us, banishing Christmas and all that ever made our England merry, sir – with the old king dead and pinch-lipped clerks in power, someone has to stay and, however briefly, sing his grace's praises.' With that, he found his befeathered hat, straightened slowly, bowed low, winced again, got the hat settled on his head, gathered himself and straightened his spine like a soldier. Then, either to drown or prosper, Nick Nevison disappeared in the direction of the dark Surrey bank.

'Oh, Nick,' cried Duval after him. 'Well said, my dear! Then it's me back to France with Prince Rupert. I'll swear there's precious little could kill a man like you, Nick. So, sweet friend, it's hi-ho for Calais and a crown!' And blowing a kiss to his friend, he was into the skiff with a bound. He threw me the rest of the rope, anticipating my joining him.

But, while they called for me to come aboard, I let the rope unwind slowly. Behind me I heard the Puritans advancing. I knew this was not the time for me to abandon my children, my responsibilities and all I cared for. I hadn't any temptation to run away to France. Maybe, if I failed to get home, I would find Nevison and join him. I didn't much like the idea of remaining there alone.

Once Barry Bayley had wondered whether those wordless voices in my head would only be stilled when I put a huge barrier of some sort between myself and them. What I now called the Whispering Swarm had to be strong enough to capture all my attention if it were to defeat me. But so far I had resisted it. As I was determined to resist anything threatening to drive a wedge between myself and my children.

I have thought a lot how my hatred of the Swarm helped me sustain my resolve. I have loved the Alsacia since that first time I rode beside Moll Midnight, with black silk masks and flintlock pistols, to rob the Hackney Flyer. I still love it. Of course I do not love those voices calling me back. Sometimes I think the Swarm still forms words, telling me its secret. Sometimes I think they call urgently; sometimes they admonish me. And sometimes I hear the sadness in them. A terrible sadness. Sometimes they almost break my heart.

I will not forget that night: *I hear rough voices behind me. I hear the brig's anchor rattling even before the last of my friends leaves the longboat. Sailors hurriedly haul the skiff bodily up the side. Straining like a wounded whale, the ship lifts herself out with the tide, almost an act of will. The wind rises, blustering. A fresh crack of lightning.*

And there it is again in glinting black and gold, the name of the ship: REMEMBER. Amsterdam. *I wish them Godspeed then turn to face my enemies. I still have my pistols and my sword. I have never deliberately harmed another person, yet I am determined to kill Clitch and Love before they can take me. No matter what else transpires.*

And there they are, a couple of strutting, seedy alley cocks. They see me and their chests swell. They sniff blood. They think they have me. They swagger a few paces ahead of their master Marvell. The two bar-room dandies almost prance in their glee at this opportunity. I draw my pistols from my sash and point them. 'No further!'

'And who would you murder today, Master Moorcock? An honest soldier? Or two honest soldiers? Two, I fear, may be your limit. No doubt you'll be glad to do the deed before witnesses!' Clitch spreads his gauntleted hand to indicate their own redcoat soldiers. Any one of them seems ready to roast me on his long pike.

'First the two of you and then it's the river for me,' I say. I hardly know where the words are coming from. I have the strangest sense of writing a Meg Midnight script. I have no intention of putting myself at further risk.

The storm mumbles and spatters its way to the west. Lightning spits again, showing silver snow still falling. Snow drifts slowly into the distance. As if it deserts me. The two unsavoury thief-takers lift large horse pistols from their sashes and then also draw their swords.

I wondered why I didn't fear death more at that point. The ice moved suddenly underfoot. I barely managed to right myself. Something in me said I deserved it. But so did they. If I died, then those ruffians would die too.

I could almost feel the cold steel sliding into my heart. I was ready for death. I knew such intense regret. 'Cowards,' I said. 'You have my promise to kill you both. You'll be glad of the company in Hell.'

'Come, come, come, gentlemen!' With a rather mysterious expression of disapproval, Captain Marvell held up one hand to make his men stop. Another hand indicated this exchange of ours should also halt. 'This business has us behaving like characters in Webster.' And he placed himself squarely between us. 'Let's see some sense here before all lie dead beneath this yielding ice!

'You, my good comrades, Messrs Clitch and Love, dutiful in fulfilling your duties as always, have captured this young innocent. For reasons of his own, he let himself be persuaded by false companions to help Charles Stuart escape justice. But he did not conspire to murder, nor attempt to seduce anyone, nor to carry them off into Catholic slavery. Master Moorcock, I know you for an honest fool. You would doubtless have helped Cromwell's cause, had I drawn you into our company first.'

'And become a spy like yourself, Captain Marvell?' I did not lower my pistols.

He smiled, addressing his men again. 'This lad's a hothead but he's neither villain nor traitor. I'll give my word to it. I've heard him talk. He does support our Lord Protector and all our principles.'

Not something I could easily argue against.

Shrugging, the regular redcoats were cheerfully satisfied with that. They immediately lowered their weapons. At this time in England all were weary of conflict. Too many had died or been ruined. People yearned for reconciliation. Only Clitch and Love frowned and grumbled. Those two had neither a sense of chivalry nor of honest compromise. They required either reward or revenge. For a moment it looked as if they planned to rebel on the spot and take a shot at me. But, setting his back to them, Captain Marvell crossed to where I stood and linked his arm in mine.

I made to pull free but he murmured urgently. 'Don't be foolish, lad, if you'd see your offspring again.'

I took a long breath. 'Perhaps I'd rather die than stroll across the ice with a wretched spy!'

He chuckled at this. 'You have a friend in me, though you'll not allow it, young Moorcock.'

And so, for Sally and Kitty, I let Andrew Marvell keep my arm. Then, for all the world like one old friend taking a stroll with another, Marvell slowly walked with me across the ice towards the dying lights of the Frost Fair. Over on the South Bank the storm still flashed and cracked.

What was Marvell's plan? The lights of the fair distant and the storm passed, we walked in silence through the darkness as the ice grew firmer underfoot. For a while it appeared Marvell and I were alone out there. The Whispering Swarm was muted, murmuring in the back of my skull. Almost as if he knew what went on in my head he reached up a hand to hold my shoulder. I felt at once under arrest, reassured and rescued from danger.

We took a long time crossing the ice. For most of that walk, with the Frost Fair still merry in the distance and the thunder grumbling amongst the flashing lightning, we said little. By the time we reached that wall of chilling fog surrounding Whitefriars Old Stairs I felt almost calm. Here we paused, looking back at the distant bridge.

'Well,' he said philosophically, 'if the wind holds and they manage to get downriver to open sea, your comrades will all escape justice.' I thought of the ship and her passengers. I wanted to ask Marvell about High India, the Black Aether, the silver moonbeam roads, 'Ketchup Cove'. He seemed aware of a great deal that was going on at the abbey. Could he explain any of these mysteries? How did the notion of worlds in parallel resonate with everything else I had experienced? Why did Marvell, who was no zealot, work so diligently for the Parliamentary cause? How had he first discovered the routes to other worlds? I supposed the answer lay in his poetry. Yet to ask Marvell such questions would not force him into answering, if he knew, and would have him thinking me mad, if he didn't. Why did it matter? Obscurely, I wanted Marvell to think well of me. Or at least sympathetically. He shook hands at the stairs. 'Godspeed, lad. You are wise to be wary of the Alsacia. It is not your children's friend.'

Without a further word, Andrew Marvell walked into the shivering night.

Only later did I wonder how he knew about my children.

Once again I went through the complicated ritual in which I followed so-called moonbeam paths. This was becoming second nature. I recalled the tarot, the numbers, the images, the shivering silver threads. I kept the images, the numbers and rhythms in my head as I stepped through that unnatural fog and this time it seemed easier to tread the silver road as I followed the Green Knight, the same Saracen warrior I had seen at prayer in the chapel of the abbey, and suddenly found myself climbing those slimed, treacherous steps back up to the cobbled quayside pulling my damp cloak around me, seeking an impossible warmth.

As usual, as soon as I was in the Alsacia, the Swarm at once fell silent. The walk up that first steep cold street, with houses that never saw light or fire, was a long one. Then at last I was again in the glow of the Alsacia, with its friendly people wrapped against the tiring chill, with cheerful oil lamps or candelabra guttering in every window and fires blazing in every grate. It warmed like home.

I got back to the square, walking a little more slowly as I recalled the first time I was there. My spirits had lifted considerably when I reached the top of the little lane. I recalled being fascinated by the girl with the tousled hair, highwayman's topcoat and tricorn who had ridden into the innyard calling for an ostler. I had fallen in love at that moment. My fascination had brought me back and kept me there.

But now I'd had enough. It was all over. Molly was no more than a fiction and the story had ended. I didn't acknowledge her even when I saw her standing, beautiful and vulnerable, outside The Swan With Two Necks. Even when she came to walk beside me, murmuring: 'We found each other. You said it, Mike. We're soul mates. I love you with all my heart and soul. Please, let me look after you.'

I still thought it was a rather unlikely ambition for a talented adventuress. I didn't say anything to her but just kept walking. I walked into the abbey, crossed the yew lawn and found my way to the chapel. The abbey seemed completely deserted. The last thing I had seen of the abbot and the monks was when they went to meet the attacking redcoats. Had they been wiped out? On the chapel's altar I saw not the Fish Chalice but a pile of well-used swords and pistols. Had they been left there by the monks?

I was no longer curious. I went to my cell and changed back into my ordinary clothes. I took everything I had brought and packed it in my bag. I left the weapons. Then I walked out.

Carrying my bag, I made my way steadily in the direction of the Carmelite Inn gate. It was shut. A few bits and pieces of weapons and armour were scattered about nearby. Signs of a skirmish. As usual, no bodies. No blood. Perhaps their owners were waiting on the other side.

Molly stepped out of the shadows and stood in front of the gates. I looked directly into her eyes. She hesitated, shrugged and stepped aside. I pulled open one of the gates. In Carmelite Inn Chambers a lifting fog softened the square. I stepped through the gate and stood for a moment letting my tension fall away. My eyes were full of tears.

I took a deep breath and stepped into the square as the Swarm began its terrifying whispering again. Meaningless yet charged with meaning. For a second, just to escape that cruel sound, I thought of returning to the Alsacia.

Then I walked away. My future was restored. I headed for Fleet Street and the Number 15 bus. I was going home to Sally and Kitty, to whatever responsibilities waited for me. I was certain I would never see the Alsacia again.

And I didn't mind a bit.